Dangerous Attraction

The Complete Serial
Aegis Group

Sidney Bristol

Inked Press

Thank you, Dayna & Jessica.

Love is a fire. But whether it is going to warm your hearth or burn down your house, you can never tell.

–JOAN CRAWFORD

Dangerous Attraction: Part One

1.

TRAVIS RATION HUNCHED over the hotel desk and flipped to the first page of the autopsy report. The lights from the Vegas strip cast globes of colored light onto the paper, but the glitz and glamour held no sway for him. Only the poor woman in the photo.

She was blonde. Like the rest. Pretty. A Vegas native named Linda. She'd been social, so her disappearance had been noted within hours by friends and family, but by then it was too late. Whoever was abducting blonde, attractive young women was good. And if the list of missing blonde women was a hint, the perpetrator had operated in the Las Vegas area for years—without anyone connecting the dots. Or maybe LVPD had and didn't want to face it. They wouldn't be the first to ignore a killer to preserve tourism. A killer who only took one victim a year was easy to hide.

There was a serial killer in Las Vegas, and no one wanted to admit it.

"Hey man, ready to go?" Mason Clark, a new hire to the Aegis Group security firm, stepped into Travis' room, one hand braced on the door.

"No, man. Hit the strip without me." Travis didn't glance away from the report.

The autopsy read almost exactly like the last one. The cause of death, to a one, was blood loss, coupled with trauma to the head and abdomen.

It was the differences that mattered.

Judging by the time of death, the women lasted for anywhere from seven to twelve months before being murdered and dumped. Except Linda. She was an exception. She'd only been missing for two months. Why keep her so short a time? Had something gone wrong? The dead woman's corpse might tell him more.

What was really telling, though, was that from the time of death to the next abduction was somewhere in the twenty-four hour mark, which meant these crimes were well thought out. The perpetrator organized and focused on the details.

"No? What are...No, you are not on that again." Ethan Turner, Travis' best friend, groaned and shouldered past Mason. "I thought you were going to take a break from this."

"I said I was taking a break from work." Travis picked up the hotel pen and jotted down the injuries and observations that were different from the previous victims. That was where he'd find the clues. The guy doing this was too methodical to deviate from his plan, so when and where he did things was important.

This was a different kind of skill set than his typical jobs with Aegis. If things were different, Travis might have retired from the SEALs and become a private investigator, if it hadn't been for the felony conviction and dishonorable discharge.

No one trusted a felon. He was just lucky the management at Aegis knew him. A couple of the guys he'd served with had vouched for him, gotten him a spot on the elite team the company threw at the worst of problems. It wasn't a bad gig, all things considered.

"What are you doing?" Mason crossed the room and peered over Travis' shoulder.

"He's playing hound dog for the FBI." Ethan popped the top on a longneck from their freshly stocked mini fridge.

"What is this?" Mason snagged the first page of the report with the autopsy pictures clipped to it and dropped it almost immediately onto the ground. "What the hell?"

Travis punched Mason in the thigh, not hard, but enough that the other man bent over and rubbed the spot.

"Don't fuck with my stuff." Travis grabbed the piece of paper and the photographs. He straightened the documents out, ensuring all of the pieces were securely in place before putting it back in the folder.

"What the hell *is* that? Why do you have pictures of a dead woman?" Mason's eyes were wide, his lip curled. They'd all seen death. Everyone who worked for the Aegis Group had served overseas. They'd all killed. But they weren't all good at it. Travis had reservations about Mason's hire, but he wasn't the boss.

"None of your damn business," Travis replied.

"Is this a job or something?" Mason glanced between Travis and Ethan, who shook his head and took another swig of his beer. The Aegis Group was a private security company—on paper. In reality, they performed a wide range of services that often skirted the law from abduction retrieval to protection details, extraction services to product procurement.

"Don't worry about it," Travis said.

"The fuck we won't." Ethan gave Travis the thousand yard stare. Travis was pretty sure Ethan was about to try to deck him for the hell of it.

"I thought we were here for a protective detail," Mason said.

"You are. I'm not." Travis flipped the folder closed. FBI and CONFIDENTIAL were stamped across the front of the brown surface.

"What did you get us into this time?" Ethan took two steps toward Travis, and stopped, the beer clenched in his right hand.

"You aren't involved," Travis replied.

"The hell I'm not. What is this?" Ethan pointed at the folder.

"Just something I'm looking into."

"Is this why you wouldn't go home for Christmas?" Ethan's gaze narrowed.

Travis studied Ethan—the bloodshot eyes, the clenched hand.

This wasn't about Travis, or his side gig researching potential cases for the Behavioral Analysis Unit, a specialized FBI team that tracked down the worst kinds of killers, something he'd gotten involved with after a copycat murderer recreated the horrors from his family's past.

"Molly refused to split Christmas with you, didn't she?" Travis shifted his weight onto the balls of his feet, ready to move if Ethan rushed him. The worst fight they'd had happened the day Molly told Ethan she wanted a divorce. Some emotions could only be worked out with fists.

For a second, no one moved or spoke. Travis was not looking forward to the hotel bill for trashing the place.

Ethan blew out a breath and sat down on Travis' bed as if a one-ton weight were on his back. The spring squeaked, and the pillows bounced under the man's bulk.

"Yeah, she did," Ethan mumbled.

Mason's brows rose, but he didn't comment. The kid had some brains.

Travis stood and stretched. No fight then, which was a good thing. He'd hate to have to break Ethan's nose, and then take his place on the protective detail because Ethan was too scary looking as a result.

"When will you get to see Nate?" Travis crossed to the mini fridge and grabbed his own beer. The case weighed heavily on him, but he'd gone through SEAL training with Ethan. Travis had been the best man at Ethan and Molly's wedding and the first one there to load out boxes of Ethan's things when he moved out. They were brothers in every sense of the word save blood.

"Before he goes back to school. The second through the fourth. Three days. Three fucking days." Ethan took another long pull on his bottle.

"Make the most of those days. Don't dwell on what you don't get." Travis clinked his bottle to Ethan's.

Travis knew what it was like to have an absent father. At least Ethan wanted to be in his son's life. Travis was pretty certain his father hadn't wanted to live, but he hadn't wanted to die bad enough to do something about it. That was the kind of mark a serial killer left on a person, and it was the same darkness that passed down to Travis.

"What's the deal with the FBI?" Mason picked up the folder from the desk and looked at the cover. "This is the real deal, isn't it?"

"Yeah. Leave it alone." Travis watched Mason, though not because he didn't trust the kid. Anyone who worked at Aegis underwent a thorough background check and multiple people had to vouch for a new hire. In the field, Travis would trust Mason with his life, but he didn't know the guy.

The younger man seemed to consider his options for a moment, and then he did the smart thing and laid the folder on the desk.

"What's the case this time?" Ethan asked.

"Some sick fuck is kidnapping young blonde women. He keeps them for months, maybe a year, then kills them." He left out the horrific parts about the abuse and the pregnancies. Some things the others didn't need to know.

What did he do with the babies?

"Why is this your problem?" Mason asked.

"Ever heard of TBK?" Ethan glanced at Travis.

If Mason hadn't already known, he would find out. It was only a matter of time until someone told him.

"Wasn't that on the news a while back? Last year?" Mason screwed up one eye and pressed his lips together. "I was getting out of the SEALs about that time. It's all kind of a blur."

"Nah, man, TBKiller and that dude are two different people. TBKiller was a copycat," Ethan said.

"My old man's family was murdered by a serial killer. Called himself TBK. Torture. Blind. Kill." Travis peeled part of the label off his beer. Murdered was putting it lightly. They'd been tortured in the most sadistic fashion, then before their deaths, their eyes were removed.

TBK had terrorized Oklahoma City before Travis had been born, but he had shaped Travis' life. TBK's last victims were Travis' grandparents, and his father had been forced to watch it all. His old man had never fully recovered. Travis and his half-sister Emma often bore the brunt of the dysfunction.

"Fuck. I didn't know," Mason said.

"It happened before you or I were born." Travis shrugged. "Last year this guy goes apeshit. Starts copying the TBK murders and leaving these sick notes for my half-sister, Emma. They killed him trying to finish Emma off. Turns out this guy, who'd worked at the corner gas station she went to all the time, is part of this...serial killer club. The BAU is—"

"BAU? What?" Mason blinked.

"Behavioral Analysis Unit. They're the FBI unit that specializes in serial killers. They're trying to track down the club members, but no one wants to have a serial murderer on their hands."

"And that's where Travis likes to help out." Ethan thumbed at Travis.

"How?" Mason asked.

Travis could see the skepticism in Mason's eyes. The kid had been around Aegis long enough to hear rumors, stories about the Zed Team. He was probably wondering what a felon like Travis could do that the FBI couldn't.

Well fuck him.

"I let their team know where I'm working. If they have any leads, I'll look into it." Travis sipped his beer and stared at the mirror.

"Why?"

"Why the fuck do you want to know?" He scowled at Mason, but couldn't blame him. The whole gig was strange. "The FBI has to be invited into an investigation, unless it crosses state lines. Like I said, no one wants to have a serial killer on their hands."

"So you, what? Find a reason for them to come here?" Mason asked. "Why you? You're just a bodyguard."

Travis gripped the edge of the dresser.

Just a bodyguard.

"What the fuck do you know?" Ethan flipped Mason off.

He was right. All Travis was good for these days was an under-the-table gig and to catch the bullets meant for someone else. But that was his own fault. Reputable people didn't hire a felon, even an ex-Navy SEAL felon, no matter what his credentials were. How he wound up in prison didn't matter, only that he'd done time. But some jobs were made for him. He'd tracked some of the worst kinds of people across deserts, oceans, and mountains. This serial killer wouldn't know what hit him.

SHE WAS PERFECT. Better than the others. She would make him a good wife and give him the child he desired. Maybe this time it would live.

Daniel checked his rearview mirror, but the street was empty and dark this late at night. The quaint old shops lined what had once been a major retail area for Las Vegas, before the casinos and the strip lured business away.

He parked the Buick Electra along a curb and killed the engine.

Wendy sat perfectly still and serene in the passenger seat.

This girl was different. He almost clapped his hands in giddy excitement. She was older, had already borne one son, but that meant she was capable of giving him what he needed. Her energy was better, too. At this point he was normally still dealing with the sobbing and the fighting back.

Wendy would make the perfect bride. She wouldn't betray him, she wouldn't fight him. They would remake history together.

Linda hadn't been good enough. She'd been selfish and unworthy, right to the end. His shoulder ached from where she'd stabbed him, so it was only fair she'd died by the same blade.

Wendy, on the other hand? He was looking forward to spending a year with this bride.

One year. One pregnancy. That was the rule. That was how he kept them from betraying him. He'd studied the greats, how they did it, what their methods were. Nothing good came from keeping her more than a year.

"What do you want?" Wendy's voice was quiet, soothing. She would be a gentle creature, which meant he needed to be mindful about how he handled her.

"I want you to marry me. Give me a son."

"I'm already married." She turned her head, and he stared into her dark brown eyes.

He punched the dashboard. The old car was sturdy and took the abuse.

How dare she speak of the other man in her life! That one was gone. She was his, now.

"I'm sorry." She recoiled, pressing her back against the car door.

"You marry me, or I kill your family. I think I'll start with your sister." He pulled a photograph of Wendy and a dark-haired woman out of his jacket pocket and laid it on the seat between them. His hidden cameras had snapped the candid shot of the two at the sister's apartment just last week.

Wendy gasped and covered her mouth.

"Or maybe I kill little Paul first?" He tossed another picture down. This time it was of a rosy-cheeked baby grinning up at the camera in his crib.

"Oh my God. How did you get that?"

"I took it. There is nowhere your loved ones will be safe from me. I'm in their lives." He laid down three more pictures. Her husband at work. Her parents in their kitchen. And lastly, a photograph of Wendy asleep in her own bed. "What'll it be, Wendy? Do you want to marry me?"

Her tears glistened in the moonlight, so precious. Each wife had to be broken so that they could be molded to his will, becoming the woman they were destined to be. The radio began playing the holiday classic White Christmas. He hummed a few bars as he took in his bride. She'd make the right choice. They always did.

Wendy nodded and swiped at her cheeks.

"If I marry you, do you promise not to hurt them?"

He leaned across the car and bumped Wendy's chin with his knuckle.

"I don't care about them, Wendy. I care about you. What do you say? Want to be Mrs. White? I like that last name. I think it'll remind us of this season."

She nodded and squeezed her eyes shut.

"Just don't hurt them," she whispered.

"I've always wanted a Christmas wedding." He shifted into drive, steering them back toward the strip and the drive-through wedding chapels, humming along to the radio.

2.

BLISS STEPPED INTO THE Vegas Police Department and removed her sunglasses. She blinked away the sunspots and glanced around. The place was hopping first thing in the morning—people picking up their drunken friends, prostitutes and petty thieves posting bail. Most hadn't even been to bed yet, but that was the nature of Vegas.

She strode to the counter, twisting the strap of her purse in her hands.

Why had she waited?

"Excuse me?" she said when the officer at the counter didn't acknowledge her.

"Yeah?" The man didn't even look up from his paperwork.

"My sister, she's missing." She laid a photograph on the counter and slid it across.

"How long has she been gone?"

Gone. Not missing.

Bliss swallowed her irritation. Popular theory was that a person had to be MIA for seventy-two hours before they could be considered missing. Popular theory was wrong, and so was the idea that Wendy was just—gone. Someone needed to be searching for her now.

"She's not at her house, and she's not answering her phone. I've been trying her since last night." Bliss loved her little sister fiercely. Ever since Wendy gave birth and fell into a depression, they'd begun the habit of getting together every couple of days, sometimes to just sit on the couch and say nothing.

"When was the last time you spoke with her?"

From the bored manner of the officer's questioning, she could guess how much attention the cops were going to pay her. As soon as she mentioned the depression, they would just roll their eyes and tell her to wait.

"Yesterday afternoon. Maybe five o' clock?"

"She's been missing, what?" The officer glanced at his watch. "Sixteen hours? You sure she isn't sleeping late?"

"No." Okay, that was a lie. Wendy could be sleeping in late somewhere, just not at her house. Maybe a hotel or a spa somewhere? But she'd have at least let Bliss know.

"Ma'am, you can fill out a report, but chances are she'll show up later today." He gestured to the line of people behind her. "Forms are on the right."

"But...she's missing. She's not well. What if something happened to her? Maybe you've seen her? My height, but skinny, blonde, brown eyes. Come on."

"Fill out the paperwork, and someone will look into it. Next." He gestured to a man and woman behind her. They shouldered past, and all Bliss could do was stare at them.

Was this happening? Her sister was missing. And no one cared.

Wendy was the fragile one. Their parents coddled her, and Bliss became her protector through school. She even transferred colleges to make sure Wendy had someone in her life she could lean on. It was a relief when Grayson fell madly in love with Wendy because it meant she'd never want for anything in her life. She was completely taken care of, thanks to Grayson's lucrative career designing buildings. But since the baby, Wendy was even more delicate than usual. If Bliss didn't find her soon, oh God, she couldn't live with herself. What would she tell Grayson when he came home? At least baby Paul was with his grandparents for a few days.

"Excuse me, ma'am?" A big, hulking man loomed over her. She took a step back instinctively. Something about him telegraphed danger in big, bold letters. He held out a slick white business card.

She glanced at the card. *Aegis Group* was printed on it in a neat type, no nonsense, no logo. Thick cardstock, with that fancy grain that spoke of understated money. These weren't bargain business cards some scam artists got off the Internet. It was the nice stuff only those who dealt with rich people used.

Her gaze traveled up the arm to his face. His short-cropped brown hair was slightly bleached, as if he spent a lot of time outside. Dark aviators hid half his face, but what she could see was his strong, angular jaw. If he were selling a product, it would be something dangerous and manly. Not guns though, he was someone who liked to use his hands. A knife, maybe something more covert.

"Can I see that picture?" He gestured to the photo she held clutched in her hand.

"Who the hell are you?"

"My name is Travis. I work with a private security company. I want to see if I can help. What's your name?"

Was this a scam? Grayson had a lot of money. What if someone picked up Wendy with the intent to ransom her back?

"Officer?" She raised her voice and side-stepped the man.

The officer sighed audibly and glanced at her, then the hulking brute.

"Who is he?" she asked.

"Some PI." The officer shrugged.

Great. Lot of good the cops were going to do her today.

"How do I know you're telling me the truth?" Bliss was running out of options. She didn't have the kind of resources Grayson did, but if she had to hire a private investigator, well, she wanted someone scary on their side, and this guy fit the bill. Hadn't he said his name? Travis?

He turned the business card over.

"Call this number. Ask them to verify for you who I am. What I do."

She took the card and studied the numbers. It was out of state. Illinois?

"Long way from home?" She dug in her purse for her phone.

"I'm here looking into a case."

"Why do you want to help me then?"

"The man I'm looking for abducts pretty blonde women born and raised in Las Vegas." She couldn't see his eyes, but the way he tipped his chin, she could feel his gaze travel the length of her body. "If your sister is anything like you, she fits the victimology."

"We're nothing alike, that's just it."

"I don't mean in looks." He leaned toward her, staring deep into her eyes. It was an intense sensation to be the focus of this man. "It's in the eyes. I can't explain it."

Bliss stared at him.

Their parents relocated to Vegas after her birth. Wendy was born in Vegas. They hadn't lived anywhere else. One of Wendy's problems, if they could be called that, was that she drew too much male attention. She was stunning, with a model's body and the sweetest disposition. People always said she had the most beautiful eyes.

"Keep talking," she said.

"The picture?" He held out his hand.

Bliss shoved the snapshot of them at him. It was from just before Wendy had given birth. She'd been tired, but happy.

Travis stared at it for several moments.

"What happens to the women?" she asked. Her mind could fill in the blanks, but she wanted to hear him say it. This couldn't be real. This kind of thing didn't happen in real life.

"Want to grab a seat? Maybe some coffee?"

"What happens to the women?"

He stared down at her, and the muscle on the left side of his jaw twitched.

"You should sit before I answer that question."

"Fine. Where?"

"I saw a café down the street."

"Lead on." She gestured the way she'd come. For some reason she didn't want Travis at her back. He gave her the shivers, but not in a creepy kind of way.

He nodded and strode back to the entry, pausing to hold the door open for her. She stepped out into the sunshine and shivered. Despite the clear blue sky, the breeze was unseasonably chilly. She shoved her hands in her pockets and gripped her phone with one hand, the business card with the other.

How crazy was this?

They were supposed to be planning Christmas...not this.

Her phone vibrated against her palm. She glanced at the screen and stopped in the middle of the sidewalk.

"Shit. It's Grayson—uh, her husband. What do I tell him?" The same panic she'd been fighting all morning wrapped around her throat, making it hard to breath. She glanced up at Travis and she had her anchor.

"The truth," he said.

Bliss squeezed her eyes shut and answered the phone.

"Hey," she said.

"Morning. Sorry for calling so late. Things got out of hand this morning. My morning. Your night. How is she?" From the ambient sounds and echoing footsteps, Bliss was willing to bet her brother-in-law was doing some sort of site walkthrough.

"I've got some bad news." She stared at Travis, who gave her a nod.

"What is it?"

"Wendy...is....she's...Oh, God, Grayson..." She nearly collapsed right there on the sidewalk. Travis caught her around the shoulders while she sobbed and guided her to a bench. He perched next to her, one arm slung around her in a protective embrace.

"Give it to me," he whispered.

"Hold on." She thrust the phone into his hand and covered her face, leaning against him.

"Grayson, my name is Travis Ration, I work for the Aegis Group, a—" He paused and glanced away. "Well, at least we don't have to do that. Sir, I'm sorry to tell you like this, but your wife appears to have gone missing...Last night. I met Bliss at the PD a few minutes ago, looking into a case I think might be involved...That won't be necessary...That would work...Here she is." Travis thrust the phone into her hands. "I'll be right over there."

He got up, and she missed his warmth and protective presence immediately. She watched him walk away, hands in his pockets, head swinging side to side, as if he were already on the lookout.

"Bliss?"

"Hey, sorry, it's me."

"Is he...is he serious?"

"Dead serious." She cringed at her poor word choice.

"I'm catching the next plane home. It'll take me at least sixteen hours from London. We're going to retain Aegis Group to find her. I don't care what it costs." He didn't skip a beat. There wasn't any shock or dismay, no denial, he just...hired Travis, a complete stranger, to do it.

"Is that...smart?" She turned and pitched her voice lower. "Who is this guy?"

"I don't know who he is, but Aegis is the best. Worth every penny."

What the hell kind of job was he doing that was that dangerous? Didn't Grayson build offices or something?

"I'm going to lose you. I'll call back in a bit. I want to know everything."

She hung up the phone and leaned forward, planting her elbows on her knees. They were supposed to be shopping today for presents. Bliss had even planned to coordinate with Priscilla to make sure the house got decorated and presents wrapped so Wendy didn't feel the crush of organizing it herself.

What if she never saw her sister again?

WENDY SAT WITH HER back to the wall of the cave. Metal bars blocked her path out of the cave or farther back into the rocks. It wasn't wide, maybe ten or twelve feet across. The bottom was smoothed out. A few rugs and pieces of furniture took up the rest of the space. It was a far cry from the Vegas mansion her husband built for them following their wedding, but at least there was no draft. There was also no light unless Daniel came back.

Her *husband*.

She shuddered and squeezed her eyes shut. The darkness spun around her, and she pitched sideways, landing on the soft, inviting bed.

Wendy scrambled to her feet and backed toward the cave entrance. She couldn't touch the furniture. For a brief period of time when the lights overhead had illuminated her prison, and she did her best to take stock of what was there. That was when she found them. Three pairs of women's panties stashed under the mattress. All different sizes.

Grayson was her husband, not this crazy psycho. Grayson, who she loved. They had a baby together. Paul.

Oh, Paul.

Her heart clenched and in that moment, she'd have given anything to hold her baby. Anything at all. She never wanted something so bad before, and now it might be too late. Her previous baby boy.

"Hey. Hey."

She pressed her hands over her ears, willing the voices to go away. She couldn't handle them. Their smell. She couldn't even deal with being there.

"Where did Linda go?"

"He killed her."

"Are you sure? She said, but Linda said there were others before us. I mean, I just thought he kept the women a long time."

"What do you think?"

"Is she Linda now?"

Wendy squeezed her eyes shut. The three men were in smaller cells behind hers, which meant that in order for Daniel to get to them, he had to go through hers. She could smell the men, or maybe it was their bandages. Was that her fate? What was going to happen to her? Would he chop off parts of her like he'd done to them?

She didn't dare attempt an escape, not when he'd kill her baby.

TRAVIS WAS FAR TOO big to fit in the only unoccupied booth in the café. He didn't dare suggest somewhere farther from the PD for fear the woman across from him might faint or cry or something. She'd seemed on the brink of falling apart outside, but she'd rallied and followed him to the café without so much as a tear.

"Here's your coffee. Can I get you anything else?" The waitress deposited a carafe on the table along with cream and sugar.

"No, thank you," he replied.

The woman across from him shook her head. Her shoulder length brown hair swished around her face, all glossy looking. For some crazy reason he wanted to touch it. To run his fingers through her pretty hair and see if it felt as soft as it looked. He kept his hands to himself. Girls like her didn't need men like him in their lives.

"Bliss, right?"

She nodded her head, sending those strands moving again.

"Yeah, sorry, I didn't introduce myself did I? I'm Bliss Giles." She cupped the empty ceramic mug with both hands.

He picked up the carafe and poured her some coffee first, then himself. This wasn't his thing. He didn't deal with clients, he wasn't the person to offer comfort or hope. His history hadn't wired him that way, but for her he'd try.

"Tell me about the last time you saw your sister. Do you mind if I take notes?"

"You said you'd tell me what happened to the other women." Her dark brown eyes focused on him. She was no longer on the verge of tears or lost in thought. He kind of liked being the center of her focus.

"You don't want to know that."

"Yes, I do. And I want to know why you think my sister might be one of them." She tapped the photograph of Wendy he'd laid on the table.

The two sisters couldn't be more different. At least on the surface level.

Wendy was petite, blonde, and almost breakable looking. Bliss was shapely, luscious, and that dark hair set off her pale, perfect skin. The one thing the sisters shared was their dark brown, almost black eyes. He'd heard someone call eyes that dark soulless eyes, but looking at Bliss, that sentiment couldn't be further from the truth. It was the intangible quality the camera captured that he'd seen in the other victim's photographs pre-death. A light. An inner brightness. This killer snuffed out truly bright flames, and for what?

He was going to find out.

"Tell me." She leaned closer.

He'd have to give her the Cliff notes version. What would he tell his sister?

No, that was a bad gauge. His sister kept a living collection of TBK documents and coverage. He'd likely tell her everything, because they'd lived through worse.

"Over the last seven years nine Las Vegas women, all blonde, have gone missing. They turn up between a couple months to a year after they were abducted. Dead. About twenty-four hours after the time of death, another girl is taken."

"What aren't you telling me? I could find that out for myself."

"Some things you don't want to know."

"I have a right to know. That's my sister."

"Then tell me about the last time you saw her. Let me find her."

"I want to know what you aren't telling me."

She was a stubborn little thing.

Travis cleared his throat and made himself relax. Their knees bumped under the table and she shifted, bumping into his other knee. Her cheeks tinged pink, and she finally looked away from him. Interesting. She'd challenge him, but a little knee bump was too much? Women were a mystery.

And better off far away from him.

He had no business thinking about Bliss that way. He was a felon. There was no place for a woman in his life.

"When was the last time you saw Wendy?" He picked up his pen. As fun as it was to share coffee with a pretty girl instead of Ethan's ugly mug, this was about life and death.

"Yesterday, around five. I left work and stopped by her place to check on her." She tore open sugar packets one at a time and upended them into her coffee. Her fingers were small, nimble, with nails in three shades of purple. The bangles on her wrist clanged and chimed as she moved, drawing his attention back to her smallest movement.

"Check on her? Was something wrong? Did she tell you anything?"

"Wendy..." Bliss bit her lip and glanced out of the window, tucking her hair behind her ear. There was a small tattoo there, partially hidden. It made him wonder if there was more ink on her body. Not that it was any of his business. "Wendy has post-partum depression. Her in-laws are babysitting Paul while her husband is out of town. They're looking for a nanny to take care of him. Well, both of them, really. She's been very out of sorts since his birth."

"She just had a baby?" He swallowed.

Fuck.

"Yeah. Why? Is that important?"

"Is the baby missing?" His gut rolled, and he gripped the pen so tight the plastic buckled under his fingers.

"No, he's with his grandparents."

"Poor kid," he muttered. "Did she say anything about seeing anyone? Someone following her? Anyone giving her the creeps?"

"No. Wendy barely leaves the house unless someone makes her. The depression is really bad."

"Have you been to her house?"

"Yeah, she was supposed to meet me this morning, but she didn't show, so I went to get her out of bed. The house is perfect. Clean. The beds all made."

"Could she be at a hotel or somewhere?"

"I don't think so. If Wendy didn't have to leave the house, she wouldn't. This depression, it's bad. If we didn't make her eat, she would starve."

"Could I take a look at the house? I might see something you don't."

"What's so bad you won't tell me?" Once more, those dark eyes focused on him, compelling him to share the worst of it with her.

"We're going to find her before that's an issue."

What the hell?

He couldn't promise her that, and yet he just had.

3.

BLOOD.

The stone below the bed was stained with blood.

Wendy gripped the bars as her stomach revolted. Bile coated her mouth, and the muscles in her abdomen and chest tensed in irregular rhythms. Dying might be less painful.

"Lady, hey lady, you got to calm down." Stumpy was in the cell right behind her. He only had one foot. The other leg was mostly gone.

"Take a deep breath." That order came from the old one. He sat on the floor, never moving out of his pile of rags.

The lights were back on, which wasn't much of an improvement. It illuminated the horrors her mind had created, making them real. Like the blood.

"Is he going to kill us?" she asked.

It was the first time she'd spoken directly to the men.

"Us? Probably," Stumpy said.

"Why?" Her knees gave out, and she sat down with her back against the bars drilled into the stone and faced her fellow prisoners. For the first time in months, she wanted something.

She wanted to live.

Depression had clouded her judgement and sucked the life out of her for so long, she forgot what it was like to feel. Emotion swirled within her. Sorrow at never being able to hold her baby and love him like he deserved. Her beautiful, miracle baby. Regret at not answering the phone when Grayson called the night before. He was so patient with her. She didn't deserve the kind of life he'd given her. Shame for leaning on her sister so much. Bliss practically managed Wendy's life, and for what? Wendy was so selfish and wretched she couldn't even say thank you. So many things.

"You don't want to know." Stumpy smiled at her. It was a sad expression. Under the dirt and flecks of blood he had a kind face, sort of boyish and round.

"Us he'll kill. You, he'll rape until you're pregnant, and keep you locked up until you give birth."

Wendy stared at the old man. Was he serious? She pressed her knees together. It had taken her four years to get pregnant with her husband, whom she loved and adored.

And now some sicko wanted her to give him a baby?

"Hush, don't tell her that," Stumpy snapped.

"She needs to know. If Linda was right, we're next. He'll clean house so she doesn't know anything. She needs to know."

"Oh God." The tears trickled down her cheeks.

Stumpy used the bars to hop-walk his way to the corner. He knelt and whispered something at the older one. There was a third behind them, but she hadn't heard more than moans coming from his cell since earlier. The two spoke in hushed voices.

Wendy wasn't going to survive this. She'd never been strong like her older sister. If Bliss were here, she'd be half-way to figuring out how to break the iron bars. The very least Wendy could do was stay put. Ensure that Bliss, Grayson, and Paul got to keep living. That was the bargain she'd made Daniel. If she kept up her part of it, he'd let them live.

"Hey, look at me." Stumpy crouched down, peering at her from across the cave. "What's your name?"

"Wendy," she replied.

"Robert is right." Stumpy put his forehead against the bars. "Daniel's probably going to kill us. Our only hope is to pass the story along, the one Linda told us. Do you think you can listen? Can you remember it?"

"Do I have to?" She shuddered. The last thing she wanted in her head was a gruesome story about her captor.

"There's not much time." Stumpy glanced behind him. "That one's dying. I've still got my leg and both my arms left, but he's going to take those soon."

"He cut your leg off?" Wendy gaped in new horror.

"He started with my toes."

"Oh, God," she chanted and covered her face.

"I have a family. They probably aren't looking for me, though. I was an addict, couch hopping. No one cares about me, but I'd like my family to know what happened."

"Why are you telling me this? If I die, too..."

Robert leaned toward her. Part of the blanket fell away and she realized...his arms were gone. "Girl, someday one of us will live, and that one has to know the story, so we all live beyond this nightmare."

She wanted to be the girl who lived, but she wasn't that strong.

BLISS LED THE WAY up the walk to Wendy's Las Vegas house. Or mansion. The place was big enough to fit her apartment in the entry alone.

"Have you considered this is a ransom job?" Travis asked.

"That was my first thought when I saw you, actually." She fit the key in the lock. "You should know, I have zero access to their money. I'm the poor one of the family." She meant it as a joke, but it fell flat. Her living might be modest, but she didn't want for anything. Okay, so she wanted a hunky guy, but she could get that on pay-per-view.

Travis did that thing again—she could feel him looking her over, but now, without the sunglasses, she knew just where his gaze lingered. There was something about it that made her pulse jump.

It had to be the coffee.

"If someone wanted money for her, you'd have heard from them by now."

"What exactly is it you do? Why does a PI work ransom cases?" She slid the key into the lock and twisted. The door swung inward, and she stepped over the threshold. The alarm beeped at her, and she left Travis to close the door while she entered the code.

"Was the alarm armed this morning?" Travis closed the door and spent a moment flipping the locks and studying the frame.

"Yes."

"Any security cameras?"

"No, but the security office should have some. Grayson was adamant they only build in a gated community with real security."

"What does Grayson do? Any enemies?" He slowly walked a circle, his gaze traveling all over the foyer, up the stairs to the second level.

"He designs buildings. Big ones."

"Where is he now?"

"He's hitting three or four big meetings all over the place. Chicago. New York. London and...Mexico City? His company is putting in bids, and he has to go present designs or whatever it is they do. Why? You think it's connected to him? I thought you said it was this other guy."

"I don't want to rule anything out." He turned to face her, those green, unreadable eyes on her now. Hot damn, he was good looking.

And yet...

He wasn't answering her questions. She didn't know what horrible things had happened to the missing women, or what this guy actually did.

"I just let you into their house, and I have no clue who you really are. Grayson seemed to know who Aegis is, but—you could be lying." Boy, was she dumb. He'd given her a card and what had she done? Gone for coffee.

"I told you, my name is Travis."

"Travis what?"

"Travis Ration. I work for Aegis Group."

"What the hell is that? What do you do?"

"It's a private security firm."

"And you're their PI?"

"Not...exactly."

"Then what are you?"

"You know the guy they send in to get a job done, no matter the cost?"

"Yeah?"

"That's me."

The way he said it...so cold, stark...it sent a shiver down her spine.

"Then why this case? It doesn't make sense to be here if you're a finisher."

"I'm doing a favor for a friend. They asked me to look into this for them, so here I am."

"What kind of friend asks you to look into murderers?"

"The kind with a badge."

"You aren't giving me real answers."

"Call the number. I'm going to look around the house. They've probably already processed the paperwork for this gig." He turned and strode through the double archway into the football-field sized living room.

She watched him go, her gaze drawn to his ass. If she were a normal girl, she was sure there would be other thoughts in her head, but she'd spent all last week helping supply dildos for a porn movie filming down the block from her warehouse. Those were always the worst. The producer was a nice woman who got way too excited about her job and overshared raw footage Bliss did not need to see.

Right. She had things to do. Like find her missing sister.

The business card was at the bottom of her purse already. She dug it out and punched in the numbers.

"Aegis Group. How may I direct your call?" The voice was professional, male. He sounded like he'd sell soap products or something domestic. Not at all sexy like the big brute stomping through her sister's house.

"Hi, yeah, I need to verify this guy I met actually works for you."

"I can do that. Do you have a case number?"

"Uh, what? No. He said paperwork was processing. I want to know what it is you do."

"Okay. Well, Aegis Group is a private security firm. Let me pull up our new cases."

"He said that much. What do you really do?"

For a moment he didn't answer.

"What do you need done?" he asked. A bit of the soap bubble clean faded away and she could hear an edge in his voice.

"My sister is missing and my brother-in-law just hired him over the phone. He wants to help me find her. I think. Or do you have her?"

"Who is your sister and who is he?"

"Wendy Horton, and he said his name is Travis Ration."

"Ah. Travis. I saw that request come through. It's marked urgent so it'll be processed before noon. Travis will find her."

"How do you know that? And how do you know this is really Travis?"

"Does he look like someone you wouldn't want to meet in an alley at night?"

"Yeah."

"That's Travis. Ask him about Port Said."

"What the hell is Port Said?"

"It's a city. In Egypt. Anything else I can do for you?"

"What the hell do you really do?"

"What we are paid to do. Travis can fill in the blanks. Good luck."

"What does that mean? Hello?" Bliss looked at the screen. Call ended.

What the hell had she gotten herself involved in? Who was Travis? What kind of company was this? She couldn't waste her time with this nonsense, except he was all she had as a means to find Wendy. She glanced at the time. Grayson would expect her or Wendy to check in soon. What would she tell him?

She searched the first floor, but Travis was nowhere to be found. How could a big man like him be so hard to find?

Bliss used the servant's stairs to get to the second floor. She paused on the landing and listened.

Nothing.

What did she know about this guy? Why was she trusting him? And how did Grayson know all about this company?

She crept toward the master bedroom on the east side of the house. The double doors were open and so were the curtains. She peered into the room, and found herself staring at a hard wall of man chest.

"Who is that outside?" he pointed at the windows.

"Shit. You scared me." She laid her hand against her pounding heart and strode to the window. "Oh. Landscaper."

"He has a key?"

"Well, yeah."

"Who else has a key to the house?"

"Priscilla, their housekeeper. The landscaper. The launderer. Um, I think there's an assistant of Grayson's. Then my parents. Oh. The babysitter service has one on file, too."

"Shit." Travis scrubbed a hand over his face.

"Why?"

"That's a lot of people to trust with things like security codes and keys. Too many chances someone got access your family didn't want here."

"What about Port Said?"

Travis' head jerked up and his gaze narrowed. She resisted the urge to take a step back. Damn, he was hot, but in a scary way. The guy on the phone was right. Travis wasn't the kind of person she wanted to meet in a dark alley, that was for sure. Or maybe she did, but only if he used his mouth.

God, she needed some alone time with her vibrator, soon.

"Who told you about that?"

"The guy who answered the phone. I didn't get a name." She shrugged. Okay, maybe asking him that was a set up.

"Christ." He shook his head.

"So...going to tell me about it?"

He sighed and took a seat on a dainty, padded bench under the windows.

"We got this emergency job once. Middle of Arab Spring. These girls were vacationing in Italy, decided to hop a boat to Egypt and got themselves kidnapped. The people who abducted them weren't the ransom kind. We had to get creative with how we found them. Nearly lost two guys on that job."

"Why would anyone want me to know that?"

"Beats me. It's not the kind of thing nice girls need to know."

Nice girl? Ha!

Somehow Bliss didn't think he was telling her the whole story. But there had to be something there. A reason why he was the person to help her find her sister.

"I think I know how the suspect got in," he said.

"What?" She stared at him. There was proof? Something they could take to the cops? "Show me."

Travis led the way back downstairs and to the rear wall of windows that provided a lovely view of the pool. He went to a knee next to the French doors and pointed at what looked to be a scuff on the wood paneling.

"What am I looking at?" she asked.

"The security lines have been looped back on themselves. Open the door."

She unlocked the door and pulled it open.

Silence had never unnerved her more.

Bliss closed the door, and opened it again.

"The system is supposed to announce when a door is opened. I was here two days ago and when Priscilla came in from the pool it announced, back door." She stared at Travis.

"Did they do any security upgrades recently?"

"I...uh....I don't know. Maybe? Around the time Paul was born, they had a lot of people in and out, prepping the house for the baby." She pressed her hand to her head. This couldn't be happening. He couldn't be right.

"Bliss?" Travis gripped her shoulders and guided her to an armchair. He took a knee and stayed right by her side.

"Oh, God. I think I'm going to throw up. What happened? Where is she? Who did this?"

"I don't know. Do you...have someone you want to stay with?"

"You are not looking for my sister without me." There were a dozen very good reasons why she should let the man do his job, but this was her sister they were talking about.

"I understand your concern. I'm very good at what I do. I'm going to go to the security offices. It's clear whoever got in here knew what they were doing. How to do it. And were able to motivate Wendy to leave with them without a struggle."

"Okay." She stood. "Ready."

Travis blinked at her.

"I meant, I'll go handle that. You should take it easy. Stay here in case someone calls."

"Wendy is my sister. Whenever she's needed help or got-ten herself in trouble, I've been there for her. You will have to lock me up to keep me out of this." Bliss didn't care how big or scary he was, she would always be there for Wendy. Especially now.

4.

TRAVIS DROVE THROUGH THE gated community, acutely aware of the tense silence between him and his passenger. He watched Bliss from the corner of his eye. She sat straight up, her hands in her lap, posture tense.

He'd had to face down a number of men and women who thought their dollars bought them a shotgun seat on the jobs Aegis was hired to do. The problem was that the moment an untrained civilian was put in the mix, things changed. Their unit was pulling bodyguard detail in addition to whatever they were hired to do. It just didn't fly. They couldn't risk being divided like that.

Then why was she sitting shotgun in his rental?

Back at the house, he'd backed down, even when every shred of training and experience said that Bliss Giles needed to stay right where she was.

He didn't need help. If a situation required backup, both Ethan and Mason were in Vegas. No doubt now that Wendy's husband was retaining their services, the others would be briefed. Which meant Travis needed to have a sitrep with the BAU. He was no longer their man on the job. His loyalty would always be to Aegis first. The management had given him a chance when no one else would.

It was the conviction. The way Bliss had stared him down, he'd known that he'd either keep her close or spend precious time checking up on her following him. He just hoped she could keep up.

"We have to have some ground rules," he said.

Bliss turned her head toward him, but didn't speak.

"If we don't find Wendy in the next forty-eight hours, chances are we won't find her. I need you to agree to do what I say, when I say it. And if you think you can't do that, stay behind."

"I understand," she said.

"Some of our guys are good with clients. They know how to keep them positive, calm. That's not me. I'm not a people person."

"Never would have guessed that, sunshine. Pull in here." She tapped the window. "If you promise to not keep secrets, then yes, I'll do whatever you say."

Secrets. His life was built on them. She didn't know what she was asking.

"First thing, don't tell anyone else Wendy is missing." He pulled into the parking spaces outside the security office and killed the engine.

"Why?"

"Whoever took her knew what they were doing. They've done this before. If the cops or FBI get involved it might escalate the situation, and he could end up killing her before his appointed time."

"Boy, you are cheerful."

"Let's go."

"Wait."

"What?"

"What's the second thing?"

He stared at her.

"You said first thing, what's the second?"

"I'll tell you when I know."

Bliss met him in front of the SUV, and together they entered the security office. An older man eyed him with obvious distrust.

"What can I do for you?" the guard asked.

"Hi. I need to review some footage from last night." Travis fished out another business card and offered it to the guard.

"Afraid I can't do that," the guard said.

"Actually, you have to. In that HOA my sister signed, it said residents can access the footage. Mr. Ration here has been hired by my brother-in-law. Grayson Horton, you know him?" Bliss leaned against the desk and smiled. He'd seen mercenaries who looked friendlier than she did right now.

"What exactly is it Mr. Horton is looking for?" The guard hadn't moved, but they had the upper hand.

"The footage?" Travis prompted.

"Over here." The guard got up and walked around a partition.

Travis followed him to a bank of monitors that showed the streets and entries into the community. It was a fairly common system.

"I can take it from here, thanks." Travis squeezed past the man and pulled out a chair. Bliss was right behind him and gave the guard a pointed *get lost* stare.

"Let me know if you need anything." The guard looked like he'd just sucked on a lemon, but he gave them space.

Travis opened the files containing the last twenty-four hours of footage for each entry and cued them up.

"What are we looking for?" Bliss bent and peered over his shoulder.

"Something that doesn't belong."

He started with one gate at five o' clock, the last time Bliss had seen her sister, and put the footage on fast forward through the night. He made notes about cars, the movements of people, anything out of the ordinary. He was starting to think the kidnapper must have used another point of entry by the time he got to the front gate. It was the least appealing entrance, based on traffic and the face to face time with the guards, and yet...

"There."

Travis paused the footage on the car leaving.

"What? What is it?" Bliss sat forward and looked up from her phone.

"This car. It arrived with a man inside, and is leaving with a passenger. Even the help drive better cars than this."

"Are you sure?" Bliss squinted at the screen.

"Yes."

He jotted down the make, model, and license. The image was too dark and grainy to get a facial on either person in the car, but it was a start.

"Come on."

Travis stood, and Bliss yelped. Her arm shot out, and her eyes went round. He reached out and snatched her before she landed on the tile floor. Her hands gripped his biceps, and her face was so close he could smell lemon on her breath and see lighter flecks of color in her dark eyes. Her body was soft, fitting against him in ways that would haunt him later.

"Everything okay?" the guard called.

"Fine." Travis cleared his throat and took a step back, putting Bliss at arm's length. "You okay?"

"Yeah, I didn't think you were going to move that fast." She laid a hand on her chest and blew out a breath. Her cheeks were pink again.

Damn. He could have touched her hair if he'd thought about it. Now that was a creeper idea. He needed to convince Bliss to stick to the sidelines, or she was going to become a distraction he couldn't afford.

"Let's get out of here." He gestured behind her, and this time, waited for Bliss to lead the way out of the guard shack.

On the way out to the SUV, he pulled out his cell phone. Did he call Aegis? They were technically on the case to retrieve Wendy. He'd updated the chain of command via text after speaking with Grayson. But the FBI might have better intel. He wouldn't mention that to their guys–it would chap their asses. Why not make two calls?

He hit dial, climbed into the truck, turned it on and flipped the heat to high. The Bluetooth activated almost instantly, and the call rang through the speakers.

"Ration!"

"Gavin?" Travis frowned. "Where's Zain?" The kid was another Zain in the making, except he had both hands. But Zain had ten plus years on Gavin and the kind of experience in covert and black ops that couldn't be bought. Plus he could tech circles around anyone, even the FBI and other government agencies who regularly courted at least half of the people on Aegis' payroll. Even Gavin.

"Captain Hook took the week off for some spacey, blue box thing. You know him, can't resist the geek beacon. He forwarded your text to me." Gavin muted whatever was playing in the background before speaking. "Zain forwarded your text. Pulled the info on the girl. She's cute for a chubby girl. Did you know she works for a sex toy store? Man, some of those things—"

"She's listening," Bliss announced at the same time Travis disconnected the Bluetooth.

"Keep your fucking opinions to yourself. I've got a license plate I need you to run," he said.

"Uh...Right, okay."

Sex toys?

He kept his gaze straight ahead, but his mind was already working overtime. What exactly did she do for them? Product testing?

"Can she hear me?" Gavin whispered. If it were possible, the kid had worse customer service skills than Travis.

"License plate." Fuck. Why did Zain have to be off on one of his nerd things?

"Right. I am so sorry, man. I'll email the stuff to you. She's clean. Well, I don't know her medical history, but otherwise, nothing hinky going on there. Unless it's in the bedroom. You think—"

Travis rattled off the plate number. Normally he wouldn't care what shit came out of Gavin's mouth, but this time it mattered. Without even looking at Bliss he was aware of her tense posture, the way she'd sat up straighter, smoothed her clothes down.

Chubby? That was not the word Travis would use. Gavin needed to grow the fuck up and stop looking at skin mags as his guide to women. Bliss was...real.

"Right. That plate traces back to a truck that was stolen," he said.

"The plates were on a car. Buick Electra, 1970s make I think, beige."

"Okay. Um, let me see what I can look up."

"Fine."

"Ration?"

"What?"

"Are you going to bang her?"

Travis rolled his eyes and ended the call.

Fucking Gavin. The guy was freakishly smart, but not where it counted sometimes. Travis remained still, waiting for the feminine explosion of rage. When Bliss didn't react, much less respond, he glanced her way. She'd pulled out her cell phone and was otherwise occupied. Should he apologize? He hadn't done anything wrong, and yet he couldn't shake the urge to make things right.

He'd call the BAU first. Maybe the right thing to do would come to him.

The call to his contact at the BAU went faster. They were no doubt working their own case and would go over the research when they could. By the time he hung up with the unit chief, he still didn't know what to say to Bliss.

"Sorry about Gavin. He's a stupid shit."

There.

That was good, right?

He reversed out of the spot and drove them out through the front gates.

"Your phone is really loud, just so you know." She glanced up. "Where are we going?"

Shit.

He was going to deck Gavin.

"Lunch? It'll take them a while to search for leads on the car. I can drop you back at your car if you like."

"No, that's fine. I told my boss I was going to be out for a few days. I have a few things I'll need to do, but they can wait."

Her at work...what did that mean? Did she test batteries in vibrators? Make them? Travis had never needed to use toys on a woman before. Everything he knew about them came from porn.

Shit. He wasn't any better than Gavin.

"You can ask me about it. My job, I mean." Bliss sighed and stared out of the passenger window.

He wanted to ask, but he wasn't sure he wanted to know.

"So...what is it you do?"

"I'm the sales manager for the Blush Shoppe. We sell a wide range of adult toys." She leaned her head against the seat and turned to watch him.

"You sell...what, exactly?"

"Have you ever seen a vibrator in person?" She chuckled.

"No."

"Oh, that was a fast reply."

He merged onto the highway but didn't miss the way Bliss rolled her eyes.

"What's that supposed to mean?" he asked.

"Guys and vibrators. You're all so intimidated by them."

"I am not."

"You're awfully defensive about it. What's wrong with a vibrator?" She turned to face him and perched her elbow on the armrest, leaning closer.

Did she have one? He was willing to bet she did by the way she spoke. Unbidden images unfolded in his mind. Bliss on her back, her hands between her legs...

"Nothing." He pulled into the first fast food restaurant he saw. The better to get out of this conversation.

"But you don't like them. Guys have porn. Why can't girls have vibrators?"

"It's not like that." He turned the SUV off and opened the door. Her sigh played on repeat to the mental image of Bliss pleasuring herself. It was damn frustrating to not be able to touch.

"Then what's the issue?" She made no move to get out of the truck.

He closed his door and faced her.

"Why need it at all?" he asked.

"Seriously?"

"A man should be able to take care of his woman's needs." Oh, if Bliss were his...she'd never have needs.

"What about everyone else? Not all of us have a man. And even the ones that do, what's wrong with it? I mean, do you only like one position for sex? Or do you change it up?" She froze, as if she hadn't intended to pose those questions to him.

This conversation should end. He needed to get out of the car, get some air, and pretend this never happened.

But he now knew one very important bit of information.

Bliss was single.

Her cheeks grew bright red.

Damn him.

"I like all the positions," he said.

Her, he'd do from behind so he could get his hands on her ass, a handful of her hair, bend her neck a bit for a hard kiss.

Bliss cleared her throat. Her hands were wrapped so tight around her phone her knuckles were white.

"That's not the point. I just meant...why limit the ways to enjoy sex?"

"That's never been a problem."

"Okay, then what if it can be different? Not better, just a little change."

"If a guy is doing it right—"

"But why does it have to be about the guy? Why can't it be about the girl?"

"It is."

"No, you keep coming at this talking about the man taking care of the woman, the man doing it right. It's about you. Not your partner. That right there is invalidating everything you say about wanting the other person to enjoy themselves, because it's about you. Let's just eat." She opened the car door and slipped out while he stared at the space she'd just vacated.

He wasn't selfish in bed. Was he?

5.

BLISS SAT DOWN IN a corner booth with her tray.

"Oh my God," she muttered to herself and buried her face in her hands.

Had she really just said that to Travis? A complete stranger? What had she been thinking?

She unzipped her hoodie and shed the outer layer. Her blush was still firmly in place, and to make it worse, she was hot all over now. The way Travis had looked at her and said...

Nope. She had to not think about that.

As if thinking of him summoned the man, he sank into the seat across from her. His legs immediately took up every available inch of below-table space she wasn't occupying. His knee brushed hers, their feet touched, tapped, and shuffled around as they situated themselves.

At least in a crowded restaurant, with children on either side of them, he'd let the conversation drop. Right?

He leaned toward her. There was a determined, focused look aimed directly at her. She squeezed her thighs together. This was not the time.

How was it she'd started working for Blush Shoppe not even being able to say the word *vibrator*, and now she was championing pleasure for all to a man she'd just met?

"I am not selfish," he said, pitching his voice low.

"Can we drop it?" she whispered, glancing around as if everyone knew what they were talking about.

"I'm not selfish," he said again.

"Okay. Fine. I'm sure you're very generous."

"What am I supposed to think, though? I don't have the right tools for the job?" He ducked his head at the word tools.

"It's not that." She unwrapped her burger. Her words needed to be chosen very carefully, not only because of where they were, but because Travis wasn't arguing against her. He was just a guy with normal guy hang-ups.

"Then what is it?"

"You're...focused on one type of tool. You don't use the same tools for every job. And I think you're only thinking about the...tab A in slot B scenario. What about everyone else? What about combinations of everyone else?" Their business served not just heterosexual couples, but every identification and sexual preference under the sun. Or close enough.

"Okay." Travis' brows were a dark line across his forehead, and his lips were pressed tightly together.

Neither of them had touched their food.

She needed another approach.

Think. Think. Think.

"Why do we have tools? Hammers, wrenches, all that stuff." She grabbed a fry and popped it in her mouth. Yeah, so Gavin what's-his-name had pegged her for being chubby. So what? She liked food.

"Because they're a more efficient way of getting a job done."

"Or...they do a job we physically cannot do. Think of...slot B...having parts that the human body cannot touch. Using the right tool you can. And...it's fun. What's wrong with that?"

He continued to stare at her for several moments.

"Nothing," he finally said.

"Are you seeing my point?"

"Maybe."

"Travis, it's not about tab A being the wrong size or length, it's about finding a fun way to get the job done. Try it some-time." She picked up her burger and took a bite.

Victory tasted like a quarter pound of beef with melty cheese. Her stomach growled, driving home the point she hadn't had breakfast.

"Mm." She licked a bit of cheese off her finger and glanced at Travis, who had yet to move.

He was staring at her, but not in the same way he had when she was speaking. Now he looked more like he had in the car.

All the positions.

All of them? In one go? Or would he spread them out over a week?

Shit.

Her sister might very well have been kidnapped, and she was sitting in a burger joint daydreaming about sex. She plucked a fry from the cup and crossed her legs, ignoring the sizzle of awareness that shot up her leg when she brushed against Travis under the table.

"What aren't you telling me about the women that were found dead?" she asked again.

The heat in his gaze died, and a predator of another nature stared back at her. She had no doubt that Travis Ration was a dangerous man. He was her dangerous man for now.

"Believe me when I say you don't want to know. We need to focus on finding your sister, fast."

"How are we going to do that? This guy, he got into their house, changed their security system, and God only knows what else." When she looked at it like that, there wasn't a lot of hope left.

He sighed and rubbed the side of his head.

"Port Said."

"What about it?" She didn't really care anymore.

"When we went into that op, we had seven guys to rescue two girls that were being held by a trafficking group. They controlled the area, took two of our guys hostage, and injured three others. That left me and another guy to make the call. I'm shit at field medicine, so he had to take care of the other three while I went to get our guys back and find the girls, but they'd moved them out of the city. I spent a couple days on my own, tracking them down to a fishing village where they were waiting for pickup."

"Shut up." Her mind painted the images—a beautiful, Mediterranean vista, white buildings, blue mosaics, and men with guns. Lots of guns. In the middle of it all was Travis. She doubted he wore camo paint on his face, but her brain supplied that feature anyway.

"Found the girls first, which was shitty luck, because they screamed every time they saw their shadow, but we all got out of there alive."

"Were you hurt?"

"Yeah."

"How bad?"

"Took a couple bullets, broke my nose." He shrugged as if it weren't an issue.

"And you walked out of there?"

"Adrenaline works for you in an instance like that."

She swallowed hard. Her brain wasn't capable of comprehending what he'd done. It played in her head like an action flick, but it wasn't entertainment. This was his life. He was the real deal.

"What were you? I mean, before Aegis?"

"I was a SEAL."

"Working for Aegis is better?"

"It's a good gig." He shrugged. "My point is, if she's out there, I'll find her."

Bliss chewed her lip. He might find Wendy, but would she be alive?

"You done?" He gestured to her folded wrapper and empty fry cup.

"Yeah." She glanced at her phone. Yet another message marked urgent hovered in her notification bar. "I need to run by my office."

"No problem. Can I ask you questions on the way?"

"What kind of questions?"

"About your sister. I'm looking for where the other victim's lives intersect."

"Sure. If it'll help, I'll answer what I can."

"Good."

Travis picked up her tray and scooted out of the booth. She followed, lagging behind a bit. He'd taken how many bullets and just kept going? He didn't limp. There was a smoothness to his stride, and his posture spoke of confidence. What good thing had she done to randomly run into him like she had?

BLISS GAVE TRAVIS DIRECTIONS to her Blush Shoppe office. Their storefront was within easy walking distance of the Vegas strip. They often got foot traffic from vacationers looking for something crazy to add to their experience. The Blush Shoppe was by far the biggest retail store in the city.

She did her best to black out the little fact that she was about to bring this man into her workspace. Her very sexual and graphic workspace. Bliss' office might be on the third story, far away from the retail areas, but they still had to go through the store and one of their storage areas. Instead, she focused on the questions Travis fired at her. They covered everything from where Wendy had gone to grade school to where she got her nails done.

"Tell me about the security system again," he said.

"They got it installed right before Wendy gave birth."

"How long ago was that?"

"Gosh, Paul is six months old, so probably eight or so months ago?"

"Who responds to the security calls?"

"I don't know. The police?"

"There's two basic kinds of security systems. Monitored and un-monitored. A monitored system will have someone who contacts the home owner, maybe through the control panel or a phone call. An un-monitored system is just that. Some of them will text the owner."

"Monitored. In the beginning there were a few times Wendy didn't arm it right, and someone would start talking to her."

"Okay."

"Why? What are you thinking?"

Travis glanced at her.

"What?" Bliss had the sneaking suspicion he wasn't telling her everything. Again.

"Just seems strange, your brother-in-law adding security before his kid is born."

"They were worried..." About what? "Is this somehow connected to Grayson?"

"I don't know the man, but he knows about us. There are two types of people who hire Aegis. The kind that are scared shitless, and the kind that scare people."

"So, what?"

"I'm not sure. But even if it's unrelated, you might want to know more about what it is your brother-in-law does. As far as right now is concerned, I need to check the other victim's files, see what I can dig up."

"You have a theory though." And she had questions.

He turned into the newly paved and painted Blush Shoppe parking lot. The three story brick structure had been painted white, with pink trim and an awning over the store front. Inviting and cheerful, or at least that's what the owner was going for. The lights and mannequins decked out like porno showgirls were all Vegas. What the heck was Travis going to say once he got inside?

This was going to be fun.

He killed the engine and turned to dig something out of the back seat.

"I need to look at some things. Want me to wait out here, or would you mind if I came in?"

"If you think you can handle it, you can come inside." But could she?

The store staff was a chatty, gossiping bunch. Travis was going to set them off, but on the other hand, she wouldn't mind their assumptions. He was one beefcake she wouldn't turn down.

She got out of the SUV and strode into the store, painfully aware of the man at her back. The bells chimed over the door, announcing their arrival. Two heads popped up from behind the glass display cases. Both sales associate's brows shot up, neither looking at her.

"Hey Bliss, boss is looking for you," the first girl said.

"I know. I know." Bliss shouldered her purse and stopped abruptly.

"Need us to entertain your friend?" the other girl offered.

Christ. The mammoth butt plugs had arrived, and the boxes were arranged like a Christmas tree right in front of the door. She eyed the tacky string of lights casting ominous red light onto the black toy.

"Who did this?" She turned toward the two crawling out from behind the cases. The new hot and cold glass dildos were out, finally. Not like she'd asked for them to do that for a week or anything. "This is not a front of the store item. A casual shopper is not going to purchase a butt plug the size of a cantaloupe. Move this. Put the red and green vibes up here, some fuzzy handcuffs. And where did the naughty elf costumes go? Fix this. Now."

Bliss didn't wait for the two to respond. The shop wasn't technically her responsibility, but damn it, they couldn't scare people off the moment they walked through the door.

She took the shortcut through the masturbation section to the stairs. There was no way to avoid the bondage area, so she lifted her chin, pushed her shoulders back and strolled past some of their more intimidating gear to the Staff Only door. She breathed a little easier, at least until she caught a glimpse of partially inflated blow-up dolls. Christ. She didn't want to know. The warehouse was not her area.

If she'd had her thinking cap on, measuring Travis' reaction to the front display would have given her the perfect ammunition when the sales associates inevitably argued about switching out the merchandise. They wanted the shop to invite men just like Travis in to purchase items for themselves and their partners, but putting an extreme toy hardly anyone purchased front and center wasn't the way to make it happen.

6.

OH GOD, TRAVIS HAD just seen the butt plugs. He couldn't handle the idea of a vibrator, what was he going to think of a butt plug? Or the floggers? Or the sheep-shaped blow up dolls?

Calm down.

Bliss kept her gaze straight ahead and walked past the industrial shelves full of boxes and carefully inventoried sex toys.

What did it matter what he thought?

Okay, he was an attractive man once she got past the scary factor, but he was responsible for finding her missing sister. That was it. Besides, she was chubby and her vibrator collection would undoubtedly scare him away.

One more flight of stairs, a hallway, and she unlocked her office, stepping into her sanctuary. She held her office door open for Travis and shut it behind him. Hopefully everyone else would take the hint and leave her alone.

"Sorry about that," she mumbled and retreated to her desk chair.

Her office was one of the more spacious ones, but that was because she was now in charge of order fulfillment to their bulk-buying clients. Namely, the adult film producers who sometimes liked an in-person meeting and demonstration of the products. Her desk was the size of Texas and she had two windows with a lovely view of the mountains. She turned on her desktop and waited for it to boot up.

"Do people...use those?" Travis sat across from her in one of the desk chairs. He had a few brown folders laid out in front of him and a frown on his face.

"Not enough to matter, and that's the point."

"But there are people who use them?"

"Yes." She tried to not bristle, but she knew the condemnation was next, and she couldn't help but take those comments personally. She might never want a cantaloupe sized thing shoved up her ass, but if she did, why judge?

"Christ...I don't think I want to know. Different strokes I guess."

Bliss glanced at him, waiting for Travis to tack on some other statement, but he was too busy looking at the walls. That was it?

"The BDSM practitioners who visit the store have a saying—*Your kink isn't my kink*. I feel like the sentiment applies to most of the stuff we sell." She relaxed marginally.

Not so bad.

She logged into her computer and brought up her email. Of course it had to be the holidays. Shipping was tricky and their sales volume was high, which was a good sign for the next year.

"Employee of the Year?" Travis' voice broke her concentration from composing a carefully worded email.

"Uh, yeah."

"How do you get that working here? Or do I not want to know?"

"What is it you think I do?" She turned to face him slightly. "You had your computer nerd run some sort of check on me. Why?"

She'd focused on the wrong part of that conversation. It wasn't just that Gavin what's-his-face knew she was chubby or that she worked in adult boutique. He had everything at his fingertips. He didn't even need to ask her questions about Wendy because he probably already had it all in his email.

"Some of the messiest jobs I've been on involved a family member who came into a lot of money being kidnapped by their brother, cousin, uncle or whatever. It's routine."

"Don't I have to sign something to let you do that?"

"No."

"What else did you learn about me?"

"Nothing you haven't told me. I haven't had time to look."

"But you have it."

"Gavin would have sent it to me, yes."

"If you want to know something, just ask. I'd do anything for my sister." She didn't have anything to hide, but it was an invasion of her privacy.

"That right there. It makes you a suspect." He leaned forward, elbows on the arm rests. Somehow he made the chairs look child-size with his bulk and height. He couldn't even stop taking up the space in her office.

"Because I love my sister?" She stared at him. That was the biggest load of bull she'd ever heard.

"Your sister sounds like a nice person, but she can't take care of herself. She needs you, her husband, family and even staff to get her through a day. I'm assuming this was true before the baby and pregnancy. Dependence like that breeds discontent. Especially now that she has money and doesn't have to work for anything. Someone like you could see it as a way to scheme some money out of them, since you've done so much for her and you're still having to work here."

Her jaw dropped. Was he serious? White-hot rage burned through her.

"That's not true," she blurted. "Any of it. I love my sister, and I'm glad she has Grayson in her life. And I like my job."

But was she being completely honest? Weren't there nights she lay in bed, alone and a tiny bit bitter that things worked out so easily for Wendy?

"Bliss, I'm not saying that's the case here. We know it isn't, but I've seen it happen. I want to clear that line of investigation so we can focus on finding her. You are not a suspect."

She jabbed the keys on her computer, pounding out the messages that had to be handled. She wasn't ready to stop being angry with him. He was still going to tromp through her life. He hadn't said he wouldn't.

"I'm not trying to say anything bad about your situation. Shit. This is why I don't talk to clients." He flipped through one of the folders in his lap. The silence drew out for several minutes, neither of them speaking. "You mind if I make a few calls?"

"Go ahead."

Bliss kept her eyes on the screen. Why the heck were producers working this close to Christmas? And clearly it was too much to ask her boss to deal with them right now.

I love my job.

"Yeah, hi, my wife and I wanted some information on getting a new system installed." Travis had one of her pens and a sticky note in front of him. Had he noticed the phallic designs yet? She didn't think so. "Do you monitor your system

yourself? Or do you have a company that does that? ...Yeah...
Oh...I understand, but we can't in good faith make a decision
without knowing who we're talking to... That would be great,
thank you. Compliance Systems? Got it. And what are your
rates? ...Perfect. I'll talk it over with the wife and get back to
you."

"What was that about?" she asked.

"2008. The only reason authorities knew Mindy was missing was because her alarm was set off by her cat trying to get
outside. He'd been locked in the house for a week without
food."

"Is that a lead?"

"Maybe." He held his phone up to his hear. "We'll find
out."

How was she supposed to concentrate on dildos right
now?

DANIEL TWISTED THE KEY in the padlock until the tum-
blers gave way. He'd debated disposing of his latest projects.
Two of them were such good subjects. The third didn't have
much promise. He wouldn't be surprised if that one expired
on its own. In truth, it was fairer to terminate them now. His
new wife would be taking up much of his time while they set
about starting their new family.

He lifted the door and opened it by force. Time and age
had worn the wood down. He was considering widening the
path and installing a better door, but that would mean putting in more permanent electricity. Right now, he flipped a
switch at the house, and power flowed out to his workshop.
Three lights illuminated the honeymoon suite, his holding
cells, and the workshop. There was only one outlet for his
power tools—everything else was done by hand.

"Good afternoon, dear. Sleep well?" He closed the door behind him to keep the wind out and shed his jacket. The keys were a heavy weight against his hip.

Wendy had her back against the bars on the far side of the suite. He hoped she liked his house and would be a good mother to his other children. He'd made sure to dust them all off in preparation for the introductions.

The subject in cell one whispered something to her, and she jumped.

His Wendy was so delicate.

"I slept well," she said.

"Good. Good. One last bit of housekeeping and we can finally be together." He smiled at her and unlocked the door to her suite. It was a bit on the rustic side. Some of his previous wives hadn't liked it much, but Wendy had good breeding and manners. She could appreciate the aesthetic.

"What are you doing?" Wendy's dark eyes widened, and she pushed to her feet. She was so thin she swayed and had to grip the bars for support. That wouldn't do. He'd need her strong and healthy, so she could give him a son.

"Taking care of some loose ends."

He locked the door behind him and strode across to the workshop entrance. Wendy thoughtfully kept out of his way, which was good.

He could not wait for their honeymoon.

"Loose ends? What does that mean?" Her voice raise in pitch, reverberating off the stone.

"He means he's going to kill us," the subject in cell one said. He was an older man, roughly sixty years old, who Daniel had picked up off a street corner. The subject was hardy and had held on, despite being separated from every major limb. It was a shame to dispose of him, but Daniel had more important things to think about.

"You're what? You can't kill them." Wendy's voice wavered.

He hated the wavering. It lead to tears, and not the regal, quiet ones Wendy had shed last night. The ones that turned noses and eyes red and shook bodies.

"Be quiet," he snarled and banged the gate.

"It's okay, Wendy," the subject in cell two said. He was younger, an addict with a resilient body.

"Do not speak to my wife." Daniel thrust his finger at subject two, who merely stared at him.

Daniel peered in at the subject in cell four, but the body was an empty husk. A pity, since that took all the fun out of it, but not having to deal with a squirming subject would be easier in the long run, and he was still healing from the knife wound.

He opened the cell and dragged the body to his workshop in the back. The old wooden table had supported many such projects over the years. Deep gouges scored the wood from blades and nails alike.

It was time to put these subjects to rest with the others. Then, and only then, could he get on with the business of starting his new family.

7.

TRAVIS HAD A LEAD. Something the BAU hadn't given him.

Of the eight victims, he'd been able to track down five with home security, and three of those were monitored by a contract company called Compliance Systems. The issue with having a killer who went a full year between kills was that it was difficult to impossible to tap into the earlier victims' lives. He needed a warrant for Compliance to obtain their data. But that would take time, especially since they would need to convince the cops they had an actual case on their hands.

He dialed one last number, but it went to the BAU unit chief's voicemail.

"Hey, Brooks, it's Travis again. Just checking on that lead. I think I've got something. Call me when you have time."

Damn it. He needed the information now, and Gavin's search hadn't turned up jack shit as of yet. If Zain were... No. He squashed that thought. Gavin had the same tools at his disposal Zain would in this instance.

"What'd you find?" Bliss breezed back into the office, carrying three small brown boxes stacked on top of one another. She set the haul on the far side of her desk and sat down.

"Our guy might work for this company that contracts out to answer home alarms."

"Really? That's good, right?"

"Yeah, except now how to tell which one he might be?" He tossed his phone onto the desk. "I need the car info to cross-reference employees, and we still need a warrant."

"Oh."

"What about you? Get everything done?" He almost wanted to know what was in the boxes. He'd never realized there was so much variety to sex toys.

"Almost. I need to pull a few other items and send a few emails still."

"How'd you get this job?"

"Craigslist. They advertised. I answered. And it's been three profitable years."

"I gotta ask, how does a girl like you work here?"

"Girl like me? What's that supposed to mean?" She turned to face him, hands in her lap and one brow quirked. He was learning to recognize her ticked-off face. He'd had one hell of a time pissing her off today no matter what he did. It was a skill he could do without.

"Just...normal." He shrugged. And not for the likes of him. He needed to remember that.

"Normal girls don't like jobs that pay them well?"

"That's not what I mean."

"You mean, why would I work for a sex toy company instead of...I don't know, a law firm or something?"

"Yes."

"At first, I just needed a job. Something to pay the bills. I'll admit, I was embarrassed in the beginning, but not anymore. Sure, it's not your typical career path, but sex sells. People like sex. And you know what? The people who work in and around this industry are incredibly nice and accepting. I've never been so comfortable just being me. There's some parts of my job I don't like, but there's so much more that I do."

"That question made me sound like an ass again, didn't it?"

"Yes."

"I didn't mean to—"

"Forget about it."

He rubbed the side of his face. He liked Bliss. She was smoking hot, smart, and she had...gumption. It was the only word he could think of for her. She was a fighter—quick on her feet and fierce when he pushed the wrong buttons. Once she'd pulled herself together, she'd actually been very useful looking over the footage at the guard shack.

There were plenty of guys who got involved with clients. In fact, the guys who did bodyguard work often called the gigs booty calls. It was a line he'd never crossed. But Bliss technically wasn't the client. She was...a source? It was more personal than that, but she was firmly in the gray area. Travis didn't like the area where lines blurred. It was an act firmly in the gray area that had screwed up his life forever, which was why he stuck to black and white. The letter of his orders. Doing exactly what he was paid to do. That way there was no confusion. But Bliss?

He was trying to come up with a reason to not act on the attraction pulling him ever closer to her. If he didn't, he was pretty sure they'd fall into bed together at some point. Was that a bad thing?

"We've already established where you are with the idea of sex toys." She chuckled and turned away from him when he didn't continue the conversation. What was he supposed to say? He'd been an ass and admitted it. Again.

"Hold on, I'm not entirely against them." He was plagued by the images of Bliss and a couple of the items he'd seen in the store. Some of them he wasn't even sure what they did, but she would know. And he was willing to bet she'd enjoy it, too.

Fuck it. Why not put it out there and let her make the call?

"Had a change of heart, have you?" She chuckled.

"You've made me rethink things."

"Well, then my job here is done." She laughed, and all he could do was stare. Her bracelets jangled as she pushed her hair back. She'd taken her hoodie off. She wore a loose, sleeveless black top that hinted at and hid what was underneath. There was a hint of ink on the back of her shoulder. He couldn't make it out, but he wanted to know what it was.

"If you were going to sell me one thing in the store, what would you recommend?" His groin tightened, and he could feel the throb of arousal in his balls.

"To use on yourself? Or a partner?"

"They make stuff for guys?"

"Oh yeah." She turned and snagged something out of the top brown box. "This is a male masturbation toy. The end looks like lips and the inside is supposed to mimic the way a mouth feels if you use it with a little lube. It's a popular item."

His mouth dried up and he had to swallow to get his vocal chords working. He was not even remotely interested in buying something to jack off with.

"What about on a woman?" He cleared his throat.

"Depends on who you're buying for. What's your girl-friend, or wife, like?"

"I'm single."

"Hm. Okay, then..." She squinted at the ceiling for a moment.

"What would you pick?"

"For myself?" She blinked at him, and if he wasn't mistaken her cheeks were slightly pink yet again.

"Well, what would you want your partner to use on you?"

"That's personal." She grabbed a stack of papers and fanned herself. "It's really hot in here, isn't it?"

"I'm pretty sure we've been dancing around the fact we're interested in each other most of the morning." He eased back in the chair, but it didn't allow any extra room in his jeans like he'd hoped.

Bliss' blush reached from her neckline to her hairline now.

They were consenting adults, right? After he found Wendy there wouldn't be any gray area. No uncertainty.

"Uh...well...I, um..."

"I'm not good at talking, and I'm worse when it comes to women. I figure the best thing for me is to be direct. If that's a problem, tell me now. You can also tell me to fuck off, if you like."

Her chest rose and fell at a slightly accelerated rate. He would know. He'd done a little study of her breasts earlier. Double Ds if he wasn't mistaken, but he'd need a hands-on inspection to be certain.

"A bullet," she said and turned to the monitor.

"A bullet?"

"Yes, and not the kind that come out of a gun, either."

He opened the browser on his phone and went to the store's site. It was better than wandering around the shop trying to figure out what the hell that was.

A bullet, huh?

She hadn't told him off, so that was one good thing so far today.

BLISS KEPT HER GAZE straight ahead. Wendy's gated community was three turns away. Bliss' car was in the drive. In a matter of minutes Travis would drop her off and go do whatever commando-type thing he did to rescue people. Or something. She wasn't sure what he would do, but her imagination supplied plenty of scenarios, some she wished would get out of her head.

"Heard anything yet?" She couldn't shake the feeling that the freaking FBI should have been able to get information sooner. After all, wasn't that how it worked on TV?

"No."

"Why?"

"Reasons." He turned the SUV into the community. The guard from earlier waved them in. From the looks of it, the guy had sucked a lemon since they last saw him.

"And those would be? How is the FBI even involved? I don't understand."

"It's complicated."

"Explain it to me."

Travis drove all the way to Wendy's house and put the truck in park. She turned to face him. If she had to make him understand, she would.

"She's my sister. I want to know what to expect. I know you think I'm some weak, crying woman, but I had my moment. It's over. I need to know if I should prepare our family for the worst. You don't get it, but things haven't always been easy with Wendy. Wendy...she tried to kill herself a couple of times in high school."

Travis turned his head and stared at her with those un-readable eyes of his. Was she getting through to him? Did he maybe understand? She'd lay it out there for him from be-ginning to end if she thought it would help.

"There weren't programs, support groups, or social media movements back then. College...we were just glad she sur-vived it, to be honest. When she married Grayson, it was like we had a new version of her. Like...I don't know, she had this real second chance. This depression, it's high school all over again. She hasn't been suicidal, thank God, but that's what we're afraid of. Our parents are still in denial about her de-pression right now, so if there's no chance she's still alive, I need to know so I can prepare them. Losing her...it'll break their hearts."

"If the guy I'm hunting took her, she's still alive."

"And if it was someone else?"

"We still have time."

"You won't tell me what happens to the girls."

"No. You don't need to know that."

"But what if it happens to Wendy?"

"It won't."

"How do you know that?"

"I just—"

His phone rang through the speakers, cutting off what he was about to tell her.

"Brooks, what did you—oh, Lali? Hi." Travis produced a pad of paper from the center console and a pen. "Right... Okay... Compliance Systems, any chance that's a current or past employer? ...God damn it, yes. I'm on my way now."

"What? Did they find her?"

Travis ended the call and tossed the phone onto the dash with a clatter. He gestured at the passenger door.

"Get out," he said.

"No."

"Bliss, I'm not fucking around. You need to get out now."

"I'm not getting out of this truck. You can haul me out, but I'll follow you. She's my sister. I've always been there for her, it's always been me picking up her pieces. If you find her, do you know what to do for her? Do you know how to handle her?"

She was pretty sure she could hear Travis' teeth grinding. They stared at each other for a moment.

"Fuck." He sat back in his seat. "One, you stay in the god damned truck. Two, you do what I say or I'll damn well hand-cuff you and put you in the back. Three, keep your head down."

"That sounds kinky."

"This isn't a game, Bliss."

"I know, I know, I'm sorry. Drive. I will do exactly what you tell me to, I promise." She buckled her seatbelt. "Where are we going?"

"Out of town a ways. The plates we got were stolen. They belonged to a guy in New Mexico. They hit on something when they cross-referenced the make and model of the car to the employee records at Compliance Systems."

"And? Should we call the police? Or what?"

"I'll call my backup. When we have Wendy, we'll call the cops in to make the arrest." He pressed the accelerator so hard they shot forward and the tires squealed.

"Then what?"

"Then you and Wendy get your lives back."

Travis snatched his phone before it scuttled across the dash to her side and made another call. She could barely focus on his side of the conversation. How would they find Wendy? Would she be okay? Or would they be picking up pieces? Should Bliss even be part of this? There was no way she was about to back out now she'd convinced Travis to bring her, but she had to wonder if it was the smartest place for her. Regardless, her points about Wendy and needing her were true.

"Fuck." Travis tossed the phone into a cup holder and gripped the wheel with both hands.

"What?"

"They can't leave for an hour. God damn it."

"Why?"

"Because they're here on another job and can't leave their client."

"Oh. So, what are we doing?"

"I'm going in. You will stay in the truck."

"What if you need help?"

"I can handle myself."

"But, what if you get into trouble? Should I call the cops after a little while?"

"Cops will just get in my way."

"Okay, but—"

"If you're going to question the way I do things, get out now."

Bliss clamped her lips together and held onto the door. Travis pushed the SUV faster entering the ramp onto I-15 headed out of Vegas. They passed the Speedway and kept going. The barren landscape spread out all around them, broken up only by rocks, shrubs, and the odd assortment of trash. Every so often his phone issued navigation instructions, leading them further away from the interstate and anything resembling civilization. They passed the occasional dirt trail leading away from the old road, but were otherwise alone.

"Where are we?" she asked after they'd driven nearly half an hour in silence.

"Northeast of Vegas."

"How close are we?"

"This should be our turn, here." He nodded at yet another path leading away from the road. This one was gravel instead of dirt.

"Why aren't you turning?" She craned her neck to look behind them.

"You don't drive up to a kidnapper's house and ask for your loved one back. That's not how this works."

She'd grown somewhat accustomed to Travis' gruff nature of speaking, but now it was different. His voice was cold, nearly emotionless. He didn't glance away from the road—he was completely focused. She didn't know if she should be scared or impressed.

"What are you going to do?"

He slowed the SUV and checked the mirrors, peering behind them before pulling off the road onto a bit of clear ground.

"You'll stay here. I'm going to have a look around." He reached into the center console and removed not one, but two black handguns and an assortment of other things.

Bliss recoiled, pressing her back to the door. She'd never seen a gun in person, at least not out of a holster. It made sense that he'd have a firearm, and she didn't want him to go into a dangerous situation without some sort of protection.

But this was her life. Her boring, typical, normal life. These things didn't happen to her.

"By yourself?"

"No, me and my army. Yes, by myself." Travis slid one gun into the top of his right boot. He shrugged into a strange shoulder harness. The second gun went into a holster that rested just under his left arm.

By all accounts, Travis should be able to take care of himself. It wasn't the story he'd told her about Egypt, it was the way he carried himself, the cool confidence, the deadly focus. Yet she couldn't help worrying about him.

"Please be careful," she said.

He stopped and stared at her from behind the aviators. Okay, having that full focus on her was way more intimidating when she couldn't see his eyes. He had big and creepy down to an art, but she could remember what his gaze felt like with heat in it.

"I'll bring your sister back."

"Thank you. But be careful with yourself, too, okay?"

His brow wrinkled as if he didn't understand her.

"Hand me that water in the door." He pointed at the three bottles.

"Should I do anything? Call anyone?" She handed a bottle over.

"No. Keep the truck running"

"I'm not used to sitting around waiting on other people to fix things."

"Be glad you don't have to wait much longer." He pushed his door open.

"Travis?" She reached across and touched his hand gripping the steering wheel.

He paused, one foot already out of the door.

"Seriously, be careful? Please?"

"Your brother-in-law isn't paying me to be careful with myself. He's paying me to get Wendy back."

"Well I'm telling you to be careful."

Again his brow wrinkled.

Were they even speaking the same language?

He pulled his leg back into the truck. His features softened, and she realized there was a lot less room between them now.

"I'll be careful," he said slowly.

She wanted to kiss those lips. It was a desire she'd been ignoring, but now, with only his mouth to focus on, she couldn't deny the urge. He was dangerous and completely not her nice-guy type, but there was something about him that rubbed her the right way.

"Bliss?"

Wow, really nice lips.

"Yes?"

They weren't thin like most men's. Not that he had full, pouty lips either. They were...nice. Enough there to toy with, nibble on, but not draw all the attention to those two bits of flesh. They were the kind of lips a girl wanted to touch.

Travis' hand cupped the back of her head and all thought ceased. She was keenly aware of the way his fingers caught in her hair, the jolt of electric arousal shooting through her body. He pulled her closer. She gasped the second before their mouths met. Her toes curled, and she reached for him, gripping his bicep and leaning into the kiss. He suckled her lower lip. His stubble scraped against her chin and cheek.

"Stay here," he said.

She blinked, but he was already gone.

Holy crap.

Bliss wanted to kiss him again.

She pressed the lock button and wrapped her arms around herself. Travis was going to get Wendy back. Then she was going to kiss the daylights out of that man.

8.

WHAT THE HELL?

Travis took a sip of water and peered at the house in the distance. He was getting closer, and he needed to stop thinking with his dick. Kissing Bliss had been...fantastic. And a terrible idea. She might not be paying him, but she was still a client. For now. Some guys might not be terribly bothered about bedding their temporary employer, but not Travis. The way he saw it, when he was brought into a situation it was always under great duress.

Bliss wasn't thinking clearly. She was emotional, and he was the man there to fix her problems. It made sense she'd flirt with him. It was a common case of hero syndrome, or whatever his boss called it. Any other month, she wouldn't look at him. A guy with his record didn't get girls like her. But for this moment in time, she did. And it was fucking with his head.

He needed to find Wendy and get her out of here so the cops could do their job and put this bastard away. Then he could go back to his normal routine of catching bullets.

The FBI's tech had a name for their serial killer.

Daniel Campbell. Fifty-four. He'd lived in and around Las Vegas for most of his life. He'd started out as an electrician before an accident ten years ago made an active lifestyle impossible. There was a string of minor charges against him for bar brawls, but otherwise nothing since his juvenile days, and those records were sealed.

The structure was a small stucco style house set in the foothills of Muddy Mountain. The terrain rolled and rose, painted a riot of color by the late-afternoon light, a bed of rocks and shrub that worked great for masking his approach. Getting away was another matter. He hoped Ethan and Mason showed up, or else he'd be hoofing it back to the truck, probably carrying Wendy. He'd done more under worse circumstances, but now he had Bliss to worry about. He should have made her stay put at the house, but when she argued her point so thoroughly, he couldn't deny her.

Travis adjusted his path, aiming for the back part of the house. There was a large rock formation that could hide his approach and allow him to get closer without tipping Daniel Campbell off. Nearly twenty minutes later he was starting to sweat, but he could finally make out details of the house and surrounding property.

The gravel drive extended all the way to the house, and sitting in plain sight was the same late model Buick he'd seen on the security cameras driving out of Wendy's gated community. The skin between Travis' shoulder blades prickled. He drew his weapon and pulled out his cell phone, but there was no signal. Not even the ghost of a bar. He was on his own. It wasn't the first time, but back-up in a hostage situation was always ideal.

He got as close as the rock cover would allow, and settled in to observe the residence. Daniel's land was a long, narrow rectangle, stretching from the road all the way back to the mountain. Most of the shrub appeared to have been burned back at some point. A few scraggly bushes sat sentinel under the windows, but otherwise the property was quiet. Nothing stirred the curtains and there were no other signs of life.

Or were there?

Travis took off his sunglasses and peered at a narrow, worn path weaving between the cacti and scrub. He glanced at the house, searching for cameras or other surveillance equipment, but didn't spot anything. He pushed off the rocks and picked his way to the path, keeping low. In places, the overgrown brush was tall enough to hide him. If he hadn't been up on the rocks, he wouldn't have spied it.

There was a good chance he was being watched right now by means of small cameras. He could be walking into a trap, but it was the nature of his job to be caught, shot at, and attacked, so long as he protected his client. In this case, that meant not only Wendy, but Bliss as well. Like it or not, he was walking out of here no matter what condition he was in.

The path led between boulders and back into a narrow crevice. Travis had to turn sideways to squeeze through. At some point the sides had been carved back and smoothed out for someone with a smaller build than his.

He peered around a bend in the path and stared at an old, wooden door with a padlock drilled into the rock face.

BLISS CHECKED HER PHONE. Again.

Time was moving too fast. It needed to slow the hell down. There hadn't been as much as a smoke signal from Travis, and the sun was starting to set. What was going on over there? Was Wendy okay? What if they were both dead?

They hadn't agreed on a time limit, and she had no way to contact Travis' friends.

Something horrible had to have happened.

She rubbed her eyes with her hands. Wendy's face, frozen in fear, filled the darkness behind her lids. A hundred nightmares of losing her sister filtered through her brain. It wasn't Wendy's fault nature had made them different. Bliss loved everything that made her sister unique.

No one could see beauty in the unexpected like Wendy.

Despite Wendy's delicate appearance, she was strong. Even when she'd been stuck full of needles by doctors, she'd never once complained.

There wasn't a person in Bliss' life who loved like Wendy.

Bliss couldn't lose her little sister.

She crawled across to the driver's seat. Her feet were a long way from the pedals, highlighting just how much taller Travis was than her. She adjusted the seat and gripped the wheel.

What was she going to do?

Travis was tough, but he was still human.

She opened the center console and peered in, holding her breath. It wasn't like he could hide a rocket launcher in there, but he had quietly stashed two guns right under her nose.

A few receipts, some business cards, and two cardboard boxes littered the bottom of the console. Tucked up against the side was a large pocketknife. It was better than nothing.

Bliss shifted into drive and whipped the SUV around, driving back toward the gravel drive. She wasn't strong like Travis, but she wasn't about to let someone hurt her sister.

In high school, Bliss had faced down the mean girls, in college she'd run off the losers. There wasn't anything she wouldn't do for Wendy. But it wasn't just her sister that Bliss was fretting over.

Travis was the kind of man she avoided on principal. The bad boys made great poster boyfriends when she was younger, but as an adult she'd always been attracted to the nice guy type. Nice guys didn't break hearts. That was her job. Travis, though, being around him made her second-guess everything she thought she knew about her love life. He was a different kind of man. She could feel it in her bones. The way he thought, his stubbornness, and how he'd kissed her. He didn't fit into a neat box, and she couldn't help being concerned about him. She didn't want him getting hurt either.

She turned the truck down the drive and pressed the accelerator. The vehicle bounced down the road, kicking up plumes of dust in her wake.

The house grew closer, solidifying into a flat roof and stucco walls. It was old and dated, but not in a good way. Wooden posts supported a sagging porch, and the windows were so dirty she couldn't tell if there were curtains or just a layer of filth.

There was no sign of Travis or Wendy.

Where were they?

The back of her neck prickled. Apprehension and adrenaline made it hard to breathe. She glanced around, searching for some movement, some sign they were there. Had she missed a turn off? Was there another house?

Her cell phone had zero bars.

No wonder Travis hadn't phoned for help.

He had to be in trouble.

She pulled the knife out of her pocket. It was too big for her hands, but the longer blade gave her a modicum of confidence.

Travis and Wendy had to be in that house. There weren't any other buildings or places to hide. The only reason Travis wouldn't be back already was if they were in trouble. It was up to her now.

Bliss killed the engine and opened the door. The thump of drums and the twang of a guitar could be heard through the house's walls. Well, if a killer was trying to drown out the noise of...she didn't want to think about it, but it made sense.

She slipped out of the SUV. Her boots crunched on the gravel, and the bitter wind sliced through her hoodie. She'd dressed for shopping, not hunting her sister's kidnapper.

Instead of heading straight for the front door, Bliss swung to her left, aiming for the right side of the house. She kept her gaze on the windows, watching for movement. Nothing stirred or maybe the windows were too dirty to tell. She put her back to the side of the house and breathed a deep breath.

In her peripheral vision she caught sight of something familiar. She peered around the house, but all she could see was the back half of a Buick. She didn't know a lot about cars, but it looked like the same one she'd seen on the security footage.

"Oh, God."

She put her hands on her knees and sucked down a deep breath.

This was real.

Her sister was here.

And so was the man who'd taken her.

Bliss gathered her scattered thoughts and collected herself. This was crazy and stupid. She wasn't the person for this job, but she was all there was. Unless she wanted to call the cops and wait for them to get there. Travis and Wendy might die before then.

She crept around the front of the house and craned her neck to try to get a look inside the house, but it was dark. And shiny.

Trash bags.

There were trash bags on the inside of the windows.

How very Dexter.

She ducked and hustled to the front door. She crouched next to it and listened to the music. After this, she'd never be able to hear country and western music without cringing.

Bliss grasped the doorknob and pushed the unlocked door inward. It swung open on squeaky hinges, casting light into an otherwise dark interior. She waited for a second or two, but no one rushed out at her with an axe and there was no screaming.

She straightened and leaned inside.

To the right, the wood paneling dated the house at forty years old. Built-in wooden shelving cut off her view of the living room. Straight ahead she could make out what looked to be the kitchen. She brushed the wall, feeling for a light switch.

A single bulb flickered on in the entry, doing little more than the fading sunlight.

Something wasn't right.

If this guy had Travis, wouldn't Travis have put up a fight? Wouldn't there be yelling, or at least someone talking?

She stepped over the threshold. Another set of light switches was farther to her right, almost inside the living room. She tiptoed toward them, cringing when a floor board squeaked. The ceiling fan spun on a wobbly base and only one light came on when she flipped the switch.

The TV on the far side of the room was the source of the music. Some singer she couldn't name belted out a tune while sparks went off behind him. Bliss crossed to the older TV and hit the power button.

Silence descended on the house. Or near-silence. Her ears rang, and she wasn't sure if she could hear herself think yet.

She held completely still, listening for any sign of life.

The hair on the back of her neck rose.

He was right behind her, wasn't he?

Bliss pivoted, lifting the knife at the same time, but she was alone.

Staring back at her from the built-ins were at least a dozen little faces.

She gasped and stumbled back, hitting the TV with her elbow.

They were babies. Some of them were so small they would have fit in her palm, while others were maybe a couple of months old. The size of Paul. They each floated in their own glass jar, surrounded by murky liquid. Their little features were bloated and distorted until they didn't look human.

"Oh my God." She covered her mouth. Her throat constricted, and her stomach began to revolt.

Travis had said there were others. Was this what he hadn't told her? That the women were broodmares for...whatever this was?

An engine rumbled up to the back of the house. Bliss ducked out of the living room and stared through the little window on the rear door. A man sat on an ATV next to the Buick.

Where had he taken them?

Bliss wasn't about to let him get away with this.

9.

"**W**ENDY... WENDY, BLISS NEEDS you to calm down." Travis gripped the frail woman's wrists to keep her from scratching his eyes out. The coppery scent of blood was thick in the air. Enough to make even him gag.

Someone had died here not long ago, and it wasn't the vic reported yesterday. That meant Daniel Campbell had other victims. Ones Travis and the FBI didn't know about.

"Wendy, damn it."

He'd been party to some tricky rescues before and, while it wasn't common, occasionally the victims didn't want to be saved. Which was too bad, because Travis had a job to do, and he wasn't about to leave a new mother to die in a filthy cave.

"No!" she wailed.

Wendy twisted one of her arms free. He groped, catching her shoulder.

"Stop it. I'm not going to hurt you," he said.

She swung her arm and hit him in the temple. His body jolted, and for an instant he was stunned. Had she really just done that? Damn woman was a lot like her sister. Wendy jerked free and scrambled to her feet. He reached out to grab her, but she evaded him, ducking through an open gate. She pulled it shut with a clang.

Travis sat back on his heels and rubbed his head. It wouldn't do to move quickly or grab her. At this rate, she'd only hurt herself.

"Wendy, I'm here to take you back to your family. Grayson is worried about you. Bliss is out in my truck waiting for me to bring you back."

"No, no, I won't let you." She leaned back, as if her slight weight mattered. Her chest heaved. By his guess, she was so panicked he'd be surprised if she didn't make herself black out.

"Won't let me what, Wendy?" Travis could grab her and haul her out, but what damage would it do to her? He wasn't the gentlest of rescuers, and Bliss had made it clear Wendy's mental state wasn't quite on an even keel. But the longer he waited for her to come around, the more time he gave Daniel Campbell to catch him in the act.

"You can't take me. You can't. You can't. You can't." She sagged against the bars, sobbing.

Chances were, Wendy was too scared and traumatized to be able to recognize the good guys. The trick was going to be minimizing the damage she did to herself. The best way to do that was with a mild sedative.

He slid his wallet out of his pocket, keeping one eye on Wendy as he slid the two-inch long injector out of the wallet. It was a standard Aegis tool. All the guys carried one. They never knew when they'd end up tossed onto a job like this one.

"Your sister is worried about you, Wendy." He let the wallet drop to the ground and took a step closer to the gate.

"He can't hurt her. I won't let him." Her voice was muffled. Her head was buried against her arm.

He reached through the bars and stuck the business end into her bicep. It was spring loaded, so once the seal on the end was broken, it pushed the sedative into the target, requiring no further contact from him.

"Wha-what did you do?" Wendy's head snapped up, and she stumbled backward, holding her arm. The injector fell to the ground, lost in the deep shadows.

"Nothing." He held his hands up.

Five…

She swiped her arm and looked down.

Four…

Her knees buckled, and she sat down hard.

Three…

Christ. She was going to cry.

Two…

He opened the gate, and she held out her arm as if to fend him off.

One.

She was out.

Travis scooped Wendy up. She weighed less than his go-bag. He used his shoulder to push through the cell door and the wooden exterior one. Squeezing past the stones was trickier. He had to turn sideways and flatten Wendy's body to his. There wasn't a way around it. The rocks scraped at him, catching on his clothes and scratching Wendy's skin.

The path between the rocks widened and Travis was able to stretch his legs. Sounds were misleading between the rocks. He'd heard something earlier, but couldn't make it out now. He took care to watch his footing, but couldn't shake the sense of urgency. He'd been gone longer than he intended to. Any minute, Mason and Ethan were going to show up, and what he really needed was a clean get-away.

He emerged from the rocks, and the path sloped down into the shrub and foothills. It was too quiet. Whatever had buzzed in the distance, it had to have gone somewhere. He peered out over the shrub and brush before descending into the thick of the ground cover.

In the distance he could see the house.

And a man getting off an ATV.

From Travis' vantage point, he was high enough to catch a glimpse of a dark-colored SUV in front of the house.

His rental.

What the hell was Bliss doing?

Was she in the house?

"God damn it," Travis muttered.

He slid down the incline a bit before hitting the more level path. He should have known better than to leave Bliss on her own. She wasn't the kind of girl to take inaction well. At the very least, he should have left her with something to protect herself with. Granted, that would have been asking for trouble.

Travis jogged, trying his best to not jostle Wendy much. His boots crunched on the gravel and dirt. Branches snagged their clothing and hair.

Any minute, Daniel Campbell would go check on the SUV or find Bliss. What then?

Travis' job was Wendy, but Bliss was equally important. He wasn't about to let either woman get hurt, regardless of what the job was.

If his boss could hear that thought, Travis would get the boot. Aegis rules were law, and they did what they were paid to do.

He reached the edge of the property in a matter of minutes, but it was already too late. Daniel wasn't anywhere to be seen.

Travis skirted the house, going around the right side and then cutting across the front to his truck. The keys were in the ignition, and the doors were unlocked. He circled to the other side and placed Wendy in the back seat, sparing a moment to bind her wrists with flexible restraints and handcuff her to the bench seat. As against being rescued as she'd been, he wasn't about to have her run away.

Bang!

His body went rigid at the report of a gun. Some sort of shotgun. From inside the house.

Bliss.

Travis pushed backward out of the truck and stared at the house through the windshield.

Not Bliss.

Something inside him broke, and he barely contained the urge to scream. She couldn't be dead. He was right here.

A small figure lurched out of the front door, dark hair obscuring her face, but he knew that figure.

Bliss.

He sprinted toward her and met her almost halfway to the house.

"Are you hurt?" His gun was in his hand. He didn't even remember drawing it.

"Run." She pushed him.

A man filled the doorway, a twelve-gauge shotgun in his hand.

Travis fired first, aiming wildly as he pushed Bliss ahead of her, shielding her with his body.

"In the truck," Travis yelled.

He fired again, but the man he assumed was Daniel Campbell was out of sight.

Bliss skidded around the front of the SUV while he climbed into the driver's seat and started the engine.

"Are you hurt?" he yelled.

Job or no, if Bliss was shot, he'd go in there, rip that shotgun out of Daniel's hands and shoot him full of buckshot.

"No, no. Where's Wendy? Oh my God, Wendy!"

Travis shifted into gear and whipped the SUV around, spraying gravel in his wake. The job wasn't over until the girls were out of danger.

BLISS CRAWLED INTO THE backseat of the truck. It bounced down the gravel road, knocking her off-balance. Wendy was always petite, but her hollowed out cheeks were gaunt and her skin was ashen.

"What—why is she handcuffed?" Bliss crouched in the floorboard and pushed Wendy's hair off her brow.

"She was traumatized," Travis said over his shoulder. "Didn't know I wouldn't hurt her."

"You—what? Knocked her out and handcuffed her?" Was that seriously how he handled hostages?

"Yes."

She glanced at the back of Travis' head. He was serious. For a moment, she was torn between outrage and relief. She couldn't find it in her to be angry with him either way. He'd found Wendy, when the cops wouldn't even pretend to look. Her baby sister was coming home. Alive.

Bliss knelt and pressed a kiss to Wendy's forehead. She held her sister's hands, rubbing some warmth back into them despite being jostled and tossed around. Travis seemed determined to push the vehicle to unholy speeds. Granted, she wanted as far away from that creep and his army of babies as possible. She still didn't even know what to think about that.

She peered out through the rear windows, but couldn't see a vehicle following them. In the movies, the kidnapper gave chase, and there was a big, dramatic end. This almost felt anticlimactic. They had Wendy, everyone was safe. That was a good thing, right?

Then why did Bliss still have a gnawing sense of dread, as if this wasn't the end of it all?

Images of the house, those jar babies, and Daniel Campbell zipped through her mind. She was going to need to shower after this, but nothing would clean those memories out of her head.

"Why didn't you stay where I told you to?" It was the first thing Travis had said since they got on the road.

She glanced out the window and saw the highway ahead. One step closer to civilization, the cops, and a hospital.

"I got worried," she said.

"You broke our agreement."

"Yeah, well, sorry." If she'd stayed put she wouldn't have the visions of dead babies in her head. Then again, she wouldn't have been there with the truck when Travis needed a place to stash Wendy.

Travis had saved her from the same fate as the women before her. Again, Bliss couldn't be angry with him.

"What happened in there? Who shot what?" he asked.

"The women, he forced them to have babies, didn't he? That's what you wouldn't tell me." Bliss sat back and stared at his profile. She could see bumps in his nose, no doubt from multiple breaks. The hard lines of his face were just like him; he either got the job done, or he didn't.

"How do you know that?" he asked finally, his voice quieter.

"Because I saw the babies."

"The children? They're back there?" The SUV slowed, and he glanced at her.

"They're dead. He has them lined up in jars. He watches TV with them or something."

"What?"

"There were over a dozen babies in jars. Most of them were probably newborns."

"They were in jars?"

"Yes!"

"What did you do?"

"What do you mean, what did I do?"

"What happened inside the house?"

"I went in, saw the babies, freaked out, and then that guy, Daniel, came inside. I tried to get out, but he grabbed me. I kicked him in the nuts, and he tried to shoot me. I ran outside and there you were."

"Don't ever do that again."

"I don't want to."

Wendy groaned and her hand curled around Bliss'.

"Wendy? Wendy, hey, it's Bliss." She bent her head.

Wendy's eyes' popped open, and she stared up at Bliss, her features twisted in horror.

"No, no, no," Wendy screamed. She tried to sit up, but her hands were bound to the bottom of the bench. Instead, she rolled off the seat and onto Bliss, trapping her against the console and the back of Travis' seat.

"What the hell?" he snapped.

The phone rang, adding to the general din.

"Wendy, it's me. Bliss. Your sister." Bliss wrapped her arms around Wendy and bear hugged her. Bliss did her best to use her weight to keep Wendy immobile.

Travis pulled into a Love's truck stop and parked the SUV. He twisted around with his phone pressed to his ear. Bliss couldn't hear what he said.

"He'll kill you," Wendy wailed. The fight left her body, and she lay limp on the seat.

"What? Me? Who will kill me?" Bliss eased her hold on Wendy and leaned back.

"Daniel." Wendy sniffled. "He said if I left, he'd kill Paul. And you. And Grayson. I don't want my baby to die. I don't want you to die."

Bliss glanced at Travis. The asshole back there had convinced her sister to stay a prisoner in exchange for her life? For the rest of Wendy's family? What did she say to that?

"Wendy, no one is going to die," Travis said. He spoke with the utmost certainty, as if Daniel Campbell would have to go through Travis to get to them.

"He killed Robert. And Stumpy. And that other guy. He killed them. In front of me. And he made me marry him." Wendy's body shook as she cried. "He—he's crazy! He's following some sort of medieval serial killer plan. He's crazy. You have to take me back or he'll kill you."

Travis reached back between them and cut the bonds around Wendy's wrists. Two police cars pulled up on either side of them. Bliss pulled Wendy into her arms and squeezed her. She wanted to rip Daniel limb from limb for what he'd put her sister through. The man was evil.

"Wendy?" The command in Travis' voice made even Bliss look at him.

Wendy sniffled and peered up at Travis. Her body shook so much Bliss worried her sister might fall apart, or forget where she was again.

Travis rest his elbow on the console and stared at Wendy.

"Listen to me, these cops? They aren't going to let anything bad happen to you, Bliss, or your baby, understand?"

Wendy nodded.

"Good."

Bliss held her sister and watched Travis exit the SUV, hands up. She was too stunned to do anything else. The whole drama outside played out in a matter of moments. More cop cars streamed past, headed for Daniel Campbell's torture chamber of horrors, hopefully, but she only had eyes for Travis. He'd promised her he'd get Wendy back, and he had.

DANIEL LOADED THE LAST of his children into the motorhome. The barn where he'd stored his get-away ride was already engulfed with flames, along with the trophies he couldn't take with him. He'd had a lot of good memories here, but it was time to sever all ties with his old life.

Because of her.

Wendy's sister.

Bliss.

She'd pay.

He'd make sure of that.

10.

BLISS PEELED HER BOOTS off and groaned. They were cute and comfortable for a mall stroll, but damn they ached after a full day of on-her-feet action, not to mention sprinting across gravel. She eased back onto the sofa and flexed her toes.

"Did you hurt yourself?"

A wave of heat traversed her body. For a split second she'd forgotten Travis' presence inside her home. She remained very still, wishing the buzz of arousal would die already. It was a completely unreasonable reaction after the day's events.

"Bliss?" His fingers brushed her shoulder. Her breath caught deep in her chest and her skin tingled.

No such luck on killing her lady boner for the man.

"No, no, I'm fine. My feet just hurt."

"Epsom salt?"

"What?" She pried one eye open. He was a lot closer than he'd been. His stubble was more pronounced, accentuating that dangerous look that fit him so well. She was beyond figuring out what it was about him that turned her on. There was always one anomaly to every proven fact, right? And the fact was she liked nice guys, and Travis was anything but nice. He still revved her engine.

"Epsom salt. Do you have any?" Travis said slowly.

"Maybe in the bathroom? I don't think so." She pushed herself up off the couch, but he caught her shoulder and pushed her back down.

"I'll look. Through here?" He didn't wait for her confirmation before striding into her jack-and-jill bath.

"You don't have to do that," she said for what felt like the hundredth time.

Not only had Travis rescued her sister, he'd stuck with them until Wendy was behind guard at the hospital, Grayson had landed, and baby Paul was back in their arms. Bliss had never seen her sister so in tune with her baby. Bliss had been shooed out by the hospital staff and back into Travis' care shortly after Paul's arrival. They'd grabbed a pizza and a couple beers at a place down the street. She'd thought he'd drop her off and leave, but he'd followed her inside.

"Seriously, you don't have to do whatever you're doing. I'll get a cab to grab my car in a few." Or maybe she'd just sit on the couch and watch bad reruns. Yeah, that sounded like a good idea.

"Can't." Travis emerged from the bathroom sans salt, but he had something else in his hand. "They have your sister's house under surveillance. They aren't releasing your car until after they go over the scene. You might not even get it back tomorrow considering they're probably short-staffed for the holidays."

She groaned and threw her arm over her face.

"Why me?" she said.

The sturdy coffee table shifted. She knew Travis was across from her. She sensed the heat of his body, and if she put her amazing horny powers to use, she could probably even measure the distance between them.

What she needed was for him to leave, so she could spend a little time with her vibrator collection and the bad-boy fantasy she'd been collecting material all day for.

His hand closed around her ankle and lifted.

"Wow—what—?"

"Relax." His growly, gravelly tone didn't invoke relaxation.

He pealed her sweaty sock off and dropped it on the floor.

"What are you doing?" And why did he have to touch her? Every time he did that, it turned up the heat burning her from the inside out.

Travis squirted a bit of her mint cream into his palm and slicked it over the ball of her foot.

"Seriously, don't." She tried to pull out of his grip, but he didn't release her.

Wasn't it enough he'd saved her sister, pulled her ass out of the stupid fire, fed her, and gotten her home? Couldn't he leave her to her private, erotic fantasies?

He proceeded to ignore her and cupped her heel, driving his thumbs into the muscles and tissue. She sucked in a deep breath, and her body went completely lax. Her eyes rolled up in her head. She couldn't decide if he was hurting her or giving her a footgasm. He continued up, into her arch, working over every bit of her. The sensation straddled that line of pleasure and pain. She clamped her lips shut, determined to keep the sounds of utter OMG, yes! inside lest she embarrass herself further.

Travis' thumbs dug into her arch and she moaned. Her mind went blank, and she was pretty sure she was one with the sofa now.

He chuckled and she couldn't scrounge up the energy to care.

"Oh, God, what are you doing?"

"Pressure points, it'll take the stress out, help you sleep after today."

"Oh, right there. Oh. My. God."

She squeezed her eyes shut. Yeah, she was embarrassing herself, but damn that felt good.

Travis left her foot perched on his thigh and grasped her other ankle. She didn't protest this time. Why should she? This was the most man-stimulated activity she'd seen in a while. By the time he finished with her other foot, Bliss was slouched down on the sofa, ready to dribble down to the floor and stay there until Christmas Eve.

"You're going to fall," Travis said.

"Don't care. Dead now." She had her eyes closed tight, the better to not see him with.

The coffee table groaned again. Her whole body seemed to vibrate, she was so completely aware of his every move. He pushed her hair off her face with a touch so gentle she might have thought she'd imagined it had she not also felt the slight puff of breath.

An image of his lips, those damn, kissable lips, filled her mind's eye. He'd kissed her once, and she wanted him to do it again.

"Bliss?" He spoke her name in that same, gravelly tone.

"Hm?" She turned her head slightly, finding him by sound and scent.

"Tell me to leave," he said.

Her eyes popped open. He filled her vision. One hand was on the couch behind her. He had a knee next to her hip. A quiver of apprehension shot through her. He was big and scary, but he'd never hurt her. At least not her body.

"Why?" she asked after a moment. Couldn't he walk out of there on his own two feet? Wasn't that what she'd wanted a few minutes ago?

He cupped her cheek, sliding his hand up into her hair. The feel of him was different from any man she'd been with before. Even his skin was rough around the edges, just like him.

"Because otherwise I'm going to kiss you, and we both know where that's going to go."

She gulped. He'd called her out on the attraction before. Did she dare?

"Kiss me," she said, before she could overthink her answer.

Travis lowered his head, wrapping an arm around her and hauling her farther up on the couch without breaking contact. His tongue delved past her lips, thrusting into her mouth. She held onto him, her head reeling as he laid her out on the sofa right where he wanted her. His weight pressed her down into the cushions, and one thick thigh shoved between hers. She wrapped her leg around his hip. She gripped his shoulders, hanging on with everything she had as he swept her up into a sensual tornado.

She'd wanted men before, but not like this. Not with an all-consuming desire she felt to her toenails. It wasn't neat or nice or even polite. His stubble scraped across her cheek and he bent her head backward with one hand dug into her hair.

"Travis," she mumbled as he kissed his way down her neck.

Bliss ran her hands over his shoulders, arms, and through his short hair. There was no illusion that she had any control here. Travis was driving this show and damn, if she wasn't glad she had a front row seat. Or something.

He shoved her shirt and bra up roughly, exposing her breasts and stomach. She sucked in a deep breath, and her eyes popped open.

Chubby.

His friend had called her chubby.

Travis caught her wrists before she registered her own attempt to shield herself.

"Don't," he ground out between his teeth.

"But..."

The smolder in his gaze was enough of a command to keep her in place.

But what if she was too fat? What if there was more of her to go around than he realized?

Travis levered up on one arm, his gaze on her chest. He grasped one nipple between his fingers and rubbed it, the calluses better than any suction toy she'd ever tried.

"Ooooh!"

Her vision unfocused and she stared at the ceiling.

"Perfect," Travis muttered.

Her?

Really?

She could point out a few less than perfect areas, but she'd take the compliment.

His mouth closed around her other nipple, laving it with his tongue. Her eyes rolled back in her head, and she arched her back, pushing more of her chest into his mouth and hand.

Yes, she wanted him. She wanted him bad.

Travis tugged at the front of her jeans until the button slipped loose and her zipper lowered. He reared up and grasped the denim around her hips and jerked it down her legs, leaving her in her panties, with her shirt and bra up under her armpits. He stared down at her and again she had to fight the urge to cover herself.

He'd pursued her. He'd called her perfect.

She fisted the cushion under her to keep her hands in place.

"W-what are you doing?" she asked.

"Trying to think of something to say."

Bliss gulped, and a tendril of doubt crept in.

"Why?" she asked.

"Because, I should say something, but I suck at talking. I don't normally do this."

"Do what?" He screamed heterosexual, so he couldn't mean he did guys.

He leaned over her, running a hand up her stomach to cup a breast.

"I don't get involved with clients. I don't do it."

"Oh..."

"You're different. I should be different." The hard line of his mouth and the dark furrows on his brow suddenly made a tiny bit of sense.

She wasn't the only one dealing with self-doubt. This larger-than-life man, this hero, had insecurities too. She smoothed her hand up his arm to his face where she traced the lines.

"I like you. Be you," she said.

He bent his head and kissed her again, and this time his mouth was soft, yielding. She greedily stroked her hands down his back to the firm globes of his ass. Man, he had a nice ass—all firm and hard.

She wrapped her arms around his neck, pulling him down on top of her, relishing the way he pressed her into the cushions. His hands blazed a path across her body, her skin tingling everywhere they touched. She grabbed handfuls of his shirt, hauling it up and over his head.

Bare skin.

She could have cheered, but she saw the scars first.

Dots, lines, and jagged scars created a topographical map of Travis' life on his skin. He hadn't been kidding when he said he was a human shield. Her heart ached for him. She pressed a kiss to his shoulder, tasting him.

He shoved his arms under her and hauled her up into his arms, cradling her close.

Bliss yelped and clung to his shoulders, cringing. He was a strong guy, but she wasn't exactly tiny. Still, he didn't miss a step or even grunt carrying her into her bedroom and the big bed she slept in alone. He laid her down and stripped her shirt and bra off her, leaving her in just her panties.

His hands traced the lace at her hip and down her thigh. Her breath caught the closer he got to her mound.

"Fuck," he muttered.

"What?"

"I'm sorry. I think my hands are too rough for this stuff. I snagged them." He smoothed out the snarl in her lace panties.

"It's okay. I have more than one pair." They were clothes. She could replace those. This moment? It was a once in a lifetime thing.

He cocked his head to the side.

"Really?" he asked.

She could hear him thinking. What was he up to?

Travis dug in his pocket and produced the same knife she'd taken earlier to defend herself. He flicked it open and she held her breath.

He wouldn't...

11.

BLISS WATCHED IN FASCINATION and a touch of fashion horror. With a gentle flick of his wrist, Travis parted the delicate lace at her hip with the blade of his knife, never once coming close to her skin. She gasped and watched him do it again on the other side, until her panties were in bits and she wasn't wearing a stitch of clothing.

"There we go," he muttered.

The knife went onto her nightstand while he pushed her thighs apart, crawling up onto the bed.

"You just..."

"I did." He kissed her inner thigh.

She fought the urge to cover herself, but it was a bit too late for that. Besides, her subconscious knew exactly what she wanted. Her lungs burned, needing oxygen, but she couldn't move a muscle.

Travis traced a winding path from her knee to the other leg and back and forth on either thigh. She'd never been so grateful to Wendy for those nightmare waxing trips they went on every so often. Stray hairs were the least of her worries.

He kissed her mound, and her breath rushed out of her lungs. She dropped her head back against the pillows and shifted her feet restlessly on either side of him. If she'd thought she'd been hot for him before, it was nothing compared to the arousal burning her up from the inside. And all he'd done was strip her down and kiss her a bit.

"Travis..." She couldn't bear to look at him. Was he having second thoughts?

"Yeah?"

She pried one eye open and peered down at him. He had one hand splayed over her left hip and his gaze on her face. Her poor lungs froze again. Desire sharpened Travis' features, his cheeks sunk in, and his deadly focus was all on her.

What did she say? What could she say?

"Where's the bullet?" he asked.

"Uh, what?"

"Earlier you said you liked a bullet. Where is it?"

"Forget it." She couldn't help glancing at her nightstand. The drawer was closed, right?

"In here?" Travis reached where her traitorous eyes led him and opened the drawer.

Two cloth bins separated out her favorite toys into daily and occasional use, each in a color-coded bag. He snagged a pink cloth bag from the back of the drawer.

"No!" She snatched the toy bag from his fingers and shoved it under the pillow.

"What is that?" Travis crawled up her body, his hand delving under the pillow to close around hers.

"Not a bullet."

Shit. That was the last thing he needed to see.

"Show me." He tugged on her hand, but didn't force her to comply.

"No." She shook her head.

Travis studied her for a moment. If he looked in that bag, she was pretty sure he'd leave right now.

"Okay, then which one is the bullet?"

"Blue bag."

"Which one?" He glanced at the drawer.

"All of them, just pick one."

"You like your bullets, huh?" He released her hand, and she breathed a sigh of relief. But it didn't last long. He picked a blue bag out of the mix and upended it on the mattress next to her.

Oh no...not that one...

Travis pinched the finger loops and lifted the pink-and-chrome toy off the sheets. The silver, egg-shaped bullet was halfway encased in a silver silicone sleeve, with two finger loops on either side of the mid-section. A clear, pink tongue curved up and over the bullet part, the surface ribbed and covered in bumps. He would pick the more outlandish look-ing toy to open.

"I don't get it," he said after a moment.

She covered her face with one hand and took it from him. Practice and plenty of time with this particular toy meant she didn't need to see it to slip her fingers into the silicone bands until the bullet rested against her middle finger and the tongue curved over her nails.

"You turn it on and...stroke."

"Oh yeah?" Travis' brows lifted and a slow grin spread over his face. "Show me."

No was on the tip of her tongue. Just this morning, the mere mention of a vibrator had repulsed him, was he really going to change his mind that fast?

If he wasn't open to it, did she really want to share her bed with him?

She twisted the bullet in her palm and it began to vibrate. At the low setting, it was a good warmup to bigger and better things.

Travis shifted to lay next to her. She reached down between them, staring at his shoulder, and gently stroked the silicone tongue over her mound. Her heated skin tingled at the touch, and she felt the vibrations down to her bones.

"Does it feel good?" he asked.

He was so close she felt the puff of his breath against her cheek. She opened her eyes, staring at the ceiling.

"Yes."

"Why do you like this one?"

"It's waterproof, and the ridges give it a nice feel." She curled her toes, fighting down the tide of embarrassment.

"Let me."

Travis drew her hand away from her mound and slid the loops off her fingers. He didn't even turn it off as he transferred it to his hand. The bands stretched around his digits and she had to wonder if that was just a prelude of what was to come. Did the big man, big cock myth hold true?

She couldn't tear her gaze from his face and the way he stared down her body. Unlike her first touch with the bullet, his was not tentative. He cupped her mound in a bold, possessive grip, resting the length of the toy along her slit. Her clit throbbed. She groaned and arched her back.

He let his hand rest there a moment before pressing his middle finger, and by extension the toy, against her. Gently, he rubbed it up and down, pressing into her. She gasped and grabbed the sheets with one hand and his forearm with the other. He shifted to lean over her, and his hot breath fanned over her nipple.

Oh, yes, her mind screamed.

He kissed her nipple and pressed his finger farther into her, massaging her vagina and teasing her clit. His knee kept her thighs open—it gave her something to grip with her knees.

His tongue swirled around her breast, teasing the stiff peak until sensation zinged from her pussy to her breasts. She wrapped her arms around his shoulders and shifted her hips, grinding against his hand.

"Oh, fuck." He laid his head against her shoulder and worked his finger back and forth through her folds. "I want inside of you right now."

"Yes!" She dug her nails into him, pulling him closer. If she didn't come soon, she would go out of her mind.

"You're damn tight."

"I want to come with you inside of me. Please, Travis?" She didn't even close her eyes when she said it.

Travis shook off her grip and vaulted off the bed. He shed both jeans and boxers at once, tossing them away to land haphazardly over her furniture. She didn't even flinch when he plucked a condom from her nightstand and ripped it open. She followed the path of his hands and gulped.

Big man, big package.

"You sure?" He put one knee on the mattress.

Bliss sat up and snatched the condom out of the package before he could stop her. She knelt facing him and reached for his erection. There was so much power in him, he could push her aside and do as he liked. She'd probably even thank him for it. Instead, he held perfectly still while she rolled the latex down his hard length.

The tendons on either side of his neck stood out, a testament to how much control he was exerting over what he wanted. Which was her. It was a powerful, heady thing to know he wanted her that badly.

She rose up on her knees and cupped his cheek, leaning in for a kiss.

As if that contact broke whatever leash he'd put on his baser instincts, he crashed down on top of her. Their legs dangled off the side of the mattress, but she didn't care. His mouth devoured hers, thrusting his tongue into her as his now empty hand palmed her breasts and coasted down her stomach.

She felt his cock nudge her thigh, and she shifted until she could wrap her legs around his waist. His now bare fingers pressed against her opening.

He tore his mouth from hers and panted against her cheek.

"God damn," he muttered.

"Travis." She lifted her hips as his finger slid deep inside of her.

"Tell me if it hurts?"

"Fuck me already," she snapped.

"All right." He chuckled and kissed the corner of her mouth.

His fingers left her, only to be replaced by the blunt head of his cock. She perched her heels on the edge of the mattress and pressed closer. He held back, depriving her of that first inch.

He shifted over her until he rose up, her leg brushing his thigh their only physical contact. She wanted to spend hours touching and kissing him. He wasn't magazine beautiful—even naked, he was a little scary looking—but right now he was her scary. Her man. And she wanted him inside of her.

Travis carefully guided his cock to her entrance and glanced at her. Their gazes locked, and he pressed into her. She gasped and wrapped her fingers around the forearm supporting his upper body.

"You okay?" he gritted out and held still.

"Yes, yes, yes." She hooked one arm around his neck and pulled him lower.

His girth stretched her, rubbing every nerve ending as he penetrated her, joining their bodies. He withdrew and thrust once more, sinking deeper. She appreciated his thoughtfulness, but she wasn't a virgin. As he thrust once more, she lifted her hips, and their bodies met in a hard slap of flesh.

She groaned, and her eyes nearly rolled back in her head. Fully inside of her, he stretched and fit her better than any toy. There were some things that couldn't be replaced. A real, live penis was one of those.

"Shit, you okay?" His body went rigid, probably with the strain of remaining completely still.

She lifted her lower body, leveraging her feet on the mattress and wiggled her ass. The things she wanted to do to this man might still be illegal in a few states. She lowered her hips, holding her breath as he slid from her body.

"Oh, fuck," he muttered.

"That's the point." She grinned.

Travis hooked one arm under her knee, robbing her of her mobility and thrust, sinking deep. The breath rushed out of her lungs as he descended on top of her. The mattress squeaked and shifted under them. She didn't care if they ended up on the floor, so long as he didn't stop.

His hips pumped, long, deep strokes in and out, while his gaze held hers. There was something about the way he stared that made her feel like he saw deep into her soul, as if he could see how she felt and raised the bet. Her insides quivered and she held onto him tighter.

"Bliss," he hissed out.

Her name on his lips sparked something deep within her. A sense of rightness, as if she'd been made to fill his arms and be filled by him. It was a soul-deep sensation that took her by surprise.

"Oh, Travis!"

A tide of pleasure swept over her, threatening to rob her of all thought and control. Her body clamped down on his cock, and he groaned, his motions becoming jerky and uneven. His mouth claimed hers as he shoved the mattress almost a foot off the box spring. She felt his muscles constrict and twitch across his back and squeezed him close, holding tight to this man who filled a hole in her life she hadn't known was there.

12.

TRAVIS STARED UP AT the ceiling and ran his fingers through Bliss' hair. It was even softer than he'd imagined. She snuggled closer, her breath fanning across his chest. The sheet clung to his damp skin.

He didn't know what to think. Sex was an itch to be scratched when it was convenient, and he never crossed the line with a client. Bliss might not be paying his check, but she was involved, and she had no idea what he was. Who he was.

"Think they'll catch him?" she asked.

"Daniel?"

"Yeah."

"Eventually, yeah." The question was, how many people would Daniel kill before they caught him? Killers on the run often splintered, going on sprees or worse. It was out of Travis' hands now—the cops had made that clear.

"I hope so." Bliss lifted her head and looked up at him. "What's your plan for the holidays?"

"Nothing, really." Tracking Daniel had been it. Now he was at loose ends until the FBI threw him another file to look over. No doubt they were knee-deep in paperwork over Daniel's case, since the transient murders crossed state boundaries, putting it squarely in their hands.

"Usually we all get together at Wendy's, but I'm not sure what we'll do this year, you know? Do you at least get time off?" She kissed his chest, and her hair slid over his skin.

Shit. He was a terrible person. If she knew the truth about him, she would have shoved him out of her life.

"Yeah, I'm off now, until the first of the year or so, maybe later. Depends on when a job comes up." He shrugged and glanced at the clock. Half past midnight. Great.

"You think you'd be interested in going out later this week? After everything dies down?"

"Bliss...I don't live in Vegas."

"What?" She blinked at him.

"I live in Illinois. I...we talked about that."

"Oh. Oh right. That...sucks. I guess I should have. Now I feel stupid." She laid her cheek against his chest.

"No, don't. I suck at talking, remember?" God, he was the worst kind of man. She had no idea who she'd gotten into bed with. He'd practically taken advantage of her.

"Don't worry about it."

"Damn it. I'm not good at this either," he muttered and scrubbed a hand over his face.

"It's okay."

"No, it's not. I shouldn't have stayed." He sat up and glanced around her bedroom, searching for his clothes.

The best thing for her was to be away from him. A guy with his record didn't deserve a nice girl. Between his time with the SEALs and in prison, he was fucked up. Throw in his serial killer roots and his baggage was more than any woman deserved. Especially one like Bliss. She was too smart and too normal for a guy like him. He'd do her a favor by leaving.

He snagged his jeans and underwear from the top of her laundry hamper and stepped into them. The silence had the hair on the back of his neck lifting.

The sound of a feminine sniffle sliced him to the bone. He turned and froze. Bliss sat with her back to the white head-board, the sheets clutched to her chest and her face turned away from him.

Was she crying?

That wasn't what he wanted.

For a second he stood there and watched her hand disap-pear behind the curtain of hair. She sniffled again, the sound muted this time, but he still heard it.

"Bliss?" He set one knee on the bed. When she didn't re-spond, he crawled across the bed to her. "Please don't cry. I don't know how to fix that."

"Go away." She grabbed the pillow that still bore the in-dention from his head and clutched it to her chest.

"Bliss...I don't know how to make you understand."

"It was a big mistake. I get it." She stared at the far side of the room, resolutely not looking at him, but he could see each tear trickling down her cheeks. They hurt worse than any bullet he'd ever taken.

"No, that's what I...God damn it, Bliss. I'm a felon. Did you know that?" He bit the inside of his cheek and waited for her to slap him.

Her brow wrinkled and she glanced at him, a frown curl-ing her lips downward.

"I'm a felon. A serial killer murdered my dad's family. I was kicked out of the SEALs, and now the only thing I'm good for is as a human shield or the FBI's blood hound. I'm fucked up, and you want no part of this." He jabbed a finger at his chest.

It was the rough, unvarnished truth of his life. Since the moment he'd been conceived, the bastard son of the Ration Survivor, his life was shrouded in darkness. His own mother couldn't stand to look at him. Why should Bliss have to accept what the woman who birthed him could not?

"I don't even know where to start with that." Bliss stared at him, which was better than avoiding him, except now he could see how red her eyes were.

"I've done hard time."

"For what?" One brow arched, as if she didn't believe him.

"Kidnapping a kid." Each word was a nail in his coffin. People got crazy when it came to kids, his prison time was proof of that.

"You kidnapped a kid? Why?"

It was Travis' turn to stare at her. Why wasn't she calling the cops on him? Wouldn't a normal girl do that? What rational woman let a felon into her home, much less her bed?

"Because his mother threatened to kill him and herself."

"And you went to prison for that?"

"Yeah."

"You shouldn't be jailed for that, you should be...I don't know, given a medal. You seriously went to prison for that?"

"A year and some change in FTC." He leaned against the headboard next to her.

"A year?"

"My sentence was longer, but it was reduced."

"I can't believe that. What happened?"

"You should kick me out, you know that?"

"Let me get this straight." She wiped her eyes. "A lot of bad stuff has happened to you, and you think—what? It means people should stay away from you?"

"I'm not a normal guy, Bliss." He couldn't translate the darkness that haunted him into words.

"I think you've had some shitty luck, and if you're afraid of more bad stuff happening, go on." She gestured to the bedroom door.

"I'm not afraid."

"Poor word choice. The big, bad SEAL would never be afraid." She didn't flinch away from meeting his gaze.

He could almost taste the sarcasm dripping from her words. Why was she so calm about this? Didn't she know he could kill her in a dozen ways without breaking a sweat? Not that he would, she was too precious to be harmed. She should have someone in her life to be there for her, protect her if it came to that. If Travis ever met the guy, he'd be hard-pressed to not punch his lights out, even if it was what Bliss deserved.

"You're still here," she said after several moments.

"I'll leave."

"If that's what you want to do." She broke their eye contact and stared at the wall again.

"Damn it, Bliss, that's not what I want to do. It's what I should do. I can't promise you anything. I won't even be here by the end of next week."

"But you'll be here for a week at least?" She reached for his hand and threaded their fingers together.

"That's the plan." He stared at their joined hands. The simple act of acceptance floored him.

"I'm okay with that. I like you. I'd like to see you again if possible."

"You should kick me out."

"Why? Because you've been dealt a shitty hand? I don't think that stuff is contagious. Besides, it's made you a strong person. I can't imagine what it's been like for you."

"You deserve someone better."

"Better than the guy who saved my sister and Christmas all in one day?" She elbowed him and a smile spread across her face. "You're pretty awesome."

He knew he needed to say something, but his mind was at a stand-still.

Once, he'd gone rock climbing while in Utah, and he crossed a precarious bit of rock. For a few seconds, if his weight had shifted even the slightest bit, he'd have fallen to his death. From the way he held his breath to how his stomach was tied up in knots, this moment was every bit as uncertain. It wouldn't be his death if he fell, but he didn't know what awaited him.

"Travis?"

"Yeah?"

"I'm not like Wendy. I'm not looking for a man to take care of me, if that's what's bothering you. I'm happy where I'm at."

He leaned toward her and fell off the mental cliff into the unknown. Bliss met his kiss, her hand cupping the back of his neck and sliding up into his hair. He meant to be gentle, but she nipped his lower lip. Arousal thrummed through his veins. He shoved the pillow aside and dragged a giggling, squirming Bliss across his lap until she straddled him.

She flattened her hands against his chest and smiled at him. Her cheeks were pink and her eyes sparkled.

It hit him in that instant.

Travis wanted to make her happy.

He didn't know the first thing about pleasing a woman out of bed. He'd kept his relationships short due to deployment, the nature of his jobs, and his history, but for her, he could be different. It was possible, wasn't it?

"I—" The sound of Bliss' phone on the charging station silenced her protest. "It's Wendy."

She climbed off the bed and snatched up her phone. He wanted to drag her back into bed but knew she needed to be assured her sister was safe. Bliss yanked on a pair of yoga pants, a sports bra and sweatshirt, as if she were leaving.

"Where are you going?" He picked up one of the cloth bags at random.

Bliss' cheeks were redder now. She shook her head as the ringtone died.

"I have no reception in here. I have to go out onto the patio to talk to anyone. She knows that. I'll be right back. Do not open the blue bag." She pointed at the other bin. "The blue ones."

"Your sex toys are color coded?"

"Yes." She laughed and fled the room, taking a pair of house boots with her.

He watched her go, listening for the snick of the latch on the sliding glass doors.

She made him feel things he wasn't used to feeling. Emotions that had no name. It was unsettling and exciting, but he needed to remember this was only for now. At best, he could give her a weekend or a week here and there between gigs, nothing like what she deserved, but if she wanted him, he wasn't about to leave.

Travis pried open the blue bag and peered at its contents. "Fuck..."

BLISS STEPPED OUT INTO the frigid evening air. She should have grabbed a coat, but her skin was so hot she'd mistakenly thought the December weather might make her feel better.

Nope.

She hit redial on her phone and pressed it to her ear, willing Wendy to answer fast. As much as Bliss wanted to know how her sister was doing, she also wanted to get back into bed instead of standing on her concrete slab of a patio.

Travis was nothing she'd expected. He was a wounded hero, and while she wasn't foolish enough to think she could fix him, she could love the man he was now. If only for a little while.

Even as the thought solidified in her mind, she knew it was silly. She couldn't love him. Maybe the idea of him, but it was too soon. They didn't know each other. And yet, she couldn't deny that her heart hadn't beat this hard for anyone in her life. Not even the man she'd thought she might marry.

"Come on, Wendy, pick up," she muttered.

A hand wrapped around her, covering her mouth. Something pricked her neck before she could strike out.

Bliss tried to draw breath, to cry out for Travis, but her muscles refused to work— even her lungs were hard to manage. Her legs gave out, and she hit the concrete. Overhead, the stars twinkled down at her, broken only by the large silhouette of a man.

"You took what belonged to me," he said.

Oh God...

Bliss tried to lift her arm, to cry out, but her vision hazed. The last thing she saw was Daniel Campbell's face before everything went black.

Dangerous Attraction: Part Two

1.

TRAVIS' BOOTS CRUNCHED WITH each step. The Nevada desert was rough terrain at the best of times. Today was not one of those.

The trail had deep ruts on either side just wide enough for an ATV to fit through. Acrid smoke hung low in the air from the house fire not even a mile away. The smoke mixed with the repugnant scent of death, decay, and animal feces, setting the tone for his foul mood.

He held his breath as he topped the hill and the crime scene unfolded in the small valley along the Muddy Mountain. A dozen or more forensics personnel from the Las Vegas police department clustered here and there around yellow markers.

Was this Bliss' fate?

Would the serial killer treat her like he had these bodies? Or would he do worse?

Daniel Campbell might be the most dangerous serial killer on the loose in decades. And Travis had put Bliss squarely in the man's crosshairs. This was his fault. The knowledge made him sick.

He should have told Bliss no when she insisted on going with him to rescue her sister, Wendy. If he'd known then that Daniel had Wendy's entire family under surveillance, he'd have made a different call.

It should have been Travis Daniel went after, not Bliss.

"Travis, thanks for joining us." Supervisory Special Agent Ryan Brooks strode toward him, arm extended. He breathed federal officer, from the close-cropped hair to the no-nonsense suit. He seemed a little out of place in the middle of the desert, but Travis wasn't about to underestimate the man. He led the FBI's Behavior Analysis Unit that specialized in serial killers.

Travis shook the agent's hand and nodded at the man and woman at his back.

"I'm sorry to meet like this." Somehow Ryan was able to cram sympathy and briskness into those few words. "This is SSR Connor Mullins and Jade Perez. The rest of our team is at the police station and Bliss' apartment."

"They find where the cameras are transmitting to?" Travis asked.

"Not yet, but our tech is working on that remotely," Ryan replied.

After calling in Bliss' abduction, it had only taken the cops thirty minutes to locate half a dozen cameras in Bliss' home and five times that many at her sister's residence.

The bastard had watched them make love, and then he'd taken her.

"Think you could walk us through what happened yesterday?" Connor's voice rolled and lilted. Wherever the man was from, it wasn't America, that was for sure. Travis's money was on Ireland.

"Sure. Where do you want to start?"

"The beginning. Right now you are our only inside view into David Campbell's life," Jade said. The chilly December breeze blew her long, red ponytail over her shoulder.

"What about family? Co-workers?" Travis glanced between them. Someone had to know David better than him.

"Family is deceased, and he worked remotely from home the last two years. To our knowledge, you're the only person that's seen him," Jade replied.

Shit.

Travis might not be an FBI agent with all the training, but he could read between the lines. This was not good news for Bliss. He glanced over Ryan's shoulder to watch a forensics guy dusting sand off a small mound.

"How many do you think are out there?" Travis nodded at the dump site.

"No telling. They've found remains starting at that stone," Connor gestured at a large rock and then flung his arm wide, "to about fifty yards that way."

"It will take a while to match all the bodies," Jade said.

"Wendy said there were three men with her. Even if he kept three men between his kidnapping and dumping of the women that's...twenty-four possible victims." Travis' stomach knotted further.

"They've already identified thirty-two skulls," Jade volunteered.

"Christ." Travis shook his head. At the least, Daniel Campbell was responsible for forty lives lost once they factored in the women, and probably more.

"I hate to push, man, but we need to know what you know." Connor took a step closer, standing between him and the scene.

"Yeah, yeah." Travis nodded and dredged up that first memory of Bliss. "I went to records yesterday morning to pull the case files on the other women, look for similarities. Bliss walked in to report that her sister was missing. I figured, it's the right time frame, the sister fits the profile, why not follow up on it? So we got some coffee, she told me what happened, that she saw her sister the night before, but yesterday she was gone. We went to Wendy's house, and that's when I found the security system had been tempered with. Digging back into the other cases, I was able to find out a few of them had security systems that were monitored by the same company. Between that, and the make and model of the car Wendy left in, we were able to track down David Campbell."

"How did you know Wendy left in that car?" Jade asked.

"Wendy and her husband live in a gated community. We had a look at the security tape from the night before." He was pretty sure those moments crammed into the security booth with her were the bedrock of this thing between them. Or maybe he'd been a goner from the moment she walked into the police station.

"But not Bliss?" Jade's gaze narrowed.

"No. Wendy's husband, Grayson, is rich. Her family isn't. Bliss lives in an apartment complex about ten minutes away."

"Why didn't you call us or tell the cops when you located David Campbell?" Ryan asked.

"Because by then, Grayson had retained Aegis Group to get his wife back. I had to obey orders first."

"Like a good soldier," Connor muttered.

Travis ignored the comment. He was a SEAL. It was who he was. If the agent didn't like it, he could fuck off.

"Why'd you bring her here? Why not leave her at her sister's house?" Connor asked louder. The man was belligerent and starting to rub Travis the wrong way.

"Her sister's mental state. She argued that I might do more harm to her than good if I had to manhandle her out of the situation. Since it appeared to be low risk, I agreed." How did he explain to them the passionate way Bliss spoke? He was still positive that if he hadn't taken her with him, she'd have done her best to follow him.

"Walk us through the rescue," Ryan prompted. He glanced at Connor, who ignored the pointed look.

"I approached the house from the northwest on foot. I didn't know at the time no one was home. I saw the path, followed it, and found Wendy. I had to tranq her to get her out of the cell. On my way back I saw that Bliss had driven up to the house. I made a beeline for the truck, secured Wendy in the back seat, and that was when I heard a shotgun blast. Bliss exited the house, followed by Daniel. I returned fire, covering her until she could get in the SUV, and we got out of there as fast as we could."

"Did Wendy mention the other victims?" Jade asked.

"Yeah." Travis nodded. "Called them Stumpy and something else. They told her about the other victims, how they wound up there."

"And that was?"

"According to Wendy, Daniel kills the men, who he calls his test subjects, around the time he takes a new wife, as he calls the women. He forced Wendy to marry him at a drive-through wedding chapel under the name of Daniel White."

"Lali was able to track down a half dozen wedding licenses we think were Daniel's aliases." Jade shook her head.

"We think he's doing that to Bliss?" Connor asked.

"She doesn't fit his profile. She's not blonde or born in Vegas," Ryan said, not looking at Travis.

"What you're saying is he's probably using her as a test subject. He wants to get back at her for taking away Wendy." Travis didn't flinch from the truth. In the SEALs, they hadn't had the luxury of ignoring the truth, and it wouldn't change now. The only difference was him. The agony of knowing these terrible things were happening to Bliss. He'd change places with her in a heartbeat if he could.

"We don't know that," Ryan said quickly. "What else do we know about the victims?"

"Did Wendy say anything about the Psycho Club?" Connor asked.

"Killer Club," Jade corrected.

"No, nothing."

"We need to talk to Wendy. Find out what she knows," Ryan said.

"Good luck with that." Travis chuckled bitterly. "Her husband has her on lockdown." He curled his hands into fists. If he had the time to worry about Grayson Horton, he'd have already decked the guy.

"Where do we think he's gone? He torched his house, abandoned his holding cells. The Buick was burned with the house. He has to have a plan," Jade mussed out loud.

"Who knows?" Connor shrugged.

"He's detail-oriented. He would have had a getaway plan. We aren't dealing with a killer on the run yet," Ryan said.

Travis had tracked criminals and terrorists across deserts, seas, and continents. He was going to find Bliss, and when he did, he would kill Daniel Campbell.

EVERYTHING HURT.

It was the first thought that swam up through the fog. Whatever party Bliss had gone to last night must have been something wild.

Who convinced her to go?

Her mouth was dry, and someone had let a herd of elephants loose in her head. It must be the landscapers. They always seemed to mow the tiny patch of grass outside her bedroom window for half an hour. They had the worst timing.

The bed lurched, and Bliss reached out to catch herself. Her hand smacked into a metal bar. Light stabbed her bleary eyes.

This wasn't her bedroom.

She gasped for breath and blinked away the crud matting her eyelashes.

This could not be happening.

No, no, no.

Bits of last night teased her memory, but she hurt so bad.

What was going on? Was she going to die?

Across from her, shelves lined the wall. Strapped in like precious cargo were glass jars.

Glass...jars...

She squinted. Where had she seen those before? It was recent.

Light slashed in through the window above her, illuminating the jars.

Oh my God.

Daniel Campbell. She'd seen them in his house.

The diesel engine chugged loud enough to block out her thoughts.

She pressed her hand to her mouth and tried to pull her legs up, but the space was too narrow for her to do anything but lie on her back or maybe her side.

What happened? Where was she? Was Wendy okay? Had he hurt Travis?

Snatches of memory swirled in her head. They'd rescued Wendy, Grayson had arrived from London, and Travis had taken her home. After that it got a little fuzzy. They'd kissed and she knew there was more she couldn't recall.

Had Daniel killed Travis? Was he dead?

Hot tears pricked her eyes.

Why her? Why this?

The overwhelming sense of dread settled on her, and the weight of it was suffocating.

Bliss didn't want to die. Not like this. Who would take care of Wendy? What about her bucket list? There were so many things she wanted to see and do before she died.

She drew in a shaky breath and covered her mouth.

Panicking never solved problems. That's what she told Wendy. When something bad happened, she needed to take stock of her situation and make a plan. That approach had weathered the storms before, why not now?

Bliss inhaled and wrapped mental arms around all her fear, anguish, and sorrow. She shoved it into a mental closet and locked the door. There was time to fall apart when she was dead. But for now she was still alive, and Daniel Campbell had no clue who he was messing with. She might not be a badass SEAL, but she'd never rolled over and given up for anyone. Someone would come for her, and when they did, she intended to be alive.

Oh, God.

She gulped down a deep breath.

Freaking out wasn't going to do her any good.

Bliss peered through the bars, taking in her surroundings. This had to be some sort of converted motorhome. The insides had been gutted. The floor was covered in metal sheeting. A table, or something, was bolted to the center of the narrow space, maybe an arm's length from her prison. She craned her neck to look toward the back of the motorhome, but it was shrouded in shadow.

The motorhome turned a wide right. She could see out through a few feet of the windshield. An awning blocked out the light. The vehicle lost speed and lurched to a stop.

A gas station.

She shoved her hands down to her sides and closed her eyes, forcing her body to relax. Playing possum was her only defense right now.

The engine died, allowing the ambient sounds of country and western music to infiltrate the motorhome.

It wasn't soundproof.

Good to know.

The driver groaned and shifted. He must have stood. One heavy footstep after another on the metal flooring made it easy to track Daniel's movements to the door. It went against her instincts to remain quiet when it squeaked open, and the motorhome shook with each step down the stairs. The door slammed shut and for a few blessed seconds she relaxed.

She was alone.

Her body hurt, but a quick wiggle of fingers and toes suggested she seemed to be okay. Nothing hurt in a bad way, and nothing was chopped off.

She shifted so she lay fully on her back and began exploring her prison by touch. The bottom was plywood with a thin egg crate laid over it. An act of kindness? Or was that to muffle her sounds? She stomped on the walls at her feet and knocked on the ones over her head. They appeared solid, but not metal like the bars holding her prisoner.

The top of her prison was heavy, but appeared to have some give in it. The hinges were up against the wall, but what was holding it closed was a mystery.

She pulled her knees up as far as she could and wedged them against the top, pushing with everything she had.

The motorhome door opened. She squinted in the sudden light and pain stabbed her behind the eyeballs. She wrinkled her nose and forced herself to see past the pain.

Daniel Campbell.

The man chuckled and climbed into the motorhome.

That sound, it was the stuff of nightmares.

Bliss sucked down air and screamed, praying someone was outside, that they would hear her.

Daniel swore and closed the door behind him.

She grabbed the bars, shook them, and screamed again.

He went to a knee, fumbling with something on the outside and moments later the lid lifted. He swung his arm and punched her, right in the face. Stars lit up her vision, and for a second she couldn't believe what had just happened. White hot pain seared her nerves. She cradled her face in her hands and rolled away from him, hunching her shoulders. It was instinct more than anything else, a weak attempt to protect everything vital.

"You shut up, or I'll slice your throat now. They'd like that—my children. You're only alive right now because you're useful." He dug a hand into her hair and pulled her backward, until she had no choice but to look up at him.

He held a syringe in his hand.

Her neck twinged, and a memory broke loose from the fog.

Wendy had called. Bliss had left her bed, no, she'd left someone.

Travis.

Travis had been in her bed.

She'd left him to go call Wendy back and something bit her.

No, it was Daniel.

She held up her arms, weakly trying to fend him off, but he jabbed the needle into her forearm. He shoved whatever was inside into her veins, watching her.

"W-why are you doing this?" she asked. There wasn't a reason she could accept in existence, but she still wanted to know.

"Because I can," he replied.

Her vision hazed, fading to black and all the fight leeched out of her.

She wasn't dying, but she might as well be. She wasn't a SEAL, she had no training. It was only a matter of time until Daniel killed her. Just like the other women.

2.

TRAVIS PEERED THROUGH THE BINOCULARS. By all appearances, the mansion on the hill was just that, a luxurious getaway outside of Las Vegas. That was, until one of the security guards came into sight. Even the most A-list celebrity didn't have security packing semi-automatic weaponry, unless they were looking for attention. From his vantage point above the outpost, Travis could document the comings and goings of all the personnel assigned to Grayson Horton's security detail.

Wendy had just become the most protected asset in America, and Bliss was paying the price.

What chapped Travis' ass the most was that these weren't just any hired toughs. These were federal agents. Badge carrying CIA officers. Which might explain some of Grayson's hesitance about speaking to the FBI. The two agencies didn't always play nicely together.

The phone in Travis' pocket vibrated. For a moment he considered ignoring the call. Chances were it was Ryan

Brooks calling him again to relay some bit of knowledge that wouldn't help him find Bliss.

It wasn't Ryan.

"Tell me something good, Gavin," Travis said.

Next to the FBI's technical analyst, Gavin might be his best shot at getting a lead on Daniel's current whereabouts.

"Bliss' cell phone last pinged off a tower off I-95 north of Vegas at four this morning." Gavin was all business, unlike yesterday. No one at Aegis liked that someone had been kidnapped from under their noses. By now, everyone at the home base would know.

"Shit. There's everything north of Vegas." Still, it cut out the lower half of the country.

"I'm still working on Campbell's history. The FBI doesn't want to share, so you might get the same thing twice." Keys clicked and things beeped in the background.

"I'm fine with that. Maybe the second time around it'll jog something lose."

"You about to go pay our CIA friend a visit?"

"Friend is a bit much."

"Cool."

"Hey, in my email I have a folder called KC. Look through it. See if it doesn't help in the search for Campbell."

"You want me to hack into your email?" Gavin asked. The sound of keys clicking in the background stopped.

"Don't you already do that?" Travis chuckled.

"Well...yeah."

"Then get to it."

"What's KC stand for?"

"Killer Club."

"Okay..."

"It's the project I've been looking into for the FBI. A club of serial killers."

"The thing with your sister?"

"Yeah."

"I'm on it."

The line went dead, and Travis pocketed his cell phone.

He rose into a crouch and waited for the guard to circle around to Travis' side of the building.

Three...

Two...

One...

Like clockwork, the CIA agent came into sight.

Travis slid off the outcrop of rock and down a sand and stone embankment. The scrub and brush kept him out of sight from the building below. He hit upon the footpath up to the radio tower at the top of the rise and got his feet under him. For the span of a few seconds he listened, testing the wind and allowing his senses to think for him.

Satisfied he was still undetected, Travis proceeded along the path. Judging from the lack of tracks, no one had bothered to scout up this far from the house.

The property butted up to the rocks with a fence on the other three sides. In theory, this house functioned as a layover and hideout for CIA operatives in the field. It also could double as a command center in case of an attack on the region.

For as high-tech as the structure was, it still had blind spots. Like the cameras that couldn't be used due to the cluster of nests built around the poles. Because the southwestern willow flycatcher was endangered, the nests couldn't be touched, and that left the whole back half of the property vulnerable.

Which just went to show that Mother Nature had the last laugh in the end.

He crouched behind the line of decorative boulders that fenced off the pool area. Grayson and Wendy Horton were twenty yards away, safe and snug inside the multi-million dollar mansion.

Travis checked his watch and counted down to the minute mark. The interior sweep at the top of the hour would be concluding, and if he was lucky, the CIA agents were bored and sloppy. If he wasn't lucky, he might end up with a few more scars to add to his collection.

The time for hiding was over.

He slithered past the rocks, landing on his feet and strode around the pool.

Despite the tinting on the wall of glass, he could still see movement inside.

Travis reached the French doors. He held his breath, bracing for the gunshot and opened the door.

It swung open.

"Oh my God, Grayson!"

Travis ducked into the house as a man threw a weak punch at the air he'd just occupied. He shoved the man against the glass and held him there with his forearm.

"Grayson Horton, I'm Travis Ration," he said.

"W-what?"

"Grayson, he's not our enemy." Wendy stood ten feet away, clutching a baby to her chest. There were dark circles under her eyes, but she'd showered and cleaned up since he last saw her.

"Ma'am? Sir?" Right on cue, a man in a suit strode into the living room, hand at his hip. From the befuddled expression, he hadn't parsed out yet how or why Travis was there. Some security detail.

"He's not hurting us," Wendy said, reaching out to stop the CIA officer with one arm and hefting the baby up with the other.

"What the hell?" Grayson snapped. Travis let Grayson shove him away. "How did you get here?"

"I walked up to the door and let myself in," Travis replied. Pampered idiot.

"Who are you?" The CIA officer frowned. He hadn't even pulled his weapon.

"Have you found Bliss?" Wendy stepped closer, her big brown eyes so much like Bliss' it hurt to look at her. The sisters were almost complete opposites, except for the eyes.

"Not yet. Got a ping off her cell phone from early this morning. Looks like he was headed north."

"Back to where...?" Wendy's voice stuttered and died on her. Chances were she wouldn't be able to speak about what had happened to her for a long time. The baby in her arms gurgled, content despite his mother's anxiety.

"No, farther north it seems. He's gone."

Wendy sat down on a cream L-shaped sofa. Her tears could have been his, if he knew how to cry. She hugged the baby closer and rest her cheek on his head.

"He's gone? Are you sure?" Grayson asked. He moved to stand next to his wife and lay a hand on her shoulder. The child waved a hand at his father. "Here. Give him to me"

Travis gritted his teeth and watched the tender exchange. Grayson took the baby and passed her a tissue, sticking close to her side while she fought a losing battle with the tears.

"Sir?" The CIA suit glanced between them.

"Get on already." Travis waved the agent away.

Grayson nodded, and the suit went without argument.

So much for security.

"Where is he taking her? What are they doing about finding her?" Wendy sniffled and dashed the tears off her cheeks, but they kept coming.

"We don't know. At this point, he's disappeared completely. We have no leads." But there were always leads. This time, Travis and the FBI didn't have them, but the CIA was another entity altogether. He'd learned that every time someone said there weren't any. The problem was asking the right people the right questions, and when necessary, applying pressure.

"He won't get you, Wendy. You're safe." Grayson took a knee and gently wiped his wife's tears away.

"But what about Bliss?" she asked.

Grayson glanced at him.

The man would do anything for Wendy—it might as well be stamped across his forehead—but he didn't give a damn about Bliss. If he did, the CIA would already be leveraging their considerable weight.

"Your husband could help," Travis said.

"He could?" Wendy glanced from Travis to Grayson, who suddenly found something interesting on the carpet.

"The people your husband work for could be very helpful." Travis watched the hunch of Grayson's shoulders, the furrows on his brow.

Wendy didn't know.

"They could? How could they help?" She blinked her dark brown eyes at her husband, and Travis knew the man was a goner.

"Honey, let me talk to Mr. Ration for a moment alone, okay?" Grayson helped Wendy to her feet and guided her to a hallway.

He watched her leave before turning to look at Travis.

"She doesn't know?" he asked.

"No. How the hell did you get in here? There are cameras and two CIA agents." Grayson strolled to the kitchen and grabbed a bottle of water.

"I'm the best." Travis accepted the water Grayson offered, but didn't take a drink. He never trusted a man backed into a corner, especially when a woman was concerned. "You going to help find Bliss? Or hope Daniel Campbell stays content hacking your sister-in-law to bits?"

"I don't want Bliss hurt," Grayson said in a rush, hand up defensively.

"But you aren't exactly calling in any favors to help her."

"I...I'm not in good standing with the CIA right now."

"That's your problem."

"I'm not paying you to rescue Bliss. Why do you care?"

Because...the reason was just there, out of view. Bliss was special. She was important.

"Because she's an innocent in all of this. She wouldn't have become a target if she hadn't have been trying to protect Wendy." Travis set the bottle on the counter and stared at Grayson. "Are you going to let her die, or are you going to do something to help?"

"What do you think I can do?" Grayson spread his hands.

The man might look like a weak patsy, but he was no fool.

"You design buildings. You figure out ways for the American government to hide their spy tech in those buildings. Which means you must know the people at the NSA. The ones who can run facial recognition software on all the security cameras they supposedly aren't watching."

Travis pulled out a photograph of Daniel Campbell and pushed it across the marble surface. Grayson frowned at the picture.

"The FBI is on the case. Why can't they do it?"

"We all know there's the NSA they tell us about, and then there's the other one. Ask them, or when Daniel Campbell is done tearing Bliss into bits, he'll come back for Wendy. A man with a plan this detailed isn't going to let a loose end go." His body was cold, numb. He'd never felt this way before. Rescuing people had mattered, but this time, it mattered to him.

Travis pushed off the counter. Time was ticking, and they didn't have a second to lose.

DANIEL STOOD ANKLE DEEP in the fresh powder and inhaled. The weather blowing in would cover his tracks off the main road, and then he could settle in for the winter. By the time spring rolled around, no one would be looking for him. Or the girl.

Speaking of, he needed to check on her. The drugs should wear off before too much longer and he'd need to do something with her. The bench cage was fine for travel, but he didn't want her underfoot.

He pulled out his keys and examined the compass attached to the ring. With his bearings set, he trudged due west through the trees, counting off his steps. After the first few years, and one close call with the law, Daniel had implemented this back-up plan. A crash spot. The clearing along the hunting path was just big enough to fit his RV, and most importantly, his secret stash.

There.

The A-frame structure was small, not even big enough for a person of any considerable height to stand upright. He pulled the thatch door open. Snow and layers of leaves fell to the ground, but the shelter was otherwise intact. The only things inside were gas cans, and judging by the layer of dirt, they hadn't been disturbed since his last trek up to check on the site.

He grabbed two cans and made the return trek back to the RV. While he could use the ATV to run out for supplies, the fewer people he saw the better. The gas in the shelter should keep him for two weeks.

A whole winter without the demands of work or society. Months to just be. And experiment. It was enough to make him almost forget the loss of his last wife.

Wendy.

He'd reclaim her someday, but not today.

A metallic clang interrupted his giddy daydreaming.

He frowned and picked up the pace, kicking up snow as he closed in on the Winnebago.

The girl.

She was bound to be a problem. Nothing like her sweet sister.

He tossed the cans down and jerked the door open. The bench top to the cage rattled. Bliss. No, he had to stop thinking of her like that. She was an object. A thing.

His newest test subject had her feet pulled up, as if to kick the lid. No doubt that's what he'd heard.

Daniel stomped into the RV, leaving clumps of snow on the floor in his wake. It was beyond time to get her settled and out of his way. It would be interesting to see how she survived in this weather, what she could stand.

He unlocked the lid and grabbed a handful of her hair.

"No! No, wait!" She grunted and clutched his wrist as he hauled her to her feet.

The nice thing about being out this far was that there was no one around to hear her scream.

She scratched at his gloves and kicked his ankle, but otherwise she was too weak and clumsy from multiple doses of tranquilizers.

He scooped a length of chain out from under the passenger seat before dragging the female subject outside.

"The air smells fresher here," he said, pausing for a second to appreciate it.

"Kill me already," the subject said.

He glanced at her but didn't respond. Her name was already fading from memory. She was no longer a person, or even a thing with feelings. She was part of his experiment. Part of his great test to figure out just how much a human body could withstand.

Daniel led the subject all the way back to the A-frame and secured his latest pet to the tree and then to the subject by way of a pair of handcuffs. He pointed at the shelter.

"Do your best to not die."

Yet.

3.

"TRAVIS, MAN, YOU GOTTA eat something." Ethan plopped a bag of fast food down on the hotel room desk.

Travis glanced at it.

He'd had burgers with Bliss yesterday. They'd talked about sex and vibrators. He hadn't cared they were in a crowded, family establishment. One day with her and now it felt as if he were missing a crucial part of himself.

"Not hungry," he said.

Travis tossed his clothes into his suitcase and carefully gathered his files while his Aegis Group co-workers, Ethan and Mason, ate. They had their own adjoining rooms, but hadn't let him be since returning to the hotel.

"Where you going?" the kid, Mason, asked. He was the newest Aegis recruit, barely out of the SEALs.

"Don't know yet." Travis zipped the duffel bag and pulled his phone out.

"Where do you think he's gone?" Ethan asked.

"Not sure yet, but he'd have somewhere outside of Vegas to run to if he needed. Some of the bodies they identified were from as far away as Flagstaff, so we know he travels. I just don't know what the Vegas connection is."

"What Vegas connection?" Ethan had forgotten his food and now leaned forward.

"The women. Every one of the women he picks are blonde, born and raised in Vegas, and until Wendy, they'd never had a child. We know he impregnated them, kept them alive until they had the kids, and then killed them. From what Bliss saw, we know he kills and keeps the babies. I'm thinking since he dumped the last two before they carried the babies to term, he just wanted to make sure the women could carry a child."

"I think I'm going to be sick." Mason's lips curled, but he didn't go anywhere.

"Why not set up here? Wait for him to come back, if Vegas is that important to him?" Ethan suggested.

"No." Travis shook his head. "He'd keep those women for a year or more if they survived childbirth. If he escapes with Bliss, I don't think we'd find her."

"Okay," Ethan brushed crumbs off his jeans and gestured to the files on the bed, "So saying he—"

Travis' phone lit up, vibrating and ringing on the bed. He snatched it up and jabbed at the screen.

"What did you find out?" Travis asked.

"We got a hit. I'm not supposed to be able to ask for this kind of favor, but someone turned a blind eye." Grayson's voice was hushed and strained. Probably trying to keep Wendy fleeced.

Good luck, buddy.

"Where?" Travis didn't give a fuck who he owed, not when Bliss' life was in danger.

"Truck stop. I-95 up around Lake Tahoe."

"That's not much of a lead. He could be anywhere up there." Travis grabbed his bags.

Both Ethan and Mason jumped to their feet, rushing into the adjoining room. Their half-eaten burgers and fries remained on the desk.

"I'll see what else I can find out, but they got the make, model, and license on that motorhome, and the trailer he's hauling."

"Wait. Trailer? What kind? How big?"

"I'll send the picture to you. It's small. There's a tarp over it, so I don't know what is there. What do your fed friends have?"

"Nothing."

"Damn. Will this be useful to them?"

"Don't know. I'm not telling them."

"What?"

"Later, Grayson."

Travis hung up and paused at his hotel room door, mentally flipping through the scene at Daniel's house that morning.

The Buick was there, but not the ATV. They'd rightly assumed he used that to get away, now they knew where to. Somewhere out there, he'd stashed an RV and the means to escape detection.

"We're ready," Ethan announced. He strode into Travis' room, bag slung over his shoulder, followed by Mason.

"What are you doing? Go home," Travis said.

"No way." Mason shook his head. The kid was stubborn.

"We can stand here and argue about it, or you can accept that we're going to fucking help you. What's it going to be?"

Travis ground his teeth together. It was almost Christmas, and they should be with their families. Except Ethan had no one, not anymore. Travis didn't know Mason well enough, but if the kid was anything like the rest of them, he probably didn't have someone keeping the light on.

"Fine. We got to book a plane to Tahoe. Tonight."

Hang in there, baby, we're coming for you.

BLISS HUDDLED UNDER THE old, moth-eaten blankets. She'd unearthed them from the pile of discarded things in the crevices of the shelter Daniel had left her in. The wind had picked up since the sun set, and icy fingers found their way through every crack and joint in the structure.

Her teeth chattered so loud she feared she might not be able to hear anything approaching. Frozen teardrops still clung to her lashes, but she didn't bother wiping them away. Instead, she gently examined the business end of a stick she'd salvaged. It wasn't old or rotten. For the last indeterminable span of time she'd worn one end down into something like a spear.

She wasn't kidding herself. Even with a collection of stones and her spear wouldn't deter anything set on eating or killing her. All she had to do was hold on. If she could just hold herself together, Travis would save her. She had to believe he was out there under the same night sky looking for her, otherwise, what hope did she have?

DANIEL PLACED THE LAST child in the half-circle. He smiled at the beautiful, shining faces. He was asking a lot of them to be up this early, but it was worth it. They needed to learn what they were. It was time they knew they weren't just men and women.

They were gods.

And today they would receive a master lesson in where they stood with the rest of humanity.

He held up his finger to his lips, willing the children to be quiet. Of course they were excited, why wouldn't they be? Most had only seen his wives. Until now, they weren't old enough to understand what they were.

The little voices hushed.

They knew what would happen next. Last night he'd let them all watch as he studied his test subject in the dark. She'd never noticed the night vision camera bolted to the top of the structure. In his long years, he saw plenty of subjects attempt to thwart their fate, so her efforts were nothing new. Just one more habit to be broken. Until it accepted its fate.

He grabbed the side of the A-frame and pulled.

The structure splintered and cracked apart.

The subject yelped and screamed. The chain clanged as she scrambled to the side, breaking free from the debris.

She never made it to her feet.

Daniel grabbed her hair and *thunked* her head against the tree.

She lost her grip on the makeshift weapon and curled in on herself, huddling in the snow like the animal she was.

He crouched next to her. Unlike this subject, he didn't need a weapon. He was the weapon. He was the creator of her fate.

"Oh my God." She gulped and stared at his children.

"Look at me," he snapped.

Her gaze returned to his face. Her pupils were slightly dilated, her focus off. Probably from the knocks to the head she'd taken yesterday and today. Well, that was her fault.

"Children, look at it." He reached out and pinched her chin between his fingers, directing her to look up so they could see her throat. "This is what we rule over. We make them listen. We make them what we want them to be. This one will be the mother of our subjects. What?"

Daniel tilted his head to catch the faintest of voices.

"No, she will not give you a brother. She's not worthy of that." He spat at her feet and stood. "She'll give us more subjects. More playthings."

TRAVIS PEERED INTO THE darkened ranger station. Just his luck people got Christmas Eve off. Tahoe City was blanketed in new snow, and the police were spread too thin this holiday season to be of much help.

They were on their own.

Snow crunched as Ethan approached, phone in hand and a frown on his face.

"Can't get anyone on the horn about a chopper," he said.

"What about a small plane? There's got to be someone who'd want to earn a buck," Mason suggested. The kid was showing a surprising amount of ingenuity. Too bad the holidays rendered every solution a moot point.

"Nah." Ethan shook his head. "They're all short-staffed and grounded thanks to last night's ice storm. Maybe we could get someone from the south side of the lake though. Sounds like they just got a dusting of powder."

"Where are the ATV rentals?" Travis asked.

"I don't know. Let's find out." Mason pulled out his phone.

Damn. Google. Why hadn't he thought of that?

Travis' brain was seriously scrambled. He should be focused, but every other second his mind went back to last night when he held Bliss. When she pulled him back to bed instead of kicking him out.

This was all his fault.

"Why ATVs?" Ethan asked.

"Daniel used an ATV to dispose of the bodies in a ravine. It was missing from the property when the cops swarmed the place. Grayson said the RV was pulling a trailer with a tarp on it. I'm guessing that was either supplies or the ATV."

"Why the hell are you just mentioning this?" Ethan scowled.

"Sorry, it was in here." Travis pointed to his head.

"You've got to get your head out of your ass," Ethan said.

"There's a bunch of ATV trails around the south side of the lake," Mason announced. He turned his phone around and showed them a cluster of red dots.

"Let's hit the road," Travis said.

"What else haven't you told us?" Ethan asked, falling into line next to Travis on their way back to the SUV rental. "Start at the beginning."

"Which beginning?" Travis asked.

"The very beginning. We've got a drive ahead of us."

The very beginning was almost a decade ago. Maybe longer. There was no telling how many bodies littered Daniel Campbell's past. If they didn't find her, Bliss could be next.

4.

BLISS HAULED THE BUNDLE of straw and thatch over the burrow she'd made for herself out of rocks and packed snow. It was slow going. She couldn't feel her hands, and most of her clothing was either caked in ice or soaked. The handcuffs were the worst. Solid bands of freezing cold metal she couldn't escape from.

One more step.

One more handful of snow.

One more rock.

Since Daniel had scared her awake that morning, that had been her mantra. *One more.*

Bliss had never been one for the outdoors. She liked her comfortable apartment and her cushy bed. Beyond trying to stay warm, she didn't know what else she could do. The stick spear had been her great, innovative idea, but even that was gone now, buried in the pile of rubble that had been the A-frame hut.

All during the trip in the RV she'd imagined a bloody, horrible death, full of screaming and pain. Freezing hadn't been on her radar until last night. Now, even with the sun reaching its zenith, she couldn't feel her toes.

Hell of a way to spend Christmas Eve.

At least Wendy was safe. The silver lining, if there was one, was that Bliss stood a better chance of surviving the elements than her sister. If there was ever a time to love her fuller figure, it was now. In her place, Wendy might already be dead.

"On your knees."

Bliss cringed and turned toward the voice. She hadn't heard Daniel's approach, not with all the noise the chain made.

"I said, on your knees!" Daniel took two ground-eating strides toward her and lifted his hand.

"Okay, okay!" She dropped to her knees, hands lifted to ward off the blow.

He pulled back at the last second, slapping one hand into the other. She cringed anyway and curled her hands into fists. Fighting back hadn't gotten her anywhere, so she needed to play along and hope she lived. At least she knew he didn't intend to kill her yet. Just have her raped for his sadistic pleasure. It would take time to put his plan into motion, so all she needed to do was hang on. Just a little while longer.

Daniel muttered something under his breath and turned to face the tree. He produced a single key—not the one to her cuffs—and unlocked her tether.

"Come on. Keep up." He jerked the chain, pulling her off balance.

Bliss threw out her hands to brace herself but still got a face full of snow. The chain rattled over the ground. She scrambled to her feet, partly crawling until she got them under her. Her frozen, numb limbs screamed at her, but she couldn't take it easy now. Just a few more minutes on her feet, and then she could collapse. Granted, she didn't know what was at the end of this walk.

It couldn't be that bad, could it? Her kidnapper hadn't had time to gather new atrocities to throw at her.

He led her back to the RV. She almost wept when he opened the door and attached the end of her chain to the chair leg of the passenger seat.

"Inside," Daniel snapped.

Inside meant the jar babies and Daniel, but it also meant warmth, maybe a potty break and water, if she were lucky. She climbed into the RV, squeezing past Daniel, and stopped on the top stair, her jaw hanging open.

It was worse.

A body—a man—lay on the rolling metal table bolted to the floor. Blood dripped off the side. Her stomach churned, and she tasted bile.

Another man was on the floor, wearing a pair of handcuffs. He groaned, curled up on his side. Blood stained his clothes, and there was a gash on his forehead.

The man on the table gasped, and blood bubbled up between his lips.

"Oh my God," Bliss whispered. She gripped the side of the built-in shelves.

"Yes, I am your god." Daniel grinned at her. "Now we can get started."

He walked to the other end of the RV. Metal cabinets stood open, each displaying their gruesome wears. Knives, kitchen utensils, tools—she didn't want to know what he used them for.

"Patch his head up." Daniel gestured to the man lying on the floor.

Bliss glanced around until she saw a small, black case with gauze sticking out of it. She could let the man die and postpone her torture. The idea repulsed her. She grabbed the case and hobbled around the table, keeping her distance from the body.

Where was Travis?

She'd thought for sure he'd find her in a day, maybe two. But...what if he wasn't looking? The only reason he'd gone looking for Wendy was because the FBI asked him to, and Grayson paid him. No one would shell out that kind of money for her. What if this was it—stitching up Daniel's victims, being tortured, and worse?

What would be the price of survival?

Could she pay it?

TRAVIS GLANCED AT HIS PHONE.

Ryan Brooks' name flashed across the screen, and the device buzzed.

Again.

Travis rejected the call and pocketed the phone.

"The feds?" Ethan asked.

"Yeah. You'd guess they'd be off for the holidays or something," Travis muttered.

They'd hit each ATV rental on the off chance one would be open on Christmas Eve, but no dice. Their leads were running out and Grayson wasn't accepting his calls. The forecast tonight was for more snow. Any trail they might find would be covered up, and Daniel Campbell would get away.

Travis pulled into a scenic turn-off overlooking the bay and slammed his fist into the dash.

"Dude, it's a rental," Ethan said.

Mason was passed out in the back seat. They were chasing ghosts across the mountains. They weren't going to find Bliss. Not at this rate.

"We're too far behind him," Travis said. He bit his thumbnail and stared out at the water.

"What do you want us to do?" Ethan turned toward him.

"In his position, what would we do?" Travis asked.

"Get out of the country." Ethan snorted.

"At this point the only way Daniel could get out of the country would be to cross into Canada or Mexico. He's on the do not fly list. So do we head for Canada and hope to find him?"

Ethan blew out a breath and laced his finger together behind his head.

"If I took Nate I'd never make it over any border. Amber Alerts would be everywhere, so I wouldn't make it five counties over. The best thing to do would be to lay low, go off grid."

"Should I know something?" Travis asked. He knew his buddy was taking the separation hard, but kidnapping his son was a whole other thing.

"No, just saying that if I wanted to take Nate and get away with it, that's what I'd do." Ethan shrugged.

"Talked to him?"

"Yeah, while we were waiting for the truck at the airport Molly let me talk to him a bit."

"Good." Travis nodded. "So, if we were Daniel, a wanted man with his mug all over the news, chances are he'd need to do the same thing."

"Didn't you say you think he's been up here before?"

"Yeah, it would make sense. He got out of Dodge fast on a direct route to his hiding grounds."

"Okay, so he's probably thinking he'll winter up here. He's in an RV, so he either needs to plug up someplace or have a generator. He'll need to be in proximity to supplies."

"He's not the hunting type. He might string people up and kill them, but he's not a hunter. He'll need to be near a store, but not anything too big. He's got the ATV so he doesn't have to move the RV so long as the weather is good."

Travis glanced in his rearview mirror. A cop car pulled off the two-lane highway behind them, easing closer.

"Company," he said.

Ethan leaned back and frogged Mason in the thigh. The kid shouted and grabbed his leg, growling at Ethan.

"Fuck. What?" Mason snapped.

"Cops," Travis said.

"What did you do now, Ration?" Mason turned in his seat, rubbing his thigh. "Where are we again?"

"Emerald Bay, off Lake Tahoe," Travis replied. He watched the cop stroll up the passenger's side in the mirrors.

"What's he doing?" Mason asked.

"Don't know." Travis pushed the button and lowered Ethan's window.

The officer stopped and pulled his sunglasses off, squinting in the afternoon light.

"Afternoon, officer," Ethan said.

Travis nodded.

"You boys okay?" The officer had to be around his mid-to-late thirties, not all that much older than Travis or Ethan.

"Yeah, just taking in the sights." Ethan gestured at the impressive view beyond them.

"You guys here on holiday, or on your way somewhere?" The officer was looking for something. What, Travis didn't know.

"We're looking for someone." Travis slipped the photograph of Bliss out of his pocket and a photocopied image of David Campbell's license. "This is Bliss and David Campbell. You might have seen something about him on the news in the last twelve hours or so."

The officer took David's picture and whistled.

"I'm Travis, this is Ethan and Mason. We work for a private security company and have been working with the FBI on this case."

"Wish it was nice to meet you boys like this. I'm Sergeant Matt Farrow. Heard about this guy. You think he's here?" He handed the pictures back to Ethan, who passed them to Travis. "Got some ID on you?"

"Yes, sir." Ethan collected Mason's driver's license and passed them to Travis. "We tracked Daniel close to the state line. Made a guess he might be in the area."

"Anyone fitting his description roll into town in a late model Winnebago?" Travis asked. Chances were the officer didn't know anything, but he had to hope.

"Sorry, haven't seen many RVs lately." Matt leaned against the door of the SUV.

It was the answer he expected, but it was still disappointing to hear.

"Two local guys did go missing this morning, though. That's why I stopped to see what you were up to," Matt said.

"Two guys?" Travis perked up. "How do you know they went missing?"

"Friends of friends. Couple of cousins. Their truck was found on the side of the road, and no one knows where they are."

"Where'd that happen?" Travis pulled out his phone. "Can you show me on here?"

"You think this is related?" Matt took the phone and tapped around on the screen.

"This guy's killed at least forty people that we know of. Probably more. He doesn't have much of a cooling-off period." Travis wasn't willing to lump the disappearances up in Bliss' kidnapping yet, but it was worth looking into.

"Their truck was found here." Matt turned the screen back to them.

"That's not that far," Ethan muttered.

"What's this?" Travis pointed to an odd dot on the screen.

"That's the Bayview Trailhead," Matt replied.

"Are there ATV trails?" Travis' stomach knotted.

"Yeah, some go all the way out to Cascade Lake."

Holy shit.

Of course.

Lake Tahoe was a major pull. But the smaller lake off to the south end? Miles of forest and seclusion?

It was perfect.

Somewhere out there, Bliss was waiting for him.

"Officer, I need you to call this number. Tell the FBI agent who answers everything you've told me." Travis scribbled Ryan Brooks' cell phone down on a bit of paper. He didn't have time to call it all in.

"I can't let you boys go out there if this guy is that dangerous." Matt took the paper and frowned.

The hell he could. Travis wasn't asking for permission.

"Travis?" Ethan held up his hand and looked at Matt. "I get it, you're the local law enforcement, and we're a truck full of guys you don't know from Adam. It's Christmas Eve. I'm guessing you've got a family. We're about to go track this guy down. Do you really want to go with us? Or would you rather spend a bit calling around, checking us out, and give us a head start on this trouble?"

Matt frowned, clearly waging a war of rules and regulations in his head. Travis shifted in his seat, ready to just gas it and be gone.

"Fine." Matt snapped cell phone pictures of their licenses and handed them back, with the addition of a business card. "Here's my info. You run into anything or if you find those boys, let me know."

Travis nodded and shifted into drive before the state trooper could change his mind. Poor guy did not want to get mired in a manhunt on Christmas Eve.

The signs for the Bayview Trailhead weren't even a mile later.

Hold on, Bliss. We're coming for you.

5.

BLISS SQUEEZED HER EYES SHUT.

Daniel grunted, and a wet, sloppy pop resounded through the RV.

"Oh, God," the man chained up on the floor next to her muttered.

Don't look. Don't look.

"There," Daniel said in triumph.

He grunted again, and something hit the floor next to her. Warm liquid splashed her hands.

Bile coated the back of her throat and her head pounded.

"You monster, freak," the hillbilly spat. He rattled the short chain that bound him to the bench. At some point the duct tape around his boots had come undone.

"Monster?" Daniel parroted back.

"Be quiet," Bliss whispered. As long as Daniel was preoccupied with the dead guy, he wouldn't bother them. It was too late for him, but she and the other man could still survive this. Couldn't they? She had to wonder if it was worth surviving. If this was going to be her life, did she want to live it?

"Freak?" Daniel's footsteps rounded the end of the table. He was just a few feet away.

"That's my cousin," her fellow captive said. Anguish twisted his voice, and she could see his horror-stricken face in her mind's eye.

Bliss pulled her knees up to her chest and wrapped her arms around them, making herself as small as possible.

This couldn't be happening.

There was no way this could be real.

"You know what the definition of a monster is? A monster is an imaginary creature." Daniel's steps came closer. "I assure you, I'm very much real."

The man grunted and Daniel yelled.

Bliss' eyes snapped open. The new captive had a knife buried in Daniel's thigh, hilt deep. Where had that come from? She stared at his leg and the blood darkening his jeans. Daniel had one hand buried in the captive's hair and the other grasped at the knife.

Bad could always get worse.

She scrambled back, crab-walking on her hands and feet. Her hand slipped in a puddle and she went down hard, knocking her head against the metal floor. She rolled to her side and face-planted in flannel.

The other man's arm.

His dismembered arm.

The scream stuck in her throat, but she shoved up into a sitting position. The captive shot to his feet, grappling with Daniel. The knife was in Daniel's hand and he held it up, poised to stab.

She froze, torn between self-preservation and the desire to fight back. Could they overpower him? She'd never before waffled on a decision. This was a whole new state of mind, and she didn't like it.

Daniel cracked the other man in the head with the butt of the knife, sending the smaller man to his knees, but not down for the count. The captive lunged forward, taking Daniel's legs out from under him. The knife clattered to the floor as the two men grappled with each other.

This was her chance.

It was time to be brave.

The choice was easy.

She shoved forward onto her hand and knees, reaching for the hilt of the blade.

Daniel took a step and kicked it out of her reach, sending it skidding across the width of the RV.

She stared up into his face, twisted in rage.

The other man had maybe two or three feet of chain. Bliss' was closer to a dozen or more. She grabbed her leash and pushed to her feet, gripping the bloody table for balance.

"No you don't," Daniel yelled.

He yanked her back by her shirt. Seams ripped, but held. She sat down hard once more. The hillbilly held onto Daniel, but the fight was gone from him. Determination was the only thing keeping him going.

"I'll teach you a lesson," Daniel growled, sounding less human by the second.

Daniel unlocked the man's chain and hauled both of them out of the RV. Bliss' feet slipped and she stumbled over her own tether. Before long, the only thing keeping her upright was Daniel's hold on her shirt.

He shoved both her and the man face down in the snow. The icy top layer broke, cutting into her hands and face. The blood from her clothes stained it pink.

"You want to attack me?" Daniel roared.

The other man was already on his feet. Free of his chains, the only thing keeping him bound were the handcuffs. She struggled to get up, but she had nothing left. Between the drugs, the elements, and nothing to eat or drink, she was done for.

"Kill me then, go on," the man yelled.

Daniel hauled back with the knife and swung, slashing the other man's arm and chest. He yelled and Bliss screamed, bringing her arms up to protect herself.

A SCREAM RENT THE AIR.

Travis stilled. He didn't even have to hold up his hand, everyone froze.

The sound reverberated on the rocks, through the trees. It was almost impossible to tell where it came from, but he knew.

That was Bliss.

She was alive.

For now.

"That way," Mason said.

"Wait, we don't know—"

"I do." Mason jabbed his finger to the south and east. Toward Cascade Lake. "I grew up tracking in the mountains. That way."

Another scream, this time shorter, spurred them on.

Mason took point, loping easily over the snow, kicking up a spray of white powder in his wake. Travis and Ethan flanked the kid to either side, keeping six to ten feet apart. The terrain was tricky, and the snow disguised roots and rocks that tried to trip them up.

Adrenaline pushed Travis onward. His hands were near frozen, so he gripped his gun and the handle of his knife tighter.

"Oh my God," Bliss yelled.

A man shouted incoherent words.

Mason veered to their left, slowing his pace.

Urgency demanded Travis surge forward, but he kept one eye on the kid and the other on the trees ahead of them. If he acted on his feelings, he would get Bliss killed.

They broke through a stand of evergreens into a scene out of a horror movie.

"Daniel Campbell, freeze," Travis roared.

His vision hazed red.

Bliss crouched on her knees, hands up. There was no way to tell if the blood on her clothes was hers or the other man's. Daniel had one of the missing men by the scruff and held a knife to his throat. More liquid shined off the butcher apron wrapped around his girth. The poor guy in his grip was soaked and gasping for air.

"Oh my God, Travis? Is that really you?" She blinked several times, as if she wasn't sure she believed he was there.

"Bliss? Stay calm." Travis couldn't look at her. If he did, he would rip Daniel Campbell limb from limb for what he'd done to her. There were other victims, other innocents, but this was Bliss. The one bright spot he could remember, and now the same darkness that poisoned him had touched her. It was a crime punishable by death alone.

"Put the knife down, buddy," Ethan side-stepped toward the front of the RV while Mason went toward the rear.

Daniel's gaze narrowed. He pivoted, putting his back to the RV and used the hunter as a shield.

"He said put the knife down," Mason repeated Ethan's words.

"I don't think so." Daniel kept the knife at the man's throat and reached behind him, drawing a six shooter he aimed at Bliss. "If you don't want me to shoot you now, stand up."

"Don't do it," Travis blurted.

Bliss glanced from him to Daniel and back.

"Do it," Daniel adjusted his aim to Travis, "or I shoot him."

"Okay," she stood on shaky legs.

"Bliss, no," Travis said.

"Easy," Ethan whispered.

"Don't hurt anyone." Bliss clutched a length of chain that attached to her wrists.

Daniel reached out and snatched the chain, yanking her close so fast Travis didn't dare squeeze off a shot.

"There we go, this is better." Daniel hugged Bliss to him, the gun pressed up under her jaw.

There was no way this was going to end well.

Variants, statistics, and past experience rattled around in Travis' brain. He'd been here a number of times with different jobs. Hostage situations at gunpoint were bad. Unless they could turn the tables somehow. But how?

What had Bliss told him about the house?

What was the one thing missing in the fire?

"You aren't getting out of here, Daniel. Think about your kids," Travis said. The jars Bliss had reported were missing in the devastation. What were the chances Daniel had taken them?

"They are my flesh and bone. I can create more," Daniel said without skipping a beat. "You want to know how this will end?"

"You dead?" Travis knew he should shut up, but that man had Bliss. He couldn't line up his shot without seeing her pale face. Her lips were almost blue and there were leaves stuck in her hair.

"I'm going to kill this man and your two friends. Then I think I will skin you alive and make her watch. She and I will leave here. No one will find your bodies, and when I'm ready to put down roots again, she will bear me new subjects to experiment on. I'll take something from her first so she doesn't get any ideas about running away, but I'll leave the important organs untouched." Daniel stroked Bliss' hair.

A tear rolled down her cheek.

She didn't think they were going to rescue her.

He tightened his grip.

He'd show her.

One way or another, Daniel was going down. He only had six bullets, and it took a lot more than that to knock Travis off his feet. He had the scars to prove it.

"There's a problem with your plan," Ethan said.

"Yeah, we already told the FBI where we were. Local cops are on their way," Mason said.

The two really did work well as a team, while all Travis could think about was how much he wanted to kiss Bliss again. Hold her.

He willed her to keep looking at him, to focus everything his way. When things went down, he hoped she didn't see any of it.

Daniel glanced around, his gaze straying to the trees.

He hadn't counted on backup.

"Nervous?" Ethan asked.

"Doesn't matter," Daniel said. "I have a plan."

Daniel squeezed the trigger and fired.

Everything happened at once.

Bliss screamed and dropped to the ground, hands over her head.

Ethan grunted and went to his knees.

Daniel's eyes bulged the second he realized he was exposed. He drew the knife blade across the other man's throat and ducked around the front of the RV Ethan was supposed to be covering.

Travis dove for the other hostage. The hunter lay crumpled on the snow, hands clutching his throat. Travis hit his knees, shoving the man's hands aside to replace them with his own. Blood leaked out from between his fingers, but it was sluggish. The man's wide eyes darted around and his mouth opened, gasping for air.

"I'm fine, I'm fine," Ethan yelled. "Go after him."

Mason sprinted around the RV, but they all heard the ATV engine in the distance. There was no way they'd catch him on foot.

Daniel Campbell was gone.

6.

BLISS PERCHED ON THE hospital bed, her hands gripping the thin blanket they'd given her. Her feet and fingers were still cold. No matter what anyone did, she couldn't seem to get warm.

The nurse said she was still in shock, or something like that.

At least the nurse had stopped talking to her and was going straight to Travis now.

Travis.

He'd rescued her.

They hadn't said more than a dozen words to each other, but he hadn't left her side. Not for a single instant.

"Bliss?" Travis' hand rested on her shoulder, shaking her out of her deep well of thoughts.

"Hm?" She blinked at him. She'd missed something important, but for the life of her she couldn't recall what had been said.

"The doctor wants to keep you here to monitor you. I'd rather keep you close."

"Yes," she said, cutting him off.

"Yes—what?"

"I want to stay with you."

Travis meant safety. With him, there was no fear, no sense of dread. So long as he was there, everything would be okay.

He's saved her.

"I'd really rather you stay for observation," the nurse said.

"A man kidnapped me, took me across state lines, and made me watch while he chopped another man up into bits. I'm not staying here." Where he could find her.

"Okay." The nurse sighed and fixed Travis with her stare. "You have her instructions?"

"Right here." He held up a folder.

"I...don't have any clothes." Bliss held the blanket around her a little tighter.

"I have you a bag in the truck. Is it okay if she stays here while I grab it?"

"Certainly. You're the only thing happening here tonight, thank goodness." The nurse smiled and breezed out of the ER bay.

Travis turned to follow in the nurses' wake.

Invisible claws raked at Bliss' back.

"Travis!"

He turned, his lips pressed into a tight line and his eyes unreadable. She couldn't deny that he was what made her feel safe and secure.

"I'm going to step out in the hall and give Mason the keys. I'll be right there. You can see me, okay?"

She nodded, hating the tremor that shook her body, hating the way she needed him, hating Daniel for picking her family out of everyone in Vegas to target.

Travis pushed the curtain aside. Men in suits, uniforms, and nurses milled around. The FBI had shown up at some point, but it was all a blur. He handed the keys off to a guy in jeans and a leather jacket. Mason. He'd mentioned the name before, but the details escaped her.

She was so tired.

But what if she went to sleep and Daniel was there?

"Hey."

Her eyes snapped open, and she stared at Travis' chest. She looped her arms around his waist and slid off the table. He eased her to the floor and kept his hold gentle.

Tears pricked her eyes. The damn things wouldn't stop no matter what she did.

"Hey, you're safe," he whispered.

She nodded.

He had to be regretting his choice to stick around right about now, but she couldn't be more grateful. Not only was Wendy safe because of him, so was she. This nightmare wasn't over, not until Daniel was caught, but at least she was with the good guys.

"Travis?"

He turned, keeping her behind him. He was so big she couldn't see around him, but a moment later he tossed a duffle bag she recognized from her apartment on the bed.

"I don't know what I got, I just grabbed things and tossed them in." He gestured at the blue bag. "I wasn't thinking straight."

"Thanks."

"Want a moment to get dressed?"

"Sure." Her knee-jerk reaction was to keep him close, but she couldn't lean on him forever.

"I'll be right here, okay?" He stepped past the curtain and pulled it almost closed. Through the narrow gap she could see his back as he stood guard.

Even that separation triggered a twinge of anxiety. She tamped down on the urge to rush to his side and instead opened the bag to see what Travis had brought for her.

She'd need a shower and food, but clothes first.

The bag was stuffed almost to bursting with jeans, workout clothes, her birth control pills, her boots, some flip flops, and random bits of clothes. She pieced together enough of an outfit to be presentable and dressed in jeans, boots, and a thin, long-sleeved shirt she was pretty sure he'd grabbed from her dirty laundry. Mixed into the clothing were other odds and ends. Some of them didn't make any sense at all, but she appreciated that he'd thought about her needs.

He'd always intended to find her. In Travis' world, there wasn't room for failure. Even when she lost faith and thought he wouldn't come for her—he hadn't allowed it.

"Bliss?"

The sound of his voice tugged the corners of her lips into a smile.

"I'm ready." She shoved the clothes and odds and ends into the bag, making sure some things went on bottom.

He pulled the curtain back and crossed to the bedside. He took her bag and slung it over his shoulder, as if that was what he was there for.

"We've got a rental ready for us." His hand settled on the small of her back, and he propelled her out of the ER and into the waiting room. "I'm right here."

Travis guided her to a waiting SUV and got into the back seat with her. The same man who'd taken the keys earlier sat behind the wheel.

"Mason?" she asked.

"That's me." He nodded at her in the rearview mirror.

He couldn't be much older than her. He lacked the hardness that radiated from Travis, but there were shadows in his eyes. Whatever he'd been through was different, but no less life changing. It was a facet of a person's character she wasn't sure she'd ever noticed before, but now she did. Was that because she was different, too? Because Daniel had left his mark on her?

"Hungry?" Travis asked.

"Yeah, that soup they gave me at the hospital is pretty much gone." Her stomach was making a meal of her spleen.

"I want to drop you two off, and then I'll go out for food, if that's okay with you," Mason interjected.

"Nothing's open." Travis sighed.

"There'll be a grocery store or something open if the restaurants are all closed," Mason replied.

"It's Christmas Eve," Bliss said. She'd known it was just a few days away, but the last few blurred together...and here it was. "Do my parents know I'm okay? What about Wendy?"

"The FBI called them and let them know you were safe. They've all been moved to secure locations until the FBI can be sure Daniel isn't monitoring them."

"He was watching them?" She stared at Travis' profile. She wasn't hungry anymore.

Travis turned his head toward her. For a moment she didn't think he would answer. "He had your whole family under surveillance. Once Wendy was no longer available to him, he latched onto you. I'm sorry, Bliss."

She sat in silence, staring at the seat back ahead of her.

Daniel Campbell had cameras in her home. He watched her most private moments. All to what end? To stalk her sister?

Travis' arm around her tightened, pulling her closer.

"We're here," Mason announced.

He pulled the SUV up to a large, two-story log cabin that was probably half the size of Wendy's home. As such, it qualified as a mini-mansion in her eyes. Several other black vehicles and cop cars sat in the circle drive, and a group of uniformed men hung around the front door.

"Any requests?" Mason turned around and smiled.

"Hot chocolate and more chocolate," she said.

"Can do."

She scooted out of the truck with Travis at her back. A couple people turned toward them, and she felt the weight of their gaze.

"Inside," Travis said for her ears alone.

He didn't take his hand off her until they crossed through the doors of the cabin. There was more activity here. A lot more. Several groups were going over maps and paper taped to the wall while another group leafed through boxes of...she didn't want to know.

"What's going on?" she asked.

"The FBI must have gotten back from the scene. I'm guessing they're coordinating the search for Daniel from here. Come on, let's find you a room upstairs away from all this. Brooks might want to ask you some questions later." He propelled her to the wide staircase leading to the second floor.

Travis poked his head in several rooms before whisking a door open and gesturing for her to enter.

She peered into the rustic room. The wooden walls were rough, while the floors and furniture were modern and smooth. There was a flat screen TV and even a small bath-room with a shower stall.

"This good?" he asked.

"Yeah. Thank you."

"There will be five agents, Mason, and me staying here. You're surrounded and completely safe." He set her bag down on the bed. "Need anything? Clothes?"

"How's your friend?"

"Ethan?"

"Yeah."

"He'll be fine. Bullet nicked a ligament. They want to do surgery to patch it up. He'll be back up in no time."

"Oh. Good." It didn't sound that minor, but what did she know? "What about...the other guy?"

"Don England." Travis blew out a breath. "They took him into surgery. Last I heard they're still going. Sounded like he was stable, and they thought he'd pull through."

She sat down on the edge of the bed. At least Don would survive.

"What next?" she asked.

"We'll eat whatever the kid brings back and get some sleep."

"What about Daniel?"

"The FBI are tracking him."

"I'm sorry."

"For what?"

"If it weren't for me you'd have caught him already. You'd be looking for him."

"No, I wouldn't. I'd have already been on a plane home. Without you, he'd have gone on killing people." He opened his mouth and closed it. "I'm sorry this happened, Bliss. I should have stopped him. I should have known—"

"You couldn't have known." She wrapped her arms around herself.

"I should have. I'd never want this for you, Bliss." His phone rang, breaking the moment. "I need to take this," he said after glancing at the screen.

"Go on." She waved him out of the room.

He looked at her for another moment. Her new skill to see the shadows on a person's soul didn't help her to decipher what he wasn't telling her. He strode out of her room, pulling the door closed behind her.

Bliss sucked in a breath and hugged herself. She was safe, wasn't she?

7.

TRAVIS STARED AT THE map without seeing it. Every fiber of his body was acutely tuned in to the woman on the sofa.

It was almost midnight. The local law enforcement were either out manning roadblocks or at home with their families, leaving the FBI, Travis, and Mason to keep watch over Bliss and formulate a plan for what came next.

Some of them were keeping a little too close to her.

Connor Mullins barked out a laugh at something Bliss said. Travis couldn't hear them. Not that he hadn't tried.

She should be in bed, getting rest, instead of down here with the rest of them. Evidence and case details were everywhere. Why the hell were they subjecting her to this?

Because she was now their best lead.

Knowing the answer didn't placate him in the least.

He wanted to bundle her up, lock her away, and keep her safe. But wasn't his involvement what got her here in the first place? If he'd made her stay put and gone in for Wendy on his own, Daniel would have fixated on him. Or split completely.

It was his fault. All of it. Bliss would live the rest of her life with memories she couldn't scrub away and a darkness no light would ever defeat.

"What is it with these white dudes doing all the really fucked up shit?" Benjamin tossed his notepad onto a table.

"Sure debunks the racial stereotypes, huh? We don't see a lot of Hispanic or black killers. What do you think the ratio is?" Dmitri asked.

Travis tilted his head, curious about the line of reasoning. He'd never thought of it that way, but the two agents would have a different perspective.

"Ask Jade, she could crunch the numbers in her head. I'm too tired."

"Okay everyone, get some sleep," Ryan Brooks announced. "We've got a lot of ground to cover in the morning."

"Don't have to tell me twice." Benjamin slapped the folder he'd been poring over down onto the kitchen table and strode after Ryan. The unit chief and communications liaison chatted on their way up the stairs.

"Come on, lass, time to get some shut eye." Connor pulled Bliss to her feet and pushed her toward the stairs.

Travis wanted to deck the guy.

Didn't Connor realize the trauma she'd just lived through?

Bliss chuckled and smiled, something he didn't think she'd have mastery of yet. It just went to show how strong she was.

One by one the agents and Mason trickled up the stairs until it was just Travis and the red-headed woman. Jade. Such a strange name for a woman with red hair.

"You can go up, I'll turn everything off," he said over his shoulder.

He wouldn't sleep much tonight. Not under the same roof with Bliss. He'd intentionally picked the room across from hers. If he couldn't touch her, hold her, he'd at least be the closest one if something happened.

Jade glanced up from her tablet, one brow arched. Her eyes were those who had seen too much. Things beyond their years. It was a little unsettling, but only because it stirred up old memories.

"Trying to get rid of me?" she asked.

"Just offering." He shrugged.

"You've been staring at the same spot for fifteen minutes. Why don't you go to bed?"

His neck burned. With all the activity, he'd hoped to fade into the background.

"How's your sister?" Jade asked.

"Emma?" He turned, taken aback by the question. Why would the agent care about that? "Good, last I talked to her."

"Is she still seeing that detective?" There was a nonchalant way about her that was too careful, too casual.

"What do you want to know?" He narrowed his gaze, studying her. She was younger than the rest, late twenties if he had to guess, yet she dressed in clothes that could have been taken out of Connor's suitcase instead of her own.

Jade sighed and set the tablet on the arm rest.

"Curiosity. They were under surveillance for a while because there was a remote, very tiny chance they were the copycat. Or one of them was. Before Lali pulled the plug monitoring them, Jacob made a conspicuous purchase."

"What did he buy?" He curled his hands into fists. Emma was still his sister; if that cop did anything wrong, he'd have to answer to Travis first.

"He bought an engagement ring. Or at least that's our guess."

Travis stared at her. Emma, getting engaged?

"I'll be damned." He crossed to the sofa where Bliss and Connor had recently been seated and sank down onto the cushions.

"It's none of my business, I know. I just...I can empathize with what it's like to grow up with a certain heritage. Seeing Emma and Jacob together it was...I mean..." She shrugged.

"It doesn't happen to all of us, you mean?"

Jade nodded.

Travis stared at her. Jade was bookish, shy, introverted, and extremely intelligent. He could tell that much just from looking at her. It was in the way she held herself apart from the others, how her focus went past people to the problem at hand. And yet, she was cute. Pretty. But she didn't interest him like Bliss.

"What's your story?" Travis asked.

"My parents were a serial killer team. They used me as bait to lure people away from groups, grabbed them, and killed them after inflicting sexual and physical torture."

"Jesus Christ. Please tell me they're dead?"

"They're in prison." She said it all so matter-of-factly, as if it didn't touch her. As if it were just a list of details to be recited. "Travis?"

"Yeah?" His head was still reeling from the list of wrongs in a few short sentences.

"Bliss."

His spine straightened and everything else ceased to matter.

"What about her?" he asked.

"She's like us now. You seem to have built a connection with her. She's going to need someone who understands her."

"Connor seemed to be handling her pretty well."

"Connor has a gift for making people like him. Talk to him. But she never answered any of his questions. She avoided them."

"Wait, he was trying to make her talk?"

"Yes. I thought it was obvious. He was doing the talking, I was supposed to take notes on anything she said. We got nothing. She's completely closed off."

"Her brother-in-law'll get her a doctor or something." Travis would make sure of that. Wendy wasn't the only one who needed care. The man had enough money to help Bliss out, that was for sure. He pushed to his feet. "I'm headed for bed."

"Don't discount yourself, Travis. Not all of us are beyond redemption."

"Lady, you don't know the things I've done."

"I probably have a list somewhere."

Jade didn't know him. He wasn't Emma. There wasn't hope for more than what he had now. And Bliss was better off without him. The sooner the better.

He turned and stalked toward the stairs. Jade didn't say anything else, just let him go. His feet thumped on the wooden boards. He wasn't tired yet, but neither should he be allowed to mingle with the others. A couple hours cooling his heels and clearing his head could be the trick.

The light under Bliss' door was off, and the hall was dark. He considered checking on her, but if she was already asleep the last thing he wanted to do was disturb her. Besides, Connor had probably tucked her in.

He pushed the door open to his room and stepped inside.

"What are you doing here?" he said before he could reconsider his words.

Bliss sat on his bed, her knees drawn up to her chest and the bedside lamp on. He closed the door behind him, more to keep the others from waking up.

"I couldn't sleep," she said.

"Did you try?"

"Yes."

"You know you're safe here? There's two patrol cars outside, and you've got a whole team of people that will protect you." Not to mention Travis would die before he let anything bad happen to her again.

"That's...nice." And yet everything about her posture, the way she wouldn't look directly at him, and the cant of her shoulders telegraphed unease.

"What's keeping you up?"

She shrugged.

"Nightmares?" he asked.

She nodded.

Damn, but he had a few of those.

He toed off his boots and circled the bed to sit next to her, his back against the headboard.

"I still have nightmares," he said.

"About what?"

"My dad's stories. My dad. Being over in the sandbox. Jobs going sideways." *Her.*

"Do they ever go away?"

"Some of them do. Mostly you just start realizing it's a dream, and it's not as bad anymore."

"How long does that take?"

"I'll tell you when it happens."

She chuckled, and an invisible fist squeezed his heart.

"I was hoping for a better answer," she said.

"I've never been good for good news."

"Good news, talking, sex, what else are you self-proclaimed to be bad at?"

"Hey, I never said I was bad at sex." As he recalled, it had been quite good. Hadn't it? "You seemed to like it."

"I did." She stared straight ahead.

He reached over and took her hand in his. Touching her calmed the anxious voice in his head that said this was all a dream. That she was still out there somewhere, waiting on him to save her.

She should be in her own room, not here with him. And yet, he couldn't make himself say those words. It was selfish, but he wanted to be near her, to assure himself that she was safe. He didn't have any right to her. In fact, she should hate him. But he still wanted her.

"You've got to get some rest." He drew little circles on the back of her hand.

"I can't be alone," she said, so quietly he didn't think he'd heard her right.

He hadn't protected her the first time, but here she was, trusting him again.

"Do you want me to stay with you? Or would you rather I go get Jade?" The two women could bunk together with little to no issue. Besides, Jade might get through to Bliss where Connor had failed.

"Would you mind?" she asked.

Travis swallowed. It was temptation straight from hell, but for her he'd do just about anything.

"No." He stood and held out his hand. "Come on. Let's go back to your room."

"Why?" She let him pull her to her feet.

"No windows. One point of entry. It's the safest place for you." He grabbed his bag from the dresser, his boots, and turned the light off.

"Oh."

He guided her out of his room and across the hall to hers. All the lights from downstairs were off. He wished Jade a peaceful sleep.

"Get in bed." He gently pushed Bliss toward the big king bed. The pillows and blankets were rumpled, as if she had attempted sleep to no success. "I'm going to use your bathroom."

That, and give her a moment of privacy.

He took his time in the bathroom while keeping one ear tuned to Bliss' movements. He brushed his teeth, flossed, and stared at his reflection for several minutes. When he ran out of things to do, he opened the door.

Bliss wore the same thermal shirt from earlier, but her jeans and boots were discarded at the foot of the bed. She stared at the ceiling, her brow lined with worry.

There was no real way for this to go well. It wasn't like he slept in much besides his boxers. Plus, he had the memory of what it was like to hold her, be inside of her, stuck on repeat. She didn't need a trip to horny town, she needed a safety blanket.

"Can we leave the bathroom light on?" she asked.

"Course." He flipped the light back on and closed the door until just a crack of light slashed through the darkness.

Travis shed his jeans and shirt before sliding into the bed.

This was about her needs, not his. He rolled to his side and stretched an arm out over her, trapping her against the mattress. Every muscle in her body was tense, ready for something to happen, and none of it good.

He wished he could take this burden from her. Clear her mind. Let her be free to not be like him.

Eventually she blew out a breath and her hands slid up to grasp his forearm. She turned, drawing him closer until he spooned her from behind. He did his best to stay relaxed, even when she wiggled her ass against his groin in a move to get comfortable. Minute by minute the tension eased, until her breathing relaxed and he knew she'd passed out. Only then did Travis allow himself to drift off to a dreamland where a beautiful, curvy woman waited for him with mischief in her eye.

8.

B LISS' NOSE ITCHED, BUT she didn't dare move. It had to be early morning sometime. Already she could hear sounds below and the occasional door open or close on their floor. Any moment Travis would wake up, and they would have to face whatever today held in store for her.

She hadn't slept as much as dozed off and on until her body just decided it was time to be awake. Though her dreams were uneasy, they hadn't terrorized her like before. A difference she attributed to Travis' presence.

It was Christmas Day.

Usually she would pack up her car and head to her parents' house for a busy morning of presents and baking. It didn't feel like the holidays anymore, though Travis had given her a present. Her freedom.

Guilt gnawed at her. Out there, she hadn't believed he would save her, and he had. Then last night, she'd doubted him again when she allowed fear to cloud her judgment. It wasn't his fault Daniel was crazier than they thought. She'd allowed herself to be in the wrong place at the wrong time.

There was no anticipating psycho.

Travis' eyes opened and he looked straight at her. There was no groggy, half-asleep period, just full alert aimed at her.

"Morning." His sleep-roughened voice was a comforting sound.

She smiled and scratched her nose.

"Merry Christmas," she said.

"Hm, it is, isn't it?" He tightened the arm around her, pulling her across the mattress until he had her pressed up against him.

Her heart beat faster for a new reason, one that had nothing to do with fear.

"Sleep okay?" he mumbled into her hair.

"Yeah. You?"

"The best."

She was only wearing a thermal top and panties. It wasn't a lot of material between them. Was it wrong to think about sex at a time like this?

A knock at the door interrupted her mental tango.

"Travis?"

"Yeah?" he called over his shoulder.

The door creaked open just a hair. She could spy Mason's profile, conspicuously looking away from them.

"Got breakfast. Doctors are taking Ethan into surgery now, thought you'd want to know," he said.

"Be out in a minute." Travis sat up, blocking her view.

The door closed, leaving them alone again. The sheets rustled and the bed bounced as he got to his feet. He clicked the lamp on and checked his phone. The dim light was more than enough to illuminate her fantasy material. Travis reached for the ceiling and stretched.

God, he was a work of art. Rough art, but still a thing of wonder.

A conspicuous bulge tented the front of his boxers. They'd had sex a few days ago, but she could still remember the feel of him inside of her.

Travis planted his knee on the bed and loomed over her, trapping her with one arm on either side of her shoulders.

"Looking at me like that gives me ideas." His voice dropped and her nipples perked up.

Ideas? The naked kind?

He buzzed her mouth with a kiss, and she stopped breathing. It was just a scant few seconds of skin-to-skin contact, but she felt it to her core.

"Up." He slapped her thigh.

She gathered the sheets and watched him step into the bathroom. Unlike last night, he didn't close the door.

What were they?

Lovers?

Fuck buddies?

Friends with benefits?

He wasn't sticking around, not for her, so it wasn't a relationship. None of those labels felt right. She cared about him. They'd been through enough together in a week that even when he left she would never forget him.

She got dressed in her same jeans and boots, but changed out the thermal top for a sweatshirt. It wasn't the height of fashion, but it was comfortable, and she was covered.

"What are we doing today?" she asked.

"Food. Check on Ethan. See what the cops dragged in." Travis was half-dressed, which wasn't a bad trade-off. She still got to see those abs. They were unreal. The kind of thing people painted on advertisements. He could sell just about anything with that bit of skin if he wanted to. Women would line up for miles to... She did not want to think about another woman touching Travis. This holiday season, he was hers.

"Any chance I can call my family?"

"I'm sure the feds can get you a line to their safehouse."

"Safehouse?" She blinked at him.

"Yeah, given how he had you all under surveillance, they thought it would be safest if your immediate family was under protection."

"Oh my God." She blew out a breath and her eyes watered. "What did I do wrong?"

"You did nothing wrong. Nothing, understand?" Travis wrapped his arms around her tight.

"Yeah, but—"

"No, buts. Daniel Campbell is a fucked up man. He picked your sister and your family based on some parameters only he knows. You did nothing wrong. Nothing."

She clung to him and buried her face against his shoulder until the tide of overwhelming fear abated.

Bliss lifted her chin and stared at him. A few days ago, she'd thought he was the sketchiest human being she'd ever seen. Now, he was her personal hero.

Travis lowered his head. Slow and tentative wasn't his style, but he understood where she was at. She lifted herself up on tiptoe and kissed him, hooking her arm around his neck. A deep-seated ache throbbed low in her belly. He went on kissing her until her toes curled in her boots, and her nipples chafed the cups of her bra.

He lifted his face from hers, and she gasped for breath.

"Please don't leave me." As soon as the words left her mouth she cringed. Her whole life, she'd been the capable, independent one. Not this.

"I'm here. Nothing bad will happen to you."

Travis squeezed her and rested his chin on top of her head.

She prayed he was right, that the nightmares were over.

TRAVIS THANKED THE NURSE and entered the ICU bay, Mason on his heels. Ethan's body was relaxed, his head lolling to one side at an angle that was bound to leave a crick.

"What the fuck are you doing here?" Ethan's words were slurred and quiet. The anesthesia hadn't worn off yet.

"Making sure they took the right leg." Travis reached over and prodded Ethan's left knee.

"You rat bastard. Stop." Ethan pushed Travis' hand away.

"Looks like they knew what they were doing." He stepped back and hooked his thumbs in his pockets.

They'd been here a few times over the years. Sometimes they'd been in beds next to each other. Every time they'd pulled through.

"What'd the doc say?" Mason asked.

"Like I fucking know." Ethan was perhaps the grumpiest when he was hurt. His soon-to-be ex-wife had often commented on his inability to handle pain or a little direction. Over the years she'd lost the fondness for his grouchy behavior. Maybe Travis should have seen their split coming, but he didn't know the first thing about relationships.

"Go find the nurse or the doc, let us know what needs doing," Travis said to Mason.

"Sure thing." Mason pushed to his feet and strode out to the nurse's station, a big smile on his face.

Nurses.

Of course.

"Where's Bliss?" Ethan asked.

"Safe from you."

Ethan flipped him the bird.

"Nah, I left her back at the cabin with the feds. They can keep an eye on her."

"Found him yet?"

"Not a whisper or a word. Snow set in and covered his tracks. ATV trails run all through that area. He could be anywhere."

"You think he's gone?"

Travis sat in one of the two chairs and rubbed his chin. The profilers probably had a better idea of what Daniel would and wouldn't do, but Travis had a gut feeling.

"He's either right under our noses, or he's long gone," he said at last.

"Think he's still after Bliss?"

"Wendy is the one he wanted, but now, who knows? He got caught because he took Bliss. If he'd left, I'd never have knocked Grayson for a favor and found her. Only reason the feds came here is because we were here. They had nothing."

"This ain't over, man."

Travis shook his head.

"Wish I had both legs under me so I could have your back. This sucks, man." Ethan sighed and let his head drop back against the pillow.

"Any idea how long you're down for?"

"Couple weeks, then PT. I bet it's two or three months before I'm back on the job." Ethan's face twisted up. They all knew the kind of work the guys on sick leave got. Menial crap that needed to get done, but the kind of stuff no one used to field work wanted to do.

"Home office is making arrangements to fly you home in a day or two, as soon as they release you. You'll be in Mamma

Dean's infirmary before you're released." One of the perks about working for Aegis Group was the medical facility on the property. Mamma Dean was a retired Navy surgeon who didn't know the meaning of taking it easy.

"Good. When you and the kid headed back?"

"I think Mason's looking at getting out of here today or tomorrow. I don't know when I'm leaving."

"Want some advice?"

"No."

"Too bad, fucktard." Ethan jabbed at the buttons on the side of his bed until he figured out which one raised the head of the bed a bit.

"That's it?"

"Fuck you."

"You're a real ray of sunshine." Travis played it fun and easy, prodding Ethan for a reaction, when inside he went over every second at the campsite yesterday. Could he have done something different to keep them all safe and get Daniel?

"You should take some time. Spend it in Vegas or wherever with her."

"Bliss?"

"Yeah."

"Why?" He couldn't deny that was what he wanted to do. Actually, he wanted to bundle her up and whisk her away to someplace where he knew she'd be safe. Somewhere Daniel wouldn't look for her.

"Don't be stupid. You like her."

"I've liked a lot of women." But none like Bliss.

"Bullshit." Ethan's words were clearer now, his face more animated. He was coming out of it, for sure.

"If it weren't for me, she wouldn't be here now."

"If it weren't for your sorry ass, I wouldn't be alive now. Sometimes we have to take the good with the bad. I'm just saying, you like her. I've never seen you take to a woman like this before, so you shouldn't let it go. Don't be like me, man." Ethan stared up at the ceiling.

Mason knocked on the door, followed by a woman in a white coat with a tablet and a folder of papers.

"Doc's here to see ya, gimp."

"Fuck you, too, Mason," Ethan said. His jaw went a bit slack when Mason moved. "Sorry about that, Doc."

"It's okay." She laughed and pulled up a seat.

Travis tuned out for most of their discussion. Bliss was still heavily on his mind. She didn't need him in her life. He was too much trouble, his schedule haphazard, and the likelihood that one day he'd come home in a body bag was high. It was a price too high to ask any woman to pay. Most of all someone with their history. But he couldn't deny that if anyone asked him what Santa could bring him today, it would be Bliss, in a smile and nothing else.

9.

ANIEL DROPPED THE TOOL belt onto the bed. The right uniform, and no one cared what he was up to. Just went to show how stupid people were. The lot of them were only good for one thing: dying.

He checked the camera feed he set up that morning. The camera didn't tell him more than who came and went at the FBI cabin headquarters, but at least he knew when certain members were there.

Bliss hadn't set foot out of the building since she went in. He'd seen her through a few windows, enough to know the FBI hadn't spirited her away somewhere else. They were making this easy for him.

By the end of the year he'd have Wendy and Bliss all to himself. And then he could get started. No one would find them, because they were all going to die.

BLISS CLUTCHED A PILLOW to her chest and tried to focus on the Christmas Day parade on the television. The FBI apparently didn't know how to take a day off and were already discussing routes of escape Daniel could have taken. Try as she might, their voices were the only thing she could focus on.

"Everyone take a half-hour," Ryan Brooks announced. Frustration vibrated through his voice. She couldn't blame him—she was frustrated they hadn't caught Daniel, too.

"Hey, Bliss?"

She looked up at the red-headed woman. There was something just a little off about her, but Bliss liked people who were different.

"I'm going to run out to pick up a few things. I didn't pack enough clothes for this trip. Need anything?"

"Sure, whatever you can grab, I'd appreciate it."

"Want to make a list? I know Travis said he had a bag for you, but..."

"Yeah, I think he got most of my dirty clothes in there." Plus a few things...she couldn't fathom how he'd grabbed those.

"Here. Write down your sizes. I can't promise I'll get anything fashionable, but at least you'll have something else to wear."

"You don't have to do that." Bliss chewed her lip. Her money and credit cards were still at home. It was the one thing she wished Travis would have grabbed.

Jade sat on the sofa next to her, holding her phone with both hands.

"I don't have to, but I want to. Just write up a list. Plus, we can't promise when you'll be able to go home. You could be living out of that bag for a while."

"Thank you." Bliss jotted down a few things and hastily added a last item with an asterisk by it.

"No problem. If you're up to it, I'd like to ask you a few questions later."

Bliss nodded. Inwardly she cringed. She was the only living person who could divulge first-person information. Last she'd heard, Don was still out cold, in a medically induced coma to allow some of his injuries to heal and improve his chances.

Jade left without another comment. The other people were all over the house, making calls, putting together a sandwich, or talking in pairs. Since Travis and Mason had left to see about Ethan's surgery more people had arrived. A few spoke to her, but most ignored her.

"Hey, Bliss?" Connor called to her from the kitchen.

She groaned to herself and got up. The guy was nice, but she was about done with him. The only person she wanted to talk to was Travis. Or her family. But they were out of the question.

"What's kicking?" she asked, glancing at the three agents.

Connor, Benjamin, and Dmitri, if her memory was to be trusted. Granted, it wasn't hard to pick them out of the crowd. Connor had the accent, Benjamin was often the only black man in the room, and she hadn't quite figured out Dmitri's ethnicity, but she was pretty sure it included both Russian and Latin heritage. The trio was pretty funny after-hours. She'd enjoyed their banter after dinner last night, though the nightmares had returned later. At least then she'd had Travis.

"Thought you'd like to put in a call to your family." Dmitri handed her the cordless house phone, his kind smile putting her at ease.

She glanced at the pre-dialed screen and back at him.

"Seriously?" She'd accepted that wasn't going to happen.

"Go for it. Keep it short, okay?" Connor patted her shoulder, and the three men moved out of the kitchen, giving her a bit of privacy.

She hit dial and pressed the phone to her face.

It rang once, twice—

"Hello?"

Bliss clapped her hand over her mouth. Her mother's voice was the best thing ever.

"Bliss? Is that you?"

"Yes, Mom, it's me," she managed to get out.

"Oh honey, it's so good to hear your voice."

"Hello? She there?" Her father's voice was distant, which probably meant he'd picked up another phone, and now she'd have to strain to hear them both. She didn't care. She got to hear their voices.

"Hi, Dad. Merry Christmas."

"Oh, Bliss, baby, we wish you were here."

"Me, too, Dad." She put her back to the fridge and squeezed her eyes shut.

"Are you okay? They wouldn't say a lot about what happened." That was her mother. Always the worrier.

"I'm fine. Just some bruises, a few scratches. I'm okay." It wasn't the outward injuries she was concerned about. "Are Wendy and the baby okay? Grayson with them?"

Her dad blew out a breath. She could imagine him sitting down and squinting at the ceiling. He always did that whenever someone asked him a question. "Last we heard from them, yes. The officers won't let us talk to them much, but we had a check-in last night. They were good. Worried about you."

"When can you come home?" her mother asked.

"I don't know. No one's told me much of anything."

The front door opened, and she glanced at the entry. Travis stepped through the door. She held her breath as he scanned the room and spotted her. Her heart did a little flip and she waved.

"They're telling us we need to get off the phone." Her mother harrumphed.

"I'm being taken care of, Mom. Love you guys."

"We love you," her parents said in unison.

Their words were an auditory hug, something she needed so very badly. Bliss hung up the phone and swiped her hands across her cheeks. Being away from her family on Christmas sucked. Given the circumstances, it was even worse.

"Hey." Travis filled her vision, blocking off the rest of the room.

"Christ, make some noise, would you?" She chuckled. It was good to have him near again. He wouldn't always be there, but for now she needed him.

"Sorry. Eaten yet?"

"No."

"I grabbed some stuff. There wasn't a lot open."

"Thanks. How's Ethan?"

"Grouchy, so that means he's good."

"Good. They want me to talk about Daniel."

"Are you ready for that?"

She shrugged.

"If you aren't, they'll understand."

"But if I don't, we might not find him."

"They might not find him even with your input."

"I know they want you to go out and help with the search, but do you think you could stick around for a little while and...I don't know, just be here for that?" She wrapped her arms around herself.

Travis wrapped her in a hug and kissed her brow.

"I'm not going anywhere."

She could face the nightmares with him by her side. She knew she could. But what would happen when he was gone?

TRAVIS GRABBED A SODA at random and a chocolate bar one of the officers had offered up. Bliss' tears were stuck on repeat in his mind, and he could still hear her trembling voice as she recounted every agonizing moment they'd been apart. He wanted to make all kinds of promises like she'd never be afraid again, that he'd never leave her, but those were irrational.

What she needed now was time to pull herself together. Sweets were one good tool to help combat the drop in blood sugar.

Jade entered the kitchen, her gaze on him. "She's upstairs. Give her a few."

He nodded. Words were out of his power now. All he wanted to do was punch something. Preferably Daniel Campbell, but he'd settle for the punching bag downstairs.

"You aren't any use to her if you can't be calm." Jade pitched her voice low, for their ears alone.

"I am calm."

"I tried talking to her, but she wasn't interested."

"I imagine she's pretty talked out." He couldn't deny the satisfaction that it was him she turned to. "What's next for her?"

"We're looking into protective custody."

"Permanently?" If she went into something like Witness Protection, he'd never see her again.

"Hopefully not. Daniel can't have that many backup plans, and having been thwarted twice, he's going to start splintering soon. We've notified the entire region to be on the lookout for his signatures." She shook her head. "I don't remember the last time we had a killer with two clear signatures like this. It's highly uncommon."

"What do you think about the Killer Club connection?"

"What we've been able to dig up on his Internet activity is nothing like what we ran into in Oklahoma. I'm not convinced he's connected."

"Have you found others?" This was a can of worms. Travis couldn't afford to think about it. Not when Bliss needed him.

"Some." She nodded. "That clown that kept popping up for a while is a good suspect. Crimes like his are clear copycats, which seem to be that group's MO. Daniel is...different. If there's ever been someone like him, it's a hell of a long time ago."

"Back to Bliss, where will you move her?"

"Can't tell you that. Unless you plan on going with her." Jade's left brow arched ever so slightly.

The idea was tempting, but he had a duty to Aegis he couldn't turn his back on. They'd given him a life and opportunities when no one else would. He couldn't leave them.

When he didn't answer, Jade continued, "She'll go back to Vegas under protection, probably put her up somewhere for a few days until long-term arrangements are made if we don't find Daniel. Maybe you could stick around."

"Maybe."

Jade checked her phone. "You should go up now."

He nodded and headed for the stairs, taking them two at a time. The need to be near Bliss was eating him up. He paused outside her door to knock, and then opened the door.

Bliss sat in the middle of the bed. Plastic bags were strewn around, and instead of jeans, she wore pajama pants and a knit hoodie. A single red and green bag sat in front of her, out of place and festive.

"Here." He handed the soda to her and ripped open the candy bar.

She took the drink and chocolate he offered without comment.

"The sugar sometimes helps the chemical fallout."

"Thank you." She patted the bed next to her.

He sat and offered her another piece of the candy bar. She took that as well and pushed the bag toward him.

"Merry Christmas."

He stared at the gift, a knot of panic lodged in his throat.

"I didn't get you anything," he said. When was the last time anyone had given him something for Christmas? Sure, he and Emma traded cards, usually with a gift certificate, but that was about it.

"It's a gift. You don't have to reciprocate. I just...wanted to do something for you. It's a lame thank you, so you don't have to keep it."

He handed her the rest of the candy and carefully pulled out each individual piece of tissue paper. The scent of leather clung to the wrappings. What the hell? And where had she found the time? He peered at the black lump at the bottom of the bag.

"I have a receipt around here if you want to take them back," Bliss said.

Travis reached in and pulled out a pair of black leather gloves. Not the cheap kind that would flake and peel with a little use, but the real deal.

"You said your hands were cold yesterday, and I just thought it might be something you could use." She kept rambling on, tearing the candy wrapper into little pieces. "I'm sure you have gloves, but whatever."

"Thank you." He slipped his left hand into a glove. They were snug, just the way they were supposed to be. "I don't think anyone has ever given me something this thoughtful."

"You don't have to—"

"I'm serious. I usually spend Christmas on the job or by myself. This is nice. You didn't have to do this, Bliss."

"I wanted to." She wrapped her arms around her legs.

"Thank you." He gestured to the bags. "What's all this?"

"Jade got me a few things."

"I got it all wrong, didn't I?" He sighed and took the glove off, setting them carefully on the night stand.

"No, but you got a bunch of my dirty clothes." She chuckled. "There's a washer and dryer, but no detergent downstairs."

"Figures." He sighed and stretched out next to her, his back to the headboard.

"I kind of want to know how you decided what to pack." She chuckled.

"There wasn't a lot of thought to it. I grabbed things, threw them on the bed. I know I knocked some stuff over and just tossed it in, too."

"Ah, that makes sense then."

"What?"

"The bags."

The way her smile made her eyes light up, he wanted to capture that memory for all time. He reached out and cupped her cheek, relishing her warmth, the kindness she showed him. Except now he was staring, and she'd said something.

"Sorry, what?"

"Nothing. Doesn't matter."

"It does. What did you say?"

"I was just saying that it made sense why you shoved some of my, ah, bags into the duffle."

"Bags?" He had to think that one over for a moment. "The bags."

Those bags.

"Yeah, that was kind of funny to find last night."

"I just thought you might need them? I'm not that thoughtful. It was really an accident."

"Why would I need a vibrator with you around?" She smirked, and he was reminded all over again why he'd first found her so intriguing. It wasn't often people argued with him, and she hadn't backed down one bit.

"I thought you liked the variety?"

"I do." She rested her head on her steepled knees. A bit of hair swept across her cheek, pointing at her mouth he wanted to kiss. "What's next?"

He rested his head against the wall and blew out a breath. Way to kill the mood.

"Depends if they find Daniel."

"If they don't?"

"Protective custody of some kind."

"Just me or my family?"

"Not sure, but you and Wendy are the main concerns."

"How long will you be around?"

"I've got a job that starts end of next week." It was a short gig. Any other guy could take his place if it came down to that, but he'd volunteered, knowing many would still be packing in the quality family time. Screw it. "I'll stick around as long as I can, if that's what you want."

"I'd like that, but I don't want you to get in trouble because of me. I know this is just a job and whatever." She shrugged.

He stared at her. The words he needed abandoned him. How did he make her understand how special she was to him?

"Or not. You don't have to."

"Bliss, I want to. It's just hard to use the right words."

"Oh. Can you use some of the wrong ones and see if I can figure it out?"

"I can't help but think this is my fault, and you'd be a lot better off without me."

"I'm going to disagree with you. Without you I'd never have found Wendy."

"I know enough about killers to know that my actions have little to no bearing on what Daniel is going to do. But I can't shake the feeling that if I hadn't spoken to you, you'd be alright."

"I'd be worse. I'd be grieving my sister."

"And this is better?" He reached out and ran his fingers across the bruises circling her wrist.

"Better than losing her? Yes."

He shook his head. No one had ever cared that much about him.

"You saved Wendy, and you saved me. Without you, I'd be a lot worse off." She grasped his hand and laced their fingers together.

He'd promised himself to give her space, to step back and let her go, but he wasn't that strong. She was this bright, beautiful thing that had become snared in his life, and he couldn't resist her pull. Everything about her was good, so different from him. No one had ever called him good at anything, except killing and keeping clients alive.

If he were really a man, he'd get up right now and walk out the door. Bliss was stronger than she realized, and given a little time, she'd be okay.

"I'm..." Words stuck in his throat.

Bliss' face was the only thing he could see. When had she gotten so close?

"Travis?" She licked her lips, and he stared in fascination at the glistening skin.

"Yeah?"

"Make love to me?"

10.

TRAVIS' EARS RANG WITH her request.

"Make love to me. I want to feel something besides fear and helplessness. Please." Her voice broke and she blinked a single tear.

"Shh." He cupped her cheek and wiped the tear away. "You never have to ask twice, darlin'. Stay right there."

She could have asked him for anything, and he'd have broken a dozen laws just to make her happy. Pleasing her, stroking her body to orgasm was no trouble at all. He wasn't a man used to soft lovemaking, but for her he could be whatever she needed.

He got up out of the bed and flipped the lock on the door with shaking hands. It wasn't much to keep anyone out, but if Jade or another agent came knocking it might give them pause before entering.

Travis turned toward the bed and paused. The other night he'd been pushed by a sense of need so sharp and deep that it might have been a dream. This time, he wanted each moment filed away in his memory so that Bliss would always be part of him.

She sat where he'd left her, legs still pulled up. If he didn't know better, this could be a moment taken from any normal day. What would it be like to come home to Bliss every day?

He should say something, but again, the words he needed were gone.

Bliss grabbed the comforter and flipped the bags off onto the floor. She glanced up at him, an uncharacteristically shy smile pulling on her lips.

He grabbed the hem of his shirt and tugged it up. The bed creaked as he tossed the garment off. Bliss stared at his chest, her brow slightly wrinkled. He wasn't perfect. Scars and incisions marked his body from head to toe, writing the story of his life on his skin.

"Do they hurt?" She flattened her palm over a long line just below his ribs.

"Nah."

"I hate knowing you've been hurt." She took a small step closer and covered an old bullet wound with her other hand.

"Part of the job."

She kissed the jagged scar along his sternum where a man had tried to knife him. His knees went a little weak. Her tongue licked across his skin and his balls throbbed. Damn, but she was something else.

This was supposed to be about her, and he was the one getting all the attention. It just wasn't right.

Travis cupped her face using both hands and nibbled her lower lip, drawing it in between his, sucking the taste of her into his mouth. She groaned and her hands slipped around his waist. He tilted her head to the side and deepened the kiss, stroking her with his tongue, inviting her to come out to play.

He slid his hands down to her ass, squeezing the round globes. She fit his hands so well. He rocked his hips against her, and she groaned into his mouth. The only hardship about taking her to bed was his impatient cock.

She wiggled her hands between them and rubbed the length of his erection. The denim was a cruel barrier, but this was not about him. He stepped back, breaking the kiss as she got the button through the tab.

Her cheeks were flushed and her lips swollen. It was a primitive satisfaction to see her turned on because of him.

He grabbed the hem of her shirt and tugged it up, breaking her fight with his zipper. His tongue stuck to the roof of his mouth as her breasts were revealed, sans any sort of bra. Her nipples were tight, dusky brown peaks he couldn't wait to taste again. The sounds she made when he licked them were the stuff of fantasies.

Bliss reached for him, but he crowded her back against the mattress and laid her down. He knelt over her, running his thumbs over her nipples, watching her squirm. She didn't shy away from his gaze, and more often than not she stared right back at him, owning this beautiful body of hers and the desire she felt for him. He loved the rounded softness of her hips, stomach, and breasts, so different from himself.

"Travis, I want you inside of me," she said without hesitation.

"Not yet." He had to put her over the edge first.

She made a frustrated sound, something between a sigh and a growl. He chuckled and kissed the tip of her nose as he shoved his hand past the stretchy waistband of her pants. He cupped her mound, pressing two fingers against her folds.

Her mouth opened and her eyes fluttered shut. He parted her folds, rubbing against her. Her hips shifted under him, but he was saving being inside of her for a few moments longer.

He sat back on his heels, tugging her pants and panties down her long legs.

This was what sex was supposed to be like. He'd deprived himself of human connection on a meaningful level besides his friendships. Caring for Bliss, and knowing she felt something for him, too, changed everything. He didn't just want to please her, he wanted—more. It wasn't just his dick, it was his heart.

He slid his hands between her knees and pushed them open, going to his elbows. She shifted and gripped the sheets with both hands. There was something erotic about the sight of a woman's breasts from this angle, especially hers. Later, he'd have to spend more time between them, but her pleasure came first.

Bliss' mouth opened, and her gaze bore a hole into his skull. She didn't shy away from what turned her on, which was just that much better.

He licked the length of her slit, tasting the slightly salty tang of her skin.

"Travis," she drew his name out for several seconds.

He spread her folds, licking her. He thrust his tongue into her pussy. Her hips came up off the mattress, and her knees squeezed his shoulders. The noises she made were even better than last time. Her hand found his hair, and her nails raked across his scalp.

"There, right there." She gasped.

He slid his fingers into her, curling them against the sensitive g-spot while sucking on her clit. Her mouth dropped open, and her back arched. He felt the spasms of her vaginal wall before her first high-pitched moan. She grabbed a pillow, muffling the sounds of her orgasm while he stroked her, keeping the steady, even pace, milking her for everything he could until she lay slack and boneless against the sheets.

God damn, she was fantastic.

He eased out of her and carefully crawled up to lie next to her. The jeans were on the extreme side of uncomfortable now, but he could manage.

"Oh my God. Oh my God." Bliss lowered the pillow to her chest and panted.

Travis allowed himself a chuckle.

"Good?" he asked.

She stared at him with wide eyes.

"Good? Great would be an understatement." She grinned without some of the tension she'd carried earlier.

Bliss rolled toward him and threw a leg over his. He stared at the ceiling and mentally ran through what ammunition he had with him. The state of his razors. Anything but the feel of her breasts against his chest, the still-hard nipples prodding him, or her thigh rubbing up against his balls.

He knew every one of her injuries, had listened as the nurses uncovered them and then again when Bliss recounted the horrors. She wanted release, and he'd give her that, but until she had more time to heal, he wouldn't presume that sex was on the table, no matter what she said.

She kissed his jaw and cupped his cheek, turning his face toward her. He hesitated—some people weren't fond of their taste on another's mouth—but she didn't show any reservation. She kissed him and slid her leg over his hips.

"Careful." He winced and adjusted his dick with one hand, the other busy copping a feel.

"Sorry."

Bliss sat up, straddling his thighs. Her smile was the stuff better men wrote songs about. She grasped his zipper and tugged it down. He hurriedly cupped his dick before it got caught in the zipper.

"Hold on." He grabbed her hands, staying away from her bruised wrists.

"What?" She frowned.

"Just, don't think you have to."

She tilted her head to the side.

"I mean, if you aren't ready," he said.

"Travis, Daniel didn't rape me."

"I know, but it doesn't mean you're ready. If you aren't."

"I don't know if I should thank you for being considerate, or slap you for being stupid." One side of her mouth screwed up.

"No slapping." He cringed and covered his erection.

Bliss chuckled and ducked her head, kissing his mouth. He couldn't keep his hands to himself. He palmed her breasts, capturing the hard nipples between his fingers. She groaned against his lips and her eyes parted.

"Are you really turning me down right now?" She stuck out her lower lip.

"No, but—"

She put her fingers over his mouth.

"Nothing good comes after *but*."

Bliss replaced her fingers with her mouth while her other hand wrapped around his cock.

"You really want to turn me down right now?" she asked.

"No. I just want what's best for you."

"Can you stop being so considerate for a little bit? Are you really going to argue with me about having sex?"

He should.

She'd been through so much.

"No," he finally said.

She smiled and planted a kiss on his mouth while her hands slid down to cup his balls.

"Any chance you have a condom?" she asked.

He sat up, pushing her back onto her heels, and slapped his wallet onto the nightstand. Tucked inside was a little precautionary protection. He grabbed it and ripped the packet open. If she was determined to have sex—with him—he was done fighting what they both wanted. He'd tried the selfless martyr route, and that clearly wasn't for them.

Travis rolled the condom on by feel alone while Bliss' mouth kept him busy. She pushed his shoulders and he lay back, cramming a pillow under his neck. This was a sight he didn't want to miss.

She grasped his cock, her eyes a little wider.

"I thought I imagined it being this big," she said.

"It's only going to get bigger the longer you look at it."

"Oh, really now?" She grinned.

She lifted up on her knees, and he grasped her hips, steadying her. Her grip tightened, holding him in place as she sank down. He held himself back, allowing her to go at her own speed. She planted her hands on his chest, her nails driving into his skin as she rose and sank, working more of his cock into her tight little pussy. Finally she sank down, taking the last bit of him into her.

Bliss sucked down deep breaths, her gaze a little unfocused.

He sat up, wrapping an arm around her waist, and kissed her. She groaned, sucking on his tongue, and clung to his shoulders. Her body relaxed further and the vice-like grip on his cock eased.

She pushed on his shoulders, and he released her, breaking the kiss and letting his hands drift down to her ass. There was no telling how long he'd last. Not long enough, that was for sure. Her body fit him better than the gloves she'd gifted him. There was a rightness to the world when he was in her.

Bliss rose on shaky knees.

"Christ." He groaned.

"Bliss." She kissed his cheek. "My name is Bliss."

"I'll remember that."

Little sparks of light were going off behind his eyelids. She rose and fell, her breasts rubbing against his chest. He dropped back to the bed, giving her free rein to move as she liked. Her hands found his chest again, and her nails dug in.

Travis lifted his hips, moving in time with her.

"Oh—oh!" Bliss tossed her head back, her hips rolling. He could feel the flutter of muscles right before her vagina tightened in orgasm.

"Fuck—Bliss." He grasped her hips, lifting her, and thrust, losing himself in the tight, hot feel of her body around his.

He squeezed his eyes shut as his orgasm spurted out of him. Bliss fell forward, collapsing against his chest, her breath fanning over his skin. He wrapped his arms around her.

If only every day could be spent with her.

11.

ANIEL LIFTED THE CIGARETTE to his lips, his gaze on the black SUV. He didn't smoke, but it gave him a reason to loiter outside the hospital. Tapping the phone lines hadn't told him anything he couldn't have guessed on his own. What he needed was another way to keep tabs on them, especially once they returned to Vegas later in the day.

Three figures climbed out of the truck. The two men automatically put the smaller woman between them, not that Bliss was worth saving. But she was for later.

He waited until they'd entered the hospital, and then waited longer, letting the cigarette burn down almost to the filter. Disposing of the butt, he kept his head down and strode out to the parking lot, peering at the other cars. No one had pulled in after the two bodyguards, but that didn't mean someone wasn't waiting for him to expose himself. So far, the cops were looking in all the wrong places, the places some other idiot would go on the run. But not him. He had a brain.

Daniel pulled the spare rental key out of his pocket and clicked the fob. The black SUV beeped.

One more glance around.

No one was watching.

He circled the truck and opened the passenger door. A few belongings littered the console and floor board. Nothing useful. He dug into the back seat and came up with several bags. One of which had Bliss' nametag already attached to it.

Perfect.

He dug into his pocket and pulled out the tiny tracking device. Disguised as a bit of garbage, it would blend into her belongings. With any luck, it would lead him right to her once they went to ground in Vegas.

A pair of black gloves stuck out of the seat pocket. He grabbed them, turning them over.

Nice.

He shoved them in his pocket and got out of the SUV, locking it with the rental key. Satisfied, it was time to get out of the city and hit the road. His new ride should be ready soon, and he needed to return the key before it was missed.

Daniel's plans were falling into place.

BLISS PEERED OUT BETWEEN the blinds. The upper-middle class house was one of many nearly identical models in the Las Vegas housing development. Except it wasn't. This one was owned by the government. Not just the police, but *the government.* An unmarked police car had delivered them here and then left. Someone was supposed to bring Travis' rental around eventually. From the talk that had gone on around her, she picked up that their arrangement was unusual.

The difference was Travis. His continued presence in her life made everything different.

"Where the fuck are they?"

She turned and watched Travis upend his bag onto the big bed that sat in the middle of the master suite. He'd marched in here and deposited both their bags on the dresser as if it were the most natural thing. She liked that. Liked knowing he would be next to her tonight when the nightmares came again. That when she needed him, he'd be an arm's length away.

But only for another week, at best.

During the flight she overheard his hushed phone call. He was passing up work to be with her, and while she appreciated that, she couldn't let his life stall for the sake of her comfort.

"What's wrong?" She crossed to the bed.

"The gloves. I had them earlier, but they aren't in any of my stuff." A few days ago, his ferocious frown might have sent her into hiding. Now she just wanted to kiss him.

"They're somewhere." She shrugged. They'd packed in such a rush to make the flight before another front blew in. She doubted he really thought about what went where.

"But they should be here."

"You'll find them." She climbed onto the bed and lay down on her side, watching him. "Heard from Ethan?"

"Yeah. He texted. Sounds like he's still being a grump."

"When will he get home?"

"Tomorrow, as long as flights aren't grounded."

"You guys seem really close."

"Should be. We've known each other since Basic."

"Yeah?" She curled her arm under her, eager to hear anything about his past.

Instead, Travis grunted and started folding his clothes.

Well, nuts.

"What was that like?" she asked.

"Basic? Bullshit."

"That's all you have to say about it?" She laughed and threw a pillow at him.

Travis caught it, folded it in half and sat on the mattress, the pillow under his forearm.

"I don't have a lot of good memories from Basic."

"Why?"

"I had a friend that enlisted with me. He couldn't hack it, got kicked out and...it's just bad memories."

"Why? What happened?"

"Carlos went on to have a kid. It was his baby momma who went crazy, threatened to kill the kid, and I grabbed the boy while Carlos talked her down."

"Oh, no."

"Yeah."

"But...what happened? You told me a little, but I'm guessing not the whole story."

Travis sighed and stretched out, cramming the pillow under his head. He stared at the ceiling, hands crossed over his stomach.

"Carlos had a bad picker. He only liked the crazy women. He knocked up Priss right before Basic, and he always said getting kicked out was good, because he got to be there for her during the pregnancy. She was never right in the head. Every time I was home, they'd broken up and been back together a couple of times."

She held her breath, dreading the end of his story.

"That last time, they were split up. She called, pissed about something that didn't even make sense, and threatened to kill their son, Manuel. Carlos, he was scared. Real scared. So we went over there, and she's hitting on this kid." He swung his hand in the air, not looking at her. "He was seven, I think. She's just wailing on him. Carlos grabs her, and I figure, this kid needs help. I grab him, get in the truck and go down the street until the cops come."

Her heart hurt. On the surface he was just rattling off the details, but she knew how much it had to bother him. Travis was a protector. He'd acted with the best interests of the kid in mind.

"We must have sat there for an hour. I thought no one was coming. I didn't have a cell phone, and all I've got is a screaming kid. Well the cops get there, yank me out, start yelling, and they haul me to prison and give the kid back to Priss and Carlos, who in that hour had patched things up and were back together. They stayed together all during my trial. Carlos, he lied through his teeth on the stand. It was awful, but he never was very strong when it came to women. Worst of it? I was in the pen maybe six weeks when I heard Priss killed Carlos on one of her crazy benders."

"No!"

"Yeah. I got paroled a couple months later."

"What happened to Manuel?"

"He lives with Carlos' mother now. I go by and see him whenever I'm home."

"Does he like you?"

"Yeah. He got all the brains his parents never had. Smart kid. Scary smart."

"What did you do after that?"

"I got out and went straight to a bar. My sister, Emma, showed up, and we drank until we were seriously fucked."

"Really?" Bliss laughed and tried to picture what Travis' sister must look like. She had to be an interesting woman.

"Yeah, you don't want to have a drinking contest with her. Our old man had her on the bottle young. She can't drink me under the table, but she can hold her own."

"Your dad got you guys drinking when you were kids?"

"My sister. My mom would have smacked him silly. Didn't stop me sneaking a few beers."

"Okay, wait..." She shook her head, rearranging the pieces.

"My dad stepped out on his wife a lot. He only had two kids though. Emma, whose mom is his wife, and me. We're about a year apart."

"And it's your dad who had the run-in with the serial killer?"

"Yeah. BTK. He murdered my grandparents and made him watch."

"That had to be rough."

"It wasn't a cake walk."

"And you said a copycat tried to kill your sister?"

"Yeah, earlier this year, guy called himself BTKiller. He was...I don't know, trying to recreate the original BTK murders because he thought he was the reincarnation of the guy. You'd have to ask Emma. He had this idea that if he killed all these people, her and this cop, he'd set his soul free or some bullshit."

"And that's how you got hooked up with the FBI?"

"Kind of. Their guys called me, asked me some questions. It went from there."

She shook her head, mind reeling. They hadn't even touched on his time in the Navy, doing whatever it was he did, or his job now. Danger was woven into the fabric of who he was. There was no use wishing him safe because, even doing something safe, he was dangerous.

"What?" he asked.

"Nothing, I'm wrapping my head around all of it."

"I'm not a good person, Bliss."

"Right." She rolled her eyes.

"You're seeing me as the man you want me to be."

"Or maybe you've decided to be a martyr because a few idiots said you were a bad apple? I can't believe that. You're a lot better than you give yourself credit for."

"I'm not."

"Fine. If that's what you want to believe." She rolled off the bed, stood and stretched.

If Travis wanted to be a martyr and believe he was some sort of awful human being because a bunch of bad stuff had happened to him, she wasn't going to change his mind. But now she understood him a tiny bit better, and she liked what she'd seen.

"Where you going?" he called out as she left the bedroom.

"Kitchen." She hadn't stopped being hungry since they'd picked her up out of the snow. Sure, another meal would go straight to her hips, but they were hers, and she wasn't about to feel guilty for being alive to eat.

TRAVIS WATCHED BLISS LEAVE the bedroom.

She didn't get it. And he didn't know how to make her understand. His life was cursed. There was a darkness he couldn't shake. He'd been born into it, and it would die with him. There was no future if she couldn't accept that.

A future?

What the heck was he thinking?

He shook his head and sat up, busying himself with putting his clothes into a drawer.

There was no denying he liked Bliss. She was special, and he would be crazy to not want her in his life. But that was a something he couldn't ask of her. He couldn't offer her a stable home like Grayson. He wouldn't be around to take her calls, have dinner or anything. She deserved better than him, and that was the end of it.

He put the last of his things away and headed downstairs, following his nose.

Bliss stood at the stove, stirring something in a pot. She was barefoot and bounced her hip in time to music only she could hear. Just the sight of her was a punch to the gut. This time two days ago he hadn't been certain he'd ever see her again. And here she was.

It was enough to make a man wonder about the future. To want something different. But even trying to live part time in Vegas to be nearer to her wouldn't be fair to her. He'd watched the stress that kind of separation put on Ethan and Molly. Sure, other guys made it work, but someone always suffered. He wouldn't ask her to do that.

Travis crossed to the entry and the brown box the officer had left for him.

"What 'ya got there?" Bliss asked.

He set the box on the kitchen counter and opened it. A couple of things for him, and two for her.

"Belated Christmas presents." He held up the two items.

"Oh, you're so thoughtful. I've always wanted my very own Taser. And Mace?"

"Will you be serious?"

"Fine. What's up?"

"I want you to keep these with you. Have you used mace before?"

"I had some in college. I know the basics. Point it away from you. Aim for the eyes. If I get it on me, don't try to wash it off with soap, use milk."

"Good. And the Taser?"

"You sure that's necessary?"

"It could be. I'd like you to have a gun, but first you need to know what to do with it."

"A gun? Seriously? Me?"

"What? You operate a vibrator. It can't be that much different."

"I'm going to pretend you didn't just say that."

"Look, I just want you safe. These are easy tools to keep around in case you need them."

She sighed and tapped the spoon on the pot.

"Fine. How do I work it?"

They left the soup on to simmer while he showed her the basics of the hand-held device. It had enough juice to stop a man in his tracks long enough for her to get away. That was the most important thing he had to drill into her.

"If you'll consider it, I'd at least like to show you how to shoot." He placed the items back on the counter. Later he'd make sure they got into her purse.

"But they said we couldn't go out."

"Not now. Some other time." He got at least a week off between gigs, sometimes more. Plenty of time to make a trip to Nevada.

"Like—what? You're just going to come back to Vegas to teach me how to shoot a gun?"

"Sure. Why not? You don't want me here?" Hadn't he just decided that was a bad idea? He had no self-control where she was concerned.

She blinked at him for a second, then stared at the soup, stirring it slowly.

"It's not that. I like you. But it's hard to lean on you and know you're going to leave any minute. I was starting to think I'd never see you once you left."

"I never said that."

"No..."

"I wouldn't mind coming back if you wanted to see me."

Bliss nodded. It wasn't the reaction he'd hoped for, not that he knew what he wanted from her. It was all so tangled and twisted inside of him. He wanted her even when he knew the best thing for her was not him.

"I don't have to," he said.

"It's just hard right now. I really like you, and I'm so very grateful you saved not just me, but Wendy... I don't know where my head is. I'd like to see you though."

"Cool."

"But what if I'm not even here? What if they move me?"

"Then we'll figure it out. Daniel can't keep hiding forever. They're going to catch him." That, or Travis would. The most important thing right now was keeping Bliss safe. Once he was assured of her well-being, he would go on the hunt.

IT WAS GOOD TO be back in his home city. Getting out of California hadn't been as difficult as he'd thought. Granted, there were a few close calls, but his disguise had passed the test.

Daniel unlocked his secret bunker and quick-stepped down the stairs. It was time to find out where his girls were and plan for their get-away.

He fired up the computer and waited for it to boot.

Wendy was easy to locate. All he had to do was follow the courier from her husband's place of work, and he'd know

where she was. Bliss, on the other hand, was better con-
cealed. Thanks to that piece of work bodyguard. Daniel
hadn't figured out how that one played into everything, but
he was ready to find out.

A few clicks of the keys, and he brought up the GPS
tracker tuned into the device he'd planted in her bag. The red
pin plopped on the map, and he zoomed in to the very street
she was sitting on.

"Gotcha."

He grinned and clicked through his other feeds. The ma-
jority of his cameras were disabled, but a small number were
still up and running. They all showed what he expected,
abandoned homes.

Now, what about the man?

Travis.

That was his name.

"Who are you, Travis? And how will you die?"

12.

BLISS PEERED INTO YET another drawer. The master bath was stocked with all kinds of things. Toothbrushes. Adult diapers. Children's diapers. First aid kit. The list went on. If she didn't have something, she now knew where it was stocked.

The digital clock on the counter ticked off another five minutes. She'd successfully hidden in the bathroom for over an hour. Travis had moved around the house, talking on his phone, chatting with her, and mostly brooding. Their conversation over dinner had consisted of a dozen or so words.

She liked him. A lot. And she did want him to come back to Vegas. At least that was her knee-jerk reaction. On one hand, she wanted more. For Travis to realize he was more than a string of other people's mistakes. That he was a caring, thoughtful guy who just needed to let go a little. That there was more than just chemistry there. On the other hand...She didn't know if she'd be living in Vegas. If he would be allowed to know where she was. And why the hell did she have such crazy strong feelings for a guy she met a couple days ago?

From the moment Travis had walked into her life, she felt like someone had her back. He believed her when she said her sister was missing. At the house she'd freaked out, and he was right there with her. When she pressed the issue of going with him, he didn't try to keep her away. At every turn he'd had her back. What would it be like to have a partner like that? She'd always been the one pulling the weight of two people.

Then there was the chemistry. It was off the charts. She didn't think it was simply switching out her nice guy type for a bad boy. It was a result as unique as Travis himself.

She was falling in love with him, and they were doomed to fail.

"Bliss?" He knocked on the bathroom door.

She flinched and turned toward the white pocket door. If she ignored him, would he go away? She couldn't be so lucky.

"Yeah?"

"You done in there?"

"Almost."

She held her breath and listened, but of course he couldn't do her the favor of making a tiny bit of sound.

Freaking man.

Bliss turned back to the mirror. She'd showered. Dried her hair. Brushed and flossed her teeth. Scrubbed and moisturized her face. Was she missing something? Could she squeeze out a few more moments alone with her merry-go-round of thoughts?

The lock on the door *snicked*.

Her spine straightened and she stood at the tiny silver lock, pointing the wrong way.

Daniel?

The door opened. Travis stood on the other side, a knife in hand.

Bliss blew out a breath and turned to face him.

"Christ, don't do that. You scared me."

"You've been in here for a long time." He closed the knife and slid it into his pocket without looking away from her.

"Yeah, so? There's not a lot to do here." She scooped up her dirty clothes.

He stepped back, out of her way. She crossed to her bag, opting to leave the worn clothing tucked behind the duffle for now.

"What's bothering you?" Travis leaned against the dresser, watching her.

"Nothing."

"Nothing is always something when a woman says it."

She glared at him.

"Ethan's ex-wife always said that."

Smart woman.

"You going to bed?" he asked.

"Might as well."

Travis had insisted they keep the TV off. If she had to guess, the news was still clogged with updates on Daniel's whereabouts and his history of crime. The FBI had mentioned something about confirming over fifty bodies attributed to Daniel.

She climbed into bed and turned away from Travis.

He still wanted to see her.

The idea of never seeing him again left an empty ache in her chest. Could she ever have him? Would he ever truly be hers? She wasn't even sure what he meant when he suggested still seeing her.

She listened to him brush his teeth and move about the room, getting ready for bed. Everyday actions that squeezed her heart in a vice. Why couldn't this be their normal?

Travis turned all the lights off, save for the bathroom. He left the door open just a crack. For her. Because she needed the security of the light.

The bed dipped under Travis' weight, and she squeezed her eyes shut. She wanted him, but she didn't want to lose him. And right now, things were too uncertain to make any sort of call about the future.

He rolled toward her and she shifted as gravity tilted her toward him. She was intently aware of his presence, the sound of his breathing, the feel of his gaze on her.

"You need to get out of your head, darlin'. You'll drive yourself crazy if you keep doing this to yourself. You're safe. I'm not going to let anything happen to you." He turned and the sheets rustled as he stretched out on his side, closest to the door.

Travis thought she was obsessing about Daniel? That mental refrain had broken some point that morning, and she'd slept without the hint of a dream. His return to her life was a very real possibility, one she didn't like, but she couldn't control.

She held very still, listening to his breathing grow shallow and even. He could probably fool her into thinking he was asleep, so she chose to believe it for now.

Bliss rolled over, letting her gaze travel the line of Travis' body. The sheet and blanket were down around his waist and the bathroom light cast just enough light she could see the tattoo on his upper arm.

She wiggled her toes and turned back toward the windows. There was no reason for her to have so much pent up energy. She'd barely slept, hadn't eaten well, and it hurt when she moved certain ways. And yet, she wasn't about to sleep anytime soon.

The digital clock ticked off the minutes, taunting her. She turned away, only to roll to her stomach and glare at the numbers.

Longest night of her life.

Or, second longest. There was no denying that night spent in the A-frame had seemed to go on forever.

She rolled to her side, tossing back the comforter tangling around her legs.

Travis sighed in his sleep. She froze, not even breathing as she counted to twenty.

The bedside lamp clicked on, casting a warm glow on the room.

"What's bothering you?" he asked.

She rolled to her back and cringed.

"Sorry. Keeping you up?"

He rolled to his side, all that muscle on display.

"What's bothering you?" he asked again.

"Nothing."

"Bliss." He tipped his chin down and gave her The Look. The one that said they both knew very well something was bothering her and she was hiding it. "I told you Daniel can't get you here. There's two sets of plainclothes cops stationed at either end of the street, plus one lives behind us. Daniel shows up, we got him."

"Wait, we're next door to a cop?"

"Yeah."

"What about his family?"

"He's single, and this is part of his job. I think he's got a cop buddy roommate."

"Oh. I'm not worried about Daniel." She rolled to her side, chewing her lip. If she told him, she would become that girl. The clingy one who always wanted more. She'd never been that girl, but with Travis...It was all different.

"Then what's got you tossing and turning?"

"You aren't so bad at talking."

"Bliss."

She blew out a breath and spent a moment fluffing her pillow. He waited her out, watching her every movement. She was only prolonging the inevitable.

"What's going to happen to us?" She couldn't even look at him when she asked.

"That's up to you."

"That's not a fair answer."

"What do you want to hear?"

"That's what I'm talking about." She flopped onto her back. "Why do you have to put this on me? It's like you're just saying that to make me feel better or safe or something."

"Put this on you? What the hell?"

"I mean..." She glanced at him and almost wanted to hide under the bed. His scowl was dark and unhappy.

"Let me get this straight, you think I'm in bed with you, fucked you, and stayed here to make sure you feel good? Darlin' there are some things you can't pay me to do and whore myself out is one of them."

"That's not what I meant!" She sat up, her restless nerves pushing her to do something.

"I'm not that kind of man."

"I didn't mean it like that. I just thought...yeah, we like each other, and you're letting me focus on us instead of Daniel when you aren't really interested."

Travis scrubbed a hand over his face before answering.

"This ain't that complicated."

"Well, what am I supposed to think when you're pushing all this on me to make the decisions? You haven't told me what you think or feel."

"I told you exactly what I thought, that it was up to you what you wanted."

She grabbed the pillow and swung it at him. He deflected it easily with his forearm before lunging at her and pining her to the mattress. She squirmed a bit, but getting away from him was a useless expenditure of energy.

"What's not clear enough about that?" he asked.

"Because what if I want something you don't? What if you like me more than I like you?"

The scowl didn't go away and he didn't move off her, but he did let go of her arm.

"Don't you get what I'm saying when it's up to you? I want it all, but I'm not about to ask a woman to put up with my lifestyle or what I do. It's not fair to you." His voice retained the same rough quality, but there were deeper, vulnerable notes.

"Oh." She let her hands rest on his biceps. Her voice trembled despite her efforts to speak clearly. "So if I said this was it, you'd be okay leaving and never seeing me again?"

"Yes." His gaze narrowed. He didn't like that answer, but she didn't doubt that he'd at least pretend he would leave her alone, per her wishes.

She got the feeling Travis was the kind of man who got what he wanted and damn the consequences, and right now he wanted her. That desire was a palpable zing of electricity in the air, arcing between them, and she was surprised they couldn't see the sparks.

"And if I said let's be crazy and get married now?" She held her breath, dying to hear how he'd send that question back at her.

"I'd say wait until the morning."

"Seriously?" She stared at him in more than a bit of shock. Travis' shoulders lifted.

He was serious. Holy cow, the idea didn't terrify her. That rational part of her brain wasn't screaming at her to stop now.

If he said yes, she'd marry him tomorrow.

Was she brave enough to ask? To put it out there?

Hell no.

Bliss licked her lips. "I'm not serious about the wedding chapel thing, but...I don't like the idea of not seeing you again. And I don't like the idea of not knowing where I stand with you. I'm not the kind of girl that just jumps into bed with a guy."

"Okay."

"Okay?"

"Yeah."

"Use more words, damn it. What does okay mean?"

"I'm good with that. And you should plan on not jumping into bed with anyone else."

She gulped and nodded.

"As far as where we stand, like I said, I'm leaving that up to you, because I can't ask you for more than what you're ready for."

Everything. She wanted it all, but who fell for a guy they just met? That kind of stuff was for girls like Wendy. Not her.

"Then...dating?"

"I'm good with that. But Bliss, I can't even tell you when I'll be back or how long you might go without hearing from me. Some of the work we do...it's important. It's not all watching rich guys like Grayson tinker around. Sometimes it's very dangerous."

"Can you at least warn me about the dangerous stuff?"

"No."

"Travis, if something bad happens I want to be prepared. Otherwise I'll worry all the time."

"I'll think about it."

"That's not fair."

"I said I'll think about it. I need to talk with Ethan. Figure out how they handled it. Molly always was chill about stuff like that. But what if I'm sent on a sensitive assignment? I can't promise that I will always be able to tell you everything, or anything. See what I mean?"

How did women and men deal with this? This wasn't just a problem unique to Travis, there were all those men and women working in dangerous fields who had to routinely leave loved ones behind. It sucked.

"Okay, so long as we can still figure that out." She could. Right? That wasn't impossible?

He stared at her for several moments, the frown lines still wrinkling his face. She could only imagine what was in his head. He'd tried scaring her away once. He was painting the worst picture possible of a relationship with him. Did he think so little of himself?

She slid her hands up to his face, applying the barest pressure with her fingers. He lowered his head, gaze locked on her lips. The first touch of his mouth was gentle. It felt as though she'd kissed him a thousand times before, and as though this were the first time. Warmth pooled in her stomach and her restless feet rubbed against the sheets. She wanted to wind her body around his, to touch him, love him, show him things could be different.

"Bliss?" His lips caressed her with each syllable.

"Hm?"

"Where'd you put the bags?"

Her sex toys.

She sucked in a breath, both thrilled and apprehensive about his participation with her collection of sexual wonders.

"They're in my duffle."

Travis climbed off the bed, heading straight for her bag.

She sat up and pulled the baggy shirt she'd worn to bed off and shimmied out of her panties. Was that too forward? She didn't think so, it was just being pragmatic. They were going to be naked so why not speed the process along?

Bliss clutched the pillow to her chest and watched him examine the contents of several pink drawstring bags. Pink was a safe color. Most of the time.

He selected three and left the rest on the dresser.

A promise for later?

Her body hummed with anticipation.

Travis crossed to her side of the bed and tossed the three bags onto the nightstand. He grabbed her pillow-shield, tugged it from her grasp, and deposited it behind her. In the blink of an eye she was flat on the mattress, his weight pressing her down once more, his mouth on hers. This time it wasn't gentle or kind, it was hungry.

She rolled her hips and hooked a leg over his waist, undulating against him. His erection strained the front of his cotton boxers at just the right angle.

Travis growled something incoherent and sat up, grabbing one of the pouches on his way. She was left breathless, spread eagle on the bed with him kneeling between her thighs. This was usually the moment where she would have a bit of fluttering in her stomach, some worry about her body or scaring him away, but not this time. It was just—perfect. They were exactly who they were supposed to be together, and nothing about this moment was wrong.

He reached into the long pouch and drew out a curved, magenta dildo with V-styled ridges circling its girth.

That one.

Of course it would be that one.

She ran her toes up his calf.

"Should I know anything?" he asked.

She shook her head. Usually she'd need a bit of lube, but not right now. She'd gone from dry to wet in an instant.

"What do you like about it?" He turned the dildo this way and that.

"It's good for g-spot orgasms. And I like the girth." The last bit she managed o get out without stammering. It was awfully pretty and just different enough that it stood out in her collection. But in the girth and length department she was pretty sure Travis won out.

He stared at the toy a few more moments, his brow wrinkled, as if he didn't know which end went in her.

She wrapped her hand around the base and tugged it from his grip. Some guys liked to watch, right?

Bliss closed her eyes, conscious of the blush creeping up her neck. She reached down, but Travis hands were there already. He spread her open while she guided the head of the dildo to her entrance. Her nerves were wound up just enough that she felt her body resist the tapered dildo.

Deep breath.

She slid the end in and out, keeping the strokes steady and slow. The ridges teased her vaginal walls. Travis' hand covered hers and the angle changed, rubbing the front of her channel. She gasped at the shift in sensations and curled her toes, giving control of the toy up to him.

This.

This was what it could be like.

13.

TRAVIS STARED, ENTRANCED BY the sight of Bliss' body taking the dildo. The silicone glistened with her arousal, and already she was making all those little sounds that drove him crazy. Her feet rubbed on the sheets, her hands fisting them. He didn't mind her eyes being closed. At least if he made a mistake she wasn't watching him do it.

The toy was harder than he'd expected, which made gripping it easy. He slid the full length of it inside of her, right up to the flared base. Her hips came up off the mattress and she gasped.

Had he found the spot?

He pumped the toy, slow and easy, fascinated by the way her body stretched around the oddly shaped dildo. It was fucking hot.

"Travis." She hissed and peered up at him through narrow slits.

The goal wasn't to make her come. At least not yet. He wanted to...play with her. This wasn't just about scratching a sexual itch. Of course he wanted to spend a day inside of her, but there was also something far more intimate in this act. Plus, the idea of making her come over and over again had plenty of appeal.

He'd show her just how generous he could be in bed.

He continued lazily stroking her with the dildo with one hand and upended another, smaller pouch onto the bed. The small bullet was nothing like what she'd shown him their first night, but it was perfect for what he wanted to do. He'd had nothing but time to consider.

Bliss's hips undulated, her motions faster, far more intent than his. He let the dildo slide from her pussy and tossed it a few feet over.

"No," she wailed.

He braced an arm across her hips, keeping her right where he wanted her, and twisted the bullet on. The second he touched her mound with it she shrieked and her knees clamped down on his shoulders. He watched in fascination as her spine bowed and her body shuddered.

Damn.

He hadn't even touched her clit or anything.

Her body went slack and he removed the tiny vibrator. He hadn't realized how much stimulation the dildo had provided. Clearly he had a lot to learn about sex toys and Bliss' body.

He was about to become the most dedicated student.

Travis turned the vibe off and crawled up her body. She looped her arms around his neck and hauled him down, wrapping her legs over his hips and kissing him deeply. He rolled them to their sides and kissed her back.

He'd made her that crazy. He'd pushed her to orgasm.

It was a surprisingly satisfying accomplishment.

Bliss reared back, wiggling out of his hold. He let her go, but instead of taking off for the bathroom, regrouping, or anything he'd expected, she slithered down his body, yanking his underwear down in the process.

"Wow, Bliss...."

He rolled to his back and stopped talking. There was something about a naked woman with intent in her eye. He couldn't pass up the opportunity to watch.

She stripped his underwear off him and straddled his thighs. God, she was amazing. He hated the dark bruises dotting her flesh, but she'd overcome them. There would be time to address the rest of it. She grabbed the bullet he'd discarded and twisted it on.

"What are you going to do with that?" He eyed the vibrator with apprehension.

"You'll see." She grinned at him and bent until her ass was in the air and her elbows pressed into the mattress.

He wasn't sure he wanted to see anything except her ass. Damn but he liked her butt. It was round and just right for his hands.

Bliss fisted his cock in a firm grasp. Nothing tentative or unsure about that. She slid her palm up and down his erection before licking up the underside, right along the vein that throbbed.

"Oh, fuck," he muttered and thrust up into her grasp.

She placed the bullet just under the mushroom cap. He gasped, his hips shooting up off the mattress. The vibrator rubbed the length of his cock. It was weird. The sensations were arousing but also fairly...ticklish. He jerked his hips back and forth, the muscles in his shoulders and neck tightening.

"Breathe," Bliss whispered.

He had a vague impression of her grinning at him, and her breasts resting on his thighs.

She leaned forward and wrapped her lips around his cock, her tongue swirling around the head. The wet heat of her mouth against his sensitized dick was amazing. Her hand wrapped around the base of his cock and she went to town twisting, licking, and sucking him.

Her hand cupped his balls and the bullet pressed right between his testicles.

He shouted and thrust far harder than he'd ever intend into her mouth. One hand wound up in her hair, the other in the sheets. His vision hazed, and he had the sensation of everything whizzing by, like they were on a bullet train.

Bliss sat up, breathing deep, and turned the vibrator off. Her chin was damp and a bit of his seed coated her lips.

He sat up and glanced at his still-erect dick.

"Did I come?"

"Uh, yeah." She chuckled and swiped her hand across her mouth.

"God damn."

BLISS SMOTHERED HER CHUCKLE behind her hand.

Oh man, he looked so confused. It was rather adorable.

"How am I still hard if I just came?"

She tracked his gaze to his erect penis. It hadn't softened much, if at all.

"Some guys can come more than once."

"Is that natural?"

"Yeah," she chuckled.

"Oh. Okay. Cool." He reached out and grabbed her arm, pulling her up the bed and into his arms.

She giggled, relishing the feeling of being manhandled. This was a first. She'd never thought the idea of being tossed around in bed was that great, but with Travis? She could become a fan.

Travis kissed her briefly while he hauled them both up to their knees. He pushed her forward and she grasped the headboard with both hands.

Things went flying from the bottom of the bed until she heard a very familiar crinkling sound.

Oh, yes! She gave a mental cheer and peered over her shoulder in time to watch him roll the condom on. He caught her gaze and her grin widened.

He palmed her bottom with both hands, leaning over her. She could feel the press of his cock against her ass.

"Do you know how long I've been thinking about this ass?"

Her breath caught in her throat. He'd been thinking about her? For as long as she'd wanted him?

"The second you walked out of that police station, fuck, I knew I wanted you."

He pulled back and the next thing she felt was the thick, blunt head of his cock. Unlike the dildo, he was warm, but just as unyielding. The teasing he'd given her earlier just wasn't enough. She wanted him to pound into her, make every fiber of her body feel.

She pushed back, impaling herself on him. A groan escaped her lips. He thrust and she dug her nails into the headboard. His arm circled her waist, holding her up or captive, she didn't know yet. He worked himself in and out, slowly, but she could feel his control eroding.

"Travis." She tossed her head back. "Fuck me."

"Like this?" He put real force behind it, enough to rock her forward and make the bed shudder.

Electric tendrils of lust snaked through her body.

"Yes," she shouted.

He wrapped one hand around her throat, but didn't squeeze. It was almost tender, the way he braced part of his hand against her chest.

Again he thrust, each pass of his cock branding her body as his. She moved with him, but it was mostly his contained power pumping into her, touching her in a way no toy would. There was no replacement for the feel of him inside of her or how he stirred her heart.

"Oh, Travis." She leaned her head back against his shoulder as her body gave itself over to the orgasm. Her muscles went lax, and he held her, supporting her weight as he fucked the daylights out of her.

She held onto the headboard until he shouted and stilled, clutching her to his chest.

"That was fucking amazing." She panted and kissed his hand.

Her heart was doing weird things in her chest. Things she didn't have a name for, yet.

14.

TRAVIS FOCUSED ON KEEPING his breathing even in an attempt to lower his heart rate.

He'd basically told Bliss he'd marry her.

What was he thinking?

He wasn't. That was the problem. He'd been half awake and horny, so he'd said whatever it took to get in her panties.

A small voice deep down inside whispered, *Liar.*

It was almost seven. He could probably slip out, book a flight home, and be gone by noon. With a little distance between them, he was sure they'd both come to their senses. It was the right thing to do. Falling for a client never went well, and Bliss didn't know what she was getting herself into. She could spout the nice line about accepting him for who he was all she wanted. Until the ugly reality set in. Life with him would never be easy.

He plugged his proverbial ears to keep from the chant of *Liar* out of his conscious thoughts.

The phone on the nightstand vibrated.

This was his opportunity.

He gently rolled her to her side, off his arm, and snagged the phone.

"Mm, Travis? What's wrong?" She blinked up at him, not even fully awake.

"Office. Go back to sleep." He hit the Answer button, grabbed his shorts and headed for the hall. "What's up?"

"Damn, I thought you'd be up," Gavin said.

"It's been a long couple of days. What's up? Find Daniel?" Travis pulled the shorts up and took the stairs down to the ground floor.

"No, man. Boss wanted me to see if you had Ethan's hospital records. They didn't come back with him."

"Mason has those." He peered out the window, looking first for the cops stationed at the end of the street. Not a soul was up yet.

"Oh, right, right. I guess he will come by today sometime then. Cool. Enjoy Vegas."

"Hey, Gavin, wait." Travis glanced over his shoulder, up the stairs. "Can you get me a flight back to base this morning?"

"Dude, seriously? I thought the boss was clearing you—"

"Yes or no?"

"Yeah, I can handle it, or I can pass it over to Ops. Actually, it'll be faster if I do it. You want the aisle, right?"

"Yeah. Thanks, man."

"See ya soon."

Travis hung up and blew out a breath.

Part of him wanted to crawl back in bed with Bliss, keep the lie of a future going a little while longer, but he couldn't do that.

Liar.

He turned the coffee pot on and tossed a breakfast burrito in the microwave.

There were cops and the FBI here to take care of her. Chances were, they'd reunite her with her sister, parents or both, and his presence would be completely pointless. It wasn't as if he'd done anything useful since finding her, and in truth, all he'd done was get Ethan hurt and waste a lot of Mason's time.

"What's going on?" Bliss descended the stairs, her steps lagging and her eyes still heavy with sleep.

"Work. They need me to get back today." The lie slid out, cold and hollow, but until they were back to being rational he would tell her whatever he needed to.

"Oh. Today? Like, right now?"

"Yeah, afraid so."

"Hey, will you stop for a second and look at me?" She grabbed his hand and tugged him to face her.

He needed to set her straight, for both their sakes.

Liar.

Travis looked down at her tousled hair, her lips still swollen from last night. She'd put his shirt on, which he didn't want to think too much about.

"I'm not sure this is going to work, Bliss. I've been going over it in my head and...I don't think it's going to work out."

Liar, liar, pants on fire.

"Wait, what do you mean?" She snatched her hand back.

"I mean us." He leaned against the counter, gripping the edge to keep from grabbing her and taking it all back. What the hell was wrong with him. "What are we going to do? Spend a weekend a month together? I can't be tied down with too many responsibilities away from the job."

"You can't be serious."

"I am."

Liar!

"Your job means that much to you?"

"I don't have to explain it to you." He grit his teeth.

A job didn't keep him warm at night or kiss him or make him feel like she did.

Bliss took a step back, her mouth working soundlessly.

LIAR!

He winced, both because that voice was right and—he didn't want to hurt her. But one way or another, he would. There wasn't a good thing about him, and the faster she learned that, the better. It would hurt her a lot less now than a year or five down the road, after they'd made all the mistakes and left all the scars that would never heal.

His phone beeped. Gavin was good. His flight information was all there in a nice, neat text. At least with work he knew where he stood, how to operate. He'd die if he stayed on with Aegis for the rest of his life. It was just a matter of time until he caught the right bullet in the wrong place. If he left Aegis, there wasn't anything for him in the civilian world. He couldn't support her, much less himself.

She was better off without him.

The voice didn't call him a liar this time, because it was the undeniable truth. He might have feelings for her, hell, he very well might love her, but that was a curse.

"I'll be out of here in less than an hour."

The microwave dinged. He grabbed the still-hot breakfast burrito and headed for the stairs.

More like he fled.

This was the right thing to do.

Wasn't it?

BLISS STOOD IN THE smaller bedroom over the garage, listening for sounds of the car.

Travis was leaving.

He was serious.

She still couldn't wrap her head around it all. Last night they'd almost said they loved each other. You didn't offer to marry someone you didn't love, right? And today they were over. Done with.

The hole in her chest was so new and raw she didn't really feel it yet. She was just...numb.

Travis' rental backed out of the garage. She stepped to the side, out of his line of sight. It was one thing to wait around, mooning and depressed, it was another for him to know how much this hurt.

What had she done wrong? What was wrong with her?

She wiped her hand across her cheek. The tears she'd promised herself she wouldn't cry streamed down her cheeks. She pressed her back to the wall and slid to the carpet.

Seven days. Was it really possible to fall in love with someone that fast?

Her broken heart said yes.

She hadn't harbored any kind of illusions. Yes, she knew that things wouldn't be easy with Travis, she'd have to be okay with less in exchange for being loved by him, but they could make it work.

God, she needed to pull it together. Jade and Connor would be here soon to—she didn't really know. Move her? Question her?

They weren't Travis.

She pulled her knees up to her chest and buried her face in her hands.

Life just wasn't fair.

SCENE BREAK.

DANIEL STARTED THE DEAD cop's car and eased out a full thirty seconds after Travis turned out of the residential area. He hadn't been able to tell how many people were inside the house, but there was only one in the truck.

He'd take his chances.

Travis had to die before he executed the rest of his plan anyway.

"KEYS, SIR?"

Travis stared at the rental keys.

What was he doing? Was this really the right choice?

He was going to spend the next five days drinking himself stupid. At home. Alone.

His pocket vibrated.

Bliss.

"Excuse me?" He yanked the phone out of his pocket.

"Sure thing." The attendant turned away, busying himself with paperwork behind the counter.

Not Bliss. Ethan.

"Hey, man," Travis said.

"What the fuck are you doing up this early?" Ethan's voice was raspy, low and slightly slurred. Drugs or alcohol? Maybe both?

"On my way to see you."

"Why the hell would you do that?"

"I don't know. You're my friend?"

"Unless you're bringing Bliss, I don't want to see your sorry ass."

Travis blew out a breath.

"What do you want, Ethan?"

"I want to know why you're making a huge, fucking mistake."

"Ethan, Bliss isn't Molly."

"Good. Because I'd beat your ass if you thought she was a good idea. The shit I've put up with. Wait—have you slept with my wife? Ex-wife?"

"What? No. Did someone say she did?"

"Oh fuck, don't tell me you don't know."

"No, man, I don't."

"Yeah, she's cheated on me. Yeah, I've caught her three fucking times. Believe me, stick with Bliss."

Travis stared at the wall.

Molly? Cheating on Ethan? But they'd seemed so perfect.

"Listen, you like her. Don't leave. Don't come back. Stay there and get a ring on it. Girls like that don't come along every day. Hear me?"

"Yeah."

If Ethan and Molly couldn't make it, what chance did they have?

"And I can hear you thinking. You aren't me, and Bliss ain't Molly. She told me she was unhappy years ago, but I asked her to stay. I ruined us and I know it."

"Are you drinking, Ethan?"

"Fuck yeah I am."

Shit. There was no telling what alcohol and the pills would do. Travis was going to have to make a few calls.

"You'll never stop wondering *what if* if you come home now," Ethan said.

Travis balled his hand into a fist. Damn Ethan for speaking his thoughts.

Travis knew the odds were against them, but what if he was wrong? Wasn't it time for something to go right in his life?

"I'll talk to you later, man. Put the bottle down." Travis hung up and fired off a quick text to Gavin. Someone needed to keep an eye on Ethan. He jangled the keys at the attendant. "I'm going to need to keep these a bit longer."

"Okay."

Travis jogged out of the rental car shop and climbed back into his SUV.

The feds weren't supposed to get to the house until noon. He had an hour and a half to beat them there and make things right.

It was crazy and he was probably stupid, but what else was there for him these days? Didn't he deserve to at least try to be happy?

And Bliss made him happy. He'd been serious about getting hitched. Yeah, they didn't know each other all that well, but when something was right it was right.

He loved Bliss.

And he was going to tell her.

DANIEL PULLED INTO THE small parking lot outside a florist's shop.

Flowers.

How typical.

His wives never needed such things. They were damn well happy with what he gave them.

The location was pretty perfect. Stores bordered the lot on three sides and a dumpster sat between him and the road. He had a straight line of sight to the SUV, now all he needed was for Travis to emerge.

He pulled out the cop's gun and checked the chamber.

Good to go.

Daniel kept his gaze on the rearview mirror. He'd need to get out fast and pick up a new ride. Things would have to happen fast once Travis was dead, or the feds would move his wife.

Oh, how he couldn't wait for Wendy to be back in his arms.

Travis strode around the corner of the building, a bouquet of roses in his hands.

Now.

Daniel pushed the door open, lifted the gun and fired— straight at Travis.

So long, asshole.

Dangerous Attraction: Part Three

1.

TRAVIS HIT THE GROUND, rolling and grabbing for the firearm in his boot holster. Every fiber of his body was hyper aware of his surroundings. His left arm burned, and he couldn't feel his fingers. There wasn't time to worry about the injury now, not with someone firing a gun at him. Adrenaline fueled his need to survive. Bliss. He had to get back to her. Had to protect her. She wasn't safe.

He rose to his knees, gun raised and pointed toward the front of the SUV where he'd glimpsed the shooter.

Daniel.

It had to be him. Travis had caught a glimpse of a familiar car. The nagging sense that something was wrong had just started low in his gut, and then he saw the blast of muzzle fire. From there he operated on instinct, dropping to the ground, narrowly avoiding the shot.

How had Daniel found him so fast? Why was he after Travis? What had changed to make him deviate from the plan? Daniel went after the girls and transient junkies.

Pinpricks of pain started in the fingers on his left hand. The good news was he could flex and move the limb, though the ache radiating down from his shoulder meant he was going to be in a world of pain after the adrenaline dump wore off.

An inhuman roar bounced and echoed off the brick walls boxing them in. There was nowhere for Travis to go but through Daniel. This was it. The end. He could finish this right now. Make it so that Bliss never had to worry about the killer ever again.

He crawled to the front of the truck. On a whim, he'd backed into the spot, which meant a faster exit, and a measure of protection for a shoot-out.

The footsteps came closer. Heavy boots thudding on the new asphalt.

Travis crouched behind the rental SUV, the front wheels to his back.

One...

Two...

Three.

He straightened, sighted his shot, and fired off two rounds. Daniel ducked, and the back window of a car shattered. He was maybe six feet away, out in the open lot. It should be like shooting fish in a barrel, but tremors shook Travis' arm.

Daniel returned fire, hitting the front of the SUV and the van behind him. Travis ducked behind his truck, his right leg almost buckling. A big piece of glass stuck out from his calf. He didn't remember getting cut, but adrenaline did funny things in the heat of battle.

Two more shots pinged off the truck.

Travis circled his truck until he had the brick wall behind him, and the SUV between him and Daniel. He took a breath and then stepped out in the open, aiming at where he expected Daniel to be.

He was gone.

Travis was alone.

Travis limped around the SUV, gun up, sweeping the lot in case Daniel was hiding. People across the street were yelling, a car alarm was going off, but no Daniel. He'd disappeared.

The florist shop window sported several new cracks. The owner peeked out from around the corner. Travis dug his laminated badge out from his back pocket and flashed it. The badge didn't have any legal weight besides identifying who he worked for, but sometimes it got civilians moving.

"Call the cops. Tell them Daniel Campbell was here. Do it. Now. Get inside."

Daniel had meant to kill him. For some reason, he was going after Travis, not Bliss or Wendy. It was a complete and total break from pattern. Daniel was going to be even more desperate now. People needed off the streets, out of his path, or the bodies were going to start piling up even more.

How close was the safe house?

He'd chosen a shop not too far away, but not too close either. The house was maybe a five minute drive.

Daniel could already be there if he had a backup vehicle in the area.

Travis turned and limped back to the truck, pushing the pain out of his mind and focusing on what mattered: Bliss' safety. Had he just put her at risk?

He should have never left her side that morning.

Stupid. Stupid. Stupid.

He'd vowed to protect Bliss, and now he might have just killed her.

Travis turned the key in the ignition, saying a silent prayer. Who knew what was torn up in there after the bullets hit it? The engine roared to life. He blew out a breath and threw the truck into reverse, glad he didn't have to track down a new set of wheels. With a piece of glass jutting out of his leg and a questionable arm wound, he wasn't in any shape to hoof it back to Bliss on foot, either.

"Call Ryan Brooks," he yelled at the Bluetooth.

"Calling Ryan Brooks."

He pulled out onto the street, cutting two cars off and tailgating a third until they turned out of his way. Steam trickled out from around the hood and the temperature gauge crept higher. Getting pulled over by a cop might actually be a good thing if he could catch a ride to the safe house.

"Pick up. Pick up. Pick up."

"Hello, this is SSA Ryan Brooks, if you will please leave a detailed message—"

"Fuck."

He jabbed the End Call button on the steering wheel and slammed on the gas. The engine's muddy roar wasn't a good sign. The truck was limping along when he needed a sprint.

It could already be too late. He'd walked into Daniel's hands, and now he could be after Bliss.

BLISS SAT ON THE sofa, mindlessly staring at the TV. She was numb to it all. Her life was done with, at least as she'd known it. And Travis was gone. The cops had already told her that the paperwork for Witness Protection was being pushed through despite the holidays, and that meant that in twenty-four hours Bliss Giles would cease to exist. She'd become someone else. A stranger. None of it mattered anymore.

Was this how it felt like for Wendy? Was this depression? She'd always fought her way through the tough times, determined to make things better but now... It wasn't worth it. Travis had made that clear.

A man had never meant so much to her before. She'd never allowed them to, if she were honest with herself. Nice guys fit into a box in her life, one where she still had time and attention to pick up the slack for Wendy. But a guy like Travis? He would demand everything she had. He readjusted her priorities, shown her what she could have with a man who deserved to be the love of her life. But clearly she wasn't important enough to him.

This sucked.

She flipped the channel again and couldn't muster the energy to care when the news popped on with a special update in the Daniel Campbell case.

He was her personal nightmare. Her kidnapper and tormenter. The man who wanted her to have babies he could torture to death. She couldn't even wrap her mind around it, and quite frankly didn't want to try. Soon, there wouldn't be a Bliss for Daniel to kidnap. She'd have a new identity, hopefully one he couldn't track.

The back door creaked.

An electric-like current of adrenaline raced down her spine. She sucked in a deep breath.

She could barely hear the light steps of the intruder on the linoleum. Her whole body was frozen to the sofa, tracking a single person's steps into the kitchen. In her head, she could hear the echo of Daniel's steps on the metal floor inside the RV. They'd been so loud and heavy, and she'd been sure she was about to die.

Fuck this gloomy shit, she wanted to live.

She wrapped her hand around the Taser tucked between the cushions at her side. It wasn't much in the way of protection, but she would go down fighting this time.

"Bliss?" A young man wearing sweatpants and a hoodie stepped out of the kitchen, a police badge in hand.

She sagged against the cushions in relief.

Not Daniel.

A cop.

All the tension left her body and she slumped against the cushions. Would it kill him to knock?

"Who are you?" she asked. There was no way she could keep them all straight, but she tried. These were the men and women she owed her life to, now.

"I'm Marcus. I live on the other side of the fence."

"Oh. Right." She blew out a breath. Travis had told her about the officer stationed behind the safe house tasked with keeping an eye on them. He and two officers positioned in cars at either end of the street were the entirety of her protective detail now that Travis was gone. Without him there, it didn't feel like enough.

"I'm going to have to ask you to get your things together."

"Why? What's wrong?" His expression was too tight, his smile fake. Her stomach clenched. "What happened to Travis?"

"Ma'am, I don't know. Last I heard he was getting on a plane. Will you please get your things together? We need to move you. Now."

She could demand answers, or she could grab her bag and get the same answers on the way to wherever they were taking her.

Bliss opted for taking the stairs two at a time up to the room she'd shared with Travis. She could still smell him in the sheets and her clothes. Even a shower hadn't washed him off her. He branded her body and soul as his, then left.

Now wasn't the time for sad, mopey thoughts. She'd been captured by Daniel once and that was an experience she didn't want to repeat. She grabbed her blue duffle bag off the dresser, tossed on a jacket, and was back downstairs in less than five minutes.

"Ready," she said. "Will you tell me what's going on now?"

"In the car."

Marcus took her arm and guided her out through the back door, moving at a brisk pace. She almost had to jog to keep up with him. The gate that joined their backyards stood open, and a uniformed officer waited for them on the other side. She didn't miss the way his hand sat on his service gun. Something was wrong.

"Is my sister okay? What about my parents?"

The officer took her bag and the two men led her to a patrol car parked in front of Marcus' house. Neither one spoke until she was locked in the backseat.

"Package has been picked up," Marcus radioed while the driver gassed it out of the driveway.

"What the hell is going on?"

She was used to Travis, who gave her answers. Travis, who didn't hide the truth from her. These officers were seriously scaring her.

"Ma'am, did anyone come to the door? Anyone at all?" Marcus twisted to look at her through the wire barrier.

"No, no one. Will someone please tell me what's happened?"

"One of the plainclothes officers is missing. His car is gone." Marcus' tone was grim.

"You think—you think Daniel did something?" Cold dread swept her. Bad things weren't accidents.

"We don't know anything yet."

"Your friend, he couldn't have gone out for coffee or anything?"

"No, he wouldn't have."

"Oh, God." She covered her mouth and closed her eyes. What kind of hell was this? What had she done to deserve this?

"Shit, look out!" Marcus threw his arm up, and the driver slammed on his brakes.

A big black SUV barreled down the road at them, smoke trailing out from under the hood, screeching to a stop so hard it rocked from side to side. The body was dented, and it looked like someone had taken a huge pencil and jabbed holes in the metal.

Bullet holes.

A familiar figure leapt out of the driver's side, heading straight for them.

Travis.

Her heart pounded twice as hard. He was supposed to be on an airplane. He left her. And yet, he was looking right at her. She slapped her hand against the window and pulled at the door—but there was no handle, not in the back of the cop car.

"What the hell?" Marcus got out and stalked toward Travis.

Their voices were too low for her to hear anything.

Travis.

He told her they weren't going to work out. By all rights, she should be furious with him. They were broken up. But she couldn't be happier to see him.

The two men had a short conversation, including a lot of pointing on Marcus' part. They must have reached an agreement, because the young officer turned and led the way back to the car. He grabbed the door handle and opened it, waving Travis in. She scooted over just in time for Travis to fold himself into the tight space.

God, she'd never seen anything so good in all her life.

A metallic odor tickled her nose and memory.

Bliss gasped.

"You're bleeding," she said.

"Don't worry about it." Travis wrapped his hand around hers and braced his other against the wire barrier. "Drive. Have you heard from the FBI?"

"No, not since earlier," Marcus replied. "What happened to you?"

"Daniel jumped me."

Bliss gasped. Daniel had attacked Travis? The rest of the conversation went on without her, but all she could focus on was that Travis was hurt because of her.

"You saw him?"

"Yeah."

"Was he in a blue car?"

"There was a blue car there." He rattled off the plates.

"That's the undercover car."

"Something happen?"

"An undercover went missing with his car."

"Damn it." Travis punched the wire. "I should have checked the damn car."

Marcus grabbed his cell phone while Travis hit dial on his. The name Ryan Brooks filled the screen. She watched it all happen, but just kept holding onto Travis' hand.

He was real, and he was right next to her.

What had happened in the hour or so since she last saw him? How had things gone so terribly wrong?

2.

TRAVIS KEPT ONE HAND on Bliss the whole walk from the car to the entrance of the police station, his gaze scanning the vehicles in the parking lot. Marcus strode ahead of them and the driver behind in a tight formation around her. Travis didn't breathe until they passed through the secured entrance. His leg twinged and his shoulder burned, but they were minor injuries as far as he could tell.

Marcus led them through the warren of departments, moving at a brisk pace. Bliss nearly jogged at his side, puffing and out of breath by the time they made it to the inner sanctum. The homicide department, if Travis had to guess.

Ryan and Jade had their heads together, staring at a file.

"Look what the cat dragged in," Connor drawled.

Travis steered Bliss to a cushy office chair.

"Shit, you're bleeding."

"Leave it," Travis snapped at Connor. He'd already pulled the glass out of his leg, and the wound on his arm was just a graze. It was the lack of sleep and focus that had been his undoing. "Did you find Wendy?"

Connor glanced at Ryan, who nodded, before answering. "Nothing yet. Husband has her locked down tight."

"If Daniel is making a move on me, and this close to Bliss, he has to know where they're at. They're not safe."

"Maybe you should sit down, let someone take a look at—"

"Shut it, Mullins." The last thing Travis needed was someone hovering over him because of a couple scratches.

"Morning, Bliss." Jade breezed past Travis and handed Bliss a cup of coffee. "Connor needs to ask Travis a few questions. Think you can come with me?"

Bliss nodded, never once looking at him.

Travis had screwed up. Not only did he allow his doubt to get the better of him, his rash actions put Bliss and others in danger. That was on him. All of it. The shootout. The potentially dead officer. His fault.

"Right. This morning, what happened?" Connor planted his hands on his hips and stared Travis down despite the difference in height.

"Home office booked my travel back, I went to the rental agency, and when I got there I changed my mind. Decided to stay. Figured it wasn't a good idea to show up empty-handed, so I stopped for some flowers." Flowers which had at least made it into the backseat of his SUV before he'd forgotten about them.

"That's when Daniel jumped you?"

"He must have tailed me. Marcus said something about one of the undercover cars missing?"

"Yeah, car and the dead cop were in the florist's parking lot."

"Shit."

"Like you said, Daniel knew where she was. Time of death was way before you bailed on her."

Fucking Irishman. Had to rub salt in that wound, didn't he?

"So, what happened? You had an OK Corral showdown?"

"I came out of the shop, Daniel stepped out of his car and fired at me. I dodged, it grazed my shoulder. Landed behind the SUV, got some glass in my calf."

"Bullet looks like it grazed you and then broke the van's window next to you. I'd say it's safe to assume that's what you got cut on."

"Okay, so I pulled my back-up weapon, returned fire, he shot at me, I returned fire, and he left on foot. Any stolen cars reported recently?"

"Nothing yet, but they're getting security footage from the area, looking for him or how he got away. This is a load of shit." Connor shook his head. "Are you even technically employed on this case?"

"Not anymore."

"Cops are going to have a field day with you if they don't catch Daniel."

"What was I supposed to do?"

"Shoot him."

Travis curled his hands into fists. The damn agent was on his last nerve.

"I'll call Dmitri and Ben, see what the scene is like. Maybe we can head this off. You've been a real pain in the ass, but you do good work."

Travis glanced in the direction Jade had taken Bliss. An hour apart and he'd lost her. God, he was a screw-up.

"What about her parents?" he asked.

"On their way in. Figure we can keep everyone under one roof until we smoke Daniel out."

"Except Wendy."

"Yeah, pain in the ass that husband is. Hey, what if you get your guy working on finding them with Lali?" Connor pressed his cell to his ear.

"Right." Travis tapped out a quick text to Gavin. The kid was going to hate this request, but they were running low on options.

Connor turned his back on Travis, exchanged a few words, and hung up.

"Right. So why you?" Connor asked.

"Me?"

"No, the asshole standing next to you. Yes, you. What happened out there when you snagged Bliss?"

"Nothing. Ethan and Mason talked to him. He shot Ethan, cut the other vic, and ran."

"But now he has you tied up in all of this. He knows you and Bliss are involved and that you'll come for her and her sister. Maybe you've become his—what? Arch-nemesis?"

"That's stupid."

"Yeah, well, you're the one with a big target on your back. He must have a plan, but he thinks you'll ruin it, so he has to take you out first." Connor's gaze slid off Travis. He stared at the wall and tapped his phone into his palm. "He hasn't really splintered or gone on a spree yet. It's more like he's adapting, which these fuckers don't always do well. What's holding him together?"

"Bliss said he has a god complex."

"Maybe this poor bastard thinks he's really in control of it all. Perhaps we need to shake his control a bit. Hold onto that thought."

Travis watched the agent retreat to the case boards set up in an adjoining conference room. The glass walls hid nothing. Table upon table of evidence and documentation. In the middle of it all were glass jars. The ones Bliss had told him about. What plan was the agent cooking up? And would it work?

"Mind giving me a hand?"

Bliss steeled her nerves and turned toward Travis. She'd avoided him since they arrived at the station, hiding out in the break room after answering Jade's questions. Her emotions were too mixed up for her to make sense of them, and she wasn't fond of making a spectacle of herself. The FBI agents were politely ignoring whatever it was she'd had with him up at the lake, but her parents wouldn't.

Travis held a first aid kit in his hand, and his jacket was folded over his other arm. Blood soaked his shirt, and there were several small scratches on his face he hadn't had when he left her that morning.

"Sure." What else was she supposed to say?

Bliss pulled out a chair and gestured for him to sit.

He plunked the kit onto the table and peeled his long-sleeved thermal shirt off. Her mouth dried up, and her fingers itched to trace his ladder-like abdominal muscles. Forget about what was really going on for just a few minutes. Pretend they were still in that happy place.

Blood smeared down his left arm and shoulder. A pencil-wide gash tore across the top of his bicep, partially scabbed over with bits of cloth stuck in it.

She must have made a face.

"It doesn't hurt that bad. Bandaging it will go faster with help."

"Shouldn't you see a doctor?"

"For this? No point." He handed her a bottle of peroxide and pulled out some bandages. "Let's do this over there."

He crossed to the sink, leaving her no choice but to follow him.

This was exactly the kind of thing he'd tried to explain to her. The dangers of his job. It was a hard thing to wrap her mind around, even with a front row seat. He considered a bullet wound no big deal. It was a perspective she didn't think she could understand.

"Do it," Travis said prompting her to action.

She poured peroxide along the length of the wound, wincing as it bubbled and fizzed. He simply stood there, staring past her to the wall beyond as if it didn't hurt at all.

"There."

He glanced at the wound and picked out a few bits of lint and stray fabric that stuck to the scab.

"Grab the bandages?"

She snagged the pre-packaged gauze and tape, plus an anti-bacterial ointment packet. He leaned down and she applied the topical medicine, not once looking at his face. She couldn't without the overwhelming tide of emotions doing funny things to her. There was something soothing to the action of patching him up, but she was still...unhappy.

He left her. He came back, but why? Out of some obligation? Because Daniel had surfaced? Or had he wanted to? Nothing made sense, and quite frankly, she was hurt.

"You have every right to be mad at me," he said.

"What? I didn't say anything."

"You don't have to. I screwed up. I woke up this morning, realized what I'd said, and freaked the fuck out. I'm sorry."

An apology was all well and good, but it didn't sooth the ache inside or bridge the chasm between them now. He'd broken the understood promise. What would stop him from running again?

The mental snapshot of Travis' face when he jumped out of the SUV on his way back to her tugged at her guilt strings. He saved her when he didn't have to. Without him, she could already be dead. They were on a rollercoaster, being jerked around. She should cut him some slack, though a part of her also wanted him to grovel for her forgiveness.

She did understand his explanation. Hadn't she freaked out? The only difference was she hadn't left. Of course it was natural to panic, considering the depth of what they'd said to each other. But he could have talked to her. He could have suggested they slow down, take some time to think about it. Instead he made a decision for both of them and left. An apology was nice, but it didn't change what had happened.

"It's fine. I'm glad you're okay."

"Are you sure it's fine?"

"What am I supposed to say?"

"I don't know. I'm not—"

"You're not good at this stuff?" She cut the last bit of tape and stepped back.

"No, I'm not. I screwed up. I realize that. What can I do to fix it?"

"I don't know. You didn't even talk to me. You wouldn't give me a chance to understand or suggest something else—it was *this is how it's going to be*. I don't know if I want to be with someone who doesn't consider how I feel or what I'm thinking before deciding things with no input from me."

"You're right."

"And what's to say you wouldn't do the same thing again? What if this is just how you are? Here one minute and gone the next. That's not okay." She sucked in a breath and blinked her eyes.

No, no, no, no tears!

"I'm not used to anyone relying on me. My longest relationships have all been shorter than this. I fuck up, but I do learn from my mistakes."

She wiped under her eyes, hating how stoic Travis could be about this situation.

He left her.

Yeah, he came back, but he left her when she'd trusted him to be there.

She didn't know if she had it in her to trust like that again. This whole ordeal, the nightmares, she blindly allowed herself to pin all her trust, with no reservations, on this man. And he failed her.

Yes, it was crazy to expect anyone to be perfect, but when she needed him there with her, he was gone.

She had to get away from him.

"Where are you going?"

"Bathroom." She wrapped her arms around herself and strode out of the break room.

It was hard to make anything out with tears making her vision hazy, but she stumbled into the women's restroom and splashed water on her face. The cold chill of it woke her brain up a bit. By some miracle she was alone. There wasn't anyone around to hear her crying or pester her about what was wrong.

Travis was an amazing man, but he wasn't perfect. She'd needed more from him than he could offer, and it had broken their trust. Whose fault was that?

The bathroom door opened on a long, slow squeak.

Great. Just what she needed. A witness to her breakdown.

She glanced at the newcomer. Was it too much to hope it was Jade?

"What are you doing in here?" she blurted out.

Travis had his shirt back on and his frown in place. He flipped the bathroom lock and stalked toward her.

"You can't be in here. This is a women's restroom." She jabbed her finger at his chest.

"You can't run from me."

"Yes, I can. You did."

The air left her lungs.

She did not just say that.

Travis' lips compressed into a tight line. She'd drawn blood with those words.

"I didn't—I shouldn't have said that." She wrapped her arms around herself and stared at his chest.

"I deserved that. Tell me you want me gone and I'm gone." He crossed his arms over his chest. Was it her imagination, or did she hear the tape pulling?

She opened her mouth and closed it.

The anguish of losing him all over again was an ache deep in her bones. She didn't want it to be over with him, but they'd lost something special. They'd lost the trust. Her blind belief in him was gone.

How did she put her feelings into words? How did she begin to tell him?

"I don't know that you're not going to leave again. I can't trust you when you say that. You left. You left me alone." Sure, he had a life and a career that didn't involve her, but for a few minutes they'd flirted with the idea. They'd wanted to make it work. Didn't that mean something? Weren't they something to each other?

Travis wrapped his arms around her, and she buried her face in his chest. She was angry with him, and she still loved him. He had more power over her than Daniel, more pull on her fears and hopes than the worst nightmare to ever walk Vegas.

"That was the worst decision of my life, darlin'. If I could go back and kick my own ass, I would. I don't deserve another chance, you're right." He kissed the top of her head, and she clung to him, melting from the inside out.

The unspoken statement hung in the air so clear she thought she heard him say, *But I want a second chance.*

"Do you want me to leave?" he asked instead.

She'd never heard Travis sound hesitant or uncertain before, and she didn't like it. If she stopped thinking about herself, she knew they were both going through something here. It wasn't just about her.

Bliss leaned back and stared up at him. She wasn't the only one scared of what was happening between them, she just chose to react in a different way.

"No."

He squeezed her a bit tighter.

"I'm used to handbooks and officers barking orders. I'm going to screw up, but I promise no repeat issues."

"I think I saw a *Relationships for Dummies* once."

"I'll get a copy. Do they have one for boyfriends?"

Oh... Her body flashed hot and cold.

"Too soon?" he asked.

"No, I'm just—processing."

"I'm not used to people relying on me outside of the SEALs, but if you'll give me another shot, I'll do better."

"It's a two-way street. People in relationships," the word and all its implications made her shiver, "rely on each other. I think it's too soon for us to stick a label on this. Don't argue with me, okay? You freaked out. I think it's reasonable to say maybe we jumped in too fast."

"I don't know any other way."

"I'm not going to change my mind." He spoke with the determination of someone with conviction. A man with his mind set on one goal. Her.

"I hope you don't."

She slid her hands up his arms and over his shoulder, mindful of his wound. They were a messed up couple, but they had each other.

Travis tightened his grip around her waist and dropped his head.

"I could take you away from here," he said.

"Where would we go?" She chuckled.

"Anywhere. Jamaica. The UK. Thailand. Somewhere far away."

She pulled back a little and looked up at him. Oh, the fantasy of it. But it wouldn't work. "I'm not leaving, and I'm not giving up my life. It's mine. And besides, if that happened you'd have longer to fly to get back to work, and I'd spend longer alone. That's not going to work for me."

"Fine. Then we'll figure something else out. I just want to keep you safe."

He wasn't perfect, but he was hers. If he forgot that again, well, she'd have to put the Taser he gave her to another use.

3.

DANIEL HUNCHED DOWN IN the front seat of the sedan. Four cars in less than two hours. He was pretty sure he'd covered his tracks, but he couldn't shake the sense that he was being watched.

Damn feds.

He was getting too old for this.

No, he couldn't be old. Gods didn't get old. Right?

He gripped the steering wheel, but his hand slid off the smooth leather. A smear of blood stained the high-end material.

Shit. Was he bleeding again?

He should have never used the officer's gun. It was different than his six shooter. He'd missed because he'd gotten cocky, and now that son of a bitch was still alive.

His plan was screwed to hell. First he botched killing the fed attached to Bliss, then he took too long to get back to the safe house and snatch Bliss from under the cops' noses. The only thing left was to pick up his wife, but even that wasn't enough for him any longer.

He needed to get revenge.

FOUND THEM.

Travis glanced at the message and instinctively squeezed Bliss' hand.

"What?" she mumbled.

"Come on." He pushed off the desk and strode toward the conference room. Since he wasn't technically on this case, he'd stayed out of the way. If Daniel were in the wilderness or hiding out in a hot zone, Travis knew what to do. Getting inside the head of a deranged serial killer and figuring out what fucked up kind of reasoning made the man tick was a place Travis didn't want to go.

Ryan glanced up from his phone as they entered. Travis pushed Bliss behind him in a vain attempt to shield her from the jar babies.

"Lali and Gavin found them," Ryan announced.

"Them, who?" Bliss glanced from Ryan to Travis.

"Your sister."

"Wendy? Are they okay?"

"They're fine. Still in CIA custody." Ryan pocketed his phone. "We can't make them do anything."

"No," Travis agreed.

"I bet she could." Connor thumbed at Bliss.

She squeezed Travis' hand, and he released the tight grip he had on her, swiping his thumb over her knuckles as an apology.

Five minutes. That's all Travis wanted with the guy. Somewhere he could punch his lights out.

"Let me talk to her," Bliss said.

Ryan held up his hand. "How sure are we that Daniel knows where Wendy is?"

"He's too detail-oriented. Wendy is his target. Bliss and Travis are bystanders in this. It's the women he focuses on. Look." Connor turned and gestured at one of the boards. Photographs of several dead blonde women lined the top of it, with coordinating information below. "The women were first. It's always been about them. He had his accident, got well, and then the first woman went missing. The best we can tell, the transient murders were a year later, after his accident. The women represent who he really is, the men are his way of expressing his rage. It's in how he disposes of the bodies. The women are left. He wants them found because they're special. The men? They're trash. He tosses them out. He's going to zero in on Wendy, and there isn't an army out there that will stop him."

"What about what Wendy said? That he's copying someone?" Bliss glanced between them, her nose scrunched up.

"If he's copying someone, it's obscure enough we can't place them." Jade sighed and glared at the floor.

"Where is Wendy?" Bliss turned to Travis. "You know I'm right. She'll listen to me. Remember how scared she was?"

Connor glanced from Bliss to Travis.

"I'll take you," Connor said.

"I'm riding with you." Travis wasn't about to let her out of his sight.

"If we do that, we're putting everything he wants in one location." Ryan scrubbed his hand across his face.

"He hasn't yet taken on more than two people." Jade gestured to another list scrawled on a dry-erase board. "Ones and twos, he'll attack one and use them to control the other. We saw that with Don, and preliminary reports on several identified remains support that theory. Don't go off on your own and he won't attack."

"Let's go then." Connor grabbed his jacket.

Travis didn't like it, but he was completely biased. Still, he grabbed Bliss' jacket, borrowed another that wasn't soaked with blood, and joined the small team heading to waylay Grayson's hideout.

"Do I want to know how you guys found her?" Bliss asked. She sat between him and Dimitri, about as safe and protected as he could make her.

"The baby." Travis stared out of the passenger window. "Paul?"

"Yeah. He gets some kind of frou-frou fancy baby formula. Lali and Gavin looked for recent purchases. Then they followed the money."

"Someone's getting in trouble," Connor said from the driver's seat.

"Why?" Bliss' brow wrinkled.

"Because a CIA agent in the field should be harder to identify. His guy nailed the fella doing the buying." Connor thumbed at Travis.

"Oh. Then...if it was that easy for them to find Wendy, it'll be just as easy for Daniel?" Bliss wrapped her hand around his and squeezed. She was holding it together so well, it was hard to remember this was all new for her.

"Not as easy, but yeah, that's what we're afraid of. We know he's got mad technical ability, but Lali was never able to track down where his stuff was kept or where the cameras transmitted to. He had another location, somewhere not at his house." Connor merged onto the highway and headed south.

Twenty minutes later they pulled into another gated, up-scale community. Connor flashed his badge to gain entry and navigated them around to a sprawling, three-story abode that was just slightly less opulent than the home Grayson already owned.

A man trimming perfect hedges turned around and stared at the minivan. Security. They weren't that discreet. But they had protected Wendy from another kidnapping. Maybe that's what Bliss needed. Round-the-clock watchdogs, but that wasn't any way to live. They had to stop this, soon, before someone that wasn't Daniel got killed.

BLISS PUSHED PAST THE man stationed at the door and glanced around the sparkling marble entry.

"Bliss?" Wendy's voice echoed, intermingled with the sounds of a TV and other people speaking.

"Where are you?" Bliss peered into the two rooms on either side, but they were empty.

Wendy strode through a grandiose arch leading to the rest of the home, baby Paul perched on her hip. Bliss stared, blinked, and couldn't believe her eyes. It was a subtle transformation, something a casual observer or a stranger wouldn't notice, but Bliss did. It was Wendy's smile, the color of her cheeks, a slight bounce in her step.

"Oh, Bliss!" Wendy wrapped her free arm around Bliss' shoulders.

She hugged both mother and son, burying her face in Wendy's hair. Paul immediately took the opportunity to pull on Bliss' ponytail, but she couldn't care less.

"What are you doing here? Is everything okay?" Wendy pulled back and glanced from Bliss to Travis.

"What the hell is going on this time?" Grayson came down the stairs, followed by another man in a suit.

"Mr. Horton, I'm Supervisory Special Agent Connor Mullins." He extended his hand.

"Bliss?" Wendy pitched her voice low, watching the men grumble and growl at each other.

"Come in here." Bliss dragged Wendy into what she guessed would be someone's office someday.

"Have you seen Mom and Dad?"

"Yes, they're at the station."

"Oh, good. How are you?" Wendy cupped Bliss' cheek.

"I'm okay. You look—good."

"I feel good." She absently stroked Paul's face and let him grasp hold of her finger.

"Yeah?"

"It's like...I woke up." Wendy tilted her head to the side and stared at the floor. "It's almost like I've been asleep, and what happened—it made me realize I want to live. I don't want to be who I was letting myself be. It was awful and terrible and...I can barely sleep, but I feel like I've got my life back."

"That's good. That's really good." Bliss could hardly believe her ears. She'd never wish this experience on anyone, but if something good could come out of it, well, she'd focus on that.

"How about you? Travis is still around?"

"Yeah. I pretty much owe him my life." She followed Wendy's gaze to where Travis stood scowling at Connor and Grayson.

"You want to tell me what's going on between you two?"

How long had it been since Bliss talked guys with her sister? Ages.

"It's...complicated," she said.

"He's not your usual type." Wendy tilted her head to the side and smiled.

"No." Bliss fidgeted and glanced away. Things with Travis were too uncertain to talk about yet. Not until she knew where they stood with each other.

"So what's up? I'm guessing you didn't stop by with a federal escort just to chat."

"I wish I did." She turned back to Wendy. "It's Daniel. He tried to kill Travis earlier, and they know he killed a cop outside the safe house where I was. They think he already knows where this house is, and they want us to all go to the station. More people. More protection."

"That's why Mom and Dad are there?" Wendy's eyes widened until they seemed to overtake her face.

"Yeah. They think he's obsessed with you, but he won't go up against a lot of people to get you."

"There's a lot of people here, though." Wendy nodded out the window where they could see the superfluous lawn guy strolling around.

"Yeah, but they thought I was safe too, and someone died protecting me. Do you want that to happen here, too?"

"No."

"Then come with us. Please?"

Wendy chewed her lip for a moment, clearly torn. And why wouldn't she be? There was a small army stationed around her, keeping her safe. The rest of them didn't have that.

"Okay. Here, hold Paul for me while I go talk Grayson into it, okay?" She handed the baby over and tweaked his nose a little.

Gestures like that were new. Before, Wendy hadn't been able to look at, much less hold, her child. The change was remarkable. A single brush with death and she was ready to live again.

Bliss followed, staying on the edges of the group while Wendy spoke with her husband in low tones.

"No. No, we aren't going to hide out with a baby at the police station. We can't stay there forever. They need to do their job and catch this man." Grayson slashed his hand in the air.

"If it was that easy, don't you think they'd have done it by now?" Wendy held onto his other hand, her composure a thing of beauty. Just last week she'd have crumbled in on herself if someone raised their voice.

"I'm not putting you at risk."

"Is it worth risking other people's lives?"

"Going to the station isn't going to fix anything. It's not like he'll walk in and hand himself over to the cops just because you're there."

"Then we bait him," Bliss said.

All eyes turned on her. She latched onto Travis's gaze.

"They can't find him. We know he's hurt. Why not bait him? We could go back to your house, set a...a...trap, right?"

From the tight set of Travis' lips she had a pretty good idea she was onto something. If he didn't like it, well, too bad. She didn't want to go into Witness Protection, and she didn't want to have to spend the rest of her life being afraid of Daniel Campbell.

"I'd do it," Wendy said.

"No," Grayson snapped.

"I don't like it either," Travis said.

"It could work," Connor pitched his voice over Wendy and Grayson's argument. "Set you up at their house. Stage the security and keep officers inside and out of sight. It could work. Nice thinking."

She didn't believe for a second Connor hadn't already considered this option. He winked at her and turned toward Travis and Grayson. Dimitri was already on the phone, probably calling Ryan to set it up.

"No, we're not doing it, and that's final," Grayson said.

"I am." Wendy drew herself up and stared at her husband as if she were ready to do battle. "You asked what you could do to help me. Do this. Help me make sure this man is behind bars and isn't a threat to us any longer. Hiding will only make it worse."

Grayson's face twisted in anguish. "I just want to keep you safe."

"I know." Wendy leaned in and kissed her husband.

Bliss glanced at Travis, who was already staring at her. She could hear a similar argument coming from his, but with a lot fewer words.

It's my choice. My future. My life.

4.

WENDY FOLLOWED THE POLICE officer and Grayson into the house.

Their home.

She saw it with new eyes. When they moved in, she was so happy. Each piece of furniture, all the colors, she chose them with care. Looking at it now, she remembered all the reasons she loved it. Her husband had designed this especially for them. A home they could raise a family in, grow old together in.

Paul gurgled and waved at her from the car seat.

"Thank you, Priscilla. Set him there on the counter." Wendy waved at the marble surface and waited for the housekeeper to put her things down.

"Glad you're home." Priscilla smiled.

"Me too. Give me a hug?" Wendy squeezed the young woman tightly. Oh, the things Priscilla had put up with over the last year. Wendy would have to bug Grayson about doing something nice for her.

"This is the last of it." Bliss set the last of Paul's things on the counter while the men tended to the luggage.

"You didn't have to get that," Wendy said. Bliss never listened. She was her big sister, always looking out for Wendy, even when she didn't ask for it.

"I need something to do." Bliss dug into the bag containing Paul's formula and bottles, separating the clean from the dirty.

"You could take a break from managing my life and, I don't know, go do something for yourself?" Wendy nodded at the big brute of a man stalking through the living room heading for the office where Grayson sequestered the federal agents.

"What? No." Bliss' frown was more telling than the way she wouldn't look at him.

"What is going on with you two?" Wendy rocked Paul and leaned against the counter. This felt like old times. When they used to talk about each other, and not just how Wendy had managed to drag herself out of bed.

"Nothing."

"Yeah right."

"I don't want to talk about it."

"Fine." Wendy shrugged. "Oh, Priscilla, where's the phone you picked up for Bliss?"

"You—what?" Bliss rolled her eyes.

"Hush. Mom and Dad will freak out if they can't stalker-call you from across the house. It's your same number, too. Don't give me that whole *I want to pay for my own stuff* crap, either."

"Fine. I love you, and you rock." Bliss wrapped Wendy in a tight hug.

This was what she was living for. To love her sister, to see her family grow old together. Depression had almost stolen this from her, but now she was ready to fight for it again.

Wendy would also have to get Travis alone at some point and bully him into being nice to Bliss. She deserved someone who made her happy, and a life that didn't involve looking after Wendy.

"THESE ARE YOUR TRACKING devices." Connor handed the girls what looked to be small pins. "Fasten them inside your clothes, somewhere we won't see them. Keep them on your person at all times, just in case."

Just in case my ass.

Travis would make sure Bliss didn't need it. He wouldn't let her out of his sight, much less out of the house. This plan set his teeth on edge for a reason he couldn't quite put his finger on. Something bad was going to happen, and he didn't know how to stop it.

"Just in case—what?" Bliss turned the tracking device over in her hand.

"We want to be prepared for everything." Connor folded his hands together. Ever since they'd stepped foot in the Hortons' house, the agent had just about bent over backward to keep everyone happy.

"Nothing better happen," Grayson muttered, staring daggers at Connor, then Travis, as if he had something to do with this.

If Travis had his way, Bliss would be across the globe already.

"Anything else?" Wendy glanced over her shoulder, toward the sounds of Paul crying. Since they were back at their home, most normal routines were being picked up and the house staff was back on the job, which meant half a dozen more people to keep an eye on.

"That should be it. Go give the little guy a bottle, eh?" Connor smiled.

The house had received a bit of a makeover in the last two hours. All of the windows had blinds and curtains drawn, whereas before they'd been left open to let in all the natural light. Clusters of officers and agents were set up to do their jobs, and the family moved in and around them all.

If they were lucky, one of the guards on the perimeter would take Daniel down before he ever set foot on the property. But that was a big if. Chances were, he'd run off, tail between his legs, and wait for a better time to strike. At least, that was what Travis would do.

Bliss followed Wendy into the main living space. She'd avoided him since proposing this plan of hers, and for good reason. He wanted to have a chat with her. This wasn't an incredibly dangerous operation, but it was far more risk than he was comfortable with.

She needed time to trust him again, but he wasn't good with giving her space to do that. Everything in him said to stay right by her side.

"Hey, sunshine." Connor stopped in front of Travis, forcing him to look at the man. "Do a security walk-through with me."

"Why?"

"Because your job involves a lot more protecting people than mine. I just find the killers after the act. Come with me."

Travis glanced at Bliss one last time before following the agent into the foyer.

"We were able to disable the cameras, thanks to Lali. He should be blind as far as inside goes."

"Is that still on?" He nodded at the security system panel. "Yeah."

"Good." Travis pulled out his cell phone and texted the agent.

Could be hacked.

Connor glanced at his phone and flashed him a thumbs up.

I'll put Lali on it. Meet me in the office.

"I think it's time I headed out," Connor said. "See you in the morning."

"Later."

Travis watched Connor open and close the door, then flip the locks. There was no way to be sure if they were being observed, but at least they'd laid the foundation for making Daniel think otherwise.

"Need to tell everyone to stay away from the panels," Travis said once they were in the safety of the office, behind closed doors.

"Texting Ryan now. He'll talk to the officers and let the girls know. All right, so we've got a lot of people out there." He turned to the office wall they'd procured to organize the sting. "There are five guys in the gates, roving around the community. We've got two guys in the pool house with eyes on us, and cops stationed near every point of entry, most of them within sight of another cop. What do you see?"

"Too many cops."

"If we went with less, Grayson would be out."

"Daniel's going to catch sight of them and we'll be stuck here twiddling our thumbs while he gets on the road. If he's smart."

"He is smart, but his obsession rules him."

"That's what I don't get about these guys. They can't kill if they're dead or caught."

"A lot of them don't think they'll get caught or they don't care. They can't control it."

"Which do you think Daniel is?"

"Neither. He thinks he's a god. He thinks he's above all this. His obsession will make him slip up. He can't leave Wendy behind, not after he abandoned his kids."

Travis shook his head. It made no sense to him, but it didn't have to. So long as he kept Bliss safe, everything else would work itself out.

"Hey guys." Grayson opened the office door and leaned in. "We're turning in."

"Good night," Connor said. "You should hit the hay. I'm going to find a couch somewhere and cat nap."

Travis nodded. He wasn't planning on sleeping anytime soon, but no one else needed to know that. The first floor was quiet, everyone out of sight and the lights turned down low. He did a circuit of the second floor and wound up outside the double doors leading into a guest room.

The light was still on inside, and he could hear the TV.

He still didn't know where he stood with Bliss, if she wanted him here or not. If she kicked him out, he'd stand watch in the hall outside her room all night long. Until Daniel was caught, or better yet, dead, he wasn't going anywhere. That thought gave him pause. Was it true? His gut said yes. That kind of conviction was hard to ignore.

Bliss meant something to him. And her safety was more important than anything else.

Travis knocked on the door and waited.

No one answered, but he heard the soft padding of feet across carpet.

"It's Travis," he said.

A few seconds later the lock on the door released and it opened. Bliss stepped back, leaning her head on the wood.

"Can I come in?" he asked.

"Please." She waved him in and closed the door behind him again.

At some point she'd showered and changed again into pajama pants and a long-sleeved shirt.

"How's everything looking?" She gestured at the house and sat down on the bed, curling her legs under her.

"Good. If he shows up, we'll catch him." He did a slow walk around the room. If he had his way, she'd be away from all the windows, but that wasn't how Grayson's house was built.

"Will you sit down and stop prowling around?"

"Just checking things out."

Did he sit on the bed, or give her space?

Bliss hugged a pillow to her chest and stared at the muted TV. Some holiday re-run was on, so at least she wasn't watching the news.

Screw it.

Travis crossed to the bed, toed off his boots, and stretched his legs out. She'd let him in, so it was something.

"You still mad at me?" he asked. Might as well get right to the point.

"What?" She scrunched up her eyebrows and glanced at him. "No."

"Then what's up?" She'd practically avoided him since they'd crashed the Hortons' CIA house.

"Did you see Wendy?"

"Yeah."

"Not like—see her, see her, with your eyes. I mean—did you look at her?"

"She seems different."

"Yeah. You know, I've been scared what all this would do to her, if she'd just give up and wither away, or live petrified of what would happen next, but...it's like she's woken up. She's awake and fighting back. Grayson said she's her old self again. But not, because she was never this...determined. It's crazy that something so bad has done her so much good."

"You're—what? Scared that's going to change?"

"A little. I think...mostly I'm at a loss for what to do with myself. I've always been Wendy's keeper. She doesn't need me right now. It's kind of sad. But I guess family always needs each other, just the way she'll need me is different now."

Travis had no clue what he could offer to the conversation. His sister was more like a guy in a lot of ways. There wasn't a problem a blow torch or a tire iron couldn't fix. The rest of his family had communicated through fists and thrown objects. How a healthy family interacted was a mystery to him.

"I'm just...unsure of myself. I've always been needed, and now no one needs me."

"What about me?"

"You don't need me."

She pushed his shoulder. He grabbed her hand before she could pull it away and tugged her closer. Need was a funny thing. He needed air to breathe, food to eat, and he needed her to fill the emptiness inside he'd always attributed to his inner demons.

He tucked her against his side and kissed the top of her head. She lifted her chin until she looked up at him, her dark brown gaze pulling him in, looking into those hidden parts of himself he didn't like to think about.

"I think I do need you. I didn't realize how much until I walked away. I thought I was doing you a favor, that it was the right thing to do, but it wasn't. I was stupid."

"I'm not going to argue with you there." She poked his chest and smiled.

Warmth unfurled in his chest. It was strange, and not quite uncomfortable, just different.

"You think we can try this again? And I mean more than wait and see how things turn out." He'd never wanted something so bad before. If she said no, he didn't know if he could let her go.

5.

TRAVIS HELD HIS BREATH, waiting for Bliss' answer. Sweat dampened his palms, along his hairline and down his spine.

"This?" she asked.

"Us."

She spread her hand out against his chest, over his heart, but didn't speak.

"You said I'd broken your trust." He ran a finger through her silky hair. He'd never touched anything so soft or sleek before.

"You did, but you came back. I shouldn't have put you on the spot like that. That was unfair. I mean, everything you've told me about yourself..."

"That I'm a fuck up?"

"No." This time she slapped his thigh. "You're being difficult."

He caught her hand and brought it to his lips. She made him smile. He liked himself when he was around her.

"I know what I am. I know what my strengths and weaknesses are. I'm not a good man, Bliss. A good man would let you make up your own mind, but I can't. I need you. It's not something I'm used to. If you need time I'll try to be patient, but I'm not good at it."

"How exactly do you plan on making up my mind for me?"

"I have a couple ideas." He smiled through the nerves. Bliss could tell him to fuck off, and he'd go. Not far, but enough to give her space.

"What is it we're trying to decide?"

There it was, that inner spark, the bit of mischief twinkling in her eyes again.

"That I'm your boyfriend." It was silly and maybe juvenile, but part of him needed more from her.

"Then you'd better get to work because I just don't know yet..."

She was playing with him. Whatever breach of trust he'd made wasn't so big that she wasn't willing to give him another chance. He had to make the most of it. Show her he could be different, that they were right for each other.

Travis scooted off the bed.

He didn't have a plan. Hell, he didn't really know what he was doing. He'd never wanted to have a girl stay part of his life before, but she was different. This whole situation with her was new.

The bags were an option. She had quite the collection, and he was warming up to her brand of fun in bed. There were a couple more items he'd glimpsed they hadn't used yet, but he didn't want a gimmick or anything between them. She had to want him. Just him. When it came down to it, that was all he had to offer her.

He circled the bed and held out his hand. She glanced from it to his face and back before placing her hand in his. He pulled her to her feet next to the bed.

No one had ever looked at him the way she did. There was lust there, but also more. Things he didn't have names for and had never allowed himself to feel for another human being.

He cupped the back of her head, relishing the way her hair felt between his fingers. So soft and smooth. She lifted her hands and grasped his forearms, her gaze never leaving his. It was all out there in the open. He didn't need to hear the words to know the depth of her feelings for him. Or that he'd hurt her. He could see it in her eyes. How much she trusted him, how he'd hurt her, the desire, and love. It wasn't a secret.

He pressed his lips to hers and her body softened against him. She tasted like Christmas morning. Everything good and happy he'd only seen on TV. He pulled her closer, their knees bumping and bodies brushing. She smiled against his mouth and slid her hands up to his shoulders.

Travis leaned back and tugged her thermal top up and off, tossing it onto the floor. Bliss lowered her arms and tried to cover herself in a playful, coy act he wasn't buying. He pushed her hands aside and cupped her full breasts, squeezing them just a bit. She arched her back, thrusting her chest forward. Her nipples were stiff points prodding his palms. Bliss tipped her chin back, offering her mouth for a kiss he couldn't give her.

Not yet, at least.

He hooked his thumbs into her pajama pants and drew them over her hips. This time her panties were a string and scrap of fabric over her mound. He eased those down her legs, leaving her in nothing at all.

His hands shook with a need so intense, so foreign, he thought he might burn up before they'd begun. Was this how it was for her, too? Was this what love did to people, drove them fuck-all crazy?

The need for her was all-consuming, to the point he had to wonder if he was safe to be around.

"Travis?" She slid her hands up his chest, worry etched into her features.

"I'm fine." He blew out a breath.

He'd never hurt her, but neither did he have to be careful about his desire. She wasn't a fragile doll.

Travis pushed her shoulders and she slowly fell back onto the mattress, her legs hanging off the side. He enjoyed the way her breasts jiggled, how she chuckled and acted without abandon. She might not know it, but she didn't need him. Not for anything. He, on the other hand, couldn't survive without her. Not after he'd seen what life could be like. What it was supposed to be like.

He knelt over her, letting his hands rove across her body, her curves. She twined her arms around his neck and kissed him, pulling him down on top of her until she got a handful of his shirt and pulled it up. He let her rob him of his shirt. His shoulder didn't even ache anymore. That, or he was too distracted to care.

Travis slid off the bed and onto his knees, a plan for seduction forming in his head. He pushed her legs apart and slid his hands under her ass, dragging her to the very edge of the bed. She yelped and kicked her leg out. He pushed her knee over his shoulder, which had the added bonus of opening her wider for him. Moisture glinted off her damp skin.

She was wet for him.

He spread her open and licked the length of her slit. The taste of her hit the back of his mouth, and his dick throbbed. Bliss' back arched, and she groaned. He slid a finger deep inside her and felt her grow even wetter. Just for him.

"Travis." She moaned. "Travis, I need you inside me now."

"In a minute."

"No, now." She pulled on his hand, her other hand in his hair.

He considered shaking her off, but why deny her what they both wanted?

Travis let Bliss guide him up her body until they were both on the bed. She shoved her hands inside his jeans. His hips bucked and his vision blurred when her hot little hands wrapped around his cock.

"God damn," he muttered.

She pumped him, root to tip, her thumb swiping over the head, slicking the moisture over his flesh. He flexed into her hold, driving deeper into her grasp, loving the feel of her on him. His jeans slid down his hips, getting caught at the top of his thighs.

Bliss hooked her leg over his hip and the head of his cock met her wet folds.

Christ, yes, this was what he wanted, to pump into her slick, wet heat until she screamed. She lifted her hips, pressing against him. Her body yielded to his, as nature intended. He pulled back, though every fiber of his body said to thrust into her.

"Condom," he got out from between clenched teeth.

She groaned and released her hold on him, falling back on the bed.

Travis stood and shed the rest of his clothing. He flipped open his wallet...and froze.

Fuck.

"I...don't have any."

"My bag." She scampered off the bed before he could get there.

God love a prepared woman. He followed her across the room to the dresser, watching her in the mirror.

Bliss fished a foil packet out of the side compartment and ripped it open. He made a grab for it, but she retreated, clutching it to her chest.

"Let me," she said.

"Do it." He leaned against the dresser, gripping the edges with both hands.

She grinned at him and wrapped her hands around his cock. Her fingers fumbled with the latex at first, but she rolled it on him with ease.

The small, shy smile was all for him.

He'd meant to be gentle, to focus on what she wanted, but other ideas were taking root, and he needed her now. Right now.

He grasped a handful of her ass with one hand and kissed her. She fell forward against his chest, clutching at his arms. He turned, breaking the kiss and pushing her up against the dresser. The artful mirror hanging on the wall gave him an excellent view of her swaying breasts, her swollen lips, and what lust did to her face.

Bliss' reflection watched him, her face flushed and eyes dilated with lust. She braced her hands against the heavy piece of furniture, as if daring him to do every wicked thing to her. He gripped her hips and pushed a knee between her legs, making room for himself.

He'd intended to be gentler, but she seemed determined to drive him crazy.

She thrust her hips back, grinding against him. Her face was flushed now, her cheeks pink, and her bottom lip caught between her teeth.

So damn sexy.

Travis grasped his cock and passed it through her folds, coating himself with her arousal. Her heat soaked into him until he felt it in his toes. Something knocked around in his chest, big and important, but now wasn't the time for that.

He thrust, burying himself inside of her. Bliss dropped to her elbows, pushing back on him, and moaned. He sucked in a breath as he sank a few inches deeper. Her body quivered around him, stretching, adjusting to his girth and this moment. It was an intense sensation, not just because it was sex and he wanted her, but because he loved her.

The knowledge didn't bring on the same kind of panic it had that morning. He loved her, and that changed everything. No matter what, he would always love her.

Travis smoothed his hands up her thighs to her hips. Her muscles tensed under his palms and she rocked back against him.

She wanted him to move?

He grinned and thrust again, driving into her so hard she went up on her tiptoes. Her mouth opened on a silent shout, and her pussy constricted around him.

She liked it.

He pulled her hips, grinding their bodies together. Her breathing hitched and her eyes closed.

"Oh, yes," she whispered.

He rocked into her. The drawers rattled and something fell onto the carpet, but it didn't matter. Bliss opened her eyes and their gazes locked. She rolled her hips, and this time, when he pulled most of the way out, she moved with him. Their bodies met in a wet slap of flesh.

"Yes," she said louder.

He pushed her pelvis up against the dresser to keep her right where he wanted her and thrust, again and again. Bliss moaned and dropped her head forward. He was vaguely aware of other things falling off the dresser, the way it bumped against the wall, but the only thing that mattered was the feel of Bliss around him. The joining of their bodies.

This was the woman he loved.

He wasn't good enough for her, but damn it, she was in every fiber of his being.

A tingling sensation started at the base of his spine. He was going to come so hard, but she had to orgasm first.

Travis covered her left hand with his, leaning over her. He flexed his hips, driving into her with short, powerful strokes. Her fingers twined with his, squeezing tight.

He reached around her and cupped her breast, rolling her nipple between his fingers. She thrust her chest into his hand and her head back onto his shoulder.

"Travis." His name became a hiss as he plucked the stiff bud.

"Come on, darlin'," he said into her ear.

"Travis." Her voice hitched at the end and she squeezed his hand even tighter.

Bliss made some sort of sound and her body tensed, rippling with pleasure. Her mouth worked silently, her head tossing back and forth on his shoulder.

He let go of the tenuous hold of control and surged into her. Bliss leaned over the dresser, up on her tiptoes while he pumped in and out of her body, losing himself in her sighs, her scent, everything about her. She made him whole in a way he'd never experienced before.

His balls drew up, and the wave of release swept up through his body. He thrust once, twice more, and then leaned over her, burying his face in Bliss' hair and squeezing her to his chest while the tremors ceased.

Now, all he had to do was convince her to let him stay. To give him a second chance, and to love him. Another screw up, and he'd lose her. He wasn't willing to make that mistake again.

Travis kissed her shoulder and straightened. He missed the feel of being inside of her immediately, but if they worked things out, maybe they could be together. And not in the temporary sense.

Bliss remained slouched over the dresser, eyes closed and her body glistening with a light sheen of perspiration.

She was perfect.

He bent and picked her up. This time she didn't squawk in protest, though she did tense up for a second.

"Your shoulder," she mumbled.

"Flesh wound."

He carried her to the bed and lay down with her, too spent to do more than hold her for the moment. What they shared was more than an orgasm and a couple hot, sweaty moments. It ran deeper than that. At least it still did on his side. He had to hope her feelings for him hadn't changed, though maybe he was reading into it. He didn't have a lot of experience when it came to loving someone.

"Hm, I still don't know." She traced shapes against his chest.

He liked the sleepy, content smile. He was pretty sure before he'd freaked out that she'd been close to telling him she loved him. Looking at her now, he didn't think much had changed.

"Yes you do. You don't want to admit it yet." He traced her bottom lip.

"Oh, really?" She propped her head in her hand and stared down at him, that mischievous light shining out from inside. Nothing could snuff that out, not even a serial killer. She'd never been more beautiful to him. "What decision have I come to, then?"

Either he put it all out on the line, or he waited and bided his time.

Screw it.

He was all in this time.

"You love me."

Her eyes widened and her mouth dropped open. Shit. Could he be wrong?

He took a deep breath and pressed on. Might as well lay it all out there for her. "Or, you think you might love me. Either way, I've decided I'm in love with you, so you should get on board with the idea."

"Bossy." She slapped his stomach, but not hard enough to acknowledge. "That's not nice."

"It's the truth." He grabbed her hand and kissed it.

"Wait—you're serious?" She sat up and blinked down at him, her mouth hanging open.

"I'm not good at joking around." He clenched the hand curled under his head into a fist. Was this a mistake? Should he have kept that to himself?

"Travis—you're serious?"

"Yes. I'm serious. I know I screwed up, but I panicked. I think I had to so I would realize what I you meant to me."

"I thought we just said we should take things slower."

"That was your suggestion. I never agreed to it."

"You love me?"

"That's what I said."

"I...don't know what to say."

She covered her mouth with one hand and her eyes got that glossy, I'm-about-to-cry look. Shit. He'd screwed up.

"Don't worry about it," he said and glanced at the bathroom. How long could he spend cleaning up?

Bliss leaned down and cupped his face, forcing him to look at her. Her dark hair brushed his jaw and she stared deep into his eyes.

"I think I love you, too," she said.

THE HOURS DRAGGED ON, one by one, but he was patient. Nothing good ever came from spur of the moment decision-making. His patience and planning were why he was the best.

The cops made another round through the gated community. In the east, the sun started its trek across the sky. Soon, it would begin.

No one glanced twice at the housekeeper's car parked in the neighbor's shed. He timed their arrival to coincide with a gap in the security sweep. This plan was perfect. Daniel was rather proud of this one. He'd never come so close to law enforcement before. It was a little disappointing they were so bad, but then he wasn't a common criminal. He was more than human.

A hollow thud broke the stillness.

"Please, he's scared," Priscilla whispered.

"He's alive. Would you rather him dead?"

"No."

"Then wait a while longer. Remember, you do your part, your son lives." He jabbed the gun into Priscilla's ribs.

"Please don't hurt my baby." She hunched over in the driver's seat.

"Shut up. Stop crying."

Damn woman was going to blow this whole thing by bawling. It was fucking frustrating that his entire plan hinged on one worthless creature playing her part. Hopefully the cops chalked her odd behavior up to nerves. Out on the street, the same late model truck rolled by. Again.

"Go on, before anyone else wakes up."

Priscilla started the car and eased it around into the alley behind the expensive homes. They went about fifty feet before turning into the utility entrance of the house everyone was watching.

Just a few more minutes, and Wendy would be his.

6.

WENDY RINSED OUT THE bottle and stuck her tongue out at Paul, who was already drifting off to sleep.

The house was quiet, caught in the drowsy hours between when most people were asleep and when they headed out for their day. It was the perfect time to get a few things done before everyone woke up.

She opened the fridge and frowned. They had practically nothing to feed the masses currently residing in her home. Priscilla was picking up the groceries, but Wendy hadn't made a list of everything she wanted between all the activity last night.

"Utility room door open," the security system announced.

Wendy turned and listened to the light footsteps and crinkling plastic.

"Priscilla! You're early. Here, let me help." She rushed to the housekeeper's side and took one of the heavy bags.

It felt good to be the woman of the house again, with things to do and people to feed. When was the last time she'd cooked a meal that didn't need to be microwaved?

"Is there more, or is this it?" She took a few cold items out of the bag and placed them in the fridge.

"There's a lot more still out in the car. I can get it."

"Don't be silly. I'm going stir-crazy stuck in here."

Plus, poor Priscilla was looking a little worn.

"You don't have to," she said again.

"Come on. Let's go." Wendy grabbed her coat from where she'd tossed it over the back of one of the stools last night. She glanced at the officer sitting silent sentinel on the sofa, his phone pressed to his ear. The officer had spent most of the morning trying to get a hold of his ex-wife and children. Wendy's heart went out to him. "Mind watching him for a minute? He's falling asleep, so he shouldn't bother you."

"Not at all, ma'am."

"Thanks. We'll just be a moment."

"Really, you should stay in here." Priscilla was showing her overprotective streak, which was one of the reasons she was so valuable to their family.

"Don't be silly. Come on."

Wendy exited through the utility room and zipped up her coat.

"How's Carlos?" she asked.

"He's under the weather. Are you still wearing those tracking things?"

Ah, a sick child. Wendy had seen Priscilla come to work exhausted and worn out after dealing with her stubborn child. The boy was going to be a hard-headed man someday.

"Grayson made me sleep with that silly thing on." She wrinkled her nose. The device might be small, but she was going to have a bruise of it imprinted on her skin. "Maybe you should take the day off, take care of him?"

They walked around to the second driveway designated for staff and utility vehicles. Priscilla's sedan was parked on the far side of the slab that could accommodate up to three vehicles.

That was odd, but then again, who knew where the cop cars were and when?

Wendy circled around to the back of the car and waited for Pricilla to open the trunk.

"I'm sorry, miss."

"What?"

Priscilla stood a few feet away, hands down at her side and fat tears rolling down her cheeks. The trunk rose on well-oiled hinges.

"What's wrong?" Wendy glanced at the trunk at the same moment she heard a car door open.

Carlos stared up at her, tape wrapped around his mouth, his eyes open wide.

"Wendy, so nice to see you again." Daniel pointed a gun at her and smiled.

"Oh, my God." Wendy gulped, her whole body freezing.

This wasn't supposed to happen. She was at home. Safe. There were dozens of cops all around.

It had to be a dream. She was asleep in her bed. Any moment now Grayson would shake her awake.

"Get in the car, Wendy."

She took a step back and ran into Priscilla, who mumbled the same words over and over again, "I'm sorry."

Wendy wasn't getting in that car. She wasn't going back to that cave. She couldn't.

She sucked in a deep breath.

Daniel moved first. He grabbed Wendy with his left hand, jerking her against him.

"Please, you said you wouldn't hurt anyone," Priscilla said. She was full-on crying now, her hands outstretched toward Daniel.

Run! Run, Wendy wanted to tell her, but her voice was frozen.

"Priscilla—"

Daniel shifted and pushed her up against the car. She caught a glimpse of him lunging at Priscilla before Wendy squeezed her eyes shut. That gurgling sound, it brought back blood-soaked memories of what he'd done to the two men right in front of her.

Oh God, that was Priscilla...

BLISS JOGGED DOWN THE stairs. She couldn't stop smiling. Her sister was going to have a lot of questions. She was pretty sure the whole house had heard them last night. But first, she needed food. She'd always known sex burned calories, but after last night and this morning she might waste away if she didn't get something in her soon.

An officer stationed in the den had the TV on, watching the morning news. It was otherwise quiet and peaceful. Two bags of groceries, and Paul, sat on the kitchen counter.

That was...odd.

She paused and listened for sounds from the pantry or maybe the bathroom. It was totally out of character for Priscilla to leave Paul unattended. When the sitting service wasn't there, the baby's care usually fell to the housekeeper, and she took her job very seriously.

"Wendy? Priscilla?"

"They're carrying in the groceries," the officer said without glancing her way.

"What's wrong?" Travis said right behind her.

Bliss shook her head and looked up at Travis. Something was wrong. Really wrong. "Priscilla wouldn't let Wendy set foot out of the house, not after that talk with Ryan yesterday. And she wouldn't leave Paul sitting on a kitchen counter."

"How long ago did they leave?" Travis asked. He was already reaching for his gun, which she hadn't even noticed.

The officer sat forward and frowned at his wrist watch.

"Five minutes ago?" he said.

"Shit."

Bliss sprinted for the utility room door, but Travis caught her, jerking her back against his chest.

"Stop. Stay here." He pushed her into the kitchen as the officer slid past. Both men were armed and on edge by the time they exited through the utility room door.

Logically, she understood why she should be inside the house. If she went out there, she was at risk. But what if Wendy was gone?

Screw this, they were not going out there without her. It was her sister who was in trouble.

She followed maybe a dozen feet behind the men. Every fiber of her body was on alert. The breeze whipped her hair around her head, making it hard to see.

"God damn it," Travis said, then rushed ahead of them.

"We have a body at the utility entrance," the officer radioed.

A body?

Bliss stumbled to a stop at the corner of the storage shed. She reached out and braced a hand on the building, gasping for air, unable to look away from the scene.

Travis knelt next to Priscilla's prone body. Her limbs were twisted at an unnatural angle, as if she had fallen and not tried to get up or protect herself. A puddle of dark liquid spread out around her on the concrete.

"Hang in there. Priscilla? Look at me," Travis said.

She was alive?

Bliss sprinted the last couple of steps and went to her knees next to Travis. Her stomach revolted at the sight of the ugly, thick slash across her throat and up the side of her face.

"Oh, my God, Priscilla." Bliss sobbed, horrified and sickened by the sight. Priscilla might be their housekeeper, but she was also a friend. Someone who loved and cared for their family.

Travis grabbed Bliss' hand and put it in Priscilla's.

"Hang in there, we're here with you," Travis said. He smoothed her hair out of her face and never once shied away from looking at her.

Priscilla opened her mouth, but no sound came out.

"No, no, don't try to talk," Bliss said. She leaned down, just as close as Travis. "We're getting help, okay? Hang on."

She glanced at Travis, but his face was grim.

Where was the help? Why weren't they there yet?

"Look at her," he mumbled.

Bliss stared down at Priscilla. Her eyes were dilated, the pupils huge. The grip on Bliss' hand went lose and a breath hissed from between Priscilla's lips.

Was that...?

Bliss sat in shocked silence for several seconds.

Oh God, she was dead.

Priscilla was dead.

And Wendy was gone.

Bliss sat down hard and stared at her hand. Priscilla's blood stained her fingers.

"Why did you do that?" she said. "She needed help."

"That's a couple pints of blood. He didn't miss her throat this time like he did with Don. He made sure to kill her. At least she didn't die alone, Bliss. That's something."

"What the fucking hell?" Connor stood over them wearing track pants and a hoodie. "Who was watching those cameras?"

Three other officers circled them, guns out.

A radio crackled.

"They've got a visual," one announced.

Officers and agents ran this way and that, but Bliss continued to sit there, staring at another casualty of Daniel Campbell's obsession.

"Bliss, you need to get inside." Travis grasped her by the shoulders.

"But what about Priscilla?" She blinked up at him.

"Think about Paul right now, okay?"

How could she, when Wendy was gone again?

"What's going to happen to Priscilla? She has a son." She let Travis pull her to her feet. She glanced over her shoulder, unable to stop looking at Priscilla, willing the woman to get up. But she didn't.

"They'll call the coroner to come pick her up. We need to move so the cops can do their job."

He guided her inside and stood guard while she washed her hands in the kitchen sink. The house was abuzz with activity now. Officers strode back and forth, agents on the phone.

"Bliss—we just heard." Her mother and father rushed into the kitchen, elbowing Travis out of the way and surrounding her. They meant to be comforting, but their nearness suffocated her.

"They're following him now," Travis said.

"You should leave," Bliss' father said, scowling at Travis.

"What good are you?" Bliss' mother wheeled on him. "You were supposed to keep my daughter safe. Now she's gone again, because you couldn't protect her."

"Mom, Mom." Bliss held onto her mother, wrapping her arms around her. "It's not Travis' fault."

"No, it's okay. I'll go." Travis backed away.

The man Bliss loved. This was a shit way of introducing them.

Paul chose that moment to let out a big wail.

"Oh, I know, honey, I know." Mom scooped Paul out of his carrier and cradled him to her chest.

Wendy was gone. Right out from under their noses.

7.

WENDY HUDDLED IN THE back seat of yet another car. She'd lost count around the second or third. Time blurred together. She had no idea where they were, except she could still see the casinos in the distance. All she knew was that Carlos was in the trunk, safe and unhurt.

What had Priscilla done? What had he done to her?

"We're here," Daniel announced.

He pulled the car under a metal carport that stretched several yards to her left. The buildings around them were warehouses, big metal structures. The street was empty of traffic or pedestrians, just them. No one to cry out to for help or report them to the cops.

She clutched her bound hands to her chest. The tracker was still there, attached to her bra strap. Priscilla had known. She'd even asked, ensuring the device was on her.

Wendy couldn't fault Priscilla for what she'd done. If Daniel threatened her family, Wendy knew the lengths to which she was willing to go to keep them safe.

"Where are we?" she asked.

"Here."

"What about Carlos?"

"Don't fucking worry about him." Rage laced his voice.

She flinched away, pressing her back against the door.

"Don't do that, don't be afraid." His tone gentled, and he reached for her, his hands careful as he patted her arm and then her shoulder. "Come here. Come here. I had to do it, so we could be together. You were made for me. This is how it's supposed to be."

"What are you going to do to me?" She couldn't stop the tears. Hadn't she survived this once? She didn't want to go back there. Not to that cave painted with death.

"First, I've got to get your sister, and then we can leave. Go anywhere. I've got it all figured out. You'll see."

"No," Wendy blurted. Not her sister. Not Bliss. She'd given up so much of her life for Wendy. If he called her, Bliss would come. It was who she was. Who she'd always been.

This time though, this time Wendy would save her. They had the same blood, the same genetics. She could do this. She could save her sister. The cops would find her first, right? That's what the tracker was for. She just needed to hang on a little longer and keep him from making contact with Bliss.

Daniel's face twisted into something ugly, almost inhuman.

Wendy's body went cold, and tremors shook her hands. Some inborn sense kicked in. She had to keep him happy. Convince him all he needed was her. It's what Bliss would do.

"I mean, why do we need her? Can't," she swallowed down the bile, "can't it just be us?"

His mouth spread into something like a smile. He reached for her, cupping her cheek in his rough hand. She clenched her fists tighter to keep from cringing away from him.

This time she would be strong.

"She doesn't matter, but I can't let her live. Just a little while longer, and then we can be happy, together."

"Why does she matter? Can't we go now?"

"She dies," he snapped and dropped the compassionate act. "Out of the car. Now."

"Okay. Okay."

A thump from the trunk reminded her that she wasn't his only victim.

"What about Carlos?" she asked. They couldn't leave him behind, could they? Should she keep her mouth shut and hope the authorities found the car?

"Get him out." Daniel popped the lock on the trunk and pushed up out of his seat, leaving her to scramble after him.

Wendy circled the car, but froze once she reached the tail light. Daniel had the gun out, pointed at the trunk. Her body shook uncontrollably, either from the cold or the fear, she didn't know which.

Be brave.

Be more like Bliss.

"What's that for?" she asked. Wasn't she cooperating?

"The kid's trouble. Get him out."

Wendy lifted the trunk and forced herself to smile at Carlos. Did he know his mother was dead? He had every right to hate her because of this. It was her fault. If Daniel weren't obsessed with her, Priscilla would still be alive.

Carlos stared up at her, his eyes big and red. There was an ugly bump on the side of his head. The duct tape around his hands and face was twisted and mangled, but hadn't torn. Yet. He was doing his best to get free. The kid was a fighter. Priscilla would be proud.

"Hey, Carlos, it's okay." She reached for his hands and held them for a second, willing him to believe her. "It's all going to be okay. Just come with me."

Please let it be okay. Please?

Wendy helped the kid out of the trunk. Like his mom, Carlos was a strong-willed personality with lots of smarts. Grayson didn't know that Wendy had pushed Priscilla to use their address so Carlos could go to a better school district. The only thing that mattered to Priscilla was giving her son the opportunities in life she never had. Now she was gone, and who would look out for Carlos?

"Walk," Daniel barked.

"Where are we going?" Wendy wrapped an arm around Carlos and hustled him away from Daniel.

"Keep walking."

"Is it really necessary to point a gun at us?"

"Wendy, Wendy, you're so sweet and kind. You'll make a good mother, but you forget you aren't my first wife. I've had others like you. I'm not stupid. You don't love me yet, but you will. You will." He picked up his pace and pushed the barrel of his gun against the back of Carlos' head. "You do as I say, or I'll kill him, understand?"

"Oh, God. Oh my God." She swallowed hard and nodded. "Yes. Yes, I understand."

She shook from head to toe, so much that it was hard to walk. Carlos stared straight ahead, supporting her as they huddled together and stumbled forward.

Wendy wasn't strong enough for this. She wasn't Bliss. She couldn't do this.

TRAVIS STALKED DOWN THE driveway. Ryan, Connor, and Jade stood in a circle with a few uniformed officers. The frigid breeze sliced through his clothes, but it was nothing compared to the damning looks from Bliss' parents.

It wasn't his fault eyes hadn't been on the perimeter, or that the house staff wasn't being watched, but he still should have known. If he were dealing with a client under threat, it's the kind of thing he'd expect to happen. But this was a deranged serial killer with a fucked up god complex, and most of Travis' rules were out the window.

"Hey Travis. How's the family?" Connor asked.

"Pissed as hell. What the fuck happened?"

"Check those locations and report back to us," Ryan said to the uniformed officers.

The cops got in their cars and zoomed off, no doubt under pressure to wrap this up. No one wanted this kind of trouble in a major tourist destination on New Year's. Shit. The days had zoomed by for him. He hadn't realized what day it was.

"Jade and I are going to the station to coordinate with the officers there. The rest of you, keep your phones on. When he makes a move, be ready to get there."

"Yes, sir," Connor said.

Travis didn't reply. He wasn't under the orders of the FBI, but for now he was going to play by their rules. Even if their rules had gotten Wendy kidnapped. Again.

Jade and Ryan climbed into one of several black SUVs and headed out after the police, leaving Travis and Connor alone on the drive, save for the cops stationed at either end of the street.

"Have they figured out what happened and how they lost him with Wendy wearing a tracker?"

"One thing at a time, mate." Connor held up his hand and sighed. "Appears Daniel got to Priscilla through her son, Carlos. Neighbors said they saw a man with him yesterday. The build fits Daniel, though none of them saw his face. Best guess is he got her when she went home last night and set this up."

"Where's the kid?" Travis asked.

"No clue. Daniel has no problem with violence toward men and women, but what he did to his children wasn't about torture or killing, it was about preserving them. I don't think he means to kill Carlos. He's just a tool, but I wouldn't bet on that. Daniel's under a lot of pressure right now, and he could do a lot of things we wouldn't expect him to do."

"Yeah. Yeah." Travis nodded. At this point all they were doing was pointless talking. "What about the tracker?"

"It's active, but it's on a delay. We're about half an hour behind him."

"Are you fucking serious?"

"Man, we don't have your resources. We're borrowing Vegas PD tech here. This is a government budget we're playing with, and we have the best tools available to us."

"You should have said something."

"And what? Your guys cost money Uncle Sam isn't going to foot the bill for, and we both know your boss don't do charity work. How the hell you're still here is beyond me."

Travis had ignored the two calls from his boss. If it weren't the holidays, his ass would have been called home already. The shit was going to hit the fan once everyone was back from the break, and then he'd pay for this. For now though, he was on his own time and dime. That still didn't mean they couldn't have found a way to get real-time tracking devices on the girls. At least Bliss was still here.

"My balls are about to freeze off. You mind?" Connor gestured at the other SUV. "I want to start driving his trail. It'll get us closer to him the next time we get a read on our girl."

Travis stalked to the truck and climbed in. He hated this whole situation. Usually, he was the guy brought in to finish a job like this, and he had no idea how to end it. They weren't dealing with anyone remotely like what he was used to. But Daniel Campbell needed to be put down. The question was when.

BLISS SAT ON HER bed, Paul cradled against her chest. Everyone was downstairs, yelling and blaming each other. She couldn't handle it anymore. Even Travis was gone, vanished to some far corner of the house where her mother couldn't heap the blame on him. She didn't fault him for getting out of the way, but she wished she knew where he was. Even if he was out looking for Wendy. But she didn't have his number programmed into her new phone yet. Next time she saw him, it was the first thing she was going to do.

Everything in the last twenty-four hours was just more weird and surreal than the last week. Except for last night.

Last night had been perfect.

Travis loved her.

She blew out a breath.

He loved her, and he meant it.

It was crazy and totally out of character for her to jump into a relationship like this, but maybe she'd been waiting for him all along. There was no rhyme or reason to why she loved him over other guys she dated—she just did. She could totally list out the reasons why she loved him, but it was more than how he listened to her when she made a point, counted her opinion about things, or what they had in common. It was how she felt about him. How he made her feel. The way he understood her.

When all this ended, if—when—they brought Wendy home and Daniel went to jail, they had some serious stuff to sort out. She wasn't willing to be apart from Travis for longer than necessary. Maybe she needed to think about moving. Blush Shoppe had a handful of remote employees. She might take a pay cut, since she couldn't manage the in-person client meetings, but there was no reason she had to be in Vegas.

Was she serious?

Moving meant being away from Wendy and Paul and her parents. If Wendy was out of the depression then maybe...but who would be there for her in the future? Could Bliss live the rest of her life revolving around her little sister?

Travis had called her on it, and he was right. As much as she loved Wendy, Bliss couldn't live her life for Wendy. If moving was what was right for Bliss, she'd do it. And Wendy would understand. Bliss hoped she would understand.

She hugged little Paul closer and kissed his sleepy face. Wouldn't it be nice to be a baby right about now? He had no idea there was anything wrong. Not a care in the world. Whereas, once again, Bliss was at a loss for what to do next.

Her phone rang, clattering like an old telephone. She jumped, unaccustomed to the default ring tone.

Unknown Number.

There were a lot of people involved in the search for her sister. Maybe someone needed to get a hold of her?

"Hello?"

"Bliss—"

"Wendy?" Disbelief. Hope. Dread. A dozen different emotions pounded at her from all sides.

8.

"**W**ENDY, WHERE ARE YOU? I'll come get you."
"Don't say anything. Don't tell anyone about this call." Wendy sounded frantic as she breathed into the phone.

"What? Why? Are you still with Daniel? Did you get away?"

"No—"

"Give me the phone," a man said in the background. *Daniel.*

Wendy hadn't gotten away. She was still a prisoner.

Bliss clutched Paul to her chest and stared at the bedspread.

Something bad was going to happen, and she couldn't stop it.

"Hello?" Daniel said.

"I'm here." She sat up straighter, refusing to cower at the sound of his voice.

"Don't get any smart ideas and tell the cops about this call. Are they listening?"

"No. I'm up in a bedroom by myself."

"Good. Good." He practically purred with approval.

Her stomach rolled and Paul grunted in his sleep. She eased her hold on him and willed him back to sleep.

"What do you want? You know the cops are looking for you."

"I'm making a one-time offer. Meet me in half an hour, and I'll trade your sister for you. Come alone. I see the cops, I shoot the kid, and then Wendy. If you're late, I shoot the kid and leave with your sister."

Seriously?

This was his offer?

It was such a steaming pile of shit. Bliss kind of wanted to pinch herself to make sure she wasn't sleeping. She knew he wanted them both. Did he really think she wouldn't figure out it was a trap?

No, because according to the feds he had a narcissistic god complex. He thought he was smarter and better than everyone.

"Bliss, time is running out."

"Yes. Fine. I'll be there."

If the cops showed up though, if they caught up to Daniel, Carlos and maybe her sister would die.

The tracking device.

The cops were already closing in on them.

They'd find Daniel before she did, and then everyone died.

"I'll text you the address. Hurry. Don't be late."

"Wait!" she blurted.

She had to do this. She had to save her sister.

"What?"

"My sister has a tracking device on her. It's probably attached to the hem of her shirt or something. I put it there.

If you don't take that off and move, I'm not responsible for the cops showing up."

She practically heard his teeth grinding before the line went dead.

"Daniel? Daniel? Damn it."

Bliss tossed the phone onto the bed.

Shit. What was she going to do?

No cops, or everyone died.

Think. Think.

A text message landed in her inbox from the same Unknown Number. One line of text, and yet it was all the hope she had.

She needed Travis...but what if there was no way to hide him? Plus, she hadn't seen him since earlier, and there wasn't time to track him down. Besides, he'd try to talk her out of this. He loved her. He'd want to keep her safe, and she couldn't really fault him for being biased, but he didn't care for Wendy like she did.

Hadn't she been a tiny bit glad it wasn't Travis who'd been shot up in the mountains?

God, that felt like an age ago.

Bliss carefully removed the tracking device from her bra strap and pinned it to Paul's onesie. First things first, she needed to hand the baby off.

She padded downstairs, quickstepping to stay out of the officers' way as they hustled back and forth.

Travis, Connor, Jade—none of the faces she recognized were there.

The living room was a sea of uniforms and more unfamiliar faces. She tiptoed down the hall to a smaller den area that Wendy had converted into a play room. The more comfortable space was where her parents and a few friends and neighbors were clustered.

"There you are. Come sit." Her mother patted the couch next to her.

"My head really hurts. I think I want to take a shower and lay down. Would you mind?" She lifted Paul a bit and smiled.

"Of course. Hand him here."

Bliss kissed Paul's forehead. If she fucked up, she might never see her nephew again. But if she didn't do something, Daniel might disappear with her sister before the cops ever found them. The feds hadn't been able to find him. Maybe it was time to try something else. Something stupid, but at least it was—something.

"Come back down and join us," her mother said.

"Will do." Her smile was forced, but it merely supported her claim of a headache.

She took the smaller staircase up to the second floor. It was quieter up here, but also rather eerie. She glanced over her shoulder. If Travis were there, he'd know something was up. So it was a good thing he was MIA.

Back in her room, she flipped the flimsy lock into place and changed into jeans, her boots, a long-sleeved shirt and a bulky sweatshirt. The Taser and mace Travis had gifted her were easy enough to stick in her pockets. But would those be enough to stop Daniel?

She needed something with stopping power.

She needed a gun.

Wasn't it serendipitous she knew someone who over-packed their firearms?

This is how accidents happen.

She opened Travis' bag and poked around.

Buried on the bottom, under a plastic traveling case with built-in locks, was another gun. She'd seen him squirrel away the three he had a few times, enough that she'd dared to hope it would be there. They were going to have to have a serious conversation about gun safety, but for now his lapse in judgment was playing in her favor.

She knew what the safety was, but other than that, she was working on blind faith. A row of shiny bullets laid waiting in the bottom of the bag. She pocketed those as well and put the rest in the hoodie pouch.

Twenty minutes and counting to make it to the meet on time.

She was being reckless, crazy, and stupid, but it was her sister. She had to do this, because so far nothing else had worked.

Bliss adjusted her clothing and headed for the hall.

Now she just had to find a car and get her ass out of here.

Her car.

Her car was still here!

She hustled down the hall and into her sister's room, pulling up short at the last minute.

Grayson and his assistant sat on the bed, papers spread out between them.

"Need something, Bliss?" he asked.

"Are you working?" She tried to not...gape...but how could he concentrate at work when Wendy was missing?

"I'm trying to stay busy, but it's not working." He got up and paced the bedroom. His assistant glared at her.

"They're going to find her, it's going to be okay," the assistant said. Bliss could never keep them straight, so she'd just stopped trying.

"Yeah. Yeah, I'm sure you're right," Grayson muttered.

"Hey, you know where Wendy kept my spare key? I wanted to see if I left a change of clothes in my trunk." Bliss smiled and hoped he believed her.

"I have it. It's in here."

Grayson strode to the closet, which was as big as her bedroom back at her apartment. He opened a small safe and rooted around inside for a moment before turning to present her with the spare key.

"Thanks."

She grabbed the key, focusing on acting natural. How exactly was she supposed to act though? It wasn't every day a serial killer proclaimed his obsessive hatred for a girl. She glanced at her phone again and cringed at the time. It was running out.

Bliss took the small staircase to the ground floor and checked the map once again. She wasn't great with directions, but the phone could also be used to track her in a pinch. At least that's what happened in the movies. So she left it on the bottom stair, waited until no one was looking, and slid out the front door. With her hood up, she hoped she looked like any one of the neighbors coming and going.

If one of the cops made her, it was all over, and Wendy was as good as dead.

She crossed the lawn and slid into her little car, shivering. Boy, it was unusually cold this year. She started the car, glancing at the cop cars every few moments. Easing it into drive, she rolled down the street, holding her breath.

Neither car moved to follow her.

No one ran out of the house after her.

She had some serious road to burn if she was going to make it.

"DO YOU THINK HE had a car waiting here? Or did he boost something parked on the street?" Travis studied the blocked-off street. He wanted to get out of the SUV and walk the scene, look for a clue, but then he'd be in the way of the professionals.

Officers and what had to be the forensics team clustered around the first car, Priscilla's. The one Daniel had driven into the gated community and right up to the house to kidnap Wendy in.

"Nah. Two hostages? He had to have something waiting." Connor twisted to look behind them.

"If they're both tied up, what's he got to worry about? Wendy's not strong enough to break loose, and the kid's probably scared shitless."

"Time. He knew we would chase him, so he needed to get away clean and change vehicles before we got too close. He had to have something waiting at this location. He knew he was coming here. Look at the street. There's no camera in sight. He knew he'd change vehicles without us knowing what to look for."

"What about there?" Travis pointed to a dome camera mounted on the cross street.

"Nah, that's blind this way. It only goes north and south. You can't see the lights, that's how he knew."

"Fuck." Travis rubbed his forehead. He'd gone up against some thorough bastards before, but they'd had teams to do the work. This was one man. "Do we have another ping on Wendy's location?"

"Yup. Patrol is in the area now looking for a car or some sign of them."

"Do we know which way they went?"

"Lali tagged every car that crossed the intersection behind us, the one up the street, the other to the left, and the three closest traffic cameras. It's a lot of cars to follow and sort through. She's requested some support, but still, that's a lot of cameras and a lot of cars."

"Needle in a fucking haystack."

"Pretty much." Connor eased the truck past the ongoing investigation. "If I wanted time alone with my sweetheart, and I knew the law was after me, where would I go?"

"What is that? Some kind of profiler trick?"

"It's easy to get into some of their heads, but Daniel is more complex. Usually we're dealing with a sociopath, mum issues, a sadist, someone who has a single driving trait. Daniel...he's a mix. He's a narcissist, yet he hasn't made contact with us. It's like he doesn't even care about us, so who is it he wants to pay attention to him?"

"Bliss said he talked a lot about his subjects."

"Maybe. We know he picked up homeless people and chopped them up, but still, he'd want someone to know about what he was doing. To show it off."

"Wendy?"

"Yeah, that's a good point. If he considers her his wife, maybe she's his equal and her affirmation of witnessing his "work" is all he needs because we are so below his notice. But..." Connor shook his head. "It's damn frustrating, man."

Travis' phone vibrated, breaking his concentration. He glanced at the screen and frowned.

"Hey, hold on. Let me answer this." He clicked the Answer button. His phone connected to the Bluetooth. "Grayson, we're—"

"Bliss is gone."

"Wait—what?" Travis sat forward. The vision of her pale, blood-splattered face leapt to mind. Gone? Bliss? She couldn't be. No, she was safe. Last he'd seen her, she was in the kitchen with her family.

"She came up to my room, asked for the key to her car to get some stuff out of the trunk. Then someone found her phone at the foot of the stairs."

"Bloody hell," Connor muttered. He pulled over to the curb and got his phone out, too.

"What about the tracker?" Travis asked. "It just pinged, right?"

"The cops are looking for the signal, but..."

"But what?"

"She deleted all the history on the phone. No calls, no texts, nothing. She's doing something."

Bliss would do anything to protect her sister. Anything. Damn it, he should have seen this coming. Cold dread settled in the pit of his stomach. She should have called him at least. He could have helped her. Together they might have been able to accomplish something. But alone? He wasn't sure she stood a fighting chance against Daniel.

"Fuck all," Connor said.

"What?" Travis glanced at the other man.

"The tracker still shows her at the house, as of five minutes ago. Ask him to look around, really check. Is she in a bathroom? Sleeping somewhere? Anything?"

"Is there anywhere else she could be?" Travis asked.

"No, we've checked every closet, room, and vehicle on the premises. Besides, they have video of her driving out the front gate ten minutes ago." Grayson's calm tone was breaking. He'd lost not only his wife, but maybe his sister-in-law as well.

"Then the tracker should have just pinged her..."

"Shit. It must be here somewhere. Damn it, Bliss."

"We have another vehicle," Connor announced. He gassed the truck and sent it barreling around the turn.

"Grayson, I'll call you when I know more." Travis hung up and gripped the side of the door. Connor could drive like a bat out of hell all he wanted, so long as it got them a little closer to Bliss.

"When did she get a bloody damn phone?" Connor said as he took a turn at a high speed.

"Last night. Grayson had Priscilla go buy her a new one."

"And no one mentioned it? God damn it." Connor slammed his hand against the steering wheel. His phone began ringing, vibrating in the cup holder. He grabbed it and shoved it at Travis. "Put her on speaker."

Travis jabbed the screen.

"Connor, are you there?" A woman's calm voice filled the cab.

"Yeah, me and Travis are here, Lali."

"I tracked the last phone call made to Bliss' phone. It's from a pre-paid cell phone—"

"Shit," Connor mumbled.

"—and that phone is still on."

"What?" Connor and Travis said at once.

"Assuming this is our guy, I'm triangulating his location now. I have Gavin cross-referencing the area with our parameters for Daniel's secondary location."

"He could have dropped the phone to get us off his tail," Connor said.

"What if he wanted to make sure Bliss had a way of contacting him?" Travis had to hope. This couldn't be how things ended.

"He could have told her to dump the phone."

Lali's voice broke through their battle of what-ifs. "Address, I just sent it to your phone and I'm updating the rest of the team."

"Thanks, Lali."

"Go save those girls."

The line went dead.

"Where am I going?" Connor asked.

Travis brought up the map.

They had a long way to go, and Bliss had one hell of a start on them. When he got his hands on her... The only thing he could think of was never being separated from her again.

He was going to marry her.

9.

B LISS CLUTCHED THE WHEEL and stared up at the large, metal building.

She was late.

Almost ten minutes late.

She'd run red lights and broken every speed limit posted, but she was still late.

Was Carlos still alive? What about her sister? Were they gone?

She pulled the gun and bullets out of her hoodie pouch. One went in the other, right? She slid the row of bullets into the gun until it clicked. Now, she just had to hope it was as simple as removing the safety and firing. Otherwise she was shit out of luck. She really should have taken Travis up on that gun lesson he talked about. If she survived this, she was learning how to shoot.

Bliss pushed her door open and stood. The bitter breeze bit into her limbs, leeching the warmth away.

It was the mountains and snow all over again.

She slid the gun into the waistband of her jeans like she'd seen Travis do. It felt weird and unnatural pressed against her spine, but at least this way her hoodie wasn't hanging down to her knees from the weight of it. She slid the Taser out of her pocket and gripped it in the safety of her pouch.

The street was empty, probably due to the holidays. She almost wished someone would happen along to stop her. This plan was crazy. There was no way it would work, but she had to do something.

Daniel hadn't given her instructions for how or where to enter the warehouse, just—the blue and white one. She reached a door with a faded red Exit sign stenciled on it and tried the handle.

It didn't budge.

"Shit," she mumbled.

Glancing up and down the street, all she saw were the big, rolling doors she couldn't possibly get through. She took a chance and jogged to her left, around the corner.

Double doors. One, jostled by the breeze, swung a few inches.

Scratch the crime show setting. This was a horror movie, and she was the stupid chick in high heels going out the front door.

At least she had a Taser, some mace, and a gun.

Bliss took a deep breath and reached for the door.

Wendy could already be gone. Carlos could be dead. But she had to see for herself.

She stood at the door, peering into darkness so thick even the daylight only penetrated a foot or two. Listening did her no good. The ambient sounds blocked out anything helpful, like cries for help from her sister.

Did she call out hello? That seemed like asking to be murdered.

She stepped into the darkness and ducked to her right, squinting and praying her eyesight adjusted.

There. That sound. Was that a foot step? It was hard to tell with the way things echoed inside the building. She was starting to make out shapes and lighter bits of darkness, but no Wendy. No Carlos. And no Daniel.

She clutched the Taser and edged forward.

A flashlight would have been super useful. But why should she have expected to need that in the middle of the day?

Tall shelves lined her path from the door into the cavernous space. It was cold, and the occasional breeze still caught her off-guard.

Shit. The place was big. If she had any hope of meeting up with Daniel after being late, she was going to have to do it.

"Hello?" she called out. "Wendy? Carlos? Are you there?"

Bliss turned in a circle, gripping the Taser so tight it hurt her knuckles.

That.

That scraping sound was not because of the wind.

"Bliss, run!"

Wendy.

Bliss whirled toward the voice, somewhere to her right. There was just enough light filtering in through opaque panels to make out the form of a man. A very large man.

He shook a body—Wendy—like a ragdoll and then dropped her. Wendy scuttled backward on her bottom until she ran up against the metal shelves.

There was no sign of the boy. Was Carlos dead? Was she too late?

Her body reacted without her consent. Palms went sweaty and cold, her stomach tied in knots, and her limbs ached with the memory of snow and ice. For a moment, she almost swore she felt the drip of warm liquid on her face. She couldn't breathe, and her heart pounded in her throat.

Daniel took two steps toward her.

Panic set in. She could run. Flee now. It's what her instincts said to do. This was her in way over her head.

She'd made a huge mistake.

"Stop!" Bliss yelled. She forced herself to let go of the Taser and hold her hands out.

"You're late."

"You know how far this is. You knew I'd never make it in time."

"Not my problem."

"Where is Carlos?"

"I killed him."

"Then we have no deal." She took a step back. What were the chances she could run faster than him? Daniel still had that leg wound, he wasn't a spring chicken, but it wasn't like Bliss was used to doing a fifty yard dash.

"Brat's alive." He took another step toward her.

"Stop right there. You agreed if I came, you would let Carlos go." She kicked her right leg back. Hopefully the Taser bulge wasn't obvious.

"I'll let him go after we cross the state line."

When they were all under his control.

"That's not what we agreed on." It was hard to hear over the pounding of her heart and the clang of metal.

"That's what's going to happen." Daniel pulled out a gun and pointed it at Wendy. "Now, get over here or I shoot her and kill the kid."

Oh, God, she'd made a mistake. A really big mistake...

TRAVIS UNCLIPPED HIS SEAT belt and leaned forward, gun in hand.

The cell phone signal was close. They had it narrowed to a four block radius. Now, to find Bliss before something else bad happened to her. If Daniel hurt her, if she died, Travis would never be able to forgive himself. Her blood would be on his hands, because he hadn't protected her.

Connor's phone rang and once more he shoved it at Travis.

"It's Lali. Answer it."

He flipped the phone to speaker and held it between them.

"What'cha got?" Connor eased them around a turn. The shopping strip was busy with post-holiday traffic. Anyone could blend in here.

"An address. Gavin—I don't want to know what he did—but he got the texts off Bliss' phone." There was furious typing in the background, a lot like what it sounded when Travis had Gavin on the line.

"What is it?" Travis glanced at the street signs.

Lali rattled off the address.

Travis brought it up on his phone and his vision hazed red.

"That's ten miles from here," he said.

"I know. I'm alerting the rest of the team, Gavin is communicating to local law enforcement. There's more."

"Hit me." Connor whipped the SUV around and gassed it, on the fastest path to the blinking red dot.

"Daniel sent a message to her that said if she wasn't there in thirty minutes the kid would die. That was forty-five minutes ago."

"They could already be gone," Travis said.

"Bliss would be hard pressed to get there in under thirty minutes." Even Lali's soothing voice broke with tension.

"And it takes time to sneak out of a house full of people there to protect you. She's late to that meet." Connor grinned and swerved around slower moving traffic, lights on.

"How long until the closest patrol gets there?" Travis had to hope there was someone closer, someone nearer than they were.

"Uh, hold on, chatting Gavin..." The keys clacked and clicked. "Best guess? Eight minutes. That address is in the middle of a bunch of warehouses. Since the recession a lot of them have become vacant, transients have moved in, and the rest appear to be on hiatus until after the holidays."

"Suppose that's where he picked up his victims?" Connor asked.

"You're the profiler," Lali replied.

"What about finding his evil guy lair?"

Lali sighed into the receiver.

"Talk to me, Lali."

"Gavin has dozens of pings off the cell number registered to Daniel in that area. I'm cross-referencing utility costs, wireless capability, but it's not a fast process. This isn't TV. It's going to take a while."

"It's safe to say his secondary base of operations is in the area though?" Travis asked.

"Yes. Connor, Ryan is beeping me. Hold on."

"Tell Ryan to fuck off." Connor spoke too late. Lali was gone.

It was strange being the outsider on this operation. He was so accustomed to working with his SEAL brothers that riding along with the feds was a unique experience of being on the outside again.

He never much cared for being on the outside. Too bad his federal record meant jobs like this were out of the question for a guy like him. He'd stick to what he was good at, tracking down the bad guys and protecting people, and leave the serial killers to the professionals.

"How close are we?" Connor asked.

"Take a left up here. Five minutes."

"The cops should be there any minute. She's going to be fine, Travis."

Travis didn't respond. Connor didn't know if Bliss was alive or not, he was simply trying to give him hope. It's what Travis would do if their situations were exchanged. He'd say whatever it took to keep the client calm. The less hysterical or upset they were, the easier they were to manage. No one wanted a screaming customer, unless it was in bed, and then the only screaming that should happen was in pleasure. Not that he ever intended to bed a customer again.

"Shit!" Travis braced his hand on the dash and grabbed the door to keep from being hurled across the SUV.

"Sorry, man, didn't see him."

"Slow the fuck down."

"Buckle up."

"Are you trying to kill us?"

"You Americans drive too slow."

"Another left, there."

They made two more turns and it was as if they entered an urban desert. No cars. No pedestrians. It was barren and desolate. Trash and refuse lay piled up in the gutters. The buildings were worn. Most had seen better days. A few company logos were painted or bolted to the structures, but few were recognizable.

A police cruiser turned, heading toward them, flashing their red and whites at the SUV. Connor waved at the cops and kept going.

"Right," Travis said.

Connor turned, and they rolled slowly down the street to the next intersection.

"There. That's Bliss' car." Travis pointed to their right.

Another cruiser eased to a stop behind the car, followed by another SUV. In moments the place would be swarming with uniforms and guns.

"You'll have to stay here," Connor said.

"The fuck I am."

"Listen, I know she's your girl and everything, but facts are you are not a law enforcement officer. You don't have a vest. Right now, you are a liability to her. Stay here. Let us do our job and bring her back safe. Cool?"

Travis ground his teeth together.

"Fine," he said.

"Good man."

Connor left the SUV running and got out, dragging his heavy Kevlar vest with him.

Travis waited for the feds to cluster before slipping out of the truck.

If Connor was stupid enough to think he was staying put, Connor clearly had something coming to him.

The police officers on scene paid him no mind. At this point, they might suspect him of being with the feds. All he needed was the badge and vest. He pulled out his phone and paused close enough to the cruiser he could listen to the radio. Ryan was on the horn, directing officers to spread out around a particularly beat-up warehouse. If Daniel was still around, he had to have a getaway car somewhere.

Travis prayed the feds were right. That Bliss might still be here.

He shoved his hands in his pockets and waited. Watching. They didn't have long.

The buildings all had slanted roofs. Bad for snipers or making a getaway. They knew Daniel had at least one leg wound, and his lingering handicaps from the accident years prior meant he probably didn't move fast. Which was why he had to be smart. Daniel might have the physical strength to snap someone's neck, but the rest of him wasn't as mobile.

Travis strode the width of the building, putting the cops and feds to his back.

If Daniel was as smart as the feds thought he was, he'd probably know Bliss' directions would lead her to that spot and that entrance. But where would Daniel park, and where would he enter the building?

What would he do in Daniel's place? Wasn't that how Connor puzzled out the killer's actions?

Travis would go for something up high. A vantage point to watch for the arrival and entrance, and then he'd sneak up behind his target and take them out. But Daniel likely couldn't do stairs.

The cameras.

That would make sense.

Travis craned his neck and looked up.

If Daniel's hideout was here, then the chances of the area being covered with cameras was high. He could be watching them now on a mobile device. A camera would also eliminate the need for a vantage point because he could watch her from a blind.

He jogged down the side of the building. A passing cruiser hailed him with a wave, and drove on past.

Sixty feet down he found a door. An unlocked door.

10.

ET OVER HERE NOW," Daniel said again.

Bliss' body shook. She had to take that step, but it was the snow and the motorhome all over again. Pure terror. She'd never known such fear. The kind that paralyzed her body and set her mind on a mental loop of those horrible hours she'd spent terrified for her life.

Daniel took a step toward Wendy. She cried out and covered her head with her hands, but he reached past her into the shadows. Daniel dragged a small, kicking form out into the open and backhanded the boy.

"No!" Bliss took a step.

"Carlos!" Wendy reached for the child, but Daniel lifted the kid by his shirt until his toes barely touched the ground.

Think.

She had to be smart.

Fear could not win. Not now.

"I'll go with you, just leave him alone," she said.

Whatever he wanted to hear, she had to say it. She needed him to lower the gun enough so she could stun him. Then she had to hope her sister and Carlos could run.

"It's your fault I had to do that anyway." Daniel shoved a whimpering Carlos away from Wendy. Her sobs were muffled, her figure shuddering.

"I'm sorry, okay?" Bliss took another step toward them.

Her eyes were adjusted better now. Bits of light filtered in here and there, making it easier to see her surroundings, gauge where the rows were.

"Get over here." Daniel pulled a long, flexible zip-tie from his pocket.

He'd used one to bind her wrists until he could get the handcuffs on her. It was a vague, almost-memory stuck in the back of her head. She'd been drugged, passing in and out of consciousness for a bit. A passenger in her own body while he kidnapped her.

Not this time.

She took two more slow steps.

Metal on metal screeched, echoing inside the warehouse.

She glanced to her right, toward the noise.

Were those voices?

Was someone else in the warehouse?

"Bliss, look out!" Wendy yelled.

Bliss brought her arms up, one hand clenching the Taser. Daniel lunged at her, his hands grasping her body. She shoved at his shoulder and stumbled backward. Her thumb slid off the button and she nearly dropped the Taser, but she squeezed it for dear life. If she lost her hold on it, she didn't think she'd be able to get out the mace or figure out the gun.

Sparks of light lit up, crackling. For a second she could see Daniel's face, slack in shock.

She jammed the Taser at the only exposed flesh she could see.

His neck.

Bliss stepped toward him and gritted her teeth as the electrical charge leapt from his body to hers. Her muscles tensed, and she could feel the current deep in her bones. Daniel's mouth moved, but she couldn't hear his words.

Finally he released his hold on her and stumbled back, bent over.

"Bliss." Wendy gripped her by her shoulders, dragging her away from Daniel.

"Fuck," he roared.

"Over there," someone yelled from across the warehouse.

"I'm going to kill you." Daniel's voice and breathing was horse, heavy, and hard to place as human.

"Run," Bliss said. She shoved at Wendy and they each hooked an arm under Carlos' shoulders, jogging and limping away from Daniel.

"Are those the cops?" Wendy asked, her voice low.

"Wifey, get back here." Daniel's voice was damaged, rasping and breathy in a way Bliss didn't think could be fixed.

"This way." Bliss dragged them down an aisle then ducked under the lowest shelf, crawling over boxes.

Daniel's steps were heavy, thudding sounds right behind them. He tracked their movements through the shelves, while the other voices sounded as if they were getting farther away.

Bliss pushed Wendy and Carlos back the way they'd come, up a dozen or so paces then into the six foot wide shelf space. If they had any luck, Daniel would keep going for a row or two before doubling back to find them.

"Here, hide, hide, hide." Wendy pulled Bliss down between stacks of—whatever they were hiding in.

"We should keep going," Carlos' voice rose.

"Shh." Bliss slapped her hand over both their mouths and held completely still.

Doors banged and every so often she could see a slash of light.

Help was there—but Daniel was closer. And he had a gun.

Gun.

Bliss felt at her back. The gun. This was what she brought it for, right?

A scuff and scrape a few feet away froze her in place.

She hunched lower, but caught a glimpse of two legs.

What were the chances Daniel would leave without them? If they could hold on, hide just long enough to be found, they'd be safe. Right?

Daniel plodded past them then paused.

Was he listening for them? Or for the cops?

Bliss held her breath. Travis was out there, looking for her. And she was going to live, damn it.

Daniel turned and limped back the way he'd come, down the row and out of her direct line of sight. The boxes were piled too high for her to tell if he was gone.

"Go." Wendy pushed her, glancing pointedly toward the sounds of people.

"No." Bliss shook her head. They didn't know that Daniel wasn't waiting for them. He'd gone to all of this effort to get them, now was he going to let them go this easily?

"I'm going." Wendy wiggled past.

Bliss grabbed her elbow and jerked back.

If anyone was going to stick their neck out first, it was her.

She slithered past the boxes, scraping her back against the shelves. She squeezed through the space between two pallets, caught her foot on the wood and rolled into the aisle, sprawling on her back.

A footstep near her head froze her in place.

She stared up at the barrel of a gun, and behind it—Daniel.

Bliss didn't think. She couldn't. She lifted the gun she'd stolen from Travis and squeezed the trigger.

Click.

Nothing.

Daniel grinned.

"No," Wendy wailed.

"Fuck—"

Bam.

Bam.

Bliss cringed and waited for the pain.

Wheezing.

Her eyes snapped open.

Daniel stared down at his chest. It was too dark to see more than a glistening, spreading spot.

He pitched forward, landing heavily on his knees. His gun clattered to the floor.

She heaved, and focused on the figure behind Daniel.

The one in a black leather jacket and jeans.

Travis.

He didn't look at her. Instead, he closed the distance in a smooth, silent stride and kicked the gun farther away.

Voices yelling and the drum of footsteps were all around them.

"Here," Travis called out.

He went to a knee, gun still aimed at Daniel, and felt his neck.

"Travis? God damn it." She knew that voice. That was Connor.

Bliss pushed up, squinting at the lights. A dozen or more people clustered around them.

"Is he dead?" someone asked.

"He's gone." Travis slid his gun into his waistband and then looked at her.

She'd have known the weight of his gaze if she were blind.

"Where's Wendy? Bliss?" Connor knelt next to her.

"Here." Wendy climbed over and through the shelved stuff, bumping into Bliss.

Hands wrapped around Bliss shoulders and hauled to her feet. Her legs were rubber, and she wasn't quite sure which way was up or down.

"Is he really dead?" She kept staring over her shoulder, down at the body.

Travis' hands clutched her closer.

"He'd better be dead," he said for her ears alone.

She rested her cheek against his shoulder.

Daniel was dead. Did that mean the nightmare was over? Were they free?

"I THINK THE POOR bastards just want to sweep this under the rug."

Travis nodded at Connor, but he never looked away from the ambulance. The EMTs were going over Carlos while Wendy and Bliss hovered around the kid.

"You listening to me?" Connor waved his hand in front of Travis' face.

"I'm lucky they aren't arresting me."

"Damn straight."

"I was doing what I had to do to protect my client."

"We both know you don't have a contract on Bliss."

"No, but I will have one post-dated by the end of the day." Travis tore his gaze away from Bliss to stare at Connor. "Considering the circumstances, there wasn't time to draft a contract, sign it, and have it notarized."

"I'm not arguing with you. If you hadn't been there they might all be dead. Good work, mate. Go see your girl." Connor slapped Travis on his shoulder and thumbed toward Bliss.

He didn't need an invitation.

Nearly an hour going over the details with the cops while they sorted it all out, and he was ready to knock a few heads together. Christ, this was why he worked for Aegis, so they could handle the tedious bits.

Bliss glanced up, the haunted look back in her eyes. He'd made sure to never be out of sight, but it wasn't good enough. He needed to feel her. Hold her. Shake some god-damned sense into her.

She took a couple steps toward him and stopped. He closed the distance until he was so close her hair swept across his jacket.

"You good to go home?" he asked.

"Yeah, they said someone's going to take us back to Wendy's."

"Connor, probably. Come on." He turned and placed his hand at the small of her back, propelling her forward. She had that brittle, about-to-cry look. Chances were, she wouldn't let it out until her sister wasn't there. "Wendy all right?"

"I guess. She's either crying about Priscilla or...just crying."

He opened the backseat of the SUV, held the door open for her, and then climbed in after her.

"What's going—"

He wrapped his arms around her and dragged Bliss into his lap. Besides the few minutes just after shooting Daniel, he hadn't touched or spoken to her. He squeezed her to his chest and buried his face in her hair.

Bliss was alive.

The icy grip on his heart relaxed.

And Daniel was really dead. It wouldn't chase the nightmares away, but at least she wasn't in danger.

"What the hell were you thinking, taking that gun?"

"I thought—I don't know what I thought. It wasn't good, anyway."

He blew out a breath and closed his eyes.

"Next week I'm taking you to the gun range and you're learning how to load a damn gun. Fuck. Bliss, you could have died."

"I know."

She unzipped his jacket and wiggled her hands in under the leather. For several long moments they sat like that, no words, just the communion of their souls. He knew her darkness, the things that haunted her thoughts and dreams. He also knew she could overcome them in time. And he intended to be right there with her through all of it.

"Cops said you fried his brains." He chuckled, recalling the baffled expression on the officer's faces.

"Did they find the Taser?"

"Yeah, but it's in evidence. I'd just as soon get you a new one."

"I'd like that."

"Promise not to use it on me?"

"Don't piss me off."

She peeked up at him and smiled.

God, she did things to him. Scary, big things that fucked with his head and screwed his emotions up into a tight, hot ball of need.

"Why didn't you call me?" he asked.

"I didn't have your number in my new phone."

"If you ever do something like that again..." He shook his head. The simmering anger made it hard to form words. He wasn't pissed at her, though hell yes, she should have called him. He was pissed at Daniel. At the cops for not watching her. At himself for going out, thinking he could help, when his duty was to protect Bliss.

"I won't. I'm going to memorize your phone number. I swear."

"The others are coming." He patted her thigh.

Bliss groaned and slid to the middle of the seat.

"I don't want to go back to Wendy's. Mom, Dad, and everyone else are just going to make a big deal out of this, and I just want to...not."

"I know." He reached for her hand and wrapped his fingers around it. "We aren't done, yet."

"No, we aren't."

They squeezed together as everyone piled into the SUV. Wendy immediately buried her face on Bliss' shoulder, crying and leaning heavily on her older sister.

He'd never had that with Emma. He didn't know what it was like to have family lean on him. His had been glad to see him go.

There was no question he wanted Bliss, from now until forever, but what did that life look like? Any other man would have options. In order to provide for Bliss, he had to stay his course. Keep putting himself in danger. And hope she understood. They'd have weekends here and there, a couple of weeks sometimes. Was it enough? Once the dust settled, would she want to be with him?

11.

BLISS WAS READY TO hurl her fancy wine glass full of punch in Wendy's neighbor's face.

The entire neighborhood was crammed into the house. At some point between being rescued and their convoy arriving home, Mom had begun cooking all the Christmas food they hadn't consumed during her abduction. There was easily enough to feed everyone and then some.

And where the hell was Travis?

She made another noncommittal sound to whatever the neighbor was saying and glanced around for the shadow-shaped man sticking to the edge of the room. It hadn't taken more than a minute to realize how uncomfortable the large gathering made him. Travis had an amazing ability to belong in any high-stakes situation, but stick him in a social group, and he was immediately lost.

There he was. Chatting with Jade in the corner with the curtains about to swallow them up. They both looked ready to bolt. She chuckled and sipped her drink.

Travis caught her eye. She lifted her eyebrows and canted her head toward the crazy, racist neighbor. Some people just made her sick.

A little help here?

"Bliss, there you are." Wendy grabbed her arm.

Oh, fun, more family drama!

Bliss groaned and let her sister haul her out of the living room, past the kitchen, and into the pantry. The red liquid sloshed over the rim and onto her hand.

"What the hell, Wendy?" She set the glass she didn't want onto a shelf and daubed the back of her hand on her jeans. At this point, there was no telling what was on them. When this day was over, they were going in the garbage. She was weary of all the people, the activity.

"Sorry, I just—CPS wants to take Carlos. They're backed up because of the holidays and asked if he could stay here a few days until they get it sorted." Wendy paced up and down the short room. Every few steps, she reached out and straightened a can or turned a box.

"Okay. He has family, doesn't he?"

"In Mexico. Priscilla's parents were illegal immigrants who got deported a couple years ago. That's why she's been on her own. She was born here, and so was Carlos."

"Wow, that's rough." Bliss blew out a breath. Daniel's actions impacted so many people. So much death and loss and sadness.

"I want to adopt him." Wendy whirled to face her, spine straight, head held high.

"Really? Wow, I mean, are you sure?"

"Yes. I've known him most of his life. He doesn't even remember his grandparents. If we do, he could get the kind of life Priscilla always wanted for him. And of course I'd want him to know his real family. We could go visit them, or something, but he'd have a better chance if he stayed with us. Wouldn't he? Or is that arrogant? I want to do what's best for him, but I also feel responsible for what happened to his mother. I mean, can I fix this? Is it a good idea?"

"Well, have you talked to him about it?"

"No. He's upset."

"Where is he?"

"Upstairs, sleeping."

"Have you talked to Grayson about it?"

"Not yet." Wendy wrung her hands. "I was kind of hoping to pitch the idea to you, first."

"I think it's a good idea, but his family has to be included on a decision like this, I think. They are his family. But, you're right. He has known you more and longer than his own family. So yeah, I think you should consider it."

"Yeah?" Wendy smiled, and it was both happy and sad.

"Do you want me to hold your hand while you talk to Grayson?" She offered up her right hand.

"Stop it." Wendy slapped her. "No, I just—is it a good idea?"

"Maybe? If it's what Carlos wants and if Grayson is okay with it, yeah. But he's not a puppy. You can't adopt just because it makes you feel good."

"I know. I love that little boy."

Bliss took a deep breath. They were going to be okay. The nightmares weren't going to go away, Wendy's depression wasn't cured, but they could take the awful things that had happened and make a new future.

"I just keep thinking...I wanted babies. Lots of them. But after Paul, I just don't think I can go through that again. Just getting pregnant was hard enough. What if this is how we do it? We adopt?"

"That's great, Wendy. You have a lot of love to give to kids. But...can I suggest waiting a bit before jumping on the adoption train? You've been through a lot this week, and I know you're feeling better, but what if tomorrow is a bad one?"

"No, no, you're right. I want to focus on Carlos first, then in a year or more, we can see about adding to it."

"Good."

"Paperwork will probably take ages."

"Right. But, you need to take things slowly. For Carlos. For you."

"I know I'm not magically better, but I do feel more alive than I have in...months. You are right. I'll probably still have some bad days, but I want to get better."

"Have you considered therapy again?" Bliss had bullied her sister into going a handful of times, but the therapist couldn't work with a mute patient.

"Yeah, and I think this time it'll be good. I just couldn't figure out how to put things into words before. Now I have a lot to talk about." Wendy sighed and faced Bliss. "I don't know if I've ever said this, but thank you. Thank you for being there for me, and propping me up and everything. I can't imagine what it's been like for you."

"That's what sisters are for." Bliss grasped Wendy's hand and pulled her in for a hug.

"I'm just trying to say," Wendy's voice trembled, "thank you, and whatever you have it in your head to do, do it. Please? For you. I'm going to be okay."

Bliss leaned back and screwed up her face.

"What do you think I'm going to do?" she asked.

"Something. You always had the more interesting life."

"You mean Travis?" Just saying his name set the butterflies going in her stomach.

"Yeah. You like him."

"I do."

"Grayson doesn't like him."

"Do I want to know why?" Just the little Travis had said about Grayson's career left big questions in her head.

"Some other time." Wendy waved her hand. "So, what is it you're going to do?"

"I...don't know yet. I like him." Love, was more accurate, but she knew that would sound crazy to anyone else. They loved each other, and she wasn't going to let that go.

"He likes you, too."

"How do you know?"

"He rescued you."

"He rescued us."

"Carlos and I were a bonus. He went in there for you. That's how I knew Grayson was the one. I was at that party you told me not to go to, got drunk, and there he was." Wendy shook her head.

"What? You mean you didn't meet Grayson in the library like you told Mom and Dad?" Bliss mock gasped. Oh man, did she remember the stories from that night.

"The last thing they want to hear is how I puked my guts up and he held my hair."

They laughed, a myriad of memories brightening up the otherwise bittersweet day.

"You were so in love with him. I mean, from day one, it was there." Bliss shook her head.

"Which is why I can say, with confidence, don't let this one go. If you don't love him already, you're going to." Wendy crossed her arms, eyes twinkling. "Do you want to slip out? Head home?"

"God, yes. I'm exhausted, and all these people..." She shuddered.

"I don't blame you, but this is my house so I can't run away. I'll go get Travis. Someone drove your car back here, didn't they?"

"Yeah, Jade did. I have the keys." She patted her pocket.

"I'll send Travis out with your coat."

Wendy opened the pantry door and left. Bliss wrapped her arms around herself and stared at the floor.

They were going to be okay. Wendy, Carlos, and her. They were going to make it. Now, she just had to convince a brooding, sexy man to spend extra time with her.

"JADE. TRAVIS."

Travis glanced up from his phone. Ryan jerked his head. The tense set of his lips, the one clenched fist...they didn't bode well. What other bad news could they get? Did Daniel Campbell have a sick, twisted twin brother? Or a partner they didn't know about?

Both Jade and Travis followed Ryan through the throng of people into the office. It was still decked out with all their information from trying to catch Daniel. Now, would they be after another ghost?

Dmitri closed the door behind them and leaned against the wall.

"What is it?" Jade asked.

"Lali has made her initial pass through Daniel's files," Ryan said.

"And?"

"We know he was in contact with the person called Black Widow. The same one we think TBKiller was taking orders from."

Travis' stomach dropped. It was the connection he'd been asked to look into. To see if these murders matched up with other copy cats, if the feds had a case to add to the potential list of Killer Club members.

"There appears to have been some correspondence. Lali sent it over." Ryan turned his tablet around to display a page of text.

"What's it say?" Travis asked. If there was another danger to Bliss or his sister Emma, he needed to know. The reach of a couple of psychopaths wouldn't be that great. He could get them out of the country, set them up somewhere safe. Thailand had always been his first option for laying low. Take them deep enough, and no one would find them. No one but him.

"Essentially Daniel petitioned for membership over six years ago, but the emails go back further. Around the time the first blonde woman disappeared. He claims to have been inspired by a sixteenth-century German serial killer who would kill people traveling deep in the forests and hide their bodies in caves."

"Christman Genipperteinga?" Jade reached for the tablet. "That doesn't quite fit."

"Who?" Travis glanced between the two.

"He murdered almost a thousand people. Got away with it because he lived so far out. In caves. He killed mostly robbers and highwaymen, which is why it took so long for people to stop him. Who cares about the person killing the bad guys? He wasn't caught until he let his sex slave-wife visit her family, and she had a nervous breakdown and outed him to the mayor."

"Sex slave?" Connor parroted back, his face screwed up on one side.

"It's the connection." Ryan gestured to the board. "Daniel Campbell was trying to be a better Christman. He killed the women so they wouldn't betray him. His god complex morphed that into creating a better race through their children."

"Not to be rude, but what does this have to do with Bliss or Emma? Are they in any danger?"

"No." Ryan crossed his arms. "In the last email with Black Widow, she told him she doesn't allow sex crimes into the club. Any raping or genital mutilation is expressly forbidden. She goes on to say that they also do not allow child crimes, either."

"That eliminates roughly half our potential pool of cases." Jade handed the tablet back. "It's smart though. Sex crimes and children get the most media attention. If she wants to keep this club secret, best to stay away from the kinds of crimes that get the most press."

"That can't work." Travis couldn't wrap his head around the idea.

"It has." Connor pointed at the tablet. "If that email is to be believed, they've been operating for seven or more years. And we're just now finding out about them."

"And you're sure we aren't in danger?" Travis asked again. He didn't give a flying fuck about what kind of crazy puffs Daniel ate, only that the two people who mattered in his life were safe. It was a callous mindset, but they could never stop all the sickos out there from killing innocents.

Ryan shook his head. "He operated alone. Plus, retaliation murders would draw attention, and everything in Black Widow's messages conveys the need for secrecy."

"Anything else?" Travis asked.

"Unfortunately, no."

"But it's more than we had. Before we didn't know the identities of the club members. Now, we know who they answer to."

"It's interesting she chose the moniker Black Widow." Jade tapped her chin.

"That is a problem for another day. I'm ready for some of that turkey and some sleep." Connor pushed up out of one of the office chairs and stretched.

"When we get back and get this sorted, I'd like to discuss a more permanent arrangement. Your help has been invaluable." Ryan extended his hand to Travis.

Yeah right, like the FBI was going to make an exception for a felon. More likely it would be under the table work. The kind that kept him on the fringes. Still, it would be better than nothing.

"You know where to find me." Travis shook Ryan's hand. "Flying out tonight?"

"The morning. We could all use some sleep."

He was running on fumes himself.

"Travis?" Wendy leaned into the office. If possible, she looked better and more alive than she had since he'd met her. Crazy to think that kidnapping had worked some good in her life.

"Excuse me." Travis stepped out of the office, closing the door behind him. "What's wrong? Where's Bliss?"

"Nothing's wrong. I'm just helping my sister get out of here." Wendy handed him Bliss' jacket. "She'll head out in a few minutes, then you guys can go do whatever."

"What about you?"

"I'm fine. This," she gestured to the people milling around in the living room, "is what I've been missing. Bliss? She's exhausted and over-peopled. Do me a favor and get her out of here, please?"

She didn't have to ask him twice.

He took the jacket, said a few goodbyes to the feds, and jogged out to Bliss' little car. Their stuff was already in the back, so it wasn't like he was leaving anything here.

A few moments later Bliss slipped out the front door, quick-stepped to the passenger side of the hatchback, and dropped in. She leaned her head against the seat and closed her eyes, blowing out a deep breath.

"Drive. Don't talk. Just drive," she said.

He chuckled. He could understand the desire for silence, especially after being in the house that felt too full.

The path to her apartment was still burned into his skull. He would never forget these turns. It was as if he'd always been here.

"Wendy wants to adopt Carlos," she said after a while.

"Oh?"

"Yeah. Thanks for skipping out with me."

He reached over and covered her hand with his, squeezing it tight. How did he convey to her what she meant to him? How important she was?

Travis had never loved before. Bliss deserved for him to not fuck this up, but that was a lot to ask of a man with a history of screwing up.

12.

BLISS SMILED AND SQUEEZED Travis' hand.

Man of few words.

He made her heart beat too fast, her head want things she hadn't realized she wanted, and her body, well, she'd never had a man set her insides on fire like Travis did. She loved him. And he'd told her he loved her. It was a curious place to be, confident and nervous all at once. Things between them were still new, and yet the more time she was around him, the more it felt as though he'd always been there. A silent, ever-present shadow watching over her.

They spent the rest of the drive to her apartment in silence. It was nice to be free of the expectation to smile and say thank you to all the well wishes for living through the holiday nightmare. She could just—be. Travis didn't need her to put on an act. He'd see through that anyway.

"We're here." Travis killed the engine.

She stretched and pushed her door open.

"Is it safe?" She stood and blinked at her apartment.

"Yeah. Cops went over it twice."

Bliss followed Travis up the walk and leaned against his back, soaking up his warmth, while he unlocked her door. Reality would hit soon, and then she'd need to sort out work, bills, and what they were going to do to make this relationship work, but for tonight she wanted to simply be with him. Like normal people. Granted, after what Daniel had done, she'd never be normal again.

He held the door for her, their bags slung over his shoulders.

She entered her apartment and paused. Things were out of place. Only a little. But she could tell people had been here. That her home had been invaded by strangers with both good and bad intent. She wrapped her arms around her and peered around.

"The cameras are all gone."

"You said that. It's just…I didn't really think about it until now."

"You want to go somewhere else? A hotel?"

"No, that's silly. I pay rent here. I live here. I'm going to have to get over it." She pushed her shoulders back and strode into the living room. This was her space. She'd have to work it out for as long as she lived here.

Travis took their bags into the bedroom. She liked his easy assumption that was where his stuff went. As if he'd accepted this thing between them wasn't optional.

She stood behind her sofa and turned in a circle, taking in the living room on one side and the kitchen-dining room on the other.

Daniel had been here. But now he was dead. She wouldn't ever be able to erase what he'd done to her from her mind, but it didn't have to rule her.

"Come here."

She turned, and there was Travis. He wrapped his arms around her, tugging her jacket off, until he had her squeezed tight. She sighed, letting go of the tension and stress. Everything would be okay, somehow, some way.

"I missed you," she mumbled into his shirt. From the moment they arrived back at Wendy's house, he'd been a wall-hugging shadow.

"I'm not going anywhere."

"Good." She tipped her head back and looked up at him.

Travis was a rough-and-tumble man. She'd never seen herself falling for anything but the nice guy, but here they were, and she wouldn't change it for the world. He wasn't what she expected, he totally screwed up her five-year plan, but maybe that's what she needed. The kind of shove out the door to do something new — and totally for herself.

He pushed his hand into her hair, cupping the back of her head. She stared at his mouth, hungry for something besides her mother's cooking.

"You never do something like what you did today ever again." His voice was hard and probably scary, but his mouth was downright fascinating to watch.

"Okay." She slid her hands up his chest.

"I'm serious, Bliss."

"Me too."

"You could have been hurt."

"I know. It was stupid. I realized that pretty early on."

"Then why didn't you get help?"

"It was too late. I didn't have a phone. And if I wasn't there on time, he'd kill Carlos. I'd already watched his mother die. I couldn't let him die if I could save him."

Travis made a frustrated growling noise deep in his throat. It rumbled in his chest and tickled her breasts where they were mashed up against him.

"I know you're angry with me, but you know you'd do the same thing."

"That's different."

"How is it different? Is it because you think you're disposable while I'm not?" Stupid, infuriating man. She jabbed her finger at his chest. "That's not how this works. I can't just replace you. You said you loved me, and that means you are just as important as me."

"It is not the same thing. I'm trained to handle these situations. You can't even load a gun properly."

"Because you haven't taught me."

"Yet."

"I'm serious, Bliss."

"And so am I. You'd have done the same thing I did. Don't act like you wouldn't."

"It's still different. You could have been killed."

"I wasn't. You were there."

And he had been. Even in those dark, awful moments in the snow, he Came through for her. He was there at every turn and bump in the road. She knew he didn't see himself as worthy, that he had plenty of baggage, but she also saw the heart of him. Despite the mistreatment from his parents, the bad decisions, and everything else, his heart was good. It took a strong person to experience those things and come out the other side putting others first.

He lowered his forehead to hers. His eyelashes tickled her brow, and their noses bumped.

"What if I hadn't been there? What then? What if I'd lost you?"

"You didn't. I'm right here."

She pushed up on tiptoes and pressed her mouth to his. At first he didn't move. She slid her hands over his shoulders and pulled him down more. He tilted his head the barest fraction, and his lips went soft.

Yes!

Travis' hands grasped her ass and lifted. She yelped, but he swallowed the sound, deepening the kiss, and carried her to the wall, pinning her there with his hips. Her head swam, and she wrapped her legs around him. She'd never had a guy even think about doing that to her. Hell, she might as well be Wendy's size for all the strain it appeared to cause him.

His tongue licked into her mouth, gliding back and forth. He held onto her with a need she felt. There weren't words to describe it, but she knew what was in him, because now she felt it, too.

They were alive.

It was time to feel like it. Time to embrace what they had and run with it.

She loved him. All of him. Even the parts she didn't like.

Travis shoved his hands up under her shirt. His rough skin gliding over her stomach to her breasts sent fissures of anticipation through her body. He pushed her bra up and cupped her breasts. She leaned back, her head against the wall and his mouth on her neck.

Back and forth, he swiped his thumb over her breast, driving her crazy. Her panties grew damp and her clit throbbed. She tried shifting against him, but her lower body was prisoner to his strength. He grasped her nipple, tugging on it just enough to make her gasp.

"Travis."

She bunched his shirt up but never got it over his chest. Her brain short-circuited as he switched breasts, tweaking the already erect nipple.

He jerked at the tab on her jeans until he yanked it open. Somehow he wedged his big hand down the front of her pants until he cupped her mound, fingers pressed into her slit.

"I'm still pissed you risked your life," he said against her cheek.

"Mm." She rocked her hips, as much as she could. If only he'd do something with that hand.

"You're mine."

Those words...she shivered.

She was his. All of her. Heart. Mind. Soul. Body. He'd taken over her at some point, become her life line, her support, her warm comfort, and now her personal jungle gym.

She loved him.

"You understand?" He curled a single finger, sliding into her.

"Yes," she hissed.

"You pull something like that again, and I'm going to be more than pissed. Got it?"

"Yeah."

"God, you feel good."

"Your cock would feel better."

He stepped back enough for her to unhook her legs and stand, though leaned was more like it. Her back to the wall, he pushed her jeans and panties to the floor and went to his knees. She kicked out of them and her shoes as fast as she could.

Travis caught her knee, pushed it over his shoulder, and leaned closer. She held her breath and flattened her hands against the wall, looking for something to hold onto. He licked the length of her slit before she was ready. She rocked up on her toes and groaned, pushing her hips forward. He rubbed his tongue over her clit, fingers pressing into her.

She panted for breath, giving herself over to the feel of him. How he made her heart sing. The way they were together.

Bliss twisted her fingers in his short hair. She could come like this. Another few licks and her bones would liquify from the pleasure, but she wanted to come with him.

"Travis!"

He did a thing with his fingers inside and outside of her. A new wave of warmth blossomed low in her belly, spreading from head to toe.

She tugged on his hair again, harder this time.

He kissed her mound, her hip, everywhere in between as he rose to his feet. She captured his face between her hands and claimed his mouth while he picked her up again. She grasped the front of his pants and jerked them open. He shifted, giving her more room to work his jeans and underwear down his hips. His cock slid free and lay against her thigh, trapped between their bodies. She wrapped her hand around it, pumping the velvety soft skin.

This was right.

This was supposed to happen.

They were meant for each other.

She shifted her hips and placed the head of his cock against her.

"Bliss—wait."

"No."

She rolled her hips and felt him slide into her.

"Christ," he groaned. The tendons on either side of his neck stood out and his face twisted up.

"I want to feel you." She grasped his shoulders and pulled him closer, squeezing with her internal muscles. Her arousal eased his entry, letting him slide deeper.

"You don't—"

"I know what I'm doing." She kissed one side of his mouth then the other. "Don't hold back, okay?"

He took a step and shifted her body with one hand on her bottom. Gravity did the rest of the work and his cock slid the rest of the way into her. She gasped and dug her nails into his skin. It was different without a condom. More intimate.

Travis moved slowly, his hips flexing, hands holding her. She closed her eyes and savored the slow glide of skin on skin. He thrust hard enough that the pots hanging on the wall rattled.

"Yes," she said again.

His hand settled at the base of her throat, not tight, but possessive. He held her against the wall while his hips moved, in and out, harder and harder. She said things, incoherent words.

"Look at me."

She opened her eyes, staring into Travis'.

Love.

She knew he loved her, but she saw it, too.

Pleasure spiraled through her body. She gripped him tighter and groaned as the orgasm shuddered through her. He surged once, twice, and stilled, head buried against her neck. She squeezed her legs around him, pulling him a little closer, deeper into her heart and body. Where he belonged.

"I love you," she whispered.

He blew out a breath.

"Are you sure?" he asked. Those three words almost broke her heart. She kissed his cheek and squeezed her eyes shut, hurting for the boy who'd never been truly accepted.

"Yes. I love you."

"I thought I dreamed that."

For several moments they stood twined around each other. It was as if she could sense the locks coming undone inside of him. These weren't just words they were exchanging, it was a promise. An acceptance of who they each were.

At long last he blew out a breath and glanced up at her. She smiled and cupped his cheek, running her thumb over his stubble. This was right.

He carried her to the bedroom and lay her down. The sheets still smelled of him, of that night—what? A week ago now? It felt like an eternity.

Travis carefully removed the rest of her clothes then escorted her into the bathroom, and left, giving her a few moments of privacy. She cleaned up, still floating on cloud nine. There was little to no chance of her getting pregnant. She'd practically lived on birth control since she was a teenager for medical reasons. In fact, she looked forward to children, someday. Travis was the kind of man who would make a better father than he ever had. Because he didn't do anything in halves. He did it with everything he was.

By the time she was done, Travis was naked in her bed. It was a pity she was too exhausted to take advantage of him, but there would be time for that later.

"Hungry?" he asked.

"Yeah, a little. We can order pizza or something in a bit. I just want to lay here for a while."

"Okay." He pulled her against his chest and kissed her brow.

Everything with him felt right. A week ago, this would have been daring and new. Now, she couldn't see her life without him in it. They'd figure out how to make this work. They had to.

"Where do you live?"

"Illinois."

"No, I mean, do you live in an apartment, own a house?"

"Oh. I rent a place. Two bedrooms. Nicer than anything I've ever lived in before. I barely use most the space. There's plenty of room if you want to come visit."

The crux of their issue. The distance. The different lives. They were going to have to find solutions.

"I was thinking about that. What if I could work remote? It would take a while to train a replacement, but I could move up there. I realize that's like, way future plans and all, but I like knowing where I'm headed. And I just thought, I like you, I want to make this work, so why not plan for moving up there?" She leaned back and looked at him to gauge his reaction.

He could say he loved her, but not want her in his space.

Travis' expression was neutral. Too controlled and closed off. They were going to have some serious battles over the Wall o' Ration if he didn't open up on his own.

"What about your family?"

"Mom and Dad have each other. Wendy has Grayson. They don't need me."

You do.

"I...don't want you to think you have to do that." He frowned, as if he didn't like the taste of the words in his mouth.

"What if that's what I feel like doing?"

He glanced away, and his hand coasted up and down her back.

"Or, I could stay here if you'd rather come visit when you can." Everything in her screamed, *No!* She wanted to be as close to him as she could be, every minute she was allowed.

"I don't like that, either."

"Then what do you suggest?"

"Move in with me. Marry me if you want."

She opened and closed her mouth.

That was a lot faster than she was letting herself think. She'd already convinced herself after Travis' bolting act that future plans needed to be broached carefully so he didn't spook, but he'd barreled through that barrier and into the deep end. Of course, her head was already there...she just hadn't thought he was, too.

"Or not." Travis shrugged. "I don't see the point of moving all the way up there to just rent another place. It's a waste when I'm not home all the time. But, your family is here, my job is there. It's...whatever."

"No."

She crawled on top of him, needing to see his face. Every so often she could see through that badass SEAL mask. His heart was too big, too bruised to be shown to many people, but he'd let her in, shown her what he was capable of.

He curled his left arm under his head. The bandage over his wound was barely hanging on. She pressed the tape down absently while she studied his face. The tight lips. The unwavering gaze. It was the hand clenched on her knee that was the real tell. Her heart thumped painfully against her ribs.

Never, in a million years, would she have thought this was where they'd end up when she met him back at the police station.

This was it.

If she jumped, he'd catch her, but she still needed the words.

"I'm just...are you serious?" she asked.

"Yes."

"Last time we kicked this around you ran away."

"I said it was a fucking mistake. What else do you want me to say?"

"That you won't do that again. That if you need space or whatever, tell me, don't just leave."

Travis nodded.

"You have to say it. None of this nodding, grunting, shrugging stuff." She poked his ribs. "And don't say that whole line about not being good at crap. That's a bullshit line."

"I'm not perfect, but yeah, I'll communicate better next time something comes up." His thumb swiped over her skin and his lips curled up. He was still broken, there were old hurts that would never heal, but together, they could be more.

She bent down and kissed him, pouring all her love into that one act. Yeah, they were still strangers, he had no clue how much she loved musicals or the rain or so many other things. But they would make it. They'd figure it out, because Bliss wasn't about to give up on him. Now, or ever.

"Let's do it, now. Tonight," she said.

He frowned.

"Look, I'm all on board this whole live life now train or whatever. I could have died. It's changed the way I look at things." She spread her hand over his heart, just below yet another scar that could have ended him. He understood her. "You love me. I love you. Why wait? I don't see the point in waiting."

"Your family might kill me."

"What? No. Mom wasn't serious. She was just stressed earlier. She'll love you."

"No I mean about getting married tonight. Wouldn't they want to be there?"

"Probably, but this is about us, not them." Silly man making valid points and crap. But, he was probably right. Her parents, and especially Wendy, would never let her live it down if she got hitched without telling them. Considering the circus that had been Wendy's wedding, Bliss was still going to be in the doghouse over a small, fast affair.

"Bliss, I'm not going to marry you and piss off your family."

"Fine." She rolled her eyes and flopped on the bed next to Travis.

His hand coasted over her thigh toward her inner leg. Her body hummed with awareness of his every movement. She held her breath...

"At least wait until the morning," he said.

"What?" She dragged her thoughts up, out of the gutter and looked at him.

"There are places that do appointments, right? We could just do something convenient for them, like after breakfast."

"Seriously?"

"I am if you are." He squeezed her leg.

"Really?"

"Yeah. I'm not a good person. I'm not going to keep telling you no when I want you with me."

"Okay. Let's do it."

She kissed him, dragging him on top of her.

There were things to figure out, people to text—and crap, where were they going to get rings and clothes and stuff? But first, the engagement sex. Because they were engaged, weren't they?

TRAVIS SWIPED THE FANCY handkerchief over his brow. Shit, this was almost as bad as being in the sandbox. The tux was a little tight across the shoulders and every time he took a breath he was sure the thing was trying to suffocate him, but Bliss had assured him he didn't look like an ass before disappearing with her sister to go do...bridal things. What-ever the hell that meant.

His phone vibrated against his thigh. He dug it out of the impossibly deep pockets.

Ethan.

"Hey, man." Travis glanced over his shoulder into the foyer. People were starting to arrive, most of them with a slightly befuddled expression on their faces.

He didn't blame them. It was pretty damn surreal to him, too.

"You're doing this?"

"Yeah." Unless Ethan had a good reason why he shouldn't. Nah. Even then, Bliss was worth it. But maybe he should have taken her up on her midnight wedding idea in-stead of waiting until ten the next morning.

"Well shit. They're about to roll me into the common room. I guess Zain got the feed hooked up to the projector in there."

"Fuck. Why the hell would he do that?"

"Because we all want to see you sweat." Ethan laughed. "I guess it'll be too late to throw you a bachelor party when you get back."

"Yeah, too late for that."

Five people in black filed into the small wedding chapel.

"Got to go," Travis said.

"Remember, the ring goes on the left hand."

"Fuck you."

He hung up, cutting off Ethan's laughter. Bliss' family, and friends he didn't know, but the feds? He hadn't expected to see them. He strode across the chapel and shook Ryan's hand, glancing down the line at the rest of his team.

"Congratulations are in order." Ryan grinned, the first unrestrained expression Travis had seen on the man. Then again, Ryan was clearly a family man.

"Thanks. I think. I thought you would be on your way out already." Travis shoved his hands in his pockets. He hadn't bothered to tell the FBI team because he figured they would be in the air, and why would they care?

"I'm pretty sure Wendy's screaming woke us up at—what was it?" Connor glanced at Jade.

"It was a little after one."

"Nearly gave me a heart attack." Benjamin grumbled.

"Anyway, we couldn't leave before Elvis sang the vows." Connor grinned. Despite how they'd butted heads, the Irishman was an okay guy.

In small doses.

"Everyone." A woman in a pale purple dress, and her hair up in a beehive stood at the chapel's entrance. "Please find your seats. For those watching at home, the service will begin in five minutes."

Shit.

Travis swallowed around the lump in his throat.

It was too late to leave, and he'd promised to talk things out with her before he did anything. Like run away from their wedding.

Their fucking wedding.

He was going to be sick.

She had no idea what she was getting herself into.

"Travis, you okay?" Jade tilted her head sideways.

"The nerves are normal. Take deep breaths, don't lock your knees, and just look at her." Ryan twisted his wedding band, a far off look in his eye.

"Thanks. Excuse me?"

He didn't wait for another word, just pushed past the small crowd and into the foyer. The air was warmer out here and sunlight streamed in through the double glass doors. A couple random people milled through the shop at the front of the chapel, but no one paid him any attention.

Travis could save Bliss the disappointment now and leave. She'd hate him for skipping out, but it might be the best thing for her. He had more baggage than anyone, she just didn't know it yet. He didn't know how to be in a healthy relationship. Even what he had with his sister or the guys he worked with wasn't what he'd call good.

He pulled his phone out of his pocket and jabbed at Bliss' contact.

It didn't get through a full ring before she answered.

"Are you planning to leave me at the alter?" Her tone was teasing, light-hearted.

He blew out a breath.

"Are you sure this is what you want?" he asked.

"You're having second thoughts."

"It's not—no, but, you don't know what you're getting yourself into."

"I know we're both going to have a big reality check. When we wake up from this, yeah, there's going to be some rough times ahead. I'm not stupid enough to think that love fixes everything, but I'm willing to work at this. If you don't want to, or if you want to put it off, tell me now before they put this veil thing on because it's going to hurt. Pretty sure they used a whole can of that Aqua Net stuff on my hair."

He chuckled, and his world shifted back into focus.

"I've never...I'm going to need a lot of patience. I'm going to screw up a lot."

"And that's fine. We'll talk about it. We'll do better. You're already doing better. You're still in the chapel, right?"

"Foyer. Chapel is too loud. Everyone was staring."

A man in a glittering white jumpsuit exited a back office and paused in front of a mirror. Elvis weddings were a much bigger thing than he'd realized. When in Vegas...

"See, already doing better. So, are we getting married or what?"

"Yeah. And forget the veil."

He hung up the phone and the sick sensation vanished. One more swipe with the handkerchief and he was himself again. This was where he was supposed to be.

"Mr. Ration, ready to make a bride a wife?" The Elvis impersonator gripped his hand and pumped it.

"I am." And he was, damn the nerves and doubts.

"Good, good. Full room today. We'll wait for the signal, then go up like we practiced earlier."

Travis nodded and checked his phone one last time.

A text from his sister Emma filled the screen.

Break a leg, bro! We r watching.

Everyone was here. Or close enough.

His blood family, his chosen family, and the people who mattered.

"That's us. Come on, let's get this show on the road." Elvis slapped his shoulder before leading the way into the chapel.

Travis kept his gaze straight ahead, all the way to the platform at the front of the room and stood on his mark.

Elvis said a few words, people snapped pictures, but none of it really mattered. He bounced his knee, just enough to feel the ring in his pocket and stared at the double doors that now stood closed at the end of the chapel.

Finally, the music started and Elvis began to sing.

Travis stopped breathing. The attendees stood as one, turning toward the doors. Elvis hit a higher note, the song lost on Travis, and the doors opened.

Bliss and her father stood at the end of the red carpet, and he'd never seen anything so beautiful in his life. His future wife. His love. His heart.

Epilogue.

Six months later.

TRAVIS JOGGED UP THE porch stairs, keeping on the balls of his feet and avoiding the squeaky board. Bliss wasn't expecting him home until tomorrow morning. These moments, coming back to the little two-bedroom house they shared, were the best. Second only to the hours of lovemaking that followed. Things weren't perfect, but they were making the best out of what they had. And it was a hell of a lot more than he'd ever expected.

He disabled the security through his phone app and let himself in the front door. For a second, he stood on the little rug and listened. Music played softly from the spare-room-turned-office, and over that he could hear her humming.

There wasn't an aspect of his life Bliss hadn't touched. From redecorating the boring house to his taste in food and music, she'd changed him. For the better. His life wasn't just work anymore. And though the long hours, days, and sometimes weeks apart sucked, he always got to come home to this.

His home. With his wife.

Travis tiptoed down the short hall and peered into their office. Or more accurately, Bliss' office. Yeah, he had a desk in the room, but she was the one who worked there five days a week.

She sat bent over his desk, her back to the door, pen in hand, signing—something.

He tapped on the door with his knuckle.

Surprising her only went so far.

There were still nightmares and panic attacks on occasion, but those were fewer and farther between.

Bliss whirled around, mouth open, eyes wide. Her hair was pulled back in a clip, and she wore one of his sweatshirts with leggings and bare feet.

"Travis!"

He grinned and crossed the room in two strides, picking her up for a thorough kiss.

Five days away, forgotten in an instant between her lips.

"What—? You weren't supposed to be back until—"

"Tomorrow, I know. I decided to hop a commercial flight instead of waiting." The cost of a one-way flight was nothing in comparison to twelve more hours together. Especially when he was facing a lengthy assignment down in the Keys.

Bliss grinned and he put her down. She kept her gaze on him and pushed the papers behind her.

"What are you up to?" He reached around her and plucked the top sheet off the stack.

"No, just—Travis!" She made a wild grab and only got his forearm.

He wrapped the arm around her and skimmed the letter.
To the governor of Oklahoma.

"What is this?" A chill swept over him.

Was Bliss unhappy? Had he upset her?

She sighed and snagged the letter from between his fingers.

"I didn't want to show you. I didn't want to get your hopes up," she said.

"Why are you asking the governor for a pardon?"

She leaned against his desk and stared up at him.

"It's the job, isn't it? You still don't like it."

"Its—no. You like what you do. I just—you really want to be a PI."

He didn't bother to nod. They'd had this conversation. That career path was closed to him thanks to his felony record, as were so many other options in life.

"I talked to a lawyer. He thinks that there's plenty of evidence and proof that your conviction could be pardoned. So yeah, I was going to send these today, see what might happen. I've got letters to both the governor of Oklahoma and the President. Worst case, they said no, you wouldn't know, and we keep on making the best of what we have." She reached for his hand, clasping it between hers. "I just want for you to be happy."

"Are you happy?"

Above anything else that mattered was Bliss. No, he didn't want to work for Aegis forever. He'd die doing this job if he stuck it out until he was too old to dodge bullets, and she didn't deserve that. Truth be told, he'd never considered a way around his conviction. It hadn't occurred to him, because good things never happened to him.

And then there was Bliss.

She was all the good he'd never had, rolled into one, sexy package.

"Are you mad at me?" She pulled his hand, urging him closer.

He let her pull him between her legs while he paused before answering, rolling her actions around in his head.

"No," he replied. "Are you happy?"

"Yeah." Her smile spread slowly across her face. "More now that you're home."

He blew out a breath and leaned down to kiss her. She tasted of oranges and tea, which meant they were probably out of food. Oh well, they could order pizza and spend more time in bed anyway.

"Note to self, next time I get a bright idea I don't want my super sneaky husband to know about, do it right after he leaves. And before I forget, Emma sent over some wedding stuff. They picked a date."

"Later."

Travis picked Bliss up, and she wrapped herself around him. There was time to figure out the logistics of a couple trips back to Oklahoma. For now, he needed to show his wife just how good they had it.

Want to know what the rest of the Aegis Group is up to?

Sign up for the New Release Newsletter at
www.SidneyBristol.com
to get inside scoops, short stories about
your favorite characters and free books.

Find out about the BAU's other cases, starting with:

Blind: Killer Instincts

He recognizes the darkness in her. It's in him, too.

Detective Jacob Payton knows the clock is ticking down. Someone is about to die, and his best suspect is also his only source of information. He's known Emma Ration's story for years—after all, a brutal serial killer left his mark on both their lives when they were still young. Meeting her is another experience altogether. She challenges his control and entices him in ways no other woman has.

But is she the killer? As the bodies pile up and their passion ignites, Jacob runs the risk of losing his control. Falling for Emma was never in his plan, but now that she's part of his life he's not about to give her up. Not even to the FBI on the trail of the very same killer.

Jacob must figure out if it's Emma in danger, or himself. If he can't uncover the identity of the copycat killer, it could be the end for both him and the woman who has fast become the center of his life

Book List

Aegis Group
Dangerous Attraction, parts 1, 2 and 3
Bayou Bound
Picture Her Bound
Duty Bound
Bound Memories
Bound & Tamed
Other BDSM Titles
Committed
Bound with Pearls
Collar Me in Paris
Festive Seduction
Electric Engagement
So Inked
Under His Skin
The Harder He Falls
His Marriage Bargain
Good Guys Wear Black
Hot Tango
Line of Duty
Standalone Titles
Falling for His Best Friend
Dream Vacation (free read)
How Zombies Stole Christmas
Anthologies
Hot Ink
High Octane Heroes

ABOUT THE AUTHOR

It can never be said that NYT & USA Today Bestselling author Sidney Bristol has had a 'normal' life. She is a recovering roller derby queen, former missionary, and tattoo addict. She grew up in a motor-home on the US highways (with an occasional jaunt into Canada and Mexico), traveling the rodeo circuit with her parents. Sidney has lived abroad in both

Russia and Thailand, working with children and teenagers. She now lives in Texas where she splits her time between a job she loves, writing, reading and fostering cats.

Sidney is represented by Nicole Resciniti of the Seymour Agency.

You can find Sidney here:

Website: www.SidneyBristol.com

Twitter: @Sidney_Bristol

New Release Newsletter:
http://sidneybristol.com/newsletter/

Facebook Page:
www.facebook.com/Sidney.Bristol.Romance.Author

Facebook Profile:
www.facebook.com/Sidney.Bristol.Author

Cheesecake Reader Lounge:
www.facebook.com/groups/CheesecakeReaderLounge

[124
2   + 130
     ‾‾‾‾
     254
     136
    ‾‾‾‾‾
    390

1- 124
2- 130
3   136

90

CPSIA information can be obtained at www.ICGtesting.com
Printed in the USA
BVOW01s1149020916

460982BV00002B/32/P

9 781519 159458